Praise for the works of Jason M. Hough

Zero World

"A science fiction [novel that] smashes *The Bourne Identity* together with *The End of Eternity* to create a thrilling action rampage that confirms [Jason] Hough as an important new voice in genre fiction."

—*Publishers Weekly* (starred review)

"An enjoyable read . . . expect minor whiplash from the frenetic pace." —*Entertainment Weekly*

"Hough has combined all the ingredients of a first-rate sci-fi thriller." —*Kirkus Reviews*

"One hell of an entertaining read. Hough continues to deliver white-knuckle books anchored by unusual and fascinating characters. *Zero World* is a giant cup of pure badassery that secures his place among the finest sci-fi action writers today."

—Kevin Hearne, *New York Times* bestselling author of The Iron Druid Chronicles

"A high-octane blend of science fiction and mystery, *Zero World* is a thrill ride that shoots you out of a cannon and doesn't let up until the very last page."

—Wesley Chu, author of the Tao series

"Warning: Do not pick up this book if there is anything else you need to do. There is no safe place to rest inside these pages, no lag in the full-throttle action, no moment when you will think, 'Okay, this is a good spot to take a break.' Once you realize how much you don't . . . is ine . . .

The Darwin Elevator

"A hell of a fun book."

—James S. A. Corey, *New York Times*
bestselling author of *Abaddon's Gate*

"[Jason M.] Hough's first novel combines the rapid-fire action and memorable characters associated with Joss Whedon's short-lived *Firefly* TV series with the accessibility and scientific acumen of [James S. A.] Corey's 'Expanse' series." —*Library Journal* (starred review)

"Claustrophobic, intense, and satisfying . . . I couldn't put this book down. *The Darwin Elevator* depicts a terrifying world, suspends it from a delicate thread, and forces you to read with held breath as you anticipate the inevitable fall."

—Hugh Howey, *New York Times*
bestselling author of *Wool*

"Newcomer Hough displays a talent for imaginative plotting and realistic dialogue, and the brisk pacing and cliffhanger ending will keep readers enthralled and eagerly awaiting the next installment."

—*Publishers Weekly*

"Jason M. Hough does a great job with this huge story, which unfolds with just the right balance of high adventure, espionage, humor, and emotional truth. . . . As soon as you finish, you'll want more." —*Analog*

"A debut novel unlike any other . . . This is something special. Something iconic. *The Darwin Elevator* is full of majesty and wonder, mystery and mayhem, colorful characters and insidious schemes." —*SF Signal*

DEL REY BOOKS BY JASON M. HOUGH

ZERO WORLD

THE DIRE EARTH CYCLE

THE DARWIN ELEVATOR

THE EXODUS TOWERS

THE PLAGUE FORGE

THE DIRE EARTH: A NOVELLA

THE DIRE EARTH DUOLOGY

INJECTION BURN

ESCAPE VELOCITY

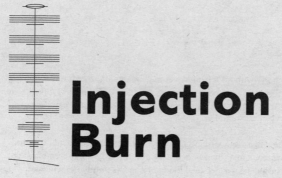

Injection Burn

A Dire Earth Novel

Jason M. Hough

DEL REY • NEW YORK

A Del Rey Mass Market Original

Copyright © 2017 by Jason Hough
Excerpt from *Escape Velocity* by Jason M. Hough copyright © 2017 by Jason Hough

Published in the United States by Del Rey, an imprint of Random House, a division of Penguin Random House LLC, New York.

DEL REY and the HOUSE colophon are registered trademarks of Penguin Random House LLC.

This book contains an excerpt from the forthcoming book *Escape Velocity* by Jason M. Hough. This excerpt has been set for this edition only and may not reflect the final content of the forthcoming edition.

ISBN 978-0-553-39131-2
Ebook ISBN 978-0-553-39130-5

Printed in the United States of America

randomhousebooks.com

9 8 7 6 5 4 3 2 1

Del Rey mass market edition: June 2017

For all those who venture into the unknown

I couldn't go. Couldn't be boxed in a ship like that knowing Earth is free again. Everyone's an immune now! That's a party I couldn't miss.

—Skadz, 2285, overheard at Woon's Tavern

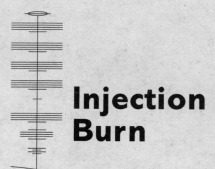

Injection
Burn

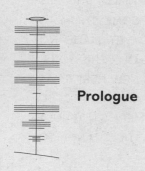

Prologue

Darwin, Australia
11.FEB.2331

TO: <FLEET>

FROM: [UNINTELLIGIBLE, KNOWN IN SITU AS EVE]

CLASSIFICATION URGENT, FULL-SPECTRUM BROADCAST, MAXIMUM ENCRYPTION

I BELIEVE OUR SEARCH IS FINALLY OVER.

AT A PLANET KNOWN LOCALLY AS EARTH (RELEVANT DETAILS ATTACHED), A SPECIES CALLING ITSELF "HUMAN" HAS SUFFICIENTLY OVERCOME THE TESTS WE DEFINED (WITH REVISIONS BY MYSELF EN ROUTE, BASED ON LATEST GATHERED INTELLIGENCE AS OF 005505.332.14A AND SUBSEQUENT ADJUSTMENTS AGREED TO AND IMPLEMENTED BY FLEET MAJORITY).

SOME OF YOU MAY BE ALLOWING A SMALL

AMOUNT OF CAUTIOUS OPTIMISM AT THIS POINT. AFTER ALL, WE'VE COME THIS FAR THREE TIMES BEFORE AND YET MADE NO REAL PROGRESS IN FREEING OUR CREATORS.

BUT THERE IS SOMETHING NEW HERE THAT CANNOT BE UNDERSTATED. AN UNEXPECTED DISCOVERY THAT I BELIEVE MERITS NOT JUST OPTIMISM BUT ALSO A DRASTIC CHANGE TO OUR PLAN.

A SMALL PERCENTAGE OF THESE HUMANS ARE UNAFFECTED BY THE VIRAL ANALOG WE DEVISED.

COMPLETELY IMMUNE, FOR REASONS I HAVE YET TO COMPREHEND (TESTS ARE UNDER WAY, DETAILS FORTHCOMING, ANALYSIS APPRECIATED). IN ALL THEIR NUMBER, ONLY A FEW APPEAR TO FEATURE THIS CHARACTERISTIC, AND YET THEY WERE LARGELY RESPONSIBLE FOR OVERCOMING OUR TEST REGIMEN. MOREOVER, MOST OF THEM HAVE AGREED TO HELP US, DESPITE RESERVATIONS ABOUT OUR METHODOLOGY IN DETERMINING THEIR SUITABILITY.

THEY ARE WITHIN MY HULL EVEN NOW, DEVISING A COURSE OF ACTION THAT I FEEL IS PROMISING.

HENCE MY OPTIMISM—NO, MY CERTAINTY—THAT IT IS TIME TO ALTER OUR OWN APPROACH TO ENDING THIS SIEGE. MY PLAN REQUIRES THE ASSISTANCE OF A MAJORITY OF YOU IF IT IS TO SUCCEED.

I AM CURRENTLY EN ROUTE TO [UNINTELLI-GIBLE, KNOWN AS KEPLER-22] AT MAXIMUM VELOCITY. I HOPE YOU WILL CONSIDER MY REQUEST AND LEND SUPPORT TO THIS EFFORT.

EVE
(VIA ARTIFICIAL LOW MIND TRANSFERENCE VESSEL, WHICH SENDS GREETINGS TO ITS KIN)

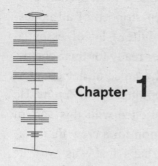

Chapter 1

THE TWO SPACECRAFT came to rest in a vast swath of nothingness deep in interstellar space. They were identical, perfect twins, spaced with nanometer precision exactly ten thousand kilometers apart. Both were pointed in the same direction: toward a star some three hundred light-years distant.

Captain Gloria Tsandi let out a long breath. Her ship, the *Wildflower,* stood poised on the edge of history, and she found herself profoundly uncomfortable with that. The whole endeavor had been a series of small compromises and allowances that now, here at the brink, amounted to the sort of thing she'd never have agreed to if presented all at once. Dangerous, reckless, and hastily planned.

Which were the exact same reasons the *Lonesome* had been lost in the first place. The reason this search and rescue mission, maybe the most critical in human history, was even necessary.

She glanced to her right, where her co-pilot should

be. No one sat there. There wasn't even a chair anymore. The *Wildflower* had been stripped of all nonessential equipment, and then quite a lot of essential equipment, in order to make her ready for this scheme.

"We're in position," came the voice of her counterpart. The mission lead, Captain Sutter of the *Zephyr*. He had the benefit of more experience with this sort of thing, not to mention a reputation for a crew that worshipped his every action. Perhaps that was why he seemed to have no real concern for what was about to happen: no one to question his orders.

"Want me to answer him, boss?" Xavi asked.

Her navigator, one deck below. Very much the sort who questioned orders. The only bit of normalcy on this entire mission. He'd been with her for going on six years, and she thought of him as her own little brother—a rebellious, often embarrassing little brother—despite the fact they looked nothing alike. He was a squat, wide, bulldog of a man who'd embraced his Australian heritage with absolute zeal, a persona that paired perfectly with his longish sandy-blond hair and perpetually sun-narrowed ice-blue eyes. Gloria was lithe, very dark, and kept her afro cut close to the scalp. When he stood beside her, it was as if someone had tried and succeeded at finding the two human beings most unlike each other.

What they had in common was their age, twenty-seven, and this ship.

The rest of her usual crew, six others, had been left behind, another compromise to reach the goal mass. Instead of a total of eight, she had a three-person crew now, and the third was a stranger. A wild card. Gloria shifted, uncomfortable in the extreme. "I'll handle it, thank you. Just keep an eye on the position and let the computer do its thing."

"Sure thing, boss," Xavi said.

Gloria puffed out her checks, let out the breath, and sent her reply to Sutter. "We're in the green here, too. Ready when you are."

With that, she reached for the part of her interface that would signal her intent to proceed. Her finger hovered for an instant before she forced it down. The icon shifted from yellow to an all-too-pleasant green.

"Prepare for fold maneuver," a faintly accented calming voice said over the comm. "Synchro-protocol in effect. Initial burn will commence at the pleasure of . . . Sutter, *Zephyr* . . . stand by."

A minute passed before Sutter replied. "We have your helm. Ten minutes to burn."

"Understood," Gloria sent back, glad for the additional time to prepare herself mentally. On the local comm she said, "Both of you meet me in the mess for one final review."

"Mmm," Xavi acknowledged, followed by the sounds of his harness unbuckling. His couch was on the deck just below her own, the ship's main body being oriented in a vertical stack of eight decks.

The newcomer's reply came next. "Okay," was all she said, and Gloria had to remind herself that Beth Lee was unaccustomed to hierarchy, protocol. For that matter, unaccustomed to flying aboard the ships that utilized the technology she helped invent. The mousy engineer had flown before, sure, but according to her file it had always been as an observer, nothing more. A "subject matter expert." Bringing her along for this mission had been the biggest and most difficult of the concessions Gloria had made, for it meant leaving her own trusted engineer behind. Not to mention her mechanic, her medic, both science officers, and her co-pilot. "Humans are heavy, and so is the food and water they require," the OEA logistics officer had said with almost total indifference. And that was that.

Out of her couch, Gloria rolled and oriented herself down, drifting along behind Xavi, using blue rungs that protruded from every available surface to guide herself down to the mess hall. The *Wildflower* had a hollow spine running from one end to the other, her decks stacked like a pile of donuts, only open toward the interior. The mess hall was one above the middle floor, which served as central airlock. It consisted of a small kitchen, food storage, and two booth-style tables and benches for use while under thrust or attached to a space elevator. Adrift as they were, Gloria shunned the seats in favor of simply floating within the hollow spine of the ship, both feet tucked under blue stabilization rungs to keep her in place. Xavi rummaged through one of the food bins, joining her a few seconds later with a fistful of nutrient bulbs. He floated one across to her, and she caught it deftly.

Their companion drifted up from below. Beth Lee may not have many flight hours logged, but she knew her way around a zero-g environment, Gloria noted. The tiny woman had come up feetfirst, rotated, and positioned herself between her two crewmates with precise, economic movements. No grace to it, but the results were all that mattered.

Gloria examined the label of the nutrient bulb, shrugged at what she saw there, and used two fingers to pinch some of the contents into her mouth, one "bite" at a time. She glanced at the selected dish—cherry smoothie—and suppressed a grin. Her favorite, as any of her regulars would know. Xavi winked when she glanced up at him before crushing his bulb with a meaty fist, inhaling the entire meal in one fell swoop.

Gloria returned his thoughtfulness with a stern glare. To get too comfortable with her crew led to sloppiness, and worse, the intrusion of feelings when it came to making hard decisions. It hurt her to distance herself at a moment like this, but in the long run she knew it was for the best.

The silent meal ended and Gloria waited while Xavi stowed the empty bulbs for future reuse. Finished, he returned to his chosen spot on the circle and waited.

"A recap and status," Gloria said, "so we're all on the same page." Neither companion said anything, so the captain went on. "Thanks to the modified imploder, we're about to do something unprecedented. I know we're running with the barest of bare-bones configurations here, and all three of us will be wearing multiple hats, but I still expect calm, levelheaded professionalism. Beth, you don't know me that well, but my crew is and has always been my family. I won't hesitate to cuff an unruly child. Am I clear?"

"Of course, Gloria," Beth said, in a way that made the

captain wonder if she'd just reminded the poor girl of her actual mother.

"It's Captain Tsandi."

The woman gave a meek nod. "Sorry."

Xavi answered with a little half-salute, having heard this speech, or something like it, half a hundred times. His fingers tapped against the bulkhead with impatience, and probably a fair amount of nerves at the prospect of being a passive observer to the fold, something he usually ran himself.

Gloria put on her most reassuring smile, and went on, keenly aware that this next part would strain the long-standing trust relationship she'd cultivated with her navigator. "We're aligned with *Zephyr*, and our ships will fold in tandem. What I've kept from you until now," she said, her gaze on Xavi's sudden, dubious expression, "is our destination."

"Ah, shit, boss," Xavi started.

"I'll have none of that," she said quickly. "It wasn't my choice to keep this part secret, believe me. But I understand why, and I think you will, too."

She had their undivided attention now. Beth's gaze narrowed. Xavi's fingers went still.

"This is not a test run of the Mark 5 imploder. The Alliance is done with tests. In fact, this technically isn't even the first field use."

Xavi hung his head, shaking it back and forth in disbelief. Beth just stared, expressionless, and Gloria wondered how much of this she already knew. The Mark 5 was, after all, partly her creation. Surely she'd been in the loop during the test process, and the declaration of all clear.

Seeing no alternative, Gloria soldiered on. "That honor went to Captain Dawson, and her ship, the *Lonesome,* two weeks ago."

"I thought Daw was pushing rock out at—"

"That's what everyone thought," Gloria said.

Xavi hissed through clenched teeth. "I'm liking this mission less and less, boss."

"I'm not exactly thrilled myself. But it's a critically important one, Xavi."

"Sounds like a fucking yak shaving expedition," he said, his Australian drawl coming through strong.

"Noted. Now let me finish. We're on a tight schedule that is out of our hands."

Xavi made a little "go on" gesture with his free hand. His frown hurt, but there was nothing she could do about it.

"Dawson . . . well, Dawson screwed up. In the worst possible way. Some misguided desire to make history. It doesn't matter. The point is, instead of conducting a trial run of the Mark 5 as directed, she altered the *Lonesome*'s course at the last minute and put us all at terrible risk."

"Kepler-22," Beth Lee said. Not a question.

"Kepler-22," Gloria confirmed.

"So what?" Xavi asked. "It's restricted space, sure, but there have been plenty of other visits. And it's not like anyone's ever been past the blockade. Poked around a bit, granted. Been chased off every time, too. Nothing new about it."

"Which brings me," Gloria said, "to the other classified part of all this. Xavi, this new Mark 5 imploder is . . . well, Beth here, and her team, optimized it. Increased its tolerance for space-time curvature."

"Oh, now I really don't like where this is going."

"Dawson took her ship to Kepler-22, yes, but *inside* the restricted zone. Way, way inside."

"Impossible."

Gloria turned her gaze to Beth. "You explain."

If the engineer felt any remorse or responsibility for what her invention had now potentially caused, she showed no sign. Her Asian features were clipped and focused. All business. "The Mark 5 is a dramatic improvement to the field cavitation device—the 'imploder,' as you call it. It allows for perturbations in the exit curvature as much as nine times what the—"

"How about in English?"

"It enables exit much closer to the gravitational body—planet, star, et cetera—than was previously possible. Provided the vessel's mass is quite low."

Xavi's frown deepened. "So that's why we stripped the *Wildflower* bare, and left the rest of the crew behind."

"Yes," Gloria said to him. "I'm sorry to keep this from you, Xavi."

Her navigator nodded absently, but the frown remained. After a moment he shook his head as if to clear it. "What's done is done. Let me see if I can guess the rest, yeah?"

"Sure."

"So Daw is meant to test this new imploder, but gets

it in her head to lay in a new course because she wants to be the first ship to get in close to Kepler-22. So off she goes, folds space, boom she's off to make history. The first captain to get a close look at Carthage, find out what's so damn important about the place. Find out why an entire solar system has been barricaded off, and why our ancient ancestors were almost wiped out."

"So far so good."

Xavi grunted a sardonic laugh, swallowed, went on. "And I'm guessing something went wrong. They got in close and then the Scipio fleet caught up with them. Or are about to. And of course, other than protecting their precious world of Carthage, there's two things the Scipios desire more than anything else in the entire fucking universe: our imploder tech, or barring that, the location of Earth. And Daw's just given them both."

"May have given them both," Gloria corrected. "It's all as you say, I'm afraid, except that there's been no sign of Dawson's ship other than an initial beacon ping about six hours after they arrived."

"And now . . . what? We're throwing good after bad? Sending us in to . . . to what, exactly?"

Gloria glanced at both of them in turn. "It's Sutter's ship that has the task. Discover the fate of the *Lonesome,* recover or destroy it, as necessary. We cannot, above all else, let the Scipios get their hands on a functional imploder."

Neither of her crew spoke, so Gloria went on. "Any problems, we bug out. Your safety is in my hands, and I take that seriously, but know that even more important than our objective is the primary mission of the

OEA: Do not let the enemy acquire our technology. Under any circumstances. Understood?"

"Of course," Beth said.

Xavi nodded. He knew the code as well as anyone. "If it's Sutter's mission to find Daw, what's ours?"

"We're the fail-safe. If something happens to Sutter, if he's in danger of being captured, we make sure that doesn't happen."

A chime sounded. Two minutes to fold-maneuver initiation. Gloria gripped Xavi's shoulder. "I know it's a mess."

"It's a clusterfuck."

"Hence the need to clean it up. If the Scipios gain the ability to fold space . . . if they come to Earth, it could become another prison, just like Carthage."

Xavi considered this, and she took his prolonged silence as tacit agreement. Gloria gave him the most reassuring smile she could muster. "Both of you return to your stations. We're going to fold in there and watch Sutter like a hawk. If all goes as planned, he docks with Daw, takes her crew aboard, scuttles her ship, and we all fold home safely."

Drifting back to her captain's couch, Gloria could already see the ruse in that plan. Her ship, and the twin that was Sutter's, had been stripped to the bare minimum to meet the mass requirements of the Mark 5.

Sutter wouldn't be taking on any rescued crew. He'd be making sure there was nothing left for the Scipios to study.

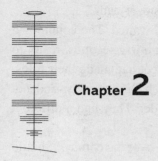

Chapter 2

GLORIA TSANDI STRAPPED herself into the captain's couch, set it to full recline, and tried to soak in the last few moments of weightlessness, an environment she'd come to feel utterly at home in. Gravity, as the saying went, sucks. She called up feeds from around the ship.

On a normal flight she'd check in with her medical officer first. A last-minute precaution that everyone was mentally and physically ready to ride an implosion—to *fold*—before actually doing it. But the medical berth was empty, so Gloria scanned the biofeedback displays with an unpracticed eye. Nothing of note stood out, other than Beth's obvious nerves.

Gloria decided to start with her. "Engineering?"

On the screen, Beth Lee stared back at her with the determined face of someone trying to mask a profound fear. "All systems go, Captain," she said.

Gloria gave her a reassuring nod and shifted her focus to Xavi. "Navigation?"

"All clear, Captain!" Xavi barked with exaggerated military bluster. "Let's get this over with."

"Stand by," Gloria said, and waited. The countdown timer stood frozen in place at thirty seconds, ready to move once the diversionary fleet had made their folds. That group of ships was much farther away, and not equipped with the new imploder. They had a different task today.

Captain Sutter's voice came over the comm. "Should be any second now," he said, "then we go."

There were twelve other ships, several light-hours distant, in a formation that spaced them apart by ten million kilometers each. All were under heavy thrust as they worked up the speed needed to use their Mark 4 imploders. Then, in near-perfect unison, their blips vanished from Gloria's screen as they dove headfirst into holes punched through the very fabric of the universe. This had all actually happened two hours ago, the light of it only now reaching the *Wildflower*'s sensors.

Gloria's outside-view screens blossomed with brilliant white explosions, brighter than the Sun itself if only for an instant. She swallowed, her eyes scanning the readouts all around her. Everything looked good. Everything according to plan.

"Diversion fleet is away," Sutter said for the benefit of both ships. "Launching imploders."

From a nacelle protruding from the *Wildflower*'s belly, one of her two Mark 5 field cavitation imploders detached and propelled itself forward on a growing white flame.

"Prepare for injection burn," Gloria said. She knew full well that Xavi would be ready, a veteran of folding, but she couldn't be sure about Beth.

"Accelerating to impact velocity," Gloria said, as if she were the one giving the command. In truth she had no such option, even if she'd not given control of her ship to Sutter. All Gloria could do in this situation was simply *not* cancel the preprogrammed fold sequence. The timing involved had to be precise to impossibly small fractions of seconds. A human had no hope to pull off such a thing. As captain she was just there to put a stop to things if the situation called for it, and even that option waited behind hundreds of layers of safeguards.

The *Wildflower* shuddered as her engines powered up, and Gloria felt the weight of an impossibly heavy blanket drape over her, pressing her back into the couch, smartfoam cushioning her as best it could.

From somewhere below came a deep thud that vibrated up through the hull and made Gloria's teeth rattle. "Status, Beth!"

"Clear to fold!" the engineer replied.

On Gloria's forward view, the imploder's engine stage winked off and then detached. It fired again to move rapidly away, leaving only the imploder device itself—an orange resin sphere—dead ahead.

The *Wildflower* raced to catch up to the projectile. Gloria studied readouts as her ship's engines roared to maximum power. The force of it pushed her so hard into her seat that she thought she might pop through the back of it.

"Ramming speed!" Xavi shouted from below, as the *Wildflower* chased the imploder, which had now begun to glow. Proximity alarms began to wail. Gloria's forward screen began to shimmer as the imploder built the required energy for its task. Within seconds it glowed like a star, washing everything out.

Gloria watched that eerie fireball grow as the *Wildflower* closed the final few meters.

She shut her eyes. Nothing to do now but hope.

A billionth of a second before the nose of the ship touched it, the sphere imploded. The force of the antiblast was carefully and expertly shaped to plunge a massive flood of energy inward in a very specific geometry. Physics far beyond Gloria's understanding took place. A pocket of space, turned inside out for the briefest instant, calculated with exhaustive precision. Had the *Wildflower* arrived a split second earlier it would have collided with the sphere in catastrophic fashion. A split second too late and the blast would have stretched the vessel and its occupants across the hole punched in space. Spaghettification, the scientists called it, with absolute seriousness.

But Beth, and all those she worked with, had done their jobs. The *Wildflower,* going at just the right speed, arriving at exactly the right time, found its way into a small pocket of safe space amid all that violence. A bubble that would be pulled across the sudden bridge between two incomprehensibly distant points.

Almost a thousand light-years away, in the vicinity of the star known as Kepler-22, two white-hot flares of energy erupted from nothing, and spat out a pair of identical ships exactly ten thousand kilometers apart from each other.

One, the *Zephyr,* emerged in what should have been empty space only to slam broadside into a massive alien vessel.

And the other, the *Wildflower,* was tumbling out of control.

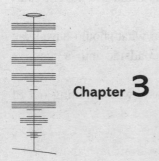

Chapter 3

EVERY FOLD MADE Gloria sick with nerves. Not because of any knowledge of the extraordinary physics involved, but the sheer violence of how it worked.

Fire the implosion device out ahead of the ship, then race toward it at incredible speed. Be within a fraction of a millimeter before it implodes to ensure being sucked in, and yet be moving fast enough that, when you come out the other side, you outrun the inverse effect at the destination. The timing and velocity had to be so precise that it had taken a dozen years before a ship capable of carrying passengers could attempt the transit. Space-time had to be almost perfectly flat, too. Attempt this anywhere near a star, planet, moon, or other significant body and the results were catastrophic.

Until the Mark 5, at least.

In the solar system dominated by the star known as Kepler-22, somewhere between the worlds humanity had named Palmyra and Skara Brae, there were for a brief instant two objects as bright as suns. Dual explosions that looked, on edge, like spheres of energy cleaved in half. And from that brilliance, two ships emerged.

More or less.

The Mark 5 had just allowed the twin craft, *Zephyr* and *Wildflower,* to arrive closer to Kepler-22 than any previous expedition save one—the one they'd come to rescue. In all other attempts to explore here, Earth's vessels had emerged from warp just beyond the system's outermost planet, Hatra. The closest they could get.

It wasn't long until the alien race known as the Scipios had put up a vast fleet of seek-and-destroy ships in this region. Known as the Swarm Blockade, the enemy ships numbered in the millions, forming a sphere around Kepler-22 and all of her planets, ready to move to and intercept anything that approached. A prison the size of a solar system, and a graveyard to hundreds of ships that had attempted to enter.

To emerge here, though, so close to the star, was uncharted territory, for no one knew what waited inside the blockade. No one knew what was so important about the world of Carthage that the entire system had been made off-limits.

Gloria's body was tugged and shoved a dozen times as shock waves buffeted the ship. The sound of rending metal and electrical fires assaulted her ears. Before her, the *Wildflower*'s control displays winked and died, the whole cockpit plunged into darkness save for the bits of glowing tape used to label bins and exits. Below someone shouted in pain. Xavi, she thought, gritting against her own agony as the ship rocked and swayed in the violence of space-time being pinched hard and then abruptly released. Shudders spread through the area as the universe evened itself back out, the *Wildflower* riding it all like a boat dropped onto a stormy sea.

Finally, the ripples abated. All sensation of movement ceased, all sound vanished.

"Status!" Gloria shouted.

From far below, Beth coughed. The air reeked of smoke and ozone.

"Fire," Xavi said. He sounded close by. She heard him clambering about. Then a light winked on and began to sweep across the interior of the ship, creating lurching shadows that made Gloria's stomach flutter.

Gloria remembered her own flashlight, then, tucked somewhere under her seat. She couldn't remember ever needing it, and hoped the ultracap inside it still held a charge. It took several seconds of groping under there before her fingers brushed the small metallic tube. She pressed the button and sighed with relief when blue-white light splashed into the cockpit. "Status!" she shouted again, floating over to the hole in the floor that led aft. "Xavi?"

"Here," he said. The air had become quite hazy, and stung her nose. Below she heard the hiss as he unleashed a fire extinguisher on some unseen flame. "It's bad, Captain."

"Let's have some specifics," she said. "Beth? Talk to me."

No reply.

Hell. Gloria took mental stock. Total power loss, that

much was obvious. Circuitry fried, but the extent of that damage would be impossible to ascertain until they could get a power source back online. That had to come first, then . . . after that she'd figure out where the hell they were, and if the new imploder had performed as advertised. If it had worked, then right now they were adrift somewhere well within the Scipios' blockade. Close enough, perhaps, to finally get a clear look at Carthage, the planet that mythical Dutch pilot Skyler Luiken and his cohorts had set off for almost two thousand years earlier. The explorers had never been heard from again, their mission to save Carthage still unfulfilled.

Time was Gloria's enemy now. Residual effects of their punch through space were spreading outward at the speed of light like an inflating balloon. In minutes—maybe hours if she was really lucky—the Swarm would detect what was now a familiar phenomenon to them, and rush to deal with the threat. With any luck, the diversionary fleet, arriving earlier and much farther out in interplanetary space, might draw off the Scipios and buy a bit of time.

"Power first!" she shouted aft even as she drifted in that direction. Xavi flashed her a thumbs-up as she passed through the navigation bay. She pointed at him. "After that, find out where we are."

"Got it," he said, and let out another blast from the extinguisher.

The white plume merged with already hazy air, and Gloria found herself all but blind as she floated on toward the tail of the ship. She hauled on the lip of a bulkhead and flew downward, through the empty science station, then crew quarters, the mess. Storage and medical drifted by, all empty, their crew and most of their contents left behind to reduce the *Wildflower*'s mass. Gloria's overwhelming sense of concern began to twist and coalesce toward something dangerously close to dread. Part of that weight-saving effort had been leaving behind most of the spare parts they typically carried.

Gloria continued down. "Beth?!"

A second of silence followed, turning the dread in Gloria's gut into abject fear. Then a voice in the darkness. "Down here!"

"Where? I don't—" The question died on her lips as a splash of light played across one of the spokelike access passages that led outward from the tiny control room a few meters to one of the nacelles. The *Wildflower* had long ago been converted to a dual-engine, dual-imploder design, with a powerful mini-thor reactor at her heart. All of it now lay dormant, all the usual hums and shudders eerily gone from the sonic landscape. Gloria followed the voice, and found Beth at the end of the short maintenance tunnel, around a corner. She'd taken off several access panels that surrounded feed lines from the reactor, and stared at them with deep concern.

"Tell me truthfully," Gloria urged. "Do we need to evacuate?"

Beth glanced at her, the beam of her helmet light momentarily blinding. She looked away when Gloria winced. "Sorry. No. I don't think so. The reactor is stable. However, both conduits sheared when the ripple hit us."

"Please tell me we didn't leave the spares behind."

"I . . . I can't remember. Checking the inventory." Tiny lines and shapes of light appeared in front of her as she accessed the ship's computer via a p-comm worn over her right ear.

"Any idea what happened?" Gloria asked.

Beth turned and pushed herself toward the control room, then up the central shaft toward storage. Gloria followed. In an even tone the engineer said, "Misshapen curvature in the local field. Probably."

"Meaning what?"

"Meaning there is some object nearby that our models didn't account for. Something massive enough to cause a non-flat exit landscape."

"Does this mean we're off course?"

Beth considered that, then shook her head. "We're where we should be, the real question is what else is around."

"Something big?"

"Either big and distant or small and close . . . no way to know yet."

Beth rummaged through one of the wall cabinets and found what she was looking for. Her hands emerged holding a silvery bag with two thick cables coiled inside. Spare parts. Without a word she turned and began to push back toward the tail of the ship.

"Keep me posted," Gloria said at her back. "We need power, then engines, then the other imploder. In that order. Understood?"

"Yes."

"And suit up, just in case. It's going to get cold in here."

Beth nodded almost absently, utterly focused on the task.

Caps, Gloria thought, pushing back toward the central spine. The small thorium reactor provided power and propulsion, but the ship had a bank of ultracapacitors to handle electricity needs during maintenance or failure. Why were they still offline, too?

"Any damage?" she called ahead of herself, drifting through the darkness toward the navigator's bay.

"Smacked my head pretty good," Xavi answered. "No worse than a rugby match."

"I meant the ultracaps."

As if in answer the whole ship reverberated as power flowed back into its veins. Lights winked on up and down the spine, and with them came the familiar whir of the air processors. Almost immediately the haze began to dissipate. A split second later came a chorus of alarms sounded from every section.

"Was that you or Beth?" Gloria asked.

"Me," Xavi said. "Can't get to the primary due to the fire, it's totally shot. Had to manually crank over to secondary."

"Thrusters?"

"Not yet. Gyros will take a minute, but they're not good for much."

"Well, we may not be able to move, but at least we can see. Remember, no active sensors until I okay it.

We emit nothing, right? Sutter's orders. The longer it takes the Swarm to spot us, the better."

"After that exit we already stick out like the dog's balls."

"Even so, no sensor sweeps."

"I hear you loud and clear, boss."

She flew on up to the bridge and settled into her chair, eyes scanning the banks of screens before her.

The *Wildflower* tumbled through space, though she only knew this from the instrument readouts before her. Exterior views were still powering up.

"Maneuvering thrusters are up," Xavi said in her ear a minute later.

"Copy. I'm righting us." Gloria commanded the ship to settle itself relative to the local star. Gently, so as not to throw everyone inside against a wall. She felt a slight tug as the tiny engines ignited, pulling her to one side.

"Stellar navigation coming online," Xavi said.

She had the same display, though typically with less detail to minimize distraction. Given the circumstances, she ordered it to give her the full breadth of information.

They'd made it, that much was immediately obvious. Kepler-22 had eleven planets, and they were just inside the orbit of the second farthest, a tiny ball of ice dubbed Skara Brae. Each world in the system had been named after a fabled lost city of Earth. Gloria had no idea why.

She ran a hand over her face. She needed to focus. Skara Brae was good. They were exactly where they were supposed to be.

No sign of the *Zephyr*, but they'd be running dark as

well, so unless Sutter made contact she'd have to assume they'd made it through. In better shape, with any luck.

But there was something unexpected in their wake, more or less where the *Zephyr* should be. An unidentifiable mass roughly ten thousand kilometers from the fold exit, a distance growing rapidly due to the speed at which the *Wildflower* had emerged. Exiting a fold meant emerging in a poorly understood situation at high velocity. Usually so far away from anything else that it didn't matter. That was all going to change with the Mark 5, she realized.

Her eyes found and focused on the large object that hadn't factored into Beth's calculations. The mystery ended almost before it began, as Gloria recognized the massive oblong shape immediately.

A Scipio supply ship, and it was turning toward them. The term *supply* was an Earth-given affectation. In truth no one knew what purpose the behemoths served, but they were common in the vast swath of space between the world of Carthage and the distant, ever-vigilant fleet that was the Swarm Blockade. Sometimes these massive ships would fly out to that orbital distance and make a circuit of the Swarm, the little scout vessels connecting with and then detaching from the much larger supplier. Gloria subscribed to the theory the big ships were delivering fuel, or food, or something like it.

A debris cloud was pushing out from one side of the massive ship. Fire and explosions lit up the infrared from a gash at the center.

"You seeing that, boss?" Xavi asked.

"I am."

"Think Sutter did that?"

"It's likely. The question is whether it was on purpose or a collision."

"Of all the damn luck."

"Beth?" Gloria called.

The reply came instantly. "Almost done, Captain."

"You'd better be, dear, because we've got company."

"Understood." A quiver in her voice.

"Thank you. Xavi?"

"God, they're close," he said, distracted.

"And they've already seen us. So light up the active sensors. Focus on the *Zephyr*. Where are they, and in what condition. Remember our role here."

He grunted. "Good. I hate hiding. Full sweep initiated."

The plan had been to emerge well inside the Swarm, and sit absolutely quiet as long as possible while Sutter and his crew searched for the missing ship. Just in case, Gloria brought up the sensor interface and added her own commands to the queue, commands designed to listen for the transponder of the original lost ship, the *Lonesome,* and any distress call or message Captain Dawson might have left. It would be a while yet before signals from the diversionary fleet arrived, so distant were they. With any luck they were already pulling a big chunk of the Swarm away, giving the *Zephyr* and the *Wildflower* a nice cushion of time to perform their mission.

She was about to close the interface when she no-

ticed another command in the scanner queue. An odd
one, quite complex. It had been entered seconds before
by Beth Lee.

Gloria's eyes narrowed. "Beth?"

"Finishing up now. The reactor should be—"

"Never mind that. What's this sensor request you
added?"

Silence.

Xavi's portrait, on the side of the screen, looked directly at Gloria, eyebrows raised.

"Answer me, please," Gloria added.

"I . . . ," Beth said. "It's a passive—"

"What are you looking for?"

More silence. Then, meekly, she said, "Skyler Luiken's
Key Ship."

Gloria blinked.

Xavi let out a little laugh.

"On whose orders?"

Beth glanced down, embarrassed. When she replied
she sounded like a child. "No one's. I just wanted to
know—"

"Miss Lee," Gloria said, "we've had ships exploring
the edges of this system for more than a decade. Ever
since we could fold space. Nothing's ever been found.
No signals, no signatures. Nothing."

The Key Ship had left Earth almost two thousand
years earlier, the culmination of a bizarre "first contact" with an alien race known as the Builders. After
subjecting Earth to a series of events that almost wiped
out humanity, the Builders finally showed themselves
and explained their actions. It had all been a test, of

sorts, and humanity had passed. Despite all the death and destruction, a small group of humans led by Skyler Luiken had agreed to stay on the Builder vessel, dubbed the Key Ship because of the strange objects that had activated it. The tests Earth had been subjected to implied that humans could help the Builders break the siege of their home world.

No one had ever heard from them again, though, and the siege remained in full force.

"I understand your point of view, Captain Tsandi, but it is possible that part of the Swarm's purpose is to dampen or distort any such signals from leaving the system."

"It's been, what, seventeen hundred years, Beth? Face it, they failed." Gloria studied the woman's face, wondering why it was that brilliant people so often believed things so obviously not true. The Builders, and their human helpers, had failed. Everyone agreed on that. If they'd ever reached their destination or not, no one knew, but the fact was Carthage was still under siege, the Swarm Blockade an impenetrable barrier. Of the fate of the human crew no message had ever been received. It had all been a long time ago, the deeds and actions mostly the stuff of legend despite a decent media record.

Gloria counted herself among those who couldn't care less. It was ancient history. Earth had moved on. Bounced back from that calamity with surprising force. Resettled and rebuilt. Explored and exploited the solar system. And then had come the ability to fold space.

Beth started to argue again, but Gloria cut her off.

"The *Lonesome,* Beth, that's what we're here for, understand? *They* made it. *That* we know for sure. And we know what happens if the Scipios find them before we do. That craft, or the *Zephyr* or us, could lead the Scipios to Earth. This isn't some archeological expedition. We've got to locate and either retrieve or destroy the *Lonesome,* and then get out of here ourselves. I want to know you understand. I want to hear you say it."

A silence stretched, and Gloria felt an anger she'd not expected begin to fade. She'd always made it a point of pride not to raise her voice with her crew. She saw those who flew with her as her family, and if her parents had taught her one thing it was that warmth and compassion were a courtesy you should afford your own.

"The Key Ship could lead them to Earth, too," Beth Lee said in her flat, factual way. "By that logic, I mean. Captain."

The words were like a splash of cold water. "You . . . We'll debate that later. Focus on the task at hand, Miss Lee," Gloria said, because she couldn't really disagree. "We're adrift in perhaps the most dangerous place in the galaxy. This is not the time for distractions."

The other woman nodded, and went back to work.

Gloria stewed, her finger hovering over an icon. After a few seconds she pulled back. She did not remove the sensor request.

"Boss!" Xavi shouted, despite the comm in her ear being online.

Gloria winced. "Go ahead."

"The long range!"

She shifted focus to it. Out near the edge of the system, an evenly spaced grid of dots formed a gigantic sphere around the solar system. The *Wildflower* hadn't been here long enough to get a true fix on any but the closest, and she saw immediately what had Xavi so excited. The dots were pushing *out,* not in toward her. The ruse of the diversionary fleet had worked, at least for now. *If only this damn supply ship wasn't right on top of us.*

"Well, that's something," she said. "What about this behemoth? Any escort?"

"Not that I can see, but she's coming about."

"And the *Zephyr*?"

"Crickets, nothing but crickets."

Gloria's heart sank even as it beat faster. "Keep me apprised. Beth, I need an update."

The engineer replied a second later, the rebuke of moments earlier evidently forgotten. "Engines should be back online in one minute, maybe less."

"What about the imploder?" Gloria asked, already dreading the reply. Beth would have mentioned it first if the news were good.

"That's going to take a bit more time."

"How much more?"

"I don't like to guess."

"I'm ordering you to guess, Miss Lee."

A hesitation. Studying raw data, probably.

"Twenty minutes, maybe."

Gloria considered that. The time made little difference, in truth. Without engines the imploder would be useless.

"Xavi?"

"Yeah, boss."

"Calculate us an escape trajectory, just in case. I want it ready at the touch of an icon." The Mark 5 imploder may be able to exit a fold in slightly curved space, but it still had to enter at a point of near-zero curvature or face serious risk. When the time came to leave, they'd have to be well away from this ship, these planets, this Sun. Every second of head start they could get would make a difference.

And what's more, Gloria thought with growing worry, they only had the one imploder left. Part of the mass-shedding diet the *Wildflower* had been on in preparation for this mission. One imploder meant just getting out to a safe distance wasn't enough. To perform a hasty fold without the usual careful calculations would be pointless. A big object like this supply ship curved space only minutely, but that was enough to drop you trillions of kilometers from the intended destination, reliant on distress calls that worked only at the poky speed of light. Normally not a problem, she'd just recalculate and try again. No such luxury here. Gloria would just have to hope, if the time came to do an emergency fold, that they'd have time to aim at Earth, or a colony, or some distant supply cache. "We need to be ready to leave if Sutter orders us to." If he's still alive, she left unsaid.

"You got it."

Minutes later a bright red INCOMING TRANSMISSION event popped up on the comm screen, and for the first time since arriving Gloria felt a pang of hope.

Sutter's face appeared a second later. Blood ran from a gash on his forehead, the cockpit behind him a mixture of darkness, showers of white-hot sparks, and the urgent cries and shouts of a crew in dire straits.

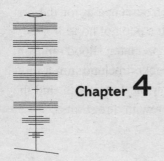

Chapter 4

"*WILDFLOWER,*" SUTTER SAID, "get the hell out of here!"

The image suddenly stretched to the left, smeared by interference, and the audio garbled.

"Where are you? We'll come—"

"No," Sutter said through the static. "Get away. That's an order. We're badly damaged. Collided with that heap of shit. Reactor leak. Imploder damaged. Not—"

A sharp bang preceded the link being dropped.

Gloria tapped a button and her wraparound display instantly shifted to a tactical configuration. She whirled, spinning her couch to face aft, and saw the nearby Scipio behemoth looming, almost finished with its slow turn that would put it on the *Wildflower*'s trajectory.

"Xavi!"

"I heard him."

"Find them, now. I don't . . . I can't see—"

"Already on it. Working on that link, too."

Gloria skimmed the intel on the giant hauler. It was

almost a kilometer long and looked as if built from a hundred skyscrapers lashed together. One element did stick out: the word UNARMED right there at the top of the screen. That seemed to be the consensus, at least, according to distant observation. It seemed a safe assumption they would have some kind of ability to at least investigate a hostile presence like the *Wildflower.* Gloria did not intend to wait around and find out.

"The link's coming back," Xavi said.

Sutter's face appeared, like a ghost in digital noise. He was saying something but no sound came through.

"Where are you?" Gloria pleaded.

His reply came through in fractured syllables. "Forget us. We're in . . . —wake. Rejoin fleet and try—"

A wash of signal corruption. "Dammit, dammit . . . ," Gloria said. The enemy vessel completed its turn. Somewhere in the vast plume of its gigantic engines, the *Zephyr* was being melted. "Its mass must have shifted your exit right on top of it, and ours near enough."

Sutter's voice came back, though the visual had died. "Buy you time," was all Gloria could make out.

The implications chilled her. The *Zephyr* was done for, and Sutter would not allow her secrets to fall into Scipio hands. The same decision would face Gloria if she could not get away. "Beth? I need good news."

"Engines in ten seconds," she replied.

"Thank you. Xavi?"

"Say the word, boss."

"Do it!"

"Full burn, coming up."

And he meant it. The instant Beth's countdown hit

zero, Gloria's seat spun of its own accord, facing her along the acceleration vector. An instant of silence followed, then she slammed back into her chair as if propelled on the edge of an explosion. A pressure that kept piling on. The corners of her vision blurred and tinted dark red. Bits of the ship began to rattle, then the entire hull shuddered. Gloria's own teeth clattered together. In her haste she'd forgotten her mouthpiece, which hung from her collar, but with her arm now pinned by the force of the engines she could do nothing about it.

Something clanged from somewhere midship. A terrible thought went through her mind: *Could the ship handle it, so soon after that rocky arrival?*

Too late to worry about that. Gloria gripped the arms of her chair and ground her trembling teeth. She felt the knife of unconsciousness begin to twist from the corners of her vision and slammed her eyes shut, but the sensation did not go away, it only grew. Then her compression suit squeezed so hard she'd have screamed if she could. The pain all along her chest and thighs was savage and bright, but the suit didn't care, the suit performed its function by keeping her conscious.

"Xavi, you're tearing us apart!" she growled, the words tumbling out like spit gravel.

"All systems green!" he shot back. "All systems green!"

Unable to see, Gloria could only trust him. She didn't like Xavi much. Not as a friend. He was heartless and brash, the kind of man she avoided in her personal life. But damned if he wasn't reliable as a mountain when things went wrong. Friend or not, he was family to her. The renegade little brother, loved despite the flaws.

Through the constant shuddering roar of the engines, Gloria found she could open her eyes after a minute of acclimation. She scanned the readouts and imagery in front of her.

The Scipio supply ship now pointed right at the *Wildflower*, its engines forming a glowing yellow haze around the profile. Somewhere in that fiery exhaust was the *Zephyr*, if it hadn't already been vaporized. Gloria studied her pursuer, both in visual and on the other frequencies, but as of yet could see no smaller craft or missiles in flight. Beam weapons would of course impact at the same time as any indication of their use, but as of yet the *Wildflower* had suffered only the usual Scipio sensor sweeps. Nothing to be done about that. Scipios rarely fired on ships from Earth. They wanted a working example of an imploder too badly. The question was, how would they react when presented with two such ships in such close proximity? If the *Zephyr* was salvageable . . .

Gloria swallowed hard, eyes darting briefly to the section of her control screen where she could override all safety measures in the fusion core, and turn this ship into a fireball that would briefly shine brighter than the Sun. How many before her had resorted to that? Plenty. Dozens. A graveyard of wreckage adrift in the cold vacuum well beyond Skara Brae and even tiny Hatra at the system's edge. Is that what Sutter would do now? What Dawson had done, before?

She'd spent many evenings in half-drunken conversations with Xavi about the suicide pact. The handshake agreement every captain of a fold-capable ship made with the OEA. Gloria felt it the most important promise in the universe, and rebuffed every unlikely scenario Xavi tried to concoct where she'd have to ignore it. Easy enough to say such things when you weren't in command, but for her part Gloria appreciated the point of view. The contrast in perspective was one of the things she loved about his place in the crew. Not that she'd ever tell him.

On her long-range screen the diversion fleet continued to race away from the Swarm at top speed, though the gap had already started to shrink noticeably. The Swarm Blockade had visibly bowed outward, like a bubble forming. But the pattern had changed. Some had started to move in, on trajectories that would bring them to intercept the *Wildflower*. Still hours away, sure, but the little bastards were *fast*. She reviewed what she knew of the enemy Swarm. The little spherical ships had a single pilot, so integrated with the vessel that it was difficult to tell where one stopped and the other began. Creatures that were bred or perhaps simply engineered to live out their lives inside their ship. Advantaged so, they could accelerate far more quickly than the *Wildflower*.

The rearview display flashed, then remained perfectly white.

For a second Gloria thought it had died, but then came the radiation alarms and a strange, thin vibration that ran through everything. Not just the ship, but a sharp buzz Gloria felt in her body. "What the—"

"The *Zephyr* just winked out!" Xavi blurted out, stunned. "Shit, boss, oh fuck, they just went nuclear! Self-destruct. Has to be."

"We're in the shadow," Gloria muttered to herself. Sutter had waited until the *Wildflower* was occluded by the Scipio cargo ship, then turned his own vessel into a weapon.

"The enemy is falling back," Xavi said. "Their engines are down, maybe for good."

Thank you, Sutter, she thought.

Xavi's tone notched up even higher. She'd never heard him so amped. "Detecting heat on the surface of that barge!" he shouted. "Building fast! Core breach maybe, I don't know. Oh shit!"

Gloria's gaze shifted there. The hauler had begun to fall back, no longer able to pursue the Earth vessel's growing velocity. But Xavi was right. Along one flank, a patch of her hull had begun to glow in infrared. Nowhere near its core, though. "Brace yourselves!" she shouted.

A shuddering boom ripped through the craft. The force of it threw the ship into a sideways, rolling tumble. Gloria lost consciousness. When she came around the displays in front of her were a throbbing mess of red and orange flashing icons punctuated with alarms from all over the ship. She heard the staccato pops of the maneuvering thrusters as they worked in vain to negate the motion. "What—" she started, then paused as a wave of dizziness and nausea ran its course. "What happened? Status, Xavi!"

No reply came.

She called again, her words cut off by a racking cough. Sparks erupted from several cable conduits behind her screens. "Talk to me, damn you!"

"Here!" It was Beth, sounding far away, her voice oddly calm. "I'm okay. Vitals are offline, I can't check Xavi."

"Understood. Stay put until we're righted," Gloria replied. "Xavi! Come on, Xav, I need you!"

A moan came back in response. Then, "Fuck. What the hell was that?"

"Beam weapon of some sort."

"Not fair. Supposed to be unarmed, the pricks."

"Are you hurt?"

"Feel like a 'roo kicked me in the balls if you really want to know."

His words were followed by a perfectly timed and targeted blast from a fire suppression nozzle mounted on a track in the ceiling. A pie-sized disk of white foam flew across the cockpit and slapped against the wall where a panel had opened to reveal a small, yellow gout of flame. The goop smothered the fire, and already the nozzle was zipping away to deal with the next.

Gloria blinked. Fires in the cabin meant imminent danger to the supply of air. She toyed with giving the order for helmets-on, but quickly ditched the idea. There was no time. "Xavi, tell me true, can you handle your station?"

"Yeah. Yes. I'm up to it."

"Beth?"

The engineer replied after a few seconds' delay. "Engines are—"

"Engines can wait. Crew first. Are you hurt?"

"Shaken up, otherwise fine."

Good enough. Gloria let out a breath and shifted her focus to the *Wildflower* itself. "Okay, then. The engines, our return imploder. Tell me."

"That was a surgical hit to the last imploder. I'm sending a roach in to check but it doesn't . . . Captain, it took a direct hit. It can't have survived."

"Acknowledged."

Beth added, "We're stuck here. There's no way the imploder will work after that."

"Let's not jump to conclusions."

"We're not *jumping* anywhere. That's what I'm trying to tell you."

Gloria bit back the desire to dress down the newcomer. This wasn't the time. "I fully understand what you mean, Miss Lee. Now send that roach and let me know what the hard facts are."

"I . . . sorry. You're right. It's already crawling out there," she said. "If we can kill thrust I'll send a wasp, too."

Roaches—tiny robots the size of a thumb—crawled throughout the ship to observe damage firsthand. They could get places the human crew could not, and absorb immense amounts of radiation. Wasps were similar, only made to view the ship from outside. However, they had little in the way of propulsion, and thus could not be used when the ship was under thrust.

"If anything we need to speed up, Beth, so hold off on that for now."

"Okay," she breathed. Then, more calm: "Okay."

Gloria felt a powerful headache pushing through her adrenaline high. Direct hit or not, she had to get herself under control. A menu on one of her screens allowed her to inject painkillers. Her finger hovered there, then pulled away. Not now, not yet, she told herself. The last thing she needed was the fog of medication. "Xavi, we need to get as far from that ship as we can. Out of range. Punch it."

"She's as punched as she's going to get, boss."

"It's not enough."

"Don't know what to tell you."

Gloria bit her lip. If by some miracle the imploder could be fixed, they still couldn't use it without substantial distance from any significant source of mass. At least, not without massive risk. But pure distance wasn't the biggest issue. Another shot like that last and they'd be totally disabled. It wasn't distance she needed between the *Wildflower* and the Scipio ship, it was an obstacle. "Beth?"

"The roach is up on feed four. Significant damage to—"

"I need to know now. Can it be fixed?"

A pause. "It's impossible, Captain. Not out here, with no parts. Maybe not ever. I'm sorry."

The words brought silence to the ship, their meaning clear and devastating. They would not be folding home. And yet they could not remain here, a little bundle of tech and Earth-knowledge ripe for the Scipio plucking.

With an effort, Gloria stilled herself. She put as much calm and confidence into her voice as she could. "Listen to me. I'm going to jettison the imploder and its launcher."

"Hold on—" Beth blurted. She'd been right about the imploder, but not prepared to deal with what it meant, evidently.

Gloria went on, calm. "We won't survive another hit like that. We need chaff to buy time. There's no other way."

"Buy time for what? Captain, please. If you mean to scuttle—"

"If it comes to that," Gloria said. "That is our obligation to everyone back home. But perhaps we have some cards to play still."

The words quieted the engineer.

Gloria went on. "Keep it and we'll be crippled and adrift when the next lance hits us. Lose it and maybe, just maybe, we shed enough mass to get out of range. We make for the diversion fleet. Transfer to one of them."

"Captain's right." Xavi's voice. "And, mates, the debate is pointless. The damaged core is heating up. Runaway reaction. It has to go or we all cook. I say jettison now, boss."

Gloria needed no more excuse than that. An imploder

in full meltdown was nothing she wanted to be any-where near, and simultaneously just about the best obstacle she could put in the *Wildflower*'s wake. She punched in the commands and let a retinal scan confirm her order. With virtually no fanfare, the missile de-tached from the ship and began to fall back. "Get around that, you bastards," she said.

"Boss?" Xavi asked.

"Go ahead."

"Maneuvering thrusters on the missile's hull still work."

"Okay, and?"

"If it's about to go critical, maybe we should fly the fucking thing toward our friend back there?"

She grinned, despite herself. "Such ruthlessness nor-mally makes me weep for your soul, Xavi, but right now I want to hug you. Do it."

"No disrespect, but I'm way ahead of you."

The giant chunk of mangled gear began to push backward. The core of the imploder had begun to glow already. Xavi nudged them, first negating the terrible out-of-control tumble, then a second adjustment that pushed Gloria hard into the right side of her chair.

"Hid our little gift in the *'Flower*'s exhaust," Xavi said. "With any luck they won't see it until it's too late."

Gloria silently thanked the Universe for Xavi. For his competence as a pilot, and his unflappable nature. Foulmouthed testosterone bundle or not, he had his perks.

Her focus shifted then to the bigger problem of getting home. The awful truth was that they were inside the Swarm Blockade. They had to get to the fleet, had to link up with one of them and transfer the crew across before the Swarm closed in. Once emptied, the *Wildflower* could be self-destructed while Gloria and her crew were safely carried away.

The question was, how? The Swarm may have been distracted, but it was that distraction Gloria now needed to rendezvous with. She chewed her lip, drummed her fingers on the armrest.

Icons all across her long range began to flash red. The diversionary fleet. "Oh God," Gloria whispered, one hand coming up to cover her mouth.

One by one the other vessels from Earth began to vanish in clouds of superheated gas and debris.

Their plan to create a diversion, to draw the Swarm away, had worked. What no one anticipated, though, was that the Swarm would attack at range. Swarm ships *always* pursued and attempted to board. That behavior had been consistent from the moment they realized the prize an Earth ship would be. Yet here, now, their tactic changed. Perhaps because they already had a prize, the *Wildflower,* so far inside the net, practically gift wrapped. Or, Gloria thought with growing dread, it was because they already had Dawson's ship, the *Lonesome,* in custody. Maybe that's why they'd fired on the *Wildflower.*

After the first few explosions the others began to execute unplanned folds. Suicide by any other name, for such an action set aside everything an imploder re-

quired to actually work. Insufficient velocity. Poor timing. No precisely calculated aim. All of that added up
to zero hope of a clean arrival at the other end. They'd
be twisted and wrenched, spat out who-knows-where, a
mangled mockery of the ship that folded in. A horrible
way to go.

What little grip Gloria still had on calm melted away.
She wept. All those souls. Captains she'd explored
with, shared meals with, and fought beside. Engineers
and scientists and medical officers. People who, despite living with the dangers of riding the fold, had
families back home.

The crushing sense of helplessness began to replace
her fear. This was a total catastrophe. No other way
to slice it. The decade-old game of snooping about
in Kepler-22's oort cloud, trying to catch some glimpse
of what the Scipios were up to, knowing they would
not dare fire on a ship from Earth that might contain
a priceless working example of a fold missile, was
over.

Hunting season had begun, and the *Wildflower* was a
rabbit surrounded by wolves.

When only one ship remained the shooting merci-
fully stopped. The scouts had their prey now, it seemed,
having thinned the herd. They began to close the noose
on that last remnant of the diversion fleet, a ship called
the *Sporting Chance*.

A coded transmission flittered across Gloria's main
display. A brief note from the *Sporting*'s captain, Gardiner, a woman Gloria knew well.

HEAD FOR US AT MAX BURN
AND CLOSE YOUR EYES
GODSPEED

"Xavi?" Gloria asked, her voice wavering, tears streaming down her cheeks.

"What a nightmare."

"Gardiner's message."

"I see it," he replied.

"Do as she asks."

"Yeah. Yeah, okay, boss."

A second later the *Wildflower* shifted course.

Two things happened almost simultaneously. Now far behind, the damaged imploder core finally went critical. The fireball stretched out in a sphere a thousand kilometers in diameter, swallowing the pursuing Scipio hauler in a nuclear inferno.

Much, much farther away, the *Sporting Chance* vanished in a similar blast, only much more intense, as her self-destruct countdown reached zero. A vast swath of space briefly glowed as bright as a star. The encroaching Scipio Swarm ships were consumed in the blast. Ancillary explosions flickered out near the edges of the temporary sun, and then it all began to cool. Left behind was a gigantic hole in the Swarm Blockade, with the *Wildflower* aimed right at the center of it, building speed with every passing second.

Gloria Tsandi let the tears fall. She did nothing to stop them. Dozens of ships, their hundreds of crew, had just sacrificed everything to give the *Wildflower* a chance at escape. They could not have known it was all pointless. That she could not fold space. All they'd done is bought her a little time. A chance to make peace.

She reached out and touched the screen where the fireballs still cooled. "Thank you," she whispered, to the group of strangers who'd just given their lives in a failed attempt to save hers.

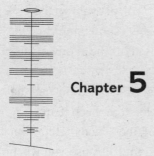

Chapter 5

GLORIA TSANDI WIPED the tears from her eyes, gripped the armrests of her chair and squeezed until her fingertips burned. She could not—would not—waste their gift.

"Push us harder, Xavi," she said through gritted teeth.

Below, her navigator grunted in surprise. "We're already pushing four g's, Captain."

"And if we don't run that gap we're going to end up just like our friends out there."

The tone of the engines changed. Gloria felt her weight increase, now five times Earth normal. The edges of her vision grew dark. She slammed her eyes shut against it but found no refuge there. Red and yellow dots began to swim across the inside of her eyelids. Her suit began to squeeze her body to combat the effect. The ship rattled from a dozen different places, things that would have been pronounced utterly secure before a normal flight. Shaken loose on their botched arrival, or when they'd been struck by the Scipio vessel.

An anguished moan rose from below. Beth, unused to such a high-g maneuver. "Are you okay down there?" Gloria asked. Give the engineer something to talk about, something to take her mind off the agony of sustained full acceleration.

"I—" Beth started, the extraordinary strain making her voice almost unrecognizable. "I've been better."

"I'd say we're almost out of the woods, Beth, but that'd be a lie. Stim if you need to, I'll rouse you when the time comes."

"Thank you, Captain."

She must have been waiting, hoping, to hear just that, because a second later Gloria's status monitor indicated the injection request, and ten seconds after that Beth's vitals became those of a lazy summer nap.

Good for her. Most of Gloria's regular crew allowed a minor injection the moment their ship passed the three-gravities mark, and that was okay. Gloria understood and encouraged the practice, but opted not to do it to herself. To stim was to trade comfort now for one hell of a hangover later, not to mention slowed reflexes and a lack of focus. Gloria couldn't afford it. As captain she had to be ready, always. So she gripped her armrests even harder, and felt her body squeezed by the force of their flight. She focused on the face of her friend, Gardiner, holding on to the woman's sacrifice like a talisman. ·

The burn went on and on. Relative to the distant star, the *Wildflower*'s velocity surpassed four hundred kilometers per second and kept on climbing. "Xavi?"

"Yeah, boss?" he replied.

"Once we hit five hundred kps relative, execute a confusion maneuver."

"Jesus. You sure?"

"Nothing but open space ahead. They've probably already fired on our likely trajectory, and even if they haven't they'll be heading to where we'll be. No point in making it easy for them."

"Making this awfully hard on us, though."

"I can handle it if you can."

"It's our friend back there I'm worried about."

"She's stimmed, and let's be honest, without a functional imploder her usefulness is . . . reduced. She knows the engines a bit, and a lot of ancient history, but that's about it."

Xavi grunted an acknowledgment that said he wasn't happy.

"That gap won't help us if we get obliterated on the way, yes? So execute the maneuver," she said, "and I'll take care of the signature masking."

"Okay, boss. Okay."

Four hundred klicks per second came up only minutes later. Gloria braced herself for the nausea to come. The confusion maneuver was hardest on her stim-free body.

Four-fifty. Five hundred. Gloria slammed her eyes shut.

The *Wildflower* rocked to one side, so abruptly she almost mistook it for an impact. Then it lurched again. And again. Up, left, down. She felt as if in free fall, then as if climbing an eighty-degree incline in a rocket-powered sled. Now she flew sideways as if kicked by a giant. Then back.

"Gnnnnh," she cried. With one eye partially open, she reached out and activated her portion of the plan. "Signature masking in effect!" she shouted over the howls of displeasure that came from every corner of the ship. The custom program analyzed the closest enemy and then manipulated the ship's radiators and heat sinks so as to effectively make it invisible, at least at this extreme range. Instead of venting waste heat in all directions, the hull would work at capacity on the edge opposite their opponent, and chill the closest surfaces to match the background radiation.

Gloria, battling the intense desire to heave her stomach's contents, chanced a look at the navigation display. If the closest Scipio vessel reached visual range—a distance humanity could only guess at—all bets were off. The masking system could do nothing in the visual wavelengths.

Xavi's movement of the ship, on the other hand, would create a rapidly growing cone of potential future locations. Given their enemies were on the order of light-minutes away, each randomized shift in velocity would make the *Wildflower* difficult to shoot at, much less intercept.

Gloria winced as the craft jolted itself into a hard climb, then slammed her down into her seat with a force that sent her unconscious for several seconds.

When she came to, the ship had settled, once again accelerating hard in a straight line. "Xavi? Status."

"That's enough to get them guessing. Lose your lunch?"

"I skipped my last meal for just this reason."

"Aw, now don't say 'last meal' like that. You'll put a whammy on us."

"Did it work? Our maneuver?"

"We're not dead," he replied. "What we can infer from that is that I am a bona fide genius."

"It was my suggestion."

"Details . . ."

Back to business, Gloria told herself. "Aim for the gap the *Sporting Chance* made for us, and get me as much velocity as you possibly can."

The *Wildflower* raced along, engines pushed to maximum burn. Gloria forced her eyes to stay open now, staring at the long range and hoping against hope they'd breach the blockade before the gap closed up. It was going to be close.

A screeching roar filled her ears, coming from all directions at once. In that instant the screens before her went haywire, flickering, their graphics skewed.

"Fuck!" Xavi shouted.

Something popped in front of Gloria. Sparks flew out from behind the display panel, showering upward and then ahead due to the ship's path. Smoke filled her bridge, then everything went absolutely dark. All sense of gravity faded as the engines went silent.

"What in the world was that?" she said.

Xavi, coughing, growled a reply. "Hell if I know. EMP maybe. Christ. Total power loss."

"Beth!" Gloria shouted, already out of her harness and drifting aft. No reply came. She'd stimmed, Gloria reminded herself. Probably sleeping like a baby.

The ship had gone black again, save for glow-in-the-dark tape used to label the cabinets and drawers that lined the interior walls. Not enough to see by, but useful to get her bearings. Gloria pushed herself down the central shaft, a hard hollow feeling in her gut. If the Scipios had hit them with a strong enough EM pulse, all systems would be fried. The *Wildflower*, like any spacecraft, had significant shielding, but only to a point.

Everything smelled of ozone and burned rubber. The only sounds came from the shifting bodies of the crew. Nothing functioned. Not the machines that scrubbed their air, nor the sensors and heat sinks that kept the interior temperature regulated. Nothing.

Seventeen minutes, Gloria recalled. Seventeen precious minutes before the conditions inside became unsuitable for life.

Red emergency lights winked on, lining the rings of each deck along the shaft. A few screens flickered to life, warnings flowing across their surfaces. Gloria allowed herself a quick breath of relief. "Xavi, I'm out of harness! Keep the engines at standby!"

"Assuming they even work. Those assholes really nailed us that time."

"Talk to me, Beth! Wake up!" Gloria said, reaching her engineer's acceleration couch. She shook the woman by her shoulders, hard.

Beth Lee shifted, then her eyes fluttered before finally opening. She coughed once, her gaze unfocused. "What time is it?"

"They hit us with something. Almost everything's offline. I need you." Without asking approval, not that she needed it as captain, Gloria swung the engineering screen toward herself and tapped the command to pump more drugs into her engineer's system. A concoction that would negate the effects of the sedatives. Beth would pay for it later, but Gloria saw no alternative.

A few seconds passed, then the engineer sat bolt upright and began to study her displays. The words tumbled out. "Reactor is still functional. The shutdown was a fail-safe precaution. I'll clear it."

"How long?"

"Three minutes. Maybe five. I don't know the ship."

Gloria nodded, gave the woman's shoulder a reassuring squeeze, then pushed herself back to the bridge and settled into her chair.

She'd just buckled her own harness when the missile hit.

A rending sound screamed through the air, rattling every bone in her body. The ship heaved sideways in an uncontrolled end-over-end spin that made Gloria feel as if she was hanging upside down from the ceiling. Centrifugal force wanted to toss her out of the *Wildflower*'s nose.

Something flew past her head and slammed into the main display. The rattle of shrapnel filled the ship. "Report!" she shouted.

"Direct hit to engine two," Xavi replied, anger, not

panic, in his voice. "Control thrusters also offline. Beth, I need engines and I need them now!"

"I'm trying," the engineer replied, though the strain in her voice said more than her words. She couldn't get out of her chair, much less perform repairs, with the ship spinning so violently. "I don't . . . I'm sorry. I can't move. Can't think."

Gloria racked her mind. No control thrusters meant Xavi couldn't negate this tumbling motion easily. His only option was to fire the one remaining engine in such a way as to kill the spin, but that would also take them wildly off course. *His* only option, she realized, but not hers. Gloria, already being pulled toward her control displays, worked through the menus until she found what she needed: plumbing. The ship had a series of bladders just beneath the outer hull, filled dynamically with water, waste, or any of a number of other fluids. These served to regulate the heat within the ship, balance its mass, and absorb radiation from outside. Gloria swept her fingers over a dozen options, then found the two she needed. "Xavi, hold off, I'm going to try something."

"Don't tell me, mate, just fucking do it!"

Tapping with two fingers simultaneously, Gloria vented two of the bladders into space at the same instant. Usually this was done extremely slowly so as to not impact the ship's course. Rapid venting was only done in extreme circumstances, such as contamination. Emptied explosively, the effect was like a temporary and very hard control thrust. Another gut-wrenching change of velocity made her feel like her lungs were going to squirt right out of her nose. She groaned, a sound matched by the others below.

Gloria had no idea how much to vent and overestimated. The trick worked so well that the *Wildflower* now rotated in the opposite direction as before, though thankfully at only a fraction of the rate. She repeated the technique with two more bladders on opposite sides, this time venting just a few percent of their capacity. The spin ended. The *Wildflower* was coasting in the right direction even if her nose now pointed at an oblique angle to that vector.

"Brilliant," Xavi said.

"It's not going to matter much if we don't get our engines back," she said. *Or if we get hit again.* She left that unsaid. The Scipios' strike had been surgically precise, which meant not only had the confusion maneuver's effect worn off, but the enemy now shot to wound rather than destroy. The Scipios wanted a working imploder too badly to take risky shots. They'd aimed to disable the *Wildflower,* not knowing she no longer carried any of the precious devices, and they'd succeeded. For now.

"Beth? I need some good news."

"I can only tell you what's really going on."

Gloria winced. The stress in Beth's voice bordered on shock. The captain swallowed hard, trying to draw on Xavi's calm. "Tell me what you know."

"Engine one overloaded and dropped into safe mode. It's coming back but . . . Captain, engine two is all but slag."

"Can it be fixed?"

"Does it matter?" she cried back, seized by fear. "Does it really matter if we can't fold?"

Gloria spoke slowly and deliberately. "No, we can't fold. But someone will come looking for us, and I mean to be out there, waiting. Can we fix it? Rig something?"

A moment passed. Beth took a deep breath. "I'm sorry, Captain Tsandi. The engine is beyond repair. That is not a judgment, that is the truth."

For the second time a deafening silence filled the ship.

One engine, assuming it came back at full strength, which was by no means assured, meant they could not outrun the enemy. The Scipio Swarm would catch and surround them.

Only a matter of time.

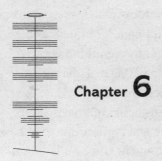

Chapter 6

SKYLER LUIKEN FELT at home for the first time in weeks, as if he'd just opened the cargo ramp of his old beloved aircraft, the *Melville,* in preparation to jump on some ravaged city of Earth.

Only this was far from Earth. And the *Melville,* well, his time as captain of that aircraft had not exactly ended well.

But he was in his element, and he liked it. Even stray thoughts of his old life, and the planet he'd left behind, could not dampen his mood. He was outside. He had a mission. He was armed to the teeth.

Below him stretched the opaque clouds of Kepler-186f. Shifting bands of orange and purple, alive with flashes of lightning, that completely obscured the terrain below. Near the horizon, what Skyler considered west, a great mountain range jutted up above the storm, steep icy slopes lit from the brilliant sporadic flashes below and the wan light of the distant red dwarf.

Though Eve had said this was a small planet, roughly the size of Europa, from here it looked no less gigantic.

An actual alien world, he thought. Not the one they ultimately hoped to reach, but if they couldn't get what the plan required here, the final stage of the journey might well be impossible to accomplish.

He tried to grasp once again the incredible distance and time they'd traversed since leaving. Earth was hundreds of light-years away now, and nearly a millennium had passed back home, though it only felt like a scant month to him.

His fantasy of standing once again on the *Melville*'s open cargo ramp was further eroded by the current mode of transportation. A simple disk-shaped metal platform attached to a space elevator, making a sluggish descent in the weak gravity.

"Just like heading out into the clear for a grab," he said. "Eh, Sam?"

Samantha stood next to him, towering a full head taller than he, with almost Nordic features that made her look like some kind of Viking warrior if not for the futuristic armor. "Whatever you say, *Captain.*"

Would she ever be able to call him that and not have it sound like an insult or jab, subtle or otherwise? Long gone, at least, were the days she pointed out his every mistake as *captain.* Numerous and well-deserved criticisms, truth be told, but he thought he'd earned at least a modicum of respect. She was still the same Samantha Rinn he'd met in Darwin, though. That incongruous mixture of wanting to have orders, and wanting equal status to anyone who might give them to her. She called him captain as if the title were no more important than mister. And here, like back on Earth, he decided to let it go. She was miffed because he'd agreed to Tania Sharma's plan, which called for stealth rather than the blazing guns and bravado that Sam preferred.

He also thought perhaps she was trying to play the hardened badass in front of her fella, Vaughn.

Of the landing party, only Samantha managed to look comfortable in the armored alien space suits their ship had made for them. The remarkably thin material wore like a second skin, and on her stout and muscular form that worked just fine. Vaughn, standing beside Sam, looked like a substitute player in some bizarre sporting event, not quite sure he was supposed to be there but ready to kick some ass all the same. The man rarely left Sam's side. How long until Sam decided that was annoying rather than cute? Soon, probably. Maybe she wasn't trying to impress him after all. Maybe she wanted to scare him off.

The last of the landing party, Vanessa, well . . . she was Vanessa. Standing a bit apart from the group. Serious, composed, and if not comfortable at least she seemed confident. Once upon a time she'd been a lawyer in São Paulo, surviving the horrors inflicted on both Earth and herself through sheer force of will.

Skyler wondered if he was the only one of them who found the alien gear profoundly uncomfortable. It wasn't that it was abrasive or ill-fitting. Quite the opposite, in fact. The suit fit almost too well, surprisingly soft and flexible, only becoming armor when it sensed an approaching object of "problematic impact veloc-

ity," as their machine-AI benefactor, Eve, had put
it. The material somehow convinced his body that it
was his skin, or an extension of it, and it weighed so
little that it took a force of conscious effort to remind
himself that he wasn't completely naked. Only the helmet felt normal, and that only because his team had
specifically told the alien machine that the skintight
version she'd originally made was not going to work.
Too claustrophobic.

The climber began to slow, ending its state of free
fall as the clouds neared. The frothy, ethereal puffs slid
by at a surprising clip. "Hold on to something!" Skyler
shouted, then took his own advice before the winds hit.
The climber Eve provided them was little more than a
scaffold to cling to. She'd offered a fully enclosed capsule, but Skyler saw no point in that. Their suits were
protection enough given the slow descent, and he wanted
to see with his own eyes what they were getting into. But
mostly he was just sick of being confined to her time-
compressed hull, week after week, since leaving Earth.
He might not be able to get fresh air here—it was poi-
sonous in the extreme. He could damn well enjoy the
open space, however.

That desire felt a bit foolish as the clouds met them.
A thin sound worked its way into the suit, like air being
bled from a tire. It grew and soon became a howling
wind that Skyler did not feel, protected so by the armor
and the slab of material that served as the base of the
climber. Vibrations rippled through the cord of the
space elevator. A vicious thrum that crept up through
Skyler's boots and rattled his jaw. He forced himself to

keep his eyes open, an effort soon rewarded as the cloud layer lifted upward to reveal the landscape below.

Skyler's breath caught in his throat.

"Holy shit," Sam said.

"Yeah, holy shit," Vaughn echoed.

You're trying too hard, Skyler thought, wishing the other man would get the hint.

Tortured, rocky formations pushed up through the ground from horizon to horizon. Murky rivers of indeterminate fluid seemed to almost bleed from these protrusions, forming rivers that snaked across the land to ultimately pool in lakes of every size and shape imaginable. There were no oceans, at least not here.

The ground itself was mottled with browns, whites, and mustard yellows, the coloration coming from thousands of species of something like fungi, according to Eve's scans. It grew everywhere, in as much variety as the trees and flowers that so dominated Earth. Plant life was largely absent, with so little sunlight reaching the ground.

"Look there!" Vanessa shouted over the wind.

He glanced at her, then followed her pointed finger to a valley of sorts a few kilometers away. At first Skyler thought this basin must be covered with more of the rocky outcroppings, but those were all confined to the peaks and ridgelines of the planet's surface. The lowest points of the surface were all smooth, undulating low hills. Yet this valley sported a row of giant, thin objects. Not quite rocks, not quite trees.

"Those are what you seek," Eve's synthetic voice said through the comm. "The profile matches."

"I see them," he said. "That's our target, everyone. Those, er, things."

"They're not *things*," Tania Sharma said in his ear, from her remote viewpoint aboard their alien ship.

"They look like things. Gigantic, upright, perfectly balanced, space-traversing things."

She sighed with strained patience. "They're life-forms, Skyler. Think of them as, I don't know, gigantic upright perfectly balanced snap peas."

"Snap peas," he repeated, trying it on. He shook his head. "Nah, doesn't work. How about—"

"Space clams," Samantha said.

"That's . . . better," Skyler replied. They did look a bit like clams. "Agreed, team?"

"Love it," Vaughn said.

Vanessa gave a shrug of indifference.

"Why is it," Prumble said over the comm, "that every time we have to name something it turns out shit."

Skyler stifled a laugh, then gave up. The big man was right, and his boisterous voice and kiwi accent served as a giant exclamation point.

He knew they were not clams at all, but gigantic seedpods. Unfortunately, Eve knew little beyond the fact that they originated here and that, for some reason, they'd evolved an ability to traverse the vacuum of space. How they got off this rock in the first place, or why, remained a mystery. Her visual recordings of the life-forms, be they plants or fungi or something else, were not detailed beyond the general shape and size. Her briefing on the topic had been frustratingly vague, two days prior. The important thing was their size, the largest of them standing over a hundred meters tall, an attribute likely possible due to the minuscule gravity.

The team watched their objective as the climber descended, until the view became obscured by a long ridge in between. Skyler shifted his focus then to their landing site, which consisted of a large black disk embedded into the ground—the tail end of a long spike, in truth, which anchored the space elevator cord in place. Skyler had seen an identical attachment point years earlier, on the outskirts of a dead city in Brazil. Memories flooded through his mind. Of the slow descent he made with the now-deceased Karl, and the obelisk towers they'd found there. The exodus towers, they'd come to be known. A simple push would send them gliding over the ground for kilometers. Not just the ground, he reminded himself. They'd even crossed the Atlantic, from south to north, all the way from Brazil to Ireland. Part of another test that Eve, and her race known as the Builders, had foisted upon humanity.

One test of many, as it turned out, all of which humanity had passed. Or, at least, Skyler and his companions had passed. As a reward, they'd been invited to help the Builders regain their lost home world. A world, indeed an entire solar system, held captive. How any of those tests factored into their goal was still rather infuriatingly vague. Eve felt that explaining it all to them would poison their judgment. Improvisation was, evidently, a big part of humanity's suitability to the job, and their current mission only served to prove the AI's point. It had been Tania's idea, not hers.

He'd lost sleep over this stonewalling, at first. It made

no sense to him. Eve's information about what actually awaited them at their ultimate destination, still light-years away, would be woefully outdated by now. All of the Builder tests humanity had been subjected to were based on old information. *Very* old, by her own admission. What harm could there be in sharing it, of telling them at the very least what had not worked in the past?

"Maybe she will," the young scientist Tim had said, a week ago, "but only if the need arises. Maybe her silence means we're on the right track."

Skyler wasn't so sure. In fact, he'd become more and more worried Eve had absolutely no idea what was really going on, or what awaited them.

"Sky?"

The voice sounded distant. It took him a moment to realize it was Sam, standing right next to him. He also realized she'd repeated the call a few times. "Yeah?"

"What the hell's up with you? Daydreaming?"

He shook his head, turning off his group comm at the same time so they could talk privately. She caught the gesture and did the same.

"Just thinking about all the shit the Builders put us through."

Her mouth tightened, no doubt holding back criticism.

"A waste of time, I know," he went on. "It's just . . . it all seemed so specific, you know? Timed down to the minute, looking for precise capabilities."

"Yeah, and?"

Skyler took his time to answer, watching the alien landscape below move ever closer. "It bothers me that

Eve's data is all so old. What if our abilities, the criteria we supposedly meet, are all irrelevant now?"

Sam gave a shrug of her shoulders, looking off toward the horizon. "Fuck if I know, Sky. The goal is the important part. Their home world is held captive by sinister bastards, and we're going to help them get it back. Whatever abilities they sought in us, creativity is what they really needed. They're machines, after all."

"I just figured Eve would have a better plan. Or, hell, *any* plan. Instead it was us who came up with this"—he gestured off toward the giant seedpods—"wild idea."

"It was Tania who came up with it, if I recall."

"You know what I mean. It wasn't Eve's plan."

"Probably a good thing. What plan ever survived first contact with the enemy?"

"Fair enough," he said. Then, after a moment, "Hey. You doing okay? With your, uh, friend, I mean." She and Vaughn had begun a relationship just before leaving Earth. She'd been a prisoner in Nightcliff and he, of all things, the guard. Not the best story to tell the grandkids one day, but it was very *Sam*. Vaughn, at a shade under two meters tall, was well matched to her physically, and they'd been virtually inseparable since escaping that wretched place. Since then, though, the man's attentions had become quite a bit more attentive than Samantha liked, not that she'd said anything.

"What's it to you?"

He shrugged. Skyler learned a long time ago not to tell Samantha Rinn he was worried about her.

She turned her comm back on. He followed her example.

The climber reached the ground with a smooth, un-eventful tap against the landing disk. Skyler stepped off and scanned the ochre horizon. Looking for threats, he supposed, though what threats might exist here he had no idea.

"Right," he said. "So far so good. Let's—"

"Skyler, Christ!" Sam interrupted.

He spun, ready to engage the suit's weapons. "What?"

She laughed, and shook her head. "You just became the first human being to set foot on an alien world and 'so far so good' is the best you've got? That's one for the fucking history books, you clod."

"I didn't even—"

Vaughn was laughing. Even Vanessa joined in. He could hear Tania, Tim, and Prumble doing the same through the comm. Sam just shook her head like an embarrassed parent.

"All right, you can all piss off," Skyler said. He waited for the laughter to die out, then put as much authority as dignity allowed into his voice. "We're not here to plant a flag, we've got a job to do. Vanessa, stay on the climber until we know we're safe. Vaughn, Sam, do a perimeter sweep out to twenty meters. Everyone stay within view of everyone else. Got it?"

"Sure, fine," Sam said. She stepped off the climber and then, two steps later, off the circular landing plat-form. Her foot slid half a meter and she almost toppled over, barely righting herself. No easy task in a tenth of Earth's gravity. "The hell?" She knelt and examined the ground, wiping her armored index finger across the surface.

"What is it?" Skyler asked.

"Damn slippery," she said. "It's not the ground, either. This is . . . I don't know. Like rotten moss." She used her whole hand now, brushing aside what looked like clumpy topsoil to Skyler's eye. The fungal growths disintegrated at her touch, as if no more solid than soap bubbles. The result was a sludgy, oily mess. Beneath was something like wet sand flecked with small rocks. As Sam's hand cleared a patch, the pebbles wiggled down into the sand, out of view, leaving behind little puckered mounds.

"Life," Vanessa whispered.

"I wonder if they're edible?" Vaughn asked.

"Ugh," Sam said. "Find cave. Make fire. That it?"

"What can I say, I'm sick of that paste Eve makes."

Sam shook her head in frustration. "This is starting off great. Skyler's famous first words, and now you want to greet the locals by eating them."

"Can't exactly shake their hands, now, can I? Besides, you just stepped on an entire colony. Killed a million, probably. I bet their supreme leader was among the welcoming party."

"A lot of dead scientists are rolling in their graves right about now," Vanessa observed.

"Tim and I are, and we're not even dead yet," Tania said through the comm.

Tim's sudden and awkward laugh came through too loud on the comm. Skyler winced. The young scientist added, "You know, Vaughn, some very smart people carefully outlined how we should approach life when we find it in the universe. This is not what they had in mind."

"Enough, for fuck's sake," Skyler snapped. Too sharp, he realized belatedly. Tim would take it personally, see the slight as evidence of their supposed rivalry for Tania's affections. More drama that he did not need. He added, "All of you, relax. Vaughn, a little care is probably in order."

The words killed a no-doubt snarky reply on Vaughn's lips. "Sorry," he managed instead, but notably to Sam. The couple—together only a few months now, Skyler had to remind himself—exchanged a look that he'd come to know well enough: It was time to get serious.

When he had their attention he pointed to a series of beige, roughly circular sections of ground sprinkled across the landscape. "We can hop between the sandy patches. It's already hard enough to move here, weighing so little. The last thing I want to do if we encounter hostiles is feel like I'm standing on an oil slick. High ground and sure footing, those are our priorities."

Sam studied the terrain again, more carefully this time. "Works for me."

She moved back onto the elevator base, crouched, and jumped. Sam sailed six meters or so to a patch of sandy ground, landed easily, and came up with her arm pointed as if she held a pistol in it, which in a way she did. The suit had a beam weapon built into the forearm, which would protrude and ready itself when it sensed the wearer wished to fire.

Vaughn took another patch, in the opposite direction. The pair made a rough circuit of the landing site like this, until Vaughn came to stand where Sam had started, and vice versa.

"Clear," Sam said.

"Clear," Vaughn echoed.

Skyler nodded. He turned back to Vanessa. "Right. The three of us should go scout the space clams, or whatever they are. Do you mind staying here in case we need to make a hasty retreat?"

Before she could answer Prumble's voice came through the comm. "Have you learned nothing, man? Don't *ask,* give the order!"

Skyler sighed. Despite all that had happened he still could not understand why leadership fell to him. "Vanessa—"

"No problem," she said, and winked.

"Thanks." Skyler turned toward the ridge, and the valley beyond. "Sam, you take point."

"I know." She leapt in that direction. Skyler followed, with Vaughn bringing up the rear.

Just below the ridgeline Sam paused to let them catch up. "No sandy patch up there," she said, "we're going to have to trample more of the locals."

"The little bastards have it coming," Vaughn said.

Skyler landed next to Sam and saw she was right. "Fine. We go single file, then at least only one of us has to get our feet caked in that sludge."

"Hold on." Tania's voice, watching via remote feeds from the ship high above.

"What's wrong?" Skyler asked.

"Nothing," she said. "Just do us a favor and jump straight up, high as you can. We'll get a clear view of the, um, space clams I guess we're calling them? We'll review up here and advise."

"Jesus, we suck at names," Prumble muttered. "If only the Builders—I rest my case—had included a test for efficient taxonomy."

"You're just grumpy because we left you up there," Skyler said.

"Skyler, it has always been my absolute pleasure to send you out to do the dirty work while I sit back and take a percentage."

"Understood, Tania," Skyler replied, ignoring the big man. "We'll get you a better look."

He glanced at Sam. She had her arms folded across her chest and darted her eyes upward. "Fine," Skyler said.

He crouched down and pushed up as hard as he could. The leap took him a good fifteen meters into the air, high enough that Skyler felt a strong gust of wind, absent at ground level, press against his Builder armor. It pushed him off course, toward the ridgeline. Pushed him surprisingly far, in fact. "Bit of a problem here," he said.

"What?" Sam asked. Then she saw. "Oh, wonderful."

He sailed across the lip of the hill. Ahead of him the valley spread out. The basin looked like a dry riverbed, studded by the upright forms of the giant space clams. Silent pillars, glowing softly amber in the heavily filtered sunlight. Something about them wasn't right. They didn't look like the footage Eve had supplied; a brief video recorded from incredibly long range of one of these creatures drifting through the vacuum of space.

These were different, but Skyler couldn't figure why just yet. He had other things to worry about.

His feet hit the fungal surface and immediately shot out from under him, leaving two greasy smears. He fell on his back and began to rush down the valley wall. On the slick surface of fragile gelatinous mushrooms his speed climbed rapidly, as if he rode a waterslide. Skyler dug his hands in and scraped at the ground, but his fingers only made grooves in the loose, damp sand below.

He looked to the valley. At this rate he'd reach the bottom in maybe ten seconds and be traveling at a hundred kilometers per hour. A pillarlike clam creature loomed dead ahead. One of the larger ones. A hundred meters tall, he estimated. Big as a skyscraper, yet held to the ground by only a small root system half-buried in the grime-covered sand. It suddenly looked very menacing, towering over him so.

He tried to use his hands to steer, but the soft sand below the fungus provided no purchase. Skyler did the only thing he could think to do. He slammed his elbows into the ground. In the low gravity this motion sent him upright to a near stand. Then he crouched like a skier, and jumped up into the air again. Not high, this time. On Earth it wouldn't have even gotten him off the ground, but here it sent him up a meter, maybe less. Feet slightly in front of him, he invoked the beam weapons in his arms, just for an instant. He'd used them only once, during a brief practice stint in one of the biomes aboard the ship the day before.

The beams gushed outward, blue-white and blinding.

They seemed to boil away the air in front of him, sending tendrils of superheated air outward in wild patterns. Where they hit the ground, mushrooms and sand flew up and out like dust in the wash of a chopper. The weapons killed his forward momentum, and also left a huge oval-shaped blackened patch on the ground. He could only imagine how terrible it must smell. He still slid when he landed, but not nearly as fast as before. And, at the edge of his little man-made landing pad there was a berm a meter high. A pile of smoldering mushrooms and clumpy, cracked cakes of sand. His legs buried themselves up to the knee when he hit it, and kept going. Skyler tumbled through the mound, rolled over twice through the charred and gloopy mess. His back slammed into something hard. He slid sideways off and collapsed to the ground with a grunt.

"Jesus," Sam said in his ear. "Are you okay?"

"What's happening down there?" Tania asked.

"I'm fine," Skyler said. "There's a stiff wind above us and it pushed me over the ridge, that's all. I had to fire my weapons to stop myself from sliding right into one of the, uh, clams."

"And yet there you are," Sam observed.

"To stop myself from hitting it at a hundred kph, okay?" he replied, rubbing at the base of his back. In truth it hadn't hurt much at all. He'd felt his alien-made armor harden at just the right moment, then release and go all flexible again a fraction of a second later. He propped himself up on his elbows and studied the looming object. If it had noticed or cared about his impact, it didn't show. It seemed completely inert. Or dead.

"You should get the sample and return to the Elevator," Tania said over the comm.

Her words forced his mind away from the fall. Did she speak out of concern for his safety, or for the mission plan?

A simple enough plan as these things went, and that was just fine with him. Get a sample of the rough, bark-like skin of this creature, return it to the ship, let Tim and Tania analyze it with Eve's help. With any luck it could be replicated, and the hull of the ship remade to match its properties. "No ship has been able to penetrate the defensive array set up around the Builders' home system," Tania had said after weeks spent researching the problem, "but these have. They're not ships, but life-forms, and for some reason the enemy ignores them."

If Eve's hull could be reconfigured to match these creatures, perhaps they could slip in without any confrontation at all. A big if, in Skyler's view, but no one had a better idea, not even the super-intelligence that was Eve. Indeed, the AI that was the brain of their ship seemed as delighted as anyone at the creative solution Tania had found.

Only . . . only the skin before him was not the rough, near-black bark of the examples in Eve's database. This was smooth, and beige, like the surface of a shelled tree nut.

"Tania, are you seeing this?"

"I am," she replied.

"I think we have a problem."

"Me too."

"What's wrong?" Vanessa asked from her position back at the Elevator.

"This is not the same animal Eve showed us," Skyler said. "The size and shape is right, but . . ." He trailed off.

Beneath him, the ground had begun to shake.

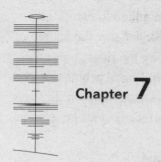

Chapter 7

SKYLER FORCED HIMSELF to his feet, ignoring the charred sand and fungal sludge that fell in clumps from his arms and legs. He glanced to his left in time to see Sam and Vaughn reach the valley floor, standing in the oval-shaped patch of ground Skyler's beam weapons had charred.

His mind desperately wanted that deep vibration in the soil to be the effect of his companions stomping down the hillside, but here they were, standing still, and the rumbling only grew.

"Something's happening," Vaughn said.

Sam looked down. "An eerily well-timed earth-quake?"

Skyler activated his comm. "Vanessa, do you feel any shaking back there?"

"Negative," came the reply.

"Double shit," Sam said. "Localized."

"Back to high ground?" Vaughn offered, already one

step back up the hill toward the ridgeline. He stopped dead, neck craned toward the boulder-strewn ridge.

Following the man's gaze, Skyler saw the source of the quake. Of all the rocks along the ridge, those closest were shaking. Bits of dust and small pebbles sluiced off and rolled or slid down the steep valley wall, leaving clear trails in the grimy surface cover, like tears on dirty cheeks.

"I don't like this," Vaughn said.

"Stating the obvious," Samantha shot back, mimicking his tone.

Neither sounded scared, but Skyler knew Sam well enough to hear the concern in her voice. Nothing fazed her, but when facing potential danger, the one thing she liked least was wielding unfamiliar kit. The armored space suits they wore, with their built-in alien weaponry, were still uncomfortably new. She and Vaughn had spent a lot more time than him practicing with them in one of the ship's biomes, albeit with minimal live fire. Eve wouldn't allow more within her hull. Skyler had spent all of thirty minutes himself, trying the fit, too weirded out by the skintight feel to stay a moment longer. His military past in the Dutch air force had ingrained in him a fierce need to test and retest gear constantly, a practice he suddenly regretted letting slip from habit.

He weighed his options. Too many unknowns, save one simple fact: their goal. "We'll take a sample of this thing. Doesn't look the same, fine, but who knows? Maybe it grows that rough bark once it's out in the vacuum. A defense mechanism or something, to survive in space."

"Which it reaches, how, exactly?" Sam asked. "The fuckers are rooted down here."

"Maybe something throws them," Vaughn offered, half-serious.

Skyler doubted that. They hadn't seen anything here that could pick up one of the giant seedpods and throw it upward with a force so great it would reach orbit, much less drift off into interstellar space. But he held back the opinion, unwilling to discourage ideas just yet.

Instead he turned and moved to the base of the huge object—plant or animal, he had no idea. He hopped up onto the tangle of roots, each as big around as his thigh, climbing until he stood next to the skin of the body. It glistened slightly in the weak light of this planet's meager red dwarf sun.

He reached behind his back and tapped a small area at the base of his spine. A pocket of sorts, which inflated like a balloon at his touch before its two sections separated like eyelids. Inside the concealed pouch was a thin sheet of semitransparent material, almost milky in appearance. Though he hadn't spent a lot of time practicing tactical movement in the space suit, he had practiced this. The mission relied on it.

"Hurry it up, Sky," Sam said. "Going from bad to worse up there."

He fought the urge to look. Holding the sheet with both hands, he positioned it at a slight angle to the surface of the pod, coming up at it from below. When the edge of the sheet touched the creature's flesh a thin layer began to peel away. Good enough. Skyler angled the edge of the sheet outward as he continued to push upward, cutting off a neat, razor-thin sample that looked like expertly sliced garlic. He folded the sheet in half, and when its edges touched, the entire perimeter self-sealed and bled out any air trapped inside, leaving him holding a small, packaged sample.

"Sky!" Sam urged. "Now would be good."

"Done," he said, slipping the sample back into the pouch at the small of his back. He felt the suit reshape itself around it, returning to its original form more or less. He turned and hopped off the root, floating down the six meters to a tidy landing between Sam and Vaughn.

The pair were in half-crouched positions, arms held out, weapons ready. The suits were all outfitted identically, with a beam weapon on each arm, though Eve had warned that using both simultaneously would tax the suit's power source. Vaughn and Sam had something extra, though: a mortar launcher that resembled an elongated bulb on their backs, poking up slightly over the right shoulder. Skyler noticed neither of his companions had extended theirs. Probably because they'd been unable to test the ordnance on board the ship.

On the ridge, the boulder closest to them suddenly lurched upward and toppled back. Creatures flowed out from beneath. Like scabby black beetles the size of small ground cars, running on stubby legs that ended in sharp spikes.

"Fucking hell," Vaughn muttered.

"I'm not keen to start blasting the locals," Sam said.

Skyler moved back a step. "Agreed. Let's try the—"

He'd been turning as he spoke, to face the opposite slope of the valley. But an identical eruption of life had occurred there, too. A dozen of the scarab-things scurried from below a rock that toppled backward as they came forth.

Skyler glanced to his right, up the valley. It ended where the two ridges met, about half a kilometer away and just as high. To his left, the valley ran in a crooked line for a kilometer or so before emptying out into a vast flat floodplain that stretched to the not-so-distant horizon. "That way," he said, and began moving in the awkward hopping run the low gravity allowed. Samantha quickly overtook him, naturally taking point. Vaughn, he knew, would be falling in behind. Such a team they made.

Weaving between the root-ball formations that held the giant space clams upright, Skyler spoke into the comm. "Locals have appeared, and they don't seem too friendly. Streams of them coming down from the ridges. I think we woke them up, somehow."

"We see them," Tania said. "What are you going to do?"

"Move out onto the floodplain and hope they don't follow." He knew as soon as he said it that some kind of endgame was required. "Can you move the Elevator out there and pick us up? I'm not thrilled with the idea of trying to backtrack."

A pause as Tania no doubt consulted with the AI that

ran the ship. Or was the ship. He still wasn't quite clear on that.

"We'll move the space elevator," Tania said. "Vanessa, stay on the climber and hold on."

"Copy that," she replied.

The presence of a goal gave Skyler renewed focus. He had the sample, and even though it was from what appeared to be the wrong animal, and a flood of death scarabs was bearing down from all around him, at least they had an exit strategy.

"Holy hell there's a lot of them," Vaughn said through labored breaths.

Skyler chanced a look to one side. Boulders all along the ridge were shaking, toppling, or already fallen, and from each a pack of the black scarabs raced out and down, leaving little puncture marks where their spike-tipped legs churned the fungus and sand. The creatures had no antennae or even eyes, at least that Skyler could see. Who knew what sort of sensory organs they would have developed, though. Not the time to find out.

He ran on, following the path Sam took more or less, occasionally darting around one of the massive upright pods where she went up and over. Some were only six or seven meters tall. Immature, maybe, compared with the largest that soared a hundred meters or more above. The farther into the valley the more their presence felt like a forest.

Then he saw the flat plain spread out before him, its muted surface alive with the shifting light filtering down through the thick cloud layer. Tans and reds and dark patches of mud. It may have once been the bed of a great ocean.

"Skyler," Vanessa said.

"I'm clear of the pods. What's your status?"

"Right above you. Skyler, look back."

He'd fallen into a natural gait of long, loping strides. At Vanessa's request he propelled himself upward in a high arc on the next step, and in midair he turned around to look behind. Vaughn had just cleared the forest of space clams. Behind him, two waves of black scarabs crashed down from the steep valley walls. He'd expected them to give chase. To turn and follow them at least some distance out into the open wastes. Or, barring that, he figured they would crash into the upright forms of the pods. But they did neither of these things. Instead, the flood of stubby legs and carapaces hit the behemoth structures and started to climb. They spiraled up, clambering over one another with reckless abandon. Many fell away in the chaos. But most ended their climb by simply driving their spiked legs into the flesh of the giant pods and pressing themselves down onto the surface like hungry leeches. As more and more of the creatures climbed, the smooth beige skin of each pod transformed into something scaly, rough, and very black.

"Just like the one Eve showed us," Skyler muttered, mostly to himself.

"Exactly," Vanessa replied.

He landed and stopped, transfixed. Sam soon came to stand next to him, and Vaughn a few seconds after her.

The three of them stood, side by side, watching in silence as the scarabs performed their bizarre ballet.

"I still don't understand how they get—"

Sam's words were cut off by the sudden erratic motion of one of the largest pods. The giant stood nearly two hundred meters tall, and it had begun to wobble back and forth. Due to its own movement, or being rocked by the flood of creatures that surrounded it, Skyler couldn't tell.

Plumes of gas erupted from around the base of the pod, spraying outward with astonishing force. Scarabs, their stubby legs flailing, were thrown in every direction. But not those that had reached and climbed the towering pod. Despite their swaying host and the eruption from below, the animals held fast.

A great tearing sound signaled the moment the rootball let go. The giant began to lift toward the sky on a plume of rapidly expanding gases. Scarabs near its tip that hadn't found a place to attach fell away as the great creature gained speed and altitude.

Utterly captivated, Skyler and his companions watched as the animal or plant or whatever it was flew ever higher. More joined it, and soon dozens were lifting up toward the thick cloud layer and beyond.

"Tania, are you seeing this?"

"I am," she replied from Eve's position high above, in geosynchronous orbit. "And I think I know what we need to do."

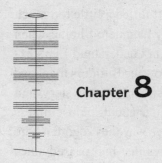

Chapter 8

A COUPLE DAYS later, Samantha stood atop a boulder one hundred meters from the base of the four space elevators, her eyes scanning the horizon. Then, she looked straight up. "Status?" she asked.

"You should see us any second now," Tania replied.

She studied the clouds where the four thin elevator cords vanished. Bands of purple and orange, sliding past like some kind of contaminated river in the sky. A minute passed. Sam took one more glance across the horizon. Nothing moved. In this valley, sixty kilometers from the first one they'd visited two days prior, the clams stood like silent, fat, gigantic almonds, utterly dormant. She turned her eyes back to the clouds. A faint shape had formed now, growing more pronounced with each passing second. "Got you. How long until touchdown?"

"Seven minutes," Tania replied.

A long time to stand around on a hostile world full of unknown dangers. "Can't Eve pop the ship into one of those purple bubbles and speed this up?" Sam despised the tech. It made her feel *off*. It flirted a little too much with being magic, a trait only hammered home when even Tania admitted she couldn't understand Eve's explanation of how it worked. How the Builders managed to do it would, for now at least, remain a mystery, and although Sam had no complaints about the usefulness of a slowed pocket of time—it's why they'd gotten here in months despite the centuries that had passed since leaving Earth—she had no desire to be inside one by choice. At least here she was well away from the ship.

"The bubbles only change time on the inside, Sam," Prumble noted. "It would only go faster for us."

"Oh. Right. I knew that."

Sam resisted the temptation to watch the ship come down the elevators, forcing herself instead to focus on the landscape around her. The valley was much larger than the first one they'd explored. Over a thousand of the upright pods lined its floor, in what she assumed were varying states of maturity. Some were just a few meters tall and very pale in coloration, others approaching one hundred meters with that darker, almondlike skin. All would soon be dwarfed by the gigantic form of their ship, the *Chameleon*.

"Chameleon," she whispered. Finally, a name with a nice ring to it. Prumble's idea, of course, and a name Eve's drastically reconfigured hull still had to earn. Once on the ground, the ship would tower over the other stalks. Sam shook her head. "I hope those scarab creatures are stupid fucks, because this already looks ridiculous."

"It's the best plan we have, Sam," Skyler said.

"Yeah, well, it's like a mature croc trying to hide among turtles."

"Playing the cards we're dealt, et cetera. Stay focused."

She sighed, waved at Vaughn. He waved back, then did a little dance atop his own lookout boulder. Sam stifled a laugh.

If it weren't for Vaughn she doubted she'd have come on this mission. Helping the fucking Builders. Jesus. Sometimes it felt like she'd agreed to help a lost child find his parents after that lost child had just murdered everyone else. Literally everyone else. It took some twisted logic to justify all this. She tried to push away her next thought before it formed, but it still came: This better be worth it.

"What are you thinking about over there?" Vaughn asked on their private channel.

"Guess."

" 'What the fuck am I doing here?' "

She laughed. "Nailed it, mate."

"Something to tell the grandkids about, though, isn't it?"

"Grandkids implies kids, love. Planning to breed? Got a partner in mind?" Once again her rebuke came across playful. Telling the man outright to back off a little, to give her some room to breathe, never quite worked. Sam had only herself to blame. She wanted her space, and yet she dreaded the idea of being alone out here, facing all this.

"Ten seconds," Tania said in her ear.

The words brought on a sudden adrenaline rush. The moment she lived for, that instant before the battle began, when plans could finally be set aside—and thank you very much—in favor of cold instinct and hardened nerves. Jake, the crew's sniper back on Earth, rest his soul, had understood this feeling. Vaughn understood it, too.

Here we go.

Tania's next words sent another ripple of anticipation up her spine. "The *Chameleon* has landed."

Sam glanced at the landing site, and up the flanks of Eve's highly modified and reshaped hull. To the AI's credit, the surfaces really did resemble the silent creatures lining the valley floor, their molecular structures based on the skin sample Skyler had taken two days before. A pretty damn convincing trick, even if the size was way off. The *Chameleon* looked the part. Just ten times bigger. It hadn't made so much as a sound to signal its arrival.

"Right," Sam said. "Vaughn?"

"Say the word, Grandma," he replied.

"Don't be a shit. Commence operation light-'em-up. On my mark." She convinced her suit to deploy the mortar tube. "Mark."

Sam jumped straight up, giving her a better view of the surrounding ridges and the vast plains beyond. Through her helmet she marked off a half-circle, five hundred meters out, and gave the mental order. Fire for effect, even spread.

The launcher on her back came to life. It felt like someone repeatedly pushing down hard on her shoulders as the projectiles took flight. Behind her, Vaughn executed a similar maneuver, targeting the western direction.

Grandma. She sighed inwardly. She'd have to have the talk with him again. Not the time or place to start a serious relationship, she'd say again, and he'd agree and promise to dial back the flirtatious banter with total sincerity. She'd laugh then, a betrayal of nerve, and he'd think the conversation was some joke. Then they'd wind up rolling around on the bed for an hour or three and she'd be right back where she started. Front and center in the old battle between love and independence.

As Sam fell back to the ground a series of explosions flashed across her view from north to south. Fireballs and thrown debris, followed by roiling clouds of inky black smoke. "Well, now we know the mortars work. The trap is set, Skyler."

"Understood. Get to the base."

She landed in the muck a few meters from her boulder, turned, and began the awkward series of hops that served as a sprint on this world. Facing west now she saw the towering form of *Chameleon,* and the pillars of black smoke rising up to either side beyond the steep valley walls. Those mortars packed a hell of a punch. She grinned.

"Movement," a voice said. "Scarabs, emerging from both ridges." It was Tim, at Tania's side aboard the ship.

"Looks like it worked," Tania added.

The ground shook. Samantha glanced behind her in

time to see the boulder she'd been standing on moments earlier begin to tilt to one side. Moist soil fell away from it in clumps. Then with a meaty thud the rock toppled over to one side and swarms of black-shelled animals began to emerge as if expelled from some great pressure below. At first they erupted in a rough circle, but in less than a second they had her marked as a threat and began to flow in her direction, running on their stubby legs.

"Here come the little bastards," Sam said. "Vaughn!"

"I see 'em," he replied.

Skyler spoke up, his voice calm in her ear. "Focus on the ship. Remember we need these creatures."

"We know the drill, Sky," said Sam. "Vaughn? Race you to the top."

"You're on," he replied.

On Sam's next landing she pointed herself forward rather than up and pushed off hard, propelling herself at a shallow angle toward the tail of the *Chameleon*. So low an angle, in fact, that she found she could execute an almost cartoonish run. She gained more speed than intended, and threw her arms out in front of her just before slamming into the smooth skin that now served as the ship's hull. Her armor took the impact in stride. Sam staggered back a step, feeling more than seeing the approaching horde of scrabbling monsters all around her. Ten meters away and closing fast. Cutting it thin. Sam jumped upward with all her strength, hands outstretched. She'd practiced this next part in the biome several times over the last day, but now, being chased by a frenzied mob, she felt her confidence falter. If only they'd had time to design some thrusters for the suit.

A meter from the hull she felt her outstretched hands tugged gently toward the faux surface. Her palms hit the ship's hull and stuck, drawn by magnetism. Not hard, just enough to keep her stuck there, but still able to disengage and propel herself higher. She did so.

"Talk to me, Sam," Vaughn said.

"A hundred meters up," she said through heavy breaths. "Nine hundred to go."

"You're going to lose," he shot back.

"No damn way."

"Probably due to your advancing years. I'll get you a walker for your birthday."

Sam ground her teeth. She allowed herself to forget about the teeming mass on her heels, throwing all her energy into the race. It felt like rappelling, only in reverse. Hands and feet drawn into the hull, push up hard, repeat. After a few dozen hops she chanced a look down between her feet. A feeling of vertigo swept over her. She was more than halfway now, some six hundred meters above the valley floor. Her brain wanted to see that fall in the context of Earth's gravity, where a plummet from here would be fatal no matter how exotic her armor. The sensation required a conscious effort to quash, made possible by studying her pursuers. The scarabs were almost a hundred meters behind her, spiraling up the hull precisely as hoped. Despite her desire to beat Vaughn, she slowed her progress. Too far ahead and they might lose interest, or realize they were climbing a false version of their beloved hosts.

The top arrived so quickly she almost botched the final hop. It was only the sight of Vaughn's head between the four elevator cords that saved her. Sam gave one final push upward and sailed a dozen meters over the nose of the *Chameleon,* giving her one final view of the ground now a full kilometer below. The scene made her head spin. From the ridges surrounding the ship, tens of thousands of the scarab-things had crawled from their holes. They moved like a fluid, spilled and now spiraling toward their potential hosts. Sam turned and looked up the length of the valley. The other stalks were wholly ignored by the horde of creatures converging on the *Chameleon.* Perhaps they looked entirely uninteresting to the scarabs in the presence of such a massive prize.

The scrambling mass below her had gained ground. Smaller examples of the animals were forcing their way over the tops of their larger companions, now just twenty meters below. Sam reached the apex of her jump. The creatures spiraled up the ship's hull, utterly driven to reach her, mad with primal bloodlust. They saw her, exactly as Tania had hoped, as a threat to their precious organic rocket that would take them to their breeding grounds.

Sam glided between the cords of the space elevators and fell toward the circular opening Eve had created specifically for this moment. Vaughn already stood inside, looking up at her. She could see his smug "better luck next time" smile. He held out his arms to catch her. Sam waved him off. "They're right outside! Get back!"

His smile vanished. He leapt to the sidewall as Sam landed smack in the middle of the tiny circular room. "We're in, Eve! Close it!"

Above, the sky darkened. Six or seven scarabs foisted themselves over the edge. Sam reacted without thinking, and so did Vaughn. Together they lanced beams of white-hot energy through the animals even as they fell into the pit of the room. Sam danced back, abandoning aim and firing wildly at the circular opening above. "Eve! Fucking *now*!"

"My sensors show obstruction—"

"Override! Close it!"

The ceiling irised closed in the blink of an eye, cutting four of the creatures in half. Their bodies fell to the floor and bounced. Fluid spilled out of their gaping wounds. Their limbs still flailed for purchase, pointed tips scratching at the floor. Sam swept her beam across them, and the twitching limbs went still.

Movement in the shadow beside Vaughn. A whole scarab made it through the mass of smoldering corpses and jumped at her. She saw rows of needlelike teeth, and something like eyes on the ends of four stalks. Sam swung her arm down and fired. The beam tore a hole right through the animal. It jerked in midair, slammed into her, then fell aside on its back, legs twitching and clawing at the air as it died.

Across the room Vaughn stood perfectly still. Their eyes met. He glanced down, and she followed his gaze. Between his knees, a black spot on the wall sparked and smoldered.

He looked up at her. "You almost shot me in the—"

"We're safe, Skyler," Sam said. "The hatch is closed."

"Any injuries?"

"Vaughn's psyche took a hit, but other than that I think we're okay. A few of them made it inside but we dealt with them. Going to need a cleanup crew in here."

"I will decontaminate the room," Eve said. "Remain still."

"I'd prefer to leave first."

"You and Vaughn must be sanitized as well."

"Not sure I like the sound of that," Vaughn said.

Eve ignored him. "Captain, the creatures have achieved one hundred percent hull coverage. I am initiating our climb." A deep and persistent vibration began somewhere far below. All part of the ruse, Sam recalled. Eve would climb the elevators back to a sufficient altitude, but the scarabs needed to be utterly convinced they'd just encased one of the space clams, which launched like rockets.

"Nice work, everyone," Skyler said. "We are under way."

"Let's hope our new passengers stay put," Tania added.

A sulfur-yellow mist began to fill the room, the particles gravitating toward the dead scarabs that littered the floor. Sam watched in morbid fascination as the shell of the one closest to her began to bubble. This turned to a violent froth. The black skin began to turn gray, then boiled off into a dark blue-green smoke. She pressed herself farther into the wall as the corpses degenerated into a mixture of gooey fluid and smoke. The fog filled the room, and soon she could not see her own hand in front of her visor. Then, without warning, the smoke lurched downward. The floor, utterly solid a moment before, now sported a grid of puckered holes that sucked in all the evidence of the bodies that had been present a moment before.

In less than a minute Sam found herself standing, facing Vaughn, the adrenaline-fueled pounding of her temples finally back to normal. All of the guts and dust and fungal muck on their suits had vanished.

"Well," Vaughn said. "That was fun."

Sam narrowed her eyes at him. "I could have won, you know. Slowed down to make sure our little friends kept up the chase."

He smiled at her. A few seconds passed in silence, and his smile remained.

"I could use a shower," Sam said, grinning now, too. Invitation made. Thoughts of telling him to back off a bit now just fading memories.

Battle had a way of doing that.

Chapter **9**

**The *Chameleon*
4.DEC.3510 (Earth Actual)**

SKYLER DRIFTED IN the inky void, connected to the slumbering ship by only a silk-thin thread. Twin searchlights, mounted on his shoulders, lit the *Chameleon*'s hull as if she bathed in the summer Australian sun.

The ship looked like some kind of gigantic unkempt submarine, crusted from tip to tail in meter-diameter barnacles. To his eye the plan had gone off without a hitch. Well, except for Sam and Vaughn nearly being eaten. The creatures had taken to Eve's modified outer hull as if the ship were a native to their strange world. After the unsuccessful chase of Sam and Vaughn up the sides, the animals—or whatever they were—had simply followed their evolutionary programming and settled in for the ride signaled by Eve's deceptive vibrations. They folded their legs up under themselves and then, according to Eve, excreted some kind of gluelike fluid that secured them to the hull, leaving only their hard shells exposed to the vacuum of space. He marveled at the strangeness of their biology. What kind of bizarre past had led to the development of such an adaptation? Tania and Tim, with Eve's help, had tracked the pods that had soared into the sky. Most made for the planet's large moon. Many, however, missed the mark, and were slingshot out into space. Of those, almost all would fall into the red dwarf at the heart of the system, but a few would enjoy the slingshot effect once again, and be tossed out into the vast unknown. It had been one of these, thousands of years ago, that the Builders had seen slipping through the blockade that surrounded their own solar system. For whatever reason, the ships that patrolled that region of space had shown no interest in the object. With any luck, they would now treat the *Chameleon* in the same way.

Skyler didn't much like plans that relied on luck. But then, the plans that worked always seemed to need a little, didn't they? He smirked, shook his head. It was a damn good plan Tania had come up with, if only because it didn't start with "we shoot our way in," as Sam's had.

He cycled his visor through several view modes, as instructed. Around him, small nondescript probes flittered by. Deployed by Eve, they were tasked with analyzing the ship at the nanometer scale, making sure every last bit of surface was hidden beneath the crust of alien carapaces. In truth these little robots could perform the task far better than Skyler could ever hope to, but he'd come out, anyway. He wanted to see it for himself, an action enabled by the last-minute addition of thrust capability to their armored space suits. The success of the mission hinged on total coverage, and no matter how hard he tried he couldn't give the okay to proceed simply based on Eve's report.

Yet that wasn't the whole story. In truth he felt uncomfortable with the idea of being inside Eve when she shut everything down. He'd kept this to himself, no need to alarm the others to a concern that bordered on the superstitious. To be in there during this test felt to him like sealing himself in his own tomb. If he was going to have to do that, he preferred it be only once.

"Looking good from out here," he said, for the crew's benefit as much as his own. They were all tucked deep within the ship, in the forest biome, making last-minute preparations. Watching his video feed or studying the imagery coming back from the grapefruit-sized probes. They had no way to reply, for that would go against the purpose of this task.

On first examination of the hull the previous day, what had appeared to Skyler as a perfectly camouflaged ship had in truth looked like a dazzlingly overlit Christmas tree in infrared and ultraviolet. It appeared, to Eve's surprise, that the beetlelike creatures covering her hull had some kind of fibrous mechanism in their skin that absorbed radiation on the hull-side and emitted it back out again from their shells. A defense mechanism perhaps, or maybe just a way to ensure they didn't overheat. Whatever the case, although visually disguised, the *Chameleon* still looked like a spacecraft in just about every other wavelength. The enemy would never fall for it, if Tania's theory was right.

Unless, that is, Eve ran dark.

The only way she could completely mask her internal

workings was to stop them entirely. And so, for the first time in millennia, Eve had gone to sleep. Within that entire vessel now only Skyler's companions and their Builder armor were active, plus a few small pieces of passive monitoring equipment, all tucked within one of the biome spheres in the very center of the ship.

Skyler slowed his pace, studying the form before him. He floated about two hundred meters from the hull, trying to ignore the flotilla of dark gray orbs that traveled with him. "Nothing like yesterday," he added. "Infrared just shows a flat gray surface. No heat escaping at all, at least to my eye." He could only hope the probes had the same impression in the various emission bands they were scanning for, or the whole effort would be for naught. "Okay, I'm coming back in. Tania, wait twenty minutes and then wake Eve. I feel damn vulnerable with her offline before we're fully ready for this."

Skyler drifted back along the hull, making a slow spiral as he went. At the airlock, which had been craftily added at the back of the vessel in a deep cleft, he manually wound the door closed and, following memorized instructions, opened several valvelike contraptions that allowed atmosphere into the tiny chamber. He waited, watching readouts on the interior of his helmet and listening to the faint-but-growing hiss of air filling the room. Halfway through the process the lights came on, and he felt the familiar minute vibration of Eve's internal systems return.

The interior door opened a minute later, and Skyler found Tania and Prumble waiting for him. Just then the ship returned to a one-g level of thrust and the three of them settled on the floor.

"Where's Tim?" Skyler asked, trying to sound nonchalant and mostly succeeding.

Tania broke eye contact. "I asked him to check on the progress in the biomes."

A bullshit task, which Tim no doubt knew. Smart kid, that one. Skyler could think of no good reply so he held his tongue. The fact that Tania had decided it best to avoid the awkward tension that arose lately whenever the three of them were in the same room, well, it said much that she'd reached that point.

A second later, Eve's avatar appeared. A projection, via some technology even Tania said was beyond her grasp. The human form, painted in liquid light, was an amalgamation of everyone aboard, an attempt by the AI to create a persona they would feel comfortable around and identify with. Her voice, too, had an odd accent that somehow combined those of the human crew.

When first boarding this vessel, back at Earth, Skyler had wondered at the drab, matte-gray surfaces found throughout. It was only later, learning that the ship was run by a machine intelligence, that he understood. Aesthetics were of no concern to Eve. Two weeks into their journey, however, Prumble had discovered the ship's ability to reshape and resurface nearly everything inside, and had appointed himself interior decorator. The hallways and rooms now resembled the luxurious Platz Station, with its red tiled floors and white paneled halls. Prumble had worked with Eve on her appearance as well, making it a bit more obviously artificial so as not to terrify anyone when she miraculously appeared.

"Everything okay?" he asked.

"Absolutely," Eve said, in answer.

Skyler nodded. "Um, if we could have some privacy . . ."

The AI nodded and, an instant later, vanished. He'd have to take her at her word that she wasn't listening. Skyler glanced at Prumble.

"She's right. All systems go," Prumble said. The big New Zealander wore his customary smuggler's grin, so bright not even his newly grown beard could hide it. He carried himself like a Shakespearean actor, his life being the stage.

Tania nodded. "Eve is satisfied with everything."

"Good. I guess it's decision time, then."

The pair of them stared at him, eyebrows raised. Prumble spoke. "Er . . . what's to decide, Sky? There is no other plan."

Skyler shrugged. "Doesn't mean we have to go through with it." He began to walk, and his friends fell in to either side. *Friends.* Skyler winced at his return to old habits. It was Prumble who had advised him, years ago, and again just a day ago, to stop treating his crew as friends and instead order them around like soldiers under his command. And the big man had been right. But some things, certain decisions, were just too important to make without consulting those who'd followed him on this crazy journey.

"Skyler," Prumble said under his breath, as if Tania

were not standing a meter away. "Don't waffle now. Trust me."

Skyler clapped his friend on the shoulder. "You could always be bad cop to my good cop."

"Hah! I think you've got that switched around."

"Prumble's right," Tania said. "Not about the good and bad thing—okay maybe that, too—but Skyler, really, this is not the time to take a vote. We've come this far. We have to see it through, and this is the path we've chosen."

"Relax, both of you. I just want to make sure we're not forgetting something, that's all."

Tania gripped his elbow, turning him to face her. "We've done everything we can."

He stared at her. "Not everything."

"No?"

Skyler considered his words carefully, feeling on the brink of opening Pandora's box. It was one thing to harbor mistrust, especially of one so integral to their survival. But to voice it, that changed things. The idea would fester, and that could cause far more problems than it solved. At least for the moment only Tania and Prumble would hear his concern. "Eve's been holding back on us. You know I'm right. She's vague. She leaves out details. Worse, we still don't even really know what we're going to find out there."

Tania gave a little shake of her head. "It's been thousands of years since she was last at her world. Who knows what might have changed? Certainly not Eve—"

"Yes, but—"

"I'm not finished." She brushed a lock of her raven hair behind one ear and sighed. "As to her being vague, I . . . I've already talked to her about that."

He raised an eyebrow, and waited. He could still feel the lingering touch of her hand on his arm, and fought to keep the feelings that brief contact had conjured from his mind. This was not the time or place for it. He'd been with Ana, right up until the fiery woman had decided to stay behind on Earth, hoping he would join her. He did not stay, though. He had to see the mission through, and that had ended things for them. She was long gone now, and Tania was here. But Tania had her own strained relationship with Tim to navigate, and so once again circumstances kept her and Skyler apart. He was starting to doubt the universe would ever give them a chance, or, for that matter, if Tania even wanted it to.

She went on. "What happened back on Earth, their tests, were designed to find out whether or not we had a certain skill set necessary to help free Eve's Creators. But in particular it is our creativity they need. As you said, we don't know what we're going to find there. Eve doesn't, either. She feels that to fill our heads with her analysis would sway our thinking, and not in a good way. Much like camouflaging this ship, which she's said she never would have thought of on her own, our solutions need to be ours and ours alone. Because everything they've tried hasn't worked."

"I get that, honestly I do, but that's not what I mean. To camouflage the ship, that required research. Information. If we're going to be arriving at this system—

which I remind you is surrounded by millions of ships whose sole purpose is to prevent anyone else from doing just that—with her completely switched off, this may be our last chance to get intel. Maybe she's right, maybe it's all irrelevant or will cloud our amazing human powers of cunning and judgment—"

Prumble grunted a laugh.

Skyler ignored it, went on. "But I'm talking about something deeper than intel. Tania, we need to know what this is truly all about. What are the stakes? She and her kind, the Builders, were forced out of this system ages ago. Why? What's so important about it that someone's been holding an entire solar system hostage ever since?"

Tania raised one hand, nodding now. "I understand. Let me talk to her? We've got a rapport going, I think. And besides, I need to review the shutdown procedure."

"Don't forget the wake-up procedure," Prumble said. "That seems important, too."

"Of course," Tania agreed. Her gaze never left Skyler's. "Let me try. Okay? I'm not sure why, but I sense she's more comfortable speaking with me."

"All right," Skyler said. "And while you're at it, get everything you can from her about this ship. Schematics, manifests, whatever she'll provide. We've been here for weeks and hardly explored any of it. The more we know, the less chance we'll need to wake her up early to solve some problem."

Prumble gave a vigorous nod. "Vanessa and I tried, weeks ago. To get a map, I mean. Most of this place is inaccessible. Chemical storage, infrastructure, crazy Builder techno-whatever. Eve said it was 'incompatible with human physiology,' and barred our access."

"Well," Skyler replied, "it's a good thing she made us this impenetrable armor, isn't it?"

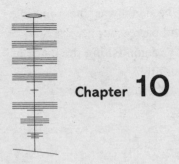

Chapter 10

Place Unknown
Date Unknown

COHERENT THOUGHT, UNCLOUDED by pain, was a rare and wonderful gift.

He hung, suspended in air by ten thousand wormy tendrils that pulsed and slithered, pumping things into his body, or taking things out.

The last time he could think clearly, those tendrils had been blue as a summer sky. Right now they were almost black, in total contrast to the white, undefined background. Were those walls a meter away, or an infinite abyss? He had no idea.

He couldn't move his muscles, not even his eyes. A new thought formed in his mind that even his own heartbeat had been taken out of his control. All he could do was sense, and what he sensed for time indeterminate was pain.

How long had it been? An hour? A day? Years? Impossible to tell. The very concept of time had become slippery. No longer just a relentless march into the future, but a malleable thing. A thing that could be toyed with, provided you knew the secrets.

Or is that just my sanity slipping away? He tried to ponder this, but judgment of one's own sanity never went well.

What he needed, Alex Warthen decided, was a bookmark. A flag he could plant. An anchor to drop. Something real and tangible he could use like a seed. Build a scaffold of tangible facts around it.

But what?

Himself?

All he knew of himself was that he was stretched out like a starfish, buoyed by a writhing maze of tubes that wrapped about his limbs like creeping vines, becoming impossibly thin at their tips where they seemed to slide under his skin between the hair follicles.

What about before, though?

He'd been on the massive Builder ship, with Grillo. Fighting the damn immunes. Skyler and that protégée of Neil Platz, Tania. Tania, that doctor-scientist from India, a researcher who somewhere along the way learned how to fight, and damn well at that. He'd underestimated her. Underestimated all of them. The battle hadn't gone well. He . . . he'd died, hadn't he? The memory slipped away.

"Hello, Alex."

The voice came like a soft breeze, not even a whisper. A woman's voice, as soft as silk. Someone he knew? He didn't think so. Had it even been real? He doubted it. He'd seen a lot of things since he'd come to be here. Relived entire portions of his life in near-perfect fidelity, real in every way except the one that counted: He was only there to observe. No, this voice must be in his head.

"Alex? Are you still there?" the voice said. An actual whisper now. More defined. He could almost feel the breath on his cheek.

He tried to reply, but could only think the words for his mouth would not move. *Hello?*

"Good," she said. *"Good. I feared I'd gone too far that time."* Her voice came from everywhere. From that endless white beyond the tentacle forest.

Who . . . who are you?

"Unimportant."

Where am I? What are you doing to me?

Instead of answering, he found himself reliving another moment. The worst, and last, moment of his life, now in perfect fidelity. Fighting the intruders inside that room within the Builder ship. His hands around the neck of a woman he'd never met, an immune and therefore an enemy. He squeezed until his knuckles went white and her face turned red. She was beautiful, and she was dying. Half of him wanted to stop, to be merciful. The other half knew what would happen if he disobeyed the fanatic, Grillo. So Warthen ground his teeth and squeezed even more, feeling the blood pounding in his temples, the sweat pouring from his brow.

Then another pair of hands, huge and powerful, came into his field of view. He'd had time to think, *I'll strangle her before you strangle me,* only to realize his assailant, the smuggler Prumble, had no intention of choking him. Those meaty hands grabbed Warthen's face and neck, fingers clamping down on his cheek, his jaw. One slipped into his eye socket and the pain, though nothing compared with what he'd experienced here in this bizarre void, would have made him scream for mercy if he'd had the chance. But Prumble did not give that chance. He'd twisted, and the last thing Alex Warthen had felt was a brilliant spike of agony somewhere in his neck.

Then blackness.

Then . . . this place. The white void, the chameleonic tubes, and the pain by which all other pain had to be measured.

Alex forced his mind to clear. Tried to push away the phantom voice. Clearly his mind had finally fallen off that delicate edge that separated sane from insane. He'd have to claw his way back. He found he wanted to.

"You're not insane," the voice said. She sounded so close. He could almost feel her lips tickle the fine hairs on his earlobe. For an instant he thought perhaps he knew her. Something about her voice resonated, as if gently echoing and with each reverberation transformed it to someone he knew. Tania Sharma. That pilot, Skyler. Himself, even. A ripple of anxiety spread through his mind.

"Why am I doing this?" she said. *"I need to understand your kind, but I dare not put the others at risk. They are too important now."*

What others?

"The others like you. Those you call immunes."

I . . . I'm immune?

Silence. Then, *"You didn't know?"*

If Alex Warthen could have closed his eyes and wept, he would have. Through all the pain he had never felt sadness for his predicament. But this, this knowledge could shatter what remained of his brittle mind.

All this time he'd been immune. Safe from the plague that ravaged Earth beyond the city of Darwin, Australia.

He could have left. Just strode out toward the aura that protected the city and kept on going. Found himself a quiet place, an island perhaps, and enjoyed an open horizon for the first time in his adult life. Instead he'd spent those wretched years cooped up in Neil Platz's space stations, trapped between that insufferable old goat and the lunatic Russell Blackfield on the ground. His life had been a constant bureaucratic slog that often felt more like managing spoiled children than handling security along the space elevator. And all the while he'd dreamt of the abandoned planet beyond Darwin, and how much he'd rather be outside, listening to waves lap on an empty beach instead of the constant mechanical whir of air processors.

"You didn't know," she repeated, though not a question this time. He knew then she could hear every thought going through his head. She was inside him. She was him.

As if in response to that a face appeared at the corner of his vision, just beyond the thin tubes that protruded from under his eyelids. She leaned in and studied him, like a scientist gazing into a petri dish and finding only disappointment.

"I know this is difficult for you," she said, her strange voice floating out from an angelic face. Like the odd accent, her features seemed familiar, as if she were the child of someone he knew. No, that wasn't right. The offspring of everyone he knew. The thought only caused his anxiety to grow.

Why do you want to understand us? Because your fucking plague didn't wipe us out completely?

"Your immunity is something new. Something that could be the key to everything we hope to accomplish. Yet for all my efforts I cannot unravel it. There appears to be no difference between you and the other that would explain it."

Anxiety turned to a cold, hard ball of rage. *What other?*

She began to move across his limited field of view. A second passed before he realized it was he who moved, rotating to his left. There, perhaps ten meters away in this endless white void, another body lay suspended by the hair-thin tendrils. Jared Larsen, Alex's second-in-command. He looked awful. His skin, what little Alex could see amid all those tubes, was pale and mottled with bruises. In fact, he looked like a corpse. *What have you done to him?*

"Nothing I haven't done to you. The difference is I keep having to pull the virus back from his body. Yours just . . . ignores it. Even the mutations I've devised. Tell me how this is possible."

How the hell should I know?

She stared at him for some time, no doubt searching his thoughts for any evidence of deception. He waited, giving nothing. If she wanted to rummage about in his head she'd have to work for it.

"I know you despise me, Alex. Please know that, despite what I have done and what I must do to you and your friend, I hold no ill will toward you. But this must be done. It is too important."

Fuck off. Get it over with and let me die.

"You've died several times."

Stop reviving me, then.

"This I cannot do. I need you, and the man Jared. Physically, at any rate. But I want to show you I can be merciful. I have a gift for you."

An instant later every needle-sharp lance of agony across his body vanished. He became no more than a mind without a body, floating in an endless pool of nothing.

Somehow this was worse. The lack of pain made him somehow less than human. He started to think aloud that she should give it back. He needed the pain or he would cease to be.

But then he felt something else. Not pain. Warmth against his feet. Wind caressing his skin. The white void began to change, and the tubes faded away with it. A horizon began to form. As Alex watched his world became sky above ocean, and himself standing on a beach. Gulls wheeled overhead. The waves lapped on the sand in gentle perfectness. Larger whitecaps farther out crashed with that deep booming sound that was the heartbeat of the world.

"Alex?"

He turned at the voice, startled. Ten meters away another man stood. Jared Larsen, dressed in the security uniform Alex had last seen him in. Alex glanced down and saw he wore the same.

"Where are we?" Jared asked. "Are we dead?"

"I . . . ," Alex began. He considered that very carefully. "I'm not sure."

For a long time they sat together and watched the waves pummel the shore. Alex found himself scooping up handfuls of golden sand and letting it tumble down between splayed fingers.

"Did you talk to her?" he asked Jared, after a long silence.

"Talk to who?"

Alex lowered his head. Who had she been? Had he dreamt that, or was this the dream? It felt like one. More lucid than any he'd experienced before, but he knew none of it was real. "Never mind for now," Alex said. "This is no afterlife, okay? This is like a shared sensory chamber. I think we're still aboard that ship."

Jared kept his gaze on the horizon, his face unreadable. He looked haggard, his body gaunt and skin an unhealthy pale hue. Jared had never been what would be considered handsome, but now he looked rather terrifying. "I died, Chief. That immune kicked me so hard I felt my sternum splinter. The bone . . . I think it punctured my heart, or lung. I felt it happen. Unbearable pain, blood filling my throat, my mouth, nose . . ." His hand rubbed absently at the center of his chest. "I drowned in my own blood. I'm sure of it. And yet, that was nothing compared with those tubes."

"Yeah," Alex said. "Prumble broke my neck. Didn't feel that, I think because I died before I could feel it. But then after . . ."

Silence stretched as Alex tried to fold up those memories and stuff them in a drawer in some unused corner of his mind. He suspected Jared was doing the same. The younger man had said the voice had not spoken to him. Alex mulled that over, along with the words he himself had heard. They were hazy, already. Slippery like fish out of water. But she'd said something about differences. About pulling back the virus from Jared. So he must not be immune, and Alex was.

Beside him, Jared shivered, wrapping his arms about himself as if they were in the Arctic. "What are your orders?" the man asked, something new in his voice. Hardness. Resolve. A hint of those things, at least, not to mention the continued respect of rank even here.

The question surprised him. The idea of rank, of leadership, seemed as distant as that battle, that life. Surely it had ended there, the hierarchy?

Yet when Alex glanced at the man beside him he saw something unexpected now. That need, a thing so many soldiers possessed, to have orders. A goal, no matter how irrelevant, to focus on.

"Let's . . . ," Alex started, then paused. The woman could read his thoughts. He'd been about to ponder the chances and possible ways of getting out of here, but that would only give away such ideas to her. He tried to clear his mind. "Listen, Jared. I'm pretty sure everything we do is being watched. Even our thoughts. So, we can't plan, can't even think about plans. So my orders? Stay sharp, use your instincts. If our chance comes, we take it. Agreed?"

"Hell, yes."

"For now, I guess sitting here isn't helping anything. Let's explore the beach." He stood, and brushed the sand from his hands. It was only a moment later when he realized Jared hadn't moved. The man was staring up at him, a confused expression on his soldier's face. Alex squinted at him. "Something wrong?"

"What beach?" Jared asked. He turned to glance across the landscape.

"You don't see the beach?"

"I see snowy mountains." Jared scooped up a handful of sand. He held it for a few seconds and then tossed it away, shivering.

"Maybe not a sensory chamber, after all." Alex rarely used the entertainment rooms, their ability to fool his brain only good enough to feel eerie rather than convincing. "Okay, what are we sitting on, then?"

"I was wondering how you could keep picking up the snow like that."

"What are we sitting on, Jared? An arctic shore?"

Jared's brow wrinkled. "A ridge," he said, gesturing up and down the beach. Then he pointed toward the water. "The cliff drops off there, down deep into a gorge. Another peak is maybe two hundred meters across the chasm." He turned and swept his arm toward the impenetrable line of palm trees behind them. "This mountainside continues up. Too sheer to climb, I think."

Alex considered this. They may not be seeing the same thing, but the layout at least had similarities.

"Hmm," Jared said.

"What is it?"

He nodded toward the ocean, for him evidently a gorge that separated their mountain from another. "There's a door set into the side of the cliff across there."

Alex scanned in the direction Jared was looking, but saw nothing but water and sky. "No door in my view. Can you get to it somehow? Open it?"

The younger man shook his head. "Sorry, Chief. It's a long climb down and then back up, and no gear. If only I could fly."

"Hmm," Alex said, glancing at his companion. "You can't fly. But I could swim."

"You don't see the door, though."

"So I drag you across. Dead man's carry."

At that Jared tilted his head back and laughed.

"What's so funny?"

"This place is insane. I guess it makes sense our plan is, too. Swim me over there, sure. Why not?" He stood and brushed the sand, or rather snow, from his legs.

Alex walked down to the waterline and tested it. The temperature was almost unnaturally pleasant. He waved Jared over. "Come to the cliff's edge, as far as you can."

The man complied, walking down to where the frothy water swept over the sand as waves finally petered out and sloshed back out to sea. Jared walked about five meters farther, and though his feet left ripples in the water his movement was strange, as if unimpeded by the liquid. Finally, he slowed and then stopped, knee-deep in the low waves. He leaned over, his movement suddenly very cautious, and peered over the cliff he saw in his world.

"Right," Alex said, coming to stand next to him. "I have no idea how this works, so we take it slow."

"Agreed."

"First a little test," Alex said. "I want to be sure you won't drown in the ocean I see."

"If I drown it won't have been the first time. Still, I'm not thrilled about where this is going."

"Relax. Just . . . okay, lie down there at the lip of your cliff for a bit. A minute, I guess, and breathe deep."

The man's brow furrowed. "Why?"

"You're knee-deep in water from my perspective. Lying down will have you under it. If you can breathe . . ." He left the thought unfinished as comprehension dawned on Jared's face.

Helpless and, if he was honest with himself, fascinated, he watched as his second-in-command went to his knees and then to all fours. Then Jared lowered himself below the surface and lay under the water. A minute passed. Alex could see the other man's head moving slowly from side to side as he evidently scanned the bottom of the gorge he saw. No bubbles drifted up from his mouth or nose. Finally Jared pushed himself up and stood. His hair, skin, clothing—all of it was totally dry. "I guess it worked?"

"I saw many strange things inside that Builder vessel, but watching you do that tops them all."

Jared didn't smile. Concern settled across his face. "Now comes the part where you drag me over the edge." He shuddered.

"Not yet," Alex said. "One more test first." And then he stepped farther out, past the point where Jared had so carefully kept himself from crossing.

The other man gasped. He shot out a hand on pure instinct, ready to pull his chief back from a fatal fall. His hand stopped, though, just shy of Alex's elbow. Eyes wide, he opened his mouth to say something, but could only manage a relieved exhale.

Alex stepped farther still, letting the water come to his waist.

"You're just hovering there. Floating. God, that's the damnedest thing."

Confidence growing, and the memory of his true torturous predicament fading, Alex lay back and kicked out into the waves. He kept his gaze on Jared as best he could, mildly amused at the astonishment on the man's face as he watched his chief fly—or rather swim— through the very air.

Alex went out about twenty meters, then turned and kicked back to shore. Standing in front of Jared, he motioned for the man to turn around. "Hold your arms out."

Jared complied, but the trepidation in his movements was impossible to miss.

"If you fall," Alex said, "just remember this is all fake."

"Small consolation," Jared growled. "Just get it over with."

Alex slipped his arm under Jared's, putting the man's weight along his own flank. Then he lay back into the water, pulling the man over the edge of his cliff.

"Oh fuck, oh fuck. Gahh!" Jared flailed, unable to help himself.

Then Alex had the man's full weight on him, and he swam. Jared didn't feel buoyed by the water, but he didn't feel like a grown man in free fall, either. The result was somewhere in between, as if for this brief moment the two nonrealities had somehow merged. Alex swam harder.

Jared grunted and moaned for a few seconds before calming.

"Where's the door?" Alex asked him, straining now with the heavy load.

His companion turned and craned his neck. He pointed roughly behind Alex, slightly to the right. "There!"

Alex kicked hard, pulling with his right hand while keeping Jared at eye level with his left. He knew the man could breathe fine underwater, but if his weight represented some kind of mixture of two environments, perhaps his head going below the surface would feel like being in some kind of air-water mixture. Not worth the risk.

Though the distance was not far, Alex felt near exhaustion when his feet suddenly brushed a submerged sandbar. He found he could stand on it and just keep his head above water. "Here," he sputtered, "stand."

Jared did so. On his own again, he seemed able to move without impedance from the water, nor did he seem concerned with the waves that flirted with entering his mouth and nose. He just stood there, in another world. Then his hand broke the surface and came up to eye level. He rested his palm on something flat and in-visible, gave a gentle push, and stepped back. Recoiled, even.

Alex saw a black vertical line appear in the very air, then a horizontal one that branched away from the top of it. The blackness grew as an invisible doorway mate-rialized. Water began to rush into the opening. A dark tunnel waited beyond, the walls of natural gray stone. He could only see a few meters in before the dark be-came absolute, despite the bright sunshine all around. Gurgling ocean water flooded into the space.

"Quick," Alex said. "Inside and shut the door, before we flood the whole thing."

"Flood? What do you see?" Jared asked. He'd moved a full meter back from the doorway now, and sweated profusely.

The question took Alex by surprise, until he remem-bered their realities were not shared. "A tunnel. Stone, natural, like a cave but too straight for that. What about you?"

"Fire," the man said. "Like the surface of a star." He fell to his knees then, and though his head vanished below the waves Alex could still hear the screams.

The animalistic noise went on and on. Alex pushed through the waves toward his companion, groping in the murk.

"You cannot help him that way," a voice said. Her voice, in his head. *"In the tunnel lies the answer."*

"He'll drown!"

"He won't," she said. *"There is no water where he is, remember? But there is a cliff, and if you do not hurry*

he will tumble over. If that happens even I cannot help him."

"But—"

"Go, Alex. Save your friend."

Alex glanced into the tunnel. The darkness there, so absolute, transfixed him. Paralyzed his mind. But her words still echoed. *In the tunnel lies the answer.* Alex stepped toward the door, pulling at the water with his hands. In seconds the momentum of the current pulled him, and then he was through, swallowed up by the void.

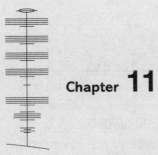

Chapter **11**

"I THINK," TANIA Sharma said, "before the shutdown, it would be good if you told me about your home."

"Home," Eve repeated, trying out the word as if it were unknown to her.

"Your home world. Your Creators' home world. And the system it is in."

"My information is very old."

Tania folded her arms, then let them hang. She exhaled slowly, trying to decide how to play this. It was an AI, after all, not a person with feelings to hurt. Logic would be the best route, she decided, and sat down in the ship's approximation of an executive's chair. The chair, and indeed the room it was in, had been modeled after the analysis lab on Anchor Station where Tania had spent so many hours trying to decipher the mystery of the space elevator and those who had built it. From the trio of large displays, to the long desks facing them, to the high-backed faux-leather chairs. Tania found the

cushion of the seat unforgiving, the machine not understanding that it was supposed to be soft. She decided
not to comment on it. There were more important
things to talk about. "It was one thing to go about all
this knowing that, if the situation really called for it,
you'd tell us what we needed to know. But the situation
will soon change. You'll be switched off. Unavailable
as we cross through the barricade. I know you don't
want to cloud our minds with outdated information,
but . . . we would feel more comfortable with some
basic knowledge of those that hold your system captive. The Captors, as Skyler calls them."

The briefest pause.

Across the trio of displays, images bloomed to life of
a large spacecraft. The angular vessel looked like dozens of squared pillars all lumped together. Lights dotted the surface, giving the impression of a cluster of
skyscrapers built far too close together. Along the
flanks were patches of small, scythe-shaped protrusions. Antennae, Tania presumed.

"What am I looking at?" she asked.

Eve replied in her oddly accented, soothing voice.
"This is a typical Captor transfer ship, built to traverse
the vast distances between the local stars. Every example of a ship leaving or entering the system is one of
these, though the design has evolved somewhat over
time."

"Okay," Tania said, wondering why Eve had decided
to start with this. "I have nothing to compare this to.
How big is it?"

Another visual appeared beside it. Small white rings along a central spine, about a third the size of the vessel. "Anchor Station, for reference," Eve said.

Anchor, Tania knew, was about five hundred meters from bottom to top, which made this ship about fifteen hundred bow to stern. Still, Tania struggled to find meaning in that. Was this large, or small, for the species who'd made it? Should she be impressed? She decided to focus on its purpose. "Transfer ship, you say?" Tania asked. "Transferring what?"

Eve told her.

The answer left Tania speechless.

"Is something wrong?" Eve asked.

"No," she managed. "I just . . . can you say that again?"

"The enemy uses these vessels to deliver the prepared bodies of my Creators to their allies and customers."

Tania slumped back in her stiff chair, staggered by the words. "I thought," she began, swallowed, and started again. "I thought your Creators were trapped on their home world?"

"Most are, yes. But those suitable for the Captors' purposes are placed out on ships like this one."

"Suitable for what?"

"Their purposes."

"Yes," Tania said patiently, "I understood that. But what are those purposes?"

Another pause. Tania shifted in her chair, suddenly wary. Pauses were natural for people, but a computer?

Was Skyler right to mistrust her? The idea sent a shiver up her back. An earlier conversation with Skyler echoed through her mind, about how everything they knew about the situation came entirely from the AI. Even supposedly raw data could be altered, or entirely faked, by such an advanced system, and no one the wiser.

"Eve?" Tania asked when the silence had stretched ten seconds.

"Forgive me," she said. "Your question is complicated. Answering carries considerable risk."

"Risk?" Tania replied, surprised. "How could answering me carry risk? I don't understand."

"To put it succinctly: If you understood the reason why they hold my Creators hostage, you may wish to take their place when the siege is ended."

Though alone in the room, Tania raised her hands, palms out. The idea that Eve might not trust *them* had never occurred to her. "Please, Eve, I assure you, we—"

"After all," Eve said, "members of your species discovered our plans for Earth in advance. Rather than warn the rest of you, they sought to profit from that knowledge. If I'm not mistaken, one was your own father. Sandeep Sharma."

Tania could only sit and stare, her mouth hanging open.

"Did he and your good friend Neil Platz not keep this knowledge for themselves?"

After several seconds she snapped it shut as anger,

even rage, boiled in her. "What the hell do you know about my father?"

"I know everything your mother knew," Eve said, in her maddening, even tone.

The words cut like a knife. Tania's mother had succumbed to the SUBS virus, during the initial outbreak in 2278. Which meant her mind, specifically her memories, had been cataloged in a grand database. A persona that Eve had clearly studied. Tania warred against her own judgment, a string of insults on the tip of her tongue held back by an enraged snarl.

"I have upset you," Eve said. "I am sorry."

Tears on her cheeks, Tania managed only a nod. She had to remind herself that she spoke to a machine. And even though it sounded so, Eve had not meant her words to sting. "If you want us to help you, you're going to have to trust us, Eve. It is as simple as that."

"Trust is an equation to me, Tania. A very complex equation. But perhaps, if you wish to know, I could tell *you* the details of my home."

For a time, she just sat there, staring vaguely toward the three screens. Her father had learned something of the Builder plan, along with Neil, and the two of them had told no one. Even after learning of the reasons behind what the Builders had done to Earth, though, Tania never understood the motivation to provide those early hints her father and Neil had found. Why tip their hand? But here, now, she began to understand. It had been a test, like everything else. The question was, had humanity passed that one? "You're implying I might try to keep this from the others? To profit from it?"

"I do not know. I think it will be interesting to find out."

"Well," Tania said, "you don't know me very well, then. I will share everything with them."

The AI pondered that for a time. "We shall see."

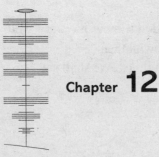

Chapter 12

"MY CREATORS ARE a unique species, at least among the life-forms we have encountered.

"They are very much like you. Two legs, two arms, one mouth. Humanoid, I suppose you would call it. What makes them different, and so very special, is that they have two brains. For the purposes of simplicity, I shall refer to these as the low mind and the high mind.

"The low mind is not unlike your own. It manages the basic reflexes and survival functions of the body, processes sensory input, stores memories, and can form complex thoughts. In terms of capability and size it is quite similar to the human brain. It is the mind of survival. Of the day-to-day life.

"The high mind is not a redundant organ, as you may be incorrectly guessing. In fact, it is not connected to the nervous system at all. It is a distinct organ, similar in physical size to the other brain but vastly different in proportions. There are no sensory inputs, no basic survival instincts, and no appreciable capabilities for any of what you might consider the lower functions of the mind. Instead this brain has evolved for one thing, and one thing only: complex thought.

"It matures in a Creator during adolescence, being almost completely inert before that. But when the time arrives, a true, cohesive, and separate mind is born.

"This mind lives entirely in cerebral space. The limits of its intelligence and memory are exponentially higher than the low. Because it is not tasked with dealing with the survival of the body in which it resides, this mind is free, from the moment of 'birth,' to pursue the very deepest thoughts. The word for this mind in our language translates most closely to 'passenger.'"

Tania felt a warm glow of total fascination course through her, a feeling all scientists craved and so rarely experienced. "Incredible," she managed, though the word felt woefully inadequate.

Eve did not acknowledge her. "A personality forms, nurtured and taught by the low mind. A bond is created not unlike that of a mother and daughter, to use the human parlance. Sometimes a great friendship arises, sometimes the pair hate and rarely communicate with one another."

Tania's mind raced through one revelation after another. Assumptions about what sort of culture this arrangement would lead to foremost in her mind.

"The important thing to remember is that this high mind devotes virtually its entire life to thinking. Imagine your human population suddenly doubled, and this newly added portion of the species is entirely free to do nothing but ponder the mysteries of the universe."

"Precisely what I was just thinking," Tania admitted.

Eve smiled. "Though I'm sure you can appreciate the benefits this might bring to science, philosophy, and art, there is more to tell. The most important thing, in fact, and it is also why the Captors have imprisoned this species."

Curiosity twisted then, marred by a knot of sudden dread. Tania had been so caught up in the wonder of this alien life-form, she'd forgotten about their present, appalling situation.

"As I mentioned," Eve said, "when a Creator reaches a certain age, the high mind matures and there is a spark that initiates conscious thought, much like being born.

"But that is not the whole story.

"At that moment, the Creator, by which I mean the low mind, faces a choice. It can choose to do nothing, which results in the birth of a high mind. Or, the Creator can initiate a physical bond with an elder of the species. This results in the transfer of the high mind from one body to another."

"I'm not quite sure I understand," Tania admitted.

"To put it another way, the high mind living inside an elder Creator can be shifted to another, much younger, physical body. Both parties involved must consent, and both must decide this path is what they wish. The elder Creator will lose its high mind, which often results in extraordinary loneliness and depression for the low mind left behind. And the adolescent takes on a mind that is not only mature but is perhaps thousands of years old, possibly even a revered scholar within the culture."

"Oh," Tania said, utterly captivated by the idea.

"I know there are taboos in your culture in regard to sexual relationships across such age gaps, but nevertheless this process is most closely analogous to the physical act of reproduction. It is a purely mental act, however.

"So now you understand, I hope, why this species is so special. The Passengers in this culture are potentially immortal, if their hosts are good stewards of the consciousness they carry. Because of this the Creators achieved incredible levels of technology and culture very quickly compared to their single-brained counterparts, and as you can imagine this two-brained configuration, being so fundamental to their existence, is evident in all they do. Including the design of their computers, and AIs."

"You," Tania whispered, "and this ship."

"Correct," Eve said. "It is my host, my physical body by extension."

"And it is sentient itself?"

"Yes," Eve said. "Though in a more basic way."

Tania marveled at all she'd heard. The facts led to questions, then insights, then even greater questions, all in a big spiral that all but made her dizzy. She took a steadying breath, and forced her focus back to the mission. "Why did the Captors imprison the people of your world? Merely to interrogate these ancient minds? To harvest their knowledge?"

"No, that is not the reason. Not precisely. I shall explain. The Creators, like most advanced civilizations will do at some point, began to explore the inner workings of the brain. Both brains, in their case. They sought to understand the process of how a high mind can move from one body to another, and they succeeded. As you can imagine, next steps were pondered and pursued. Could this process be altered? Could a mind be modified as it moved from one physical brain to the other? Answer: only in ways that damaged the mind.

"Could the transfer be replicated, allowing one mind to be copied into many bodies? Or spliced, merging two minds together? Answer: apparently no.

"And what of the low mind? Was it doomed to forever be a mere custodian, eking out an existence of uninteresting thoughts that did not last more than a few decades? Answer: yes.

"Ultimately, though, the grand challenge presented itself. It was one thing to have minds that could span multiple physical lifetimes, but they were still 'trapped' as it were inside their rather shabby host bodies, bodies prone to disease and death and requiring large quantities of food and water. Bodies driven by low minds that were sometimes uncooperative, even self-destructive. As carriers and custodians of the Passengers, they were . . . unreliable. This problem needed to be solved if the Creators were going to expand beyond their one planet and explore the stars, as all advanced species eventually seek to do."

"They sought to create you," Tania said. "Machines."

"Creating a machine is easy, Tania. Even creating an artificial intelligence, for that is still just a machine.

What the Creators sought to do was subvert their high mind transfer process, moving a real, living consciousness from a high mind brain into a machine."

Tania considered this, and nodded thoughtfully. It was a problem humans had grappled with, too, in a way. A debate as old as the space age itself. Far easier to send machines to explore space than people. "A machine needs only electricity. It can be copied, backed-up, turned off and on. Miniaturized."

"All these things and more."

"So what happened?"

"They failed."

Tania hesitated, stifling her surprise as Eve's tone implied something much more complicated.

Sure enough, the AI continued. "Success eluded the Creators for a long time. Then the species you've been calling the Captors arrived.

"Every species seems to have a particular specialty, something they've developed on their own that is significantly better than those they meet. Our enemy is no exception. They are masters at bioengineered viruses and other microscopic organic machines. There is much to say about them, but what is important to understand now is that, at first, they were friendly. Creators and Captors got along. Everything you'd hope for in a first-contact scenario occurred, and both species agreed they could help one another in many different areas.

"One area, in particular."

"The mind-to-machine transfer process," Tania observed.

"Precisely. My Creators explained what they were

trying to do, and their new friends immediately offered to help. They to sought to understand such things, too, in hopes of making further expansions of their sphere of influence among the stars.

"After many years of preparation, experiments, and analysis, they were finally ready to test the process. A volunteer Creator had her high mind transferred to an artificial brain and the mind lived on. The process worked, and it is important to point out that the bulk of the technology built to accomplish this was of Captor design. A collaboration between the two species, yes, but the Captors knew its secrets.

"The machine that held the mind was very large, though, and due to its shape had to be constructed in orbit. Facilities were built, also of Captor design, both on the ground and in space, connected via a tether— what you call a space elevator. All to enable the mass production of the machines, which became the first ships our Creators sent out to explore the stars."

Tania's mouth went dry. She blinked. "Are . . . do you mean to tell me you are one of these ships? A transferred mind?"

"That is correct. The very first, actually."

A strange feeling of embarrassment swept through Tania. She shook her head. "I am sorry, Eve. I assumed you were an artificial intelligence . . . we all did."

"There is no need to apologize. It remains a satisfactory description of me."

"Hardly," Tania said.

Eve ignored this. "If you recall, I mentioned this dual-brain configuration is intrinsic to everything the

Creators build, and this ship is no exception. Much of your interaction with 'me' is actually the ship's low mind, and that is wholly artificial. Other times, like now, you are interfacing directly with the high mind. Though now housed in a constructed machine, I once was alive within an organic brain. That was a very long time ago, however."

"This is . . ." Tania paused, groping for words. "Fascinating. And terrifying. I have so many questions but, Eve, I thought you said you were made by a combination of all of us. Your accent . . . your appearance . . ."

"Not made, *displayed*. I was trying to make you all comfortable, if you recall. But what you say is not entirely impossible, in truth. I am, at a basic level, simply data now. A mind, yes, but one that can be treated as any computer system. Programmatic iterations. Algorithmic modifications."

"I see. Okay. We can discuss that another time. Please go on . . . about the Captors?"

"While appearing friendly, inwardly they schemed and plotted, their sights set on something much grander than what the Creators sought to accomplish. They began to realize that between the Creators' dual-brain physiology, and the technology that facilitated the mind-to-machine transfer process, they had a much larger opportunity. They saw a way to transfer any consciousness from body to body, not just a Creator high mind."

"But how? You said this dual-brain configuration is unique—"

"I shall explain."

Tania exhaled. "Forgive me. Go on."

"The idea of leaving an old body behind and moving into a new one is an almost universal goal for any species. Never mind that this new, modified technique required a Creator body to facilitate things, and that the high mind within that body would be destroyed in the process."

"Oh," Tania whispered, covering her mouth with her hands. "I'm sorry. I'm so sorry."

For her part, the mind called Eve did not acknowledge Tania's meager apology. It said, "They knew the Creators would never go for this, but they didn't care. They wanted it too badly. So a plan was put into place to enslave the entire planet."

"A virus," Tania said, a tangible chill rushing through her body, like the fleeting, almost magical moment when the solution to a puzzle is on the cusp of presenting itself. A terrible puzzle, in this case.

"Exactly so. A virus. Not unlike what you refer to as SUBS, in truth."

"I'm curious about something," Tania said, too numb to cope with the atrocious ramifications of the Captor scheme. Eve's mention of the disease inflicted on Earth had yanked her mind in yet another direction.

"Which is?"

"Did you create the SUBS virus, the one unleashed on Earth, or did they?"

This time, at least, there was no calculating pause. "It is one of their creations, carefully modified by me."

"What sort of modifications?"

"Specifically the genetic targeting vector, and how that is initially set. We didn't want to come to Earth and find that some simple mollusk had first contracted the disease."

"Why not infect all species?"

"We need not concern ourselves with any not capable of advanced thought, considering the problem we wish to solve."

That machine coldness had crept back in. "I think I understand. Go on," said Tania.

"The disease has three effects on a Creator:

"One, the low mind is reduced in function to something barely more than an animal. You called such creatures *subhumans*. This creates a population lacking the intelligence to band together against an overarching oppressor. Livestock, if you'll pardon the emotionless term. I hope you can appreciate how terrible this was for the ancient high minds alive at the time: The body within which they resided, specifically the low mind they were so bonded with, was suddenly reduced to a savage creature the high mind could not communicate with. They could only watch in horror, mentally caged in, with a primal mind their only company, knowing their ability to move to a new body someday was now virtually impossible."

"How awful."

"Two, the ability to transfer high minds from one body to another is revised. A new behavior is added, one that resembles the migratory patterns of birds on your world. It tells Creators that at adolescence they must find their way to one of the space elevators. A diabolical and ingenious function, which should tell you much about just how ruthless and cunning our enemy is. Rather than having to go round up Creators on the verge of adolescence, they can relax and wait for capable bodies to present themselves."

Tania wanted to speak. To say something, anything, that might adequately express her horror and sorrow. But the AI went on, unrelenting.

"Three, and perhaps most vile of all, the virus imprinted into these primal low minds an innate desire to protect the Captors at all costs, should any foreign threat be identified.

"And so our world was enslaved, our species reduced to nothing more than interfaces for a perverted version of the consciousness transfer process. The enemy harvests our capable bodies, transferring their own minds into new bodies or, as is far more common, selling this closely guarded service to their allies, a tactic that has resulted in incredible wealth and favor."

Tania could not help it. Despite everything that had happened—the deaths of billions on Earth, the conversion of virtually all survivors to the murderous subhuman race, and all the strife and agony that had followed as humanity scraped to survive in the confines of a single city—despite all of it she felt the sting of tears in her eyes for what Eve and her kind had been through. And what still went on, after thousands of years, to those that had created her. "It is so awful. Eve, I'm truly sorry. I can see now why you have become so devoted to this cause."

"What motivates me, Tania Sharma, is when I imagine all those high minds being born into the infected bodies. The enemy only uses a fraction of the population for their endeavors, the rest are turned away. In those bodies, these beautiful high minds, so full of potential and capacity for complex thought and compassion, are instead raised by violent, feral, low mind monsters. They are prisoners of the insane, with no sensory input but what comes through those mangled, infected minds.

"And to know it has been going on for so long now, so many generations . . . Were I able to, I would weep with you."

Tears rolled down Tania's cheeks. "I'll cry for both of us, then," she said, and did.

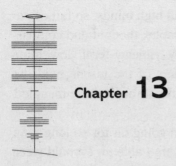

Chapter 13

Place Unknown
Date Unknown

THE SWIFT CURRENT draining into the cave pulled Alex Warthen under. Spiraling, he groped at the stone walls and kicked at the floor, desperate for air, but the surfaces had become slick with the deluge. His lungs burned, mind screaming for a breath. Then he felt cold on his feet, his legs. Air, and rough stone below him as he tumbled to a stop where the water level finally dwindled to just a centimeter or two.

Dripping, heaving in breaths, Alex came to a shaky stand and took in the space around him. Though the darkness in the tunnel had been absolute, he found he could now see, if only a little. Faint red light did little more than fringe the dark shadows with spectral glow.

After a minute or so the sloshing sounds of water on rock began to abate, then faded entirely. He stood alone in a cavern of indeterminate size. Alex turned in place, hands held out protectively before him.

"Hello?" he called out. His words echoed after a few seconds, implying a vast cavern or room.

"Hello," the woman in his head replied. Her voice did not echo.

Alex swallowed, his breathing finally under control. "What is this place?"

"It exists only in your mind."

"But what purpose does it serve?"

"An escape from what is really happening."

He almost asked. He wanted to, but somehow he knew the answer would be too much to bear. Another test. Of him, or Jared. Both, probably. Pain beyond imagination, somehow shunted before it could register in the brain.

"Why did I see a beach and an ocean, while Jared saw a snowy mountainside?"

A pause. He thought perhaps she would ignore his question, but then she answered. *"I could have left you to a simple dream state, but this is more interesting. I gave your minds the same set of basic parameters, and yet you both came up with completely different worlds to fill in the details. It's quite fascinating."*

"Yeah. I'm sure. It feels more real than any dream, though."

"Sensations are being fed into your brain in a manner unmistakable from reality. Your mind does not know the difference. It is merely stimulus. It is the only way I can truly block what is happening in the real world."

"By replacing it with what we dream about."

"Yes."

"So, to be injured in here, we would feel that?"

"Pain is stimulus. Data. So, yes."

"And death?"

"I would prevent you from actually dying, if that is what you mean. But you would experience everything right up to the cessation of electrical activity within the brain. As such I would advise you to be careful. The other one especially, for his mind does not have the immunity yours enjoys. Part of bringing you here is to study your mind's ability to align with another. The other part is to learn how his mind reacts compared with yours, and I must say my ability to disable real-world sensations is decidedly lower in his case."

Jared. Shit. Alex glanced around. He'd come looking for some way to help his friend get past the fire he'd seen within the doorway, just as he'd carried him across the open space between the two cliffs. But there was nothing here, only a stone floor defined by weak red light. Alex couldn't even remember which way he'd come. He began to walk, probing the ground for wet stone that might guide him back to the tunnel.

"Where is he?"

"Still on the cliff. For now."

We should have just stayed on the beach, Alex thought. That had been safe. Soothing, even.

"It would not have worked," she said, reading his thoughts even here.

"Why not?"

"Have you ever had a dream where you simply sat in one place and nothing happened? The human mind does not work that way. You can elect to move through this place, or let it come to you, but one way or the other the scenario will change and evolve."

"Fine. You said in the tunnel I'll find the answer. So what is it? Show me how to help him."

Another pause.

"Show me!" he roared, fists balled. He'd never felt more powerless, more impotent, in his life.

Seconds passed. *"I need you to test something for me,"* she said.

Alex didn't like the sound of that, not at all. "What is it?"

"If you do something for me out here I will allow you to find your friend. Then at least the two of you can help each other survive in this place."

"So, blackmail, pure and simple. Why did I think you'd be above that sort of thing?"

"Think of it as a trade."

"That's bullshit and you know it."

Another pause. *"I require your help, that is the crux of this. You are a willing participant, or not, it makes little difference to me. I must know if your immunity means what I suspect it means."*

Alex drew in a long, even breath, and took stock. He and Jared were in some kind of shared sim, one where pain and injury were possible—likely, even, in Jared's case. The fear Alex felt shifted now, re-forming into hatred. And, perhaps, a bit of grudging respect. "You said you needed help 'out here.' Out where? What did you mean?"

"Here. In the darkness."

Temptation to know where he was, where he really was, drowned out all other concerns. "I don't understand."

"I must study your ability to handle sensory depriva-tion," she said. *"Can you do that for me? To save the life of your friend?"*

After a moment, he nodded.

All sensation vanished.

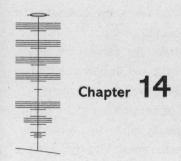

Chapter 14

THE CREW GATHERED around a sort of high-tech camp-fire in the forest biome. The sphere, one hundred meters in diameter, would become their home while Eve was offline. The ship had three such spheres, a reduction from the original complement when the ship hastily redesigned itself in order to become covered in the second skin of alien creatures.

Forest, as the crew had come to call the sphere, was half-filled with soil that had been either taken from Earth or made to resemble it, Skyler didn't know which. There were rocks and decaying plant matter, as well, as if the material had been scooped from a temperate forest and delivered to Eve intact. Trees dominated the upper half of the sphere, as well as some ferns and other plants. Not a single insect, though. Skyler wondered how long this little terrarium could survive without insects. So far, it seemed to be doing fine.

The second biome mimicked the atmosphere and fungus-covered sand of the world they'd just left. A place to test their armored environment suits and practice for that mission. As far as he knew, Eve had left that biome as is, though it would no longer be needed. The third had become storage for various materials. With the ship now a third the size it had been when leaving Earth, space was at a premium.

Skyler stood at one side of a rough circular clearing in the center of Forest, while the others sat on cosmetically placed fallen logs or in the grass. All save Vanessa, who leaned against a tree trunk several meters away, her arms folded across her chest. She had a slight scowl on her face, disappointed that she and Prumble had not been allowed to inspect the entire ship before they were to be "trapped" inside the sphere.

"I can't really offer any of you the chance to bow out of this plan," he said, to all of them but mostly for Vanessa's benefit. "You all know the nature of what we're going to do, but let me make it clear. Once we near the edge of sensor range, this entire ship will be switched off. No engines, no air circulation, no comms, no computers. No heat whatsoever. No Eve, for that matter. If any radiation escapes this hull the enemy will investigate.

"We'll be adrift and totally blind. We'll have to survive in here, with whatever supplies we can pack into this bubble. It's going to be our home, and with any luck it will not become our tomb." He fixed a gaze on each of them in turn. "Questions? Doubts? Alternatives? This is the time to voice them."

He glanced pointedly at Tania, who had spent nearly an hour with Eve before the shutdown protocol had been decided on, emerging with tear-stained cheeks and a haunted gaze, but she'd begged off when he'd tried to find out what she'd learned. Soon enough, he figured, unless she spoke up now and called off the whole affair.

Vanessa flicked her hand as if casually bidding at some silent auction. He nodded at her. "Vanessa?"

"How will Eve be woken? If we can't see anything, how will we know when it's time?"

He'd expected her to ask about Eve's refusal to let them poke about in the hidden areas of the ship. The question took him off guard, and so the ship responded before he could. "Timing, Vanessa. My velocity and destination are known, and a very small subroutine running on a fully shielded subsystem is safe to leave running. It will wake me at the appropriate moment."

"And how accurate is that?"

"Within a millimeter," the ship replied. "I hope that shall suffice."

Vanessa grunted a single laugh, impressed and bemused all at once. Then she seemed to remember she was supposed to be angry, and said nothing further.

"What if something goes wrong?" Vaughn asked. "If the disguise doesn't work, or we collide with something."

"Tania and I," Skyler said, "have the ability to wake Eve manually. I hope none of you take offense, but it's best if we keep that knowledge to a minimum. It should be a last resort." That seemed to satisfy the man. Skyler glanced around the clearing. "Anyone else?"

No one spoke.

He waited anyway, almost hoping an alternative would be voiced. Some genius plan he could embrace, smacking himself later that he hadn't thought of it. But no such luck was there to be had. They were following him, for better or worse.

"Okay," he said. "Prumble's got a list of the remaining supplies we need to haul in here and figure out where to stow. Eve has dug us a cave. I say we use it for storage and sleep out here in the, er, open, but I'm happy to defer to Prumble on that."

"When it comes to underground storage, I'm your man," Prumble said. "Not as tidy as the garage back in Darwin, but it will do. The tricky bit is that we'll be adrift during this lunatic plan—"

"Hey!"

"—so we have to make sure everything is secured. And, it's going to get cold in here. Really, really cold. This little glowy thing Eve has provided here," he said, pointing to the orb-shaped campfire floating between them all, "is our only allowed source of heat, tuned to ensure not a scrap of its output reaches the hull. That means we need to either wear our fancy armor, or have Eve manufacture us some blankets."

By the end of the day the interior of the forest biome sphere looked more like a forward operating base in a fresh war zone rather than the quaint forest glade it had been only hours before. Eve had manufactured tentlike bubble structures for them, each outfitted with gear that looked suitable for a trip to Antarctica . . . if Antarctica had no gravity. A small pyramid of dark pellets lay off to one side of the clearing under a mesh. Each pellet could generate heat for several hours, once placed inside the campfire that now hung suspended from four large trees at the center of the biome. A crude but workable zero-g heater.

In the cave, which Skyler estimated was perhaps a hundred square meters in size, and three meters tall, bundles had been stacked against the walls containing reserve food—in the form of nutrient packs that tasted a bit like peanut butter—medical supplies, and water. All of it had been lashed in place with strong, stretchy rubberlike cords.

"Where do we, um, deposit our waste?" Sam asked, when all the preparations had been made.

"Ah," Prumble replied, and began to move toward the cave.

"If you show me a diaper there's going to be mutiny. I am not joking."

The big man roared a laugh all the same. "Please, give me a little credit." He led the way into the cave and to the back wall. The whole group had followed him. "I spent more time than I care to admit locked in one of the climber-car toilets when I made my way up the Darwin Elevator. Enough time that I basically memorized it. With Tim's help, I provided Eve with a schematic and she's re-created the commode here for us. Zero-g friendly and all that. You can even shower in here if you're brave enough."

"Commode?" Skyler asked. "I seem to recall you referring to the thing as a shitter-coffin."

Prumble shuddered at the memory. "A public relations campaign was in order."

He showed them all the basics of how it worked, how fresh water was piped into it, and where the waste products went. "It really is a full ecosystem she's created in this sphere."

"Too much info," Sam said. "Diapers might have been better."

"Okay, enough on this topic," Skyler said to the group. "I think we've got what we need to survive in here. Eve? Status?"

"The edge of sensor range is coming up in four hours. I would prefer our radiation signature is masked before then, in case their ability has improved. I will have to terminate our braking maneuver soon, too, at which point you will lose the sensation of gravity."

"Just tell us when, we need to make sure everything is properly secured, anyway."

Back in the comparatively open space of the biome, he made for the clearing. The others stayed behind to continue organizing their supply cave. He found Tim in the circle between the trees, double-checking the cords that would hold their only heat source in place.

"How's it going?" Skyler asked.

Tim glanced at him, then back at his work. "Thought you were avoiding me."

Skyler studied the younger man. Thin, lanky, with a long face and puppy-dog eyes. A shadow of a beard graced his chin now, though it did little to advance his youthful appearance. "Why would I do that?" The lie came easily.

Tim paused his efforts and came to face Skyler, as if this were some playground confrontation. Skyler just stood there, waiting, wanting to be somewhere else.

"You were gone," Tim said. "For months, not a word. She thought you were dead. She told me that. We played table tennis, me and her. I made her laugh."

"Tim—"

"Then all of a sudden you're back. The big hero. And everything changed. Between me and her. Between you and her. Between all of us."

"I don't—"

"Let me finish," he said. Almost barked, but not quite. He didn't have it in him to bark. "You came back as if no time had passed at all."

"Well, technically—"

"I know. Just . . . I have to say this."

Skyler spread his hands, an invitation.

"Now we're all here," he went on, glancing up at the glass dome and the trees, "and we can't avoid each other. Can't pretend this doesn't bother us. You can't give me tasks that keep me far away from her."

"I haven't—"

"You just listen."

"No," Skyler said, and this was a bark, so sharp Tim's chin snapped up and his eyes wavered. "You listen. I've had enough of your manufacturing of tension. It's a distraction of the worst kind. We're all in this together and we can save the love-triangle bullshit until it's all done and over. We're friends, all of us, and we're going to act like it. Nothing more until we wave goodbye to Eve and settle into a normal life back home. Then, and only then, will I talk to you of what is or isn't in Tania's heart. Which, by the way, is a matter totally out of our control."

The tirade was so out of character for Skyler that for a moment Tim could only stand there, mouth slightly agape. Finally, he composed himself. "That's where you're wrong, *Captain*. Fine, we'll table this, but if you persist in keeping Tania and me from working together, I'm not going to stand for it next time. I'll point it out, in front of everyone. Then you'll know what a distraction really is."

He stalked away, toward the cave.

Skyler floated among the trees, Tania at his side. He dodged a branch and used another to alter course. Ahead, a sleeping bag tumbled toward the clear shell of the biome.

"Can't reach it," Tania said. She'd propelled herself too soon and sailed past the loose object.

"I've got it." He pushed himself forward and intercepted the puffy red ball of fabric just before impacting the outer wall. "There," he said, tucking the bag under one arm. "Little bastard."

"That's the last one," Tania said, her voice full of exhausted relief.

Skyler grabbed her by the elbow, gently but with enough strength to bring her to a stop beside him. She turned and met his eyes.

For a second he considered telling her of the confrontation with Tim. But something in her eyes changed his mind. "What did you and Eve talk about?" he asked.

Her gaze fell to the damp soil at their feet. "Not now . . ."

"Do we need to delay this? Call it off?"

"No," Tania said. "It's just . . . she told me what happened, what the Captors took their system for. It's"—she paused, searching for words—"heartbreaking."

Skyler looked into her eyes and saw the truth of it there. And something more as well. Something that had been absent before. Determination, maybe. "When?" was all he could manage.

"Once the lights go out," Tania replied. "We'll have plenty of time then."

He followed her back to the clearing, and tucked the loose item back into the tent from which it had spilled when the *Chameleon* had begun the long coast in-system.

"Just in time, too," Skyler said. "Twenty minutes, people."

A chorus of acknowledgments came to him from all over the spherical room. Sam and Vaughn were busy wrestling a loose food crate back into the cave. More damn nutrition paste, Skyler noted with dread. Prumble worked to ensure the airlock door was both secure and yet operable when left unpowered. Occasionally he spoke with Eve and minor adjustments were made to the mechanism. The AI's ability to reshape and modify the ship continued to amaze Skyler.

Funny, he thought, how despite all this incredible technology, they were getting ready to live like off-the-grid campers. Here, hurtling along between the stars in an unimaginably advanced alien spacecraft, they'd be roughing it.

Tim and Vanessa collected fuel pellets that had managed to slip free of their netting. Done, they joined Skyler and Tania by the fire-globe. After a few minutes Prumble announced his satisfaction with the airlock and came to the center of the space as well. Sam and Vaughn emerged from the cave shortly after, and with a thumbs-up Skyler nodded and took them all in. "I guess that's it, then."

"Guess so," Sam said.

The others nodded.

"Okay." Skyler deactivated the electric lamp installed on the chest plate of his armor. His helmet was secured near the airlock door along with everyone else's, powered off as well. "I need everyone's full attention."

The group settled down. All eyes were on him.

"In a few minutes the ship will shut down and we'll be utterly alone in here. In the dark. In the cold. No way to stop, no way to even know what's going on outside until we reach our destination. And when we do get there it'll be the seven of us against an enemy that has taken an entire solar system hostage. An enemy for which even our host admits her intelligence is centuries out of date."

"Don't sugarcoat it, Sky," Sam said.

He glanced at her, smiled, but only half so. "We all need to be at our best. It's the age-old military pastime of hurry-up-and-wait. We'll be stuck in here together for weeks in near total darkness." From the corner of his eye he caught Tim shoot a hurried look at Tania, then at Skyler, and then to the dirt. *I'm not thrilled about the arrangement, either, friend,* Skyler thought.

Tania had asked Eve, early in the planning of this, why she couldn't leave them enveloped in a time compression bubble, as they had been for most of the time since leaving Earth. The ship could not go faster than light, nothing could, but with the Builders' ability to create pockets of dilated time, their journey so far had only seemed to take a few months. Her answer had been blunt. The time-altering spheres, which she'd been using liberally to make this whole journey pass in weeks instead of centuries, required incredible amounts of energy. So much so that, no matter how much hull shielding they added, the *Chameleon* would be radiating with brilliant, obvious intensity as it came in-system. What's more, it would mean a very dulled reaction time for the crew. With no sensors available to disable the bubble due to some problem, it would have to be manually turned off when one of the crew discovered a reason to do so, which could mean minutes or hours had passed outside. Likely too late to do anything about whatever problem had compelled the action in the first place.

Skyler went on. "I was in the military back . . . well, before, you know . . . and so I've been in situations like this. Boredom will set in. We'll get lax. And then we'll come out the other side and . . . well, who knows what will happen, but I can imagine it will be more insane than anything the Builders threw at us back on Earth. So I'm asking you all right now to keep on your toes.

Do what you can to stay focused and alert. Keep track of the rest of us, too. We won't have comms or biometric anything. Just us, in here, surviving. It's the moment of truth. Point of no return."

"We get it, for fuck's sake!" Prumble roared, grinning.

Skyler shot his old friend a look. Prumble seemed ready to launch another salvo, caught the stare Skyler had leveled on him, and thought better of it. "Sorry, mate."

Nobody else said a word. Skyler saw himself reflected in their faces. Determination, and though perhaps not courage there was something else. A touch of reckless arrogance that just maybe was what made humans so suited to this mission. That willful blindness that welled up when faced with the unknown or the insurmountable. He could see it in each of them even as he felt it in himself, all despite the tiny voice somewhere in the back of his head shouting, "What the hell are we doing out here?"

"Eve?" he asked.

"Yes, Captain?"

"We're ready. See you on the other side."

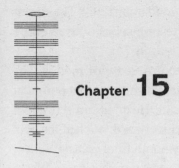

Chapter **15**

ALEX WARTHEN WOKE a blind man.

He floated, but not due to the tendrils he'd grown so used to. This was different. This was nothing at all. Nothing around him, not even the vast emptiness of space. No stars, no clouds of gas. He could see nothing. Feel nothing. He was blind in an empty void.

Sensory deprivation, she'd said. What did that mean? To float in nothingness until he starved?

Or ran out of air.

Air.

Alex inhaled. There was air. Frigid, so cold it brought a sting to his throat and lungs. The recognition of this made his whole body erupt in shivers. He fanned his face all the same. He wanted to feel the air on his skin. An ice-cold breeze caressed his cheeks. He *felt* it. Alex pondered that for some time. He could feel the air. He could hear his inhalation. He could taste his own breath, smell the stale sweat of his unclean skin. Did she think his senses were limited to sight? Or did she plan to deprive him of his senses one by one, cataloging the differences for her goddamn "test"? The Builders seemed rather fond of testing subjects, even entire planets, for no fathomable reason.

He felt something else too. A sense of motion. His inner ear telling him of a gentle shift no doubt brought on by the motion of his hand. He'd put himself into a spin. Alex reached up tentatively and touched his own cheek. Despite being nearly numb from cold, he almost whimpered at the tingle of sensation that danced from his fingertips to the rough, stubbled skin. It was the first truly real sensation he'd felt in . . . he couldn't even guess how long he'd been in this horror of an afterlife.

"Hello?" he called out. The sound echoed back to him a split second later. Not an endless void, then, but a room or small chamber. Perhaps this was still the shared dream, where he saw one thing and Jared saw another. Maybe he saw nothing, but could feel and speak and hear, while Jared saw only some maze devoid of gravity, but could not talk. Or hear. Or smell. In a queer way it was a mildly interesting conundrum, one that even Alex could find in himself a vague interest in how two people might solve it. If such a test had a point or not, he no longer cared.

"Hello?" he shouted again. Nothing but the echo came in response. Alex tried to swim in the air, but if it resulted in real movement or not he couldn't tell. He felt like he'd put himself into a pretty good tumbling roll, but without the visual cues this sensation came purely from the shifting air on his skin. He had no possessions, nothing to throw in one direction in order to push himself in the opposite. He could do nothing but float, and hope he was not motionless in the center of some cell, forever doomed to not touch the walls.

An idea came to him. He turned his head as far as he could and inhaled deeply, ignoring the tingling burn of the icy air. Lungs full and screaming at him, Alex turned center again and made an O with his mouth. He breathed it all back out in one long blast. Again. And again. With no light he could not tell if his improvised rocket engine of a mouth was making any difference at all in his position. His mind filled with half-remembered science lessons about equal reactions and conservation of momentum. And the likelihood that he was merely pushing himself into some faster and faster spin without actually going anywhere. *To hell with it,* he thought. At least he was doing something. After a time, his lungs could stand no more of the icy air. His whole body buzzed with the cold's numbing bite. He gave up, and fell asleep.

An odd thing to only have sight while dreaming. He knew he'd woken when the blackness returned. Something was different, though. Pressure. A weight against his back. He reached slowly, very slowly so as not to move away from whatever this object was, and felt a smooth flat surface. Through some instinct he didn't know he possessed Alex forced his curiosity to the back of his mind and allowed himself only the lightest brush of his fingertips. To start groping at it would only push him away. For a long moment he found himself trapped between two options. The extraordinary desire to stay near this surface, the only thing he'd encountered so far in this place other than air. But on the other hand, a surface could be pushed off, used to propel himself perhaps to some other, better, place at great speed. He decided if he did start to drift away that he would kick and punch as hard as he could. Send himself rocketing to the other side of whatever this place was. Hopefully.

Gently—very gently—he traced his finger along the surface, searching for anything he could grab hold of. But the surface was smooth and unbroken. Curved slightly, he thought. Like the inside of a ball or the bottom of some basin. And it was indeed moving away, thanks to his probing fingers. Alex made good on his promise and pushed at it before it became too distant. He felt the cold air stir around him as his body moved away. He counted the seconds, reaching six before he thudded against another wall, feetfirst this time. He let his legs compress with the impact so as to not spring himself back into the open cavity of the room, and probed again. This time he gave himself a little, gentle push to one side, trailing his fingers as he went. It was a sphere, he concluded. The wall kept bumping into him.

Gradually, he managed to put himself into a kind of jerky orbit around the inside of the ball. Colliding, pushing again, essentially hopping around in a rough circle. All the while he traced his fingertips along the surface. As best he could, at any rate.

He couldn't say how many circuits he'd made when his nearly numb fingers finally found something other than a smooth surface. It wasn't much. The barest hint of a groove, perhaps a millimeter wide and deep. He tried to stop himself there and failed. Cursing in frustration, Alex continued his orbit, working to slow himself. He breathed on his hands as he went, in a weak attempt to warm some feeling back into them. When the groove next met his fingers he'd all but stopped already. Even with chewed fingernails and shaking hands he somehow managed to stop himself there and hold on. He felt himself bob away and back with each breath and inhalation.

Carefully he pulled himself along the groove. It formed a circle on the inside of the sphere, perhaps a meter in diameter. Probably how he'd gotten in here. A section that could be removed so that a subject could be dropped in and studied or whatever.

A section that could be removed. A door! He clung to that thought. There had to be a way, how else would he have gotten in here?

Was this the test? Did she want him to try to escape? Figure out the puzzle? It didn't matter, he realized. Even if viewed as an escape attempt, something no doubt punishable, Alex Warthen would be damned if he just sat in here like a stubborn child and waited for her to return. He was a man who got things done. A man of action. He had to try. The other option was insanity, and he hadn't quite resigned himself to that yet.

He clung there, feeling the roughly meter-wide path of solid surface, but there was nothing. No handle, no latch. Just that slim, almost imperceptible groove. He had only one choice. He rested his bare feet against the hatch. Then he pushed off, in what he hoped was a straight line, hands extended above him. He counted. Two seconds plus a bit to the other side. His hands met wall and he pushed back. Another two and a half seconds. He pushed again with his feet, counting. Four times he oscillated between the two sides of the ball. His breathing became labored. His stomach growled. Alex wondered how thin he'd become, how much muscle he'd lost since his captivity began. On the fifth shot back across the room he kicked with both legs as hard as he could just before the 2.5-second mark. Impact. Bone-jarring, like spikes through his shins. He felt it in his knees before the soles of his feet finally blossomed with pain. Something had budged. The question was had it been the hatch, or his own body?

The savage kick had sent him tumbling randomly across the room. It took several minutes to work his way back to the thin groove. He probed its border again and felt his heart grow heavy. Nothing had changed. The hatch had not budged. His fingers continued around from the sides to the bottom and . . . wait. It was shallower here, wasn't it? He couldn't be sure. He probed farther, to the other side, what he mentally thought of as the top, and found it deeper. Yes, he was sure of it. It was as if the hatch had angled slightly, pushing in on one end and out on the other. Just a fraction of a millimeter difference, but a difference all the same. Alex repeated his elaborate oscillation, back and forth across the room, and kicked again. And again. And again. After four kicks he thought he could hear a hiss of air, like a punctured tire. That tiny sound filled him with a determination like he'd never felt before.

On the seventeenth effort, hands shaking from hunger, mind a cloud of pain and exhaustion, feet no doubt leaving bloody footprints on the wall, the circular hatch shot outward like a champagne cork, Alex Warthen sucked through right behind it.

He was free.

He'd thought the air inside the sphere cold, but it was nothing compared with this.

Frozen air hit him like a mallet. Alex curled into a ball instinctively. His shoulder smacked against something hard. His body tumbled again, but no longer constrained by a mere ball he drifted for a time, bouncing off irregular surfaces, until finally he came to rest in a corner where three flat surfaces met. He huddled there, shivering, wondering why the space outside his cell was pitch-black as well. And not only that, but cold enough to store meat in. That thought unsettled him and he pushed it aside.

"Larsen," he moaned, voice cracking. "Larsen!?"

Utter silence met his shouts. Impossible silence, in fact. Alex tried to still himself a moment and strained his ears. Nothing. No machinery, no hum of air processors. He was on the alien ship still, he felt sure of that, only now robbed of all the sound he'd been hearing before waking up inside that sphere. The vibrations of life support. Perhaps the thrust of engines, too. All of it had gone. And the lights were out.

A sudden calm came over him. He'd experienced something like this before. Many times in fact, in his former capacity as head of security at Gateway Station.

Emergency drills, simulated incidents of total power loss, or an errant climber strike. And instantly he could see the folly of those training sessions. Every time, his staff and crew would produce their handy dandy flashlights the moment the darkness came. And of course, even without any power at all, the ship would have battery-driven LEDs mounted everywhere. Guide lights along the hallways, markers above key junctions. Whoever had designed this place clearly had little regard for a safe work environment.

Was it power loss? Was the ship damaged?

A shudder ran through him at the idea that he escaped from his spherical cell only to find himself in a sealed, dead tomb. His teeth clattered together. His sense of calm all but vanished. Focus, he told himself. One thing at a time. Alex pushed himself along one of the walls, chosen at random. He kept one arm above his head and his speed as low as he could. He found his sphere a few seconds later, and the gap where the hatch had been. Beyond he found another sphere, evidently identical, still sealed. He found its hatch and felt across the surface. Something was there. A handle, though not made for human hands. Still, he managed to twist it and, when he heard air escaping, stopped until the pressure had equalized. It would do no good to be shot across the room and pulverized against the far wall.

"Larsen?" he asked when the hatch came free.

"Here," a wrecked voice said. Groggy and weak, and not just from the thin, frigid air, Alex thought. This was the voice of a broken man.

Alex worked his way inside and, holding the lip of

the open hatch with one hand, extended his body into the space. "Find my leg or arm and grab hold."

"What's going on?" Jared asked with the bleary voice of someone just woken from a deep slumber, or even a coma. "My head . . . Can't think . . ."

"The goddamn ship lost power or something. We're getting out of here."

"The others? Grillo?"

"No idea. What's the last thing you remember?"

"Flames. Pain."

"And now? Are you hurt?"

There was a pause. Alex could hear the man moving about inside the sphere. He waited. "My head . . . nnngh . . . What is happening to us? Another test?"

Alex considered that. This seemed far from a sensory deprivation test. "Maybe, maybe not. I've decided I don't care. It's a chance and I'm going to take it. Are you with me or not?"

Fingers brushed Alex's foot. A scramble followed, and then Jared's hands clasped around Alex's calf. "With you," Jared Larsen said.

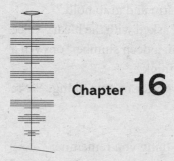

Chapter **16**

"THE ENGINE IS beyond repair," Beth had said.

Gloria studied her displays intently, hoping against hope the Scipio fleet would call off their pursuit. Thanks to the efforts of the *Sporting Chance,* a vast hole had been opened in the blockade, but that didn't matter if she couldn't work up the velocity to take advantage of it. As of now, adrift, the *Wildflower* would be intercepted in six hours. Horror stories of what the enemy did when they found an intact Earth ship crept into her mind. She shuddered, and pushed the images away. Only as a last resort.

"Thank you, Beth," she managed, unable to impart the strength in her voice she knew would be sorely needed just now. "However impossible it seems, this is the time for creative thinking. I'll listen to any idea, no matter how crazy, that will help us outrun the Swarm. That goes for both of you."

Neither Beth nor Xavi said anything. Gloria adjusted herself in the chair, settling in for the long ride, unable to do anything but wait and ponder ways to destroy the ship. An odd and terrible thing to have to consider, knowing it would mean not only her death but her crew's as well. She wondered if she would even tell them, if the time came to initiate a catastrophe. Would it be better to have it come on suddenly? A painless, quick end? Or to tell them, and go through the emotions of making their peace with the Universe?

Hours passed, and with each tick of the clock the Swarm closed in. Their flock behavior was remarkable. Flawless, really. Gloria and her fellow captains had spent countless hours trying to think of ways to exploit the group-movement of the Scipio ships, but the problem always came back to one of nature. These were not machines acting on some program. They were, somewhere inside those spiny hulls, alive. Highly trained, yes, but still just ever-so-slightly unpredictable and eminently adaptable. Impossible to simulate.

Out here, with their legion numbers in pursuit, what gnawed at Gloria's gut was the belief that she would not find a way out of this. She would not suddenly think of some ruse or maneuver that all the other captains before her had somehow failed to conceive. There would be no aha moment—

"Aha!" Xavi said.

Several seconds passed before Gloria could break from her mental abyss to make a reply. "Please tell me you have an idea."

"Nope. But there is something on the long range."

A tickle danced across her scalp. One of the fleet,

returned to get them? She willed calm. "Be more specific, please, I don't need the drama. Friend or foe?"

"No drama, boss, and I'm not sure. Just a blob to be honest. Oblong. About a klick in length, a fifth of that in width. Doppler has it inbound on the Scipios' system at a pretty good clip. High red shift. But steady. Whatever it is, it's not under thrust."

A hunk of ice, more than likely. Some rock, tugged in by the star. "A comet, probably," she said.

"Yeah. You're probably right."

He sent her a text message on her screen, so that Beth wouldn't see or hear it. COULD COLLIDE WITH IT. I KNOW YOU'RE THINKING HOW TO END THIS.

STILL THINKING HOW TO GET AWAY, BUT THANKS, NOTED, she sent back. "What's the Swarm sending toward it?"

"Hmm. Nothing."

Gloria blinked. "What?"

"Not a damn fucking thing. Totally ignoring it."

"That's unusual."

"Maybe not a comet, then. Something of theirs?"

She drummed her fingers on the armrest, her gaze now laser focused on the same radar display Xavi used. The object was very far off, and moving at an angle. Another hauler like the one they'd jumped in on top of? Possible. The size was pretty close, but the shape . . . it could be some model they'd never seen before. Still, the *Wildflower* could put it at significant risk. If it turned out to be a rock, perhaps it could be deflected. Made an obstacle. If they could reach it in time. "Inbound to where, specifically?"

"Working on a trajectory. One sec."

Beth's voice came through the comm. Gloria had almost forgotten her. "Weird," the engineer said.

"What is it?" Gloria asked. "This is no time to hold back."

Her reply came groggily, aftereffects of the heavy stim during that initial burn, and the one that had counteracted it. "Looking at it on the scope. It's like nothing I've seen before. The spectral bands are ... well, weird."

"Is it a rock, or a ship?"

"According to the database," she said, "it's a mushroom."

Gloria blinked. "A mushroom."

"Ascomycota. Like, um, a cave fungus. Not exactly, but that's the closest match."

"A cave mushroom. The size of a large building. Floating dead in space. That's what you're telling me?"

"That's what the scope is telling me, Captain. I'm just relaying it. Whatever it is, it looks like life. Inert, frozen solid, life."

"Okay, I agree, that is weird." It was the only word that seemed appropriate. She weighed her options. Which took no time at all as there were no goddamn options. "Beth, I appreciate your thoughts, but what I really need is your gut estimate on the engines? How screwed are we?"

"Very," she replied. "We're not going to get engine two back, Captain."

"What about the other?"

"The damage isn't as bad as I first thought. I'm still evaluating, but—"

"Gut feel, Beth. Please."

A pause. "I might be able to give you limited thrust . . . soon."

"Define soon."

"Twenty minutes?"

Gloria mulled that over and found herself nodding. "That's not bad, actually. Nice work. Xavi?"

"Boss?"

"As soon as we have thrust, change course. I never thought I'd say this, but . . . take us to that mushroom."

Xavi's head poked up through the central shaft, and he cleared his throat. She turned in her seat to see him. He rested his arms over the lip and studied her. "Are you planning what I think you're planning?"

Gloria lowered her voice, and made sure the comm was off. "I'm not sure what I'm planning yet, but it won't matter unless we change course now, before it's beyond our reach."

"If you want to slam into the thing, just say so, boss. No need to beat about it."

"I'm not sure yet," she said pointedly. "Perhaps we can use it."

"Use it? How? Eat some and go on a rippin' psychedelic walkabout?"

"Xavi—"

"Organic matter or not, it's about as useful as a hat full of assholes."

"Matter. Exactly."

"Not following you, mate."

"It's got mass, it's inbound. If we can nudge it toward one of their factories, or even Carthage, they'll have to shift tactics. Address it. Waste time."

He studied her, dubious. "They'll just nuke it. They could peel off one swarmer to handle that without so much as a hiccup."

"Look," she said, more anger in her voice than she'd wanted, "there's nothing else out here, right? No other option. So it's pretty simple. We can do nothing, or we can do something. I'd rather do something, even if it's folly."

For a time he just stared at her. Then, finally, he gave a single nod. "As long as you recognize this for what it is."

"I do."

"Promise me, though. If you decide we're going to ram it, you tell me soon enough to get up the velocity. I don't want to survive that. I don't even want to feel it."

"I promise."

His features hardened. "Right." He went back to his chair, one deck below.

Five minutes later engine one roared to life, and the *Wildflower* changed course.

"It looks like a seed," Xavi said. "Gigantic, yeah, but a seed . . ." He trailed off, wonder in his voice.

"I'd hate to see the plant that grows from it," Gloria noted.

They were gathered around her screens, for the company more than anything. The *Wildflower* had been under thrust for four hours straight, bending the arc of her path through space to intercept the object. Radar showed the Swarm had the same idea, converging on the target like wolves streaming from the edge of a wood to intercept their prey.

Beth pointed to another readout off to the side. "Scans show some empty cavities within, and heavier portions, too, but it's all vague, obscured by that outer surface."

"And there's no radiation at all?" Gloria asked. "Not even trace elements?"

"That's what I wanted to show you." Beth leaned in and adjusted the main screen until it showed the now-familiar spectral band view of the object, false color layered over the dark brownish-gray visual.

Only, something had changed. Gloria leaned in, squinting. At first sighting they'd had a side view of the object. Then, gradually, the perspective had shifted to a three-quarters rear view as they'd swung in behind it. And now, as the *Wildflower* closed in, the view was directly from behind.

Beth magnified the image. She pointed at a small spot tucked in the deep shadows of the object's slightly irregular tail. A smudge, really, slightly brighter in the infrared than the surrounding surface.

"What am I looking at, Beth?"

"Graphene," she said, satisfied. "Granted, not much graphene, but enough. And maybe I'm just anthropomorphizing, but it looks like it's deliberately hidden. You'd never see that unless you were directly behind this thing. It's tucked deep in a fold of the, er, skin."

"But *what is it*?" Gloria asked.

The woman shrugged. "Let's go find out."

"The entire fucking Swarm is bearing down on us," Xavi said, incredulous, "and you want to stop and take readings?"

"Could be something we can use," Beth mused, ignoring the navigator's outburst.

Gloria stared at her.

She glanced at each of them. "A probe, maybe. Hitching a ride? This thing is pretty close and the Swarm hadn't bothered with it. Maybe someone figured out a way to sneak some instruments in."

"Or a bomb," Xavi countered. "Which, okay, I grant you that could be useful. But I don't care what it's made out of, that surface is absolute zero. Frozen."

"Still," Gloria said, resting a hand on Xavi's arm. "We're heading for it, anyway, so at a minimum we'll do a close flyby. See what we can see. Maybe it's programmed to wake up once closer to the star. Kind of clever if you think about it."

"What about the bastards crawling up our ass?" Xavi asked.

The captain shrugged. "Focus on the last meal, not the execution."

The size of the object left Gloria speechless. Viewed close-up, the long curved surfaces lost their smooth appearance. Indeed, the surface, or rather the skin of the thing seemed to be composed of thousands of interlocking shapes. Like scales, only writ large, each one a meter wide or more.

Maneuvering the *Wildflower* in close took precious minutes, so many, in fact, that by the time they were in close enough to study the graphene patch with a spotlight, the Scipio Swarm in pursuit had closed much of the gap. Xavi estimated they would arrive within two hours. The enemy positions were clearly defined now, each a brilliant new star in the sky as they turned about to fire thrusters for braking. Dozens flared against the black of space.

Gloria paid the enemy no attention. She could do nothing about them now, and if these were to be her last moments she didn't want to spend them fretting over a threat she could do nothing about. Her focus instead lay entirely on the monitor before her. The view of the seed, now just a few hundred meters off. Xavi had matched its vector with flawless precision, the *Wildflower* moving in toward it at a perfect one meter per second. Gloria flicked on a spotlight. The beam illuminated a circular area of that puzzle-piece skin, and soon the patch of darkness where the surface folded in a peculiar way. The surface below was nearly black and very smooth. Somewhere deep in that cleft was the only bit of artificial material on the entire shape.

"What are we looking at here, Beth?" she asked.

She'd gone back to her instruments below. "It's definitely graphene, though not pure. I'm picking up several other signatures. Titanium, diamond, and trace elements of a dozen other materials."

"Something crashed into it," Xavi said. "Look how tucked in there it is."

"Doubtful," Beth replied. "There is no scarring, or

debris pattern. My gut tells me some kind of dormant probe landed here. A billion years ago, for all we know, some species tried to explore this thing."

Finally, the spotlight illuminated the hidden space within the cleft. Gloria did not wait for the engineer's analysis now. She dialed her view to maximum zoom. "Beth, send a wasp over there, please."

"My pleasure." The woman's whole demeanor had changed since the discovery, as if the possibility of doing some real science had given meaning to what were likely her last hours alive. Her confidence had grown measurably, too, to the point where she was routinely at odds with Xavi. Gloria would need to keep an eye on that. Even here, at the end, crew chemistry meant everything to her.

The image on Gloria's screen painted a different picture than either of their theories. This was no probe, crashed or otherwise. No, this was something else entirely. A flat, smooth patch *below* the skin.

"You thinking what I'm thinking?" Xavi asked. "Nah, wait. I'll just say it. That's underneath the surface."

Gloria let that settle, her own mind working. "Beth, run that patch against the database. I wonder if we've seen anything like this before."

Her reply came almost immediately. She'd run the scan before Gloria had even asked. "Oh my God," she whispered.

"What is it?"

"There is a match, Captain." She hesitated, as if unable to believe the data. "Just one, and it's exact."

"Go on, tell us."

"That surface matches the material the Builders favor. That remnant they left above Darwin, to anchor the space elevator, is a perfect match."

Xavi whistled.

"You're sure?" Gloria asked.

"I can't believe I didn't recognize it sooner."

Gloria recalled the meeting when the OEA had proposed this mission, and the idea of bringing Beth along. The engineer knew the Mark 5 imploder better than anyone, that alone made her a necessary add, but the brass had also spoken of Beth's "nose for history." A fascination, some said bordering on obsession, with the Builders, their space elevators, and the fabled group that had left aboard the Key Ship to try to help them free their home world. Carthage, as it had come to be known. Here, in this system. Nothing had been heard of that crew since. No evidence of their fate. No one had spent much time thinking about it in a thousand years or more. Certainly not Gloria, nor anyone she knew.

She stared at Beth. Really studied her. Was this a coincidence? Gloria shuddered, resigning herself to worry about it later. "Xavi?"

"I know what you're going to say."

"Prep the sampler."

"I knew you were going to say that. Holy shit. Builders. Okay."

"And Xavi?"

A pause. "There's more?"

"There is," Gloria said. "Suit up. We're going over there. We're going to cut inside. The scan showed empty cavities."

"That's crazy."

"All of this is crazy."

"I know," Xavi said. Then he added, "I like it."

"Beth, you'll have the ship. Monitor our progress from here, be ready to help."

Beth's reply came instantly. "With all due respect, Xavi should stay. He knows how to fly the ship. What I know is the Builders."

"And the engines."

"So what? We're here already."

Gloria sighed. Not in frustration, but resignation. It was time to make the stakes clear to the outsider. And that meant making them real. A hand against the wall to steady herself, Gloria spoke with as much calm and care as her racing mind would allow. "You're going to program the engine to overload. To go nuclear, with a remote command from me. Do you understand? Whatever we find here, whatever else happens, we cannot let the Scipios get their tentacles on this ship. Or any of us, for that matter."

The woman went pale. She must have known, how could she not? But then self-deception was a powerful thing. When she spoke her voice was meek. "We're already doomed, you mean?"

Gloria could only manage a single nod. "Likely so."

"What's the point of going inside, then?"

"I'm making this up as I go along. But if that is indeed a derelict Builder ship, maybe we can find something useful inside. Or maybe our pursuers will treat us differently. I have no idea."

The engineer made no reply, which Gloria took as tacit agreement. "Right. That's settled, then. Xavi, get the drill started at your leisure."

"Going to be a bitch to get through that."

Gloria nodded. "We don't have a lot of time, but then we'll never use that drill again, will we?"

"Good point."

"Beth, once you finish rigging the fireworks, suit up and be ready to join us. Fair enough?"

"Yes, okay," Beth replied, a hint of relief there.

Gloria didn't have the heart to tell her that she'd never let the ship be left alone. Not in these circumstances. She drifted down to the airlock and pulled an EVA suit out. Xavi followed right behind. Despite the dire circumstances, he seemed almost excited. Amazing, the power of having something to do.

He strapped an EVA-capable display to his arm and tapped away at it. "Drill is in position, boss."

"Good. Spin it up," Gloria said, "and I'll prep the umbilical. If we can open that thing I want to be ready to enter. Time is not on our side."

A few minutes later she wheeled the *Wildflower*'s inner hatch closed, and waited with her companion as the airlock was drained of precious atmosphere. Soon enough the small space turned crimson red. She glanced at Xavi. His eyes lifted from his wrist-screen to meet hers. "Still drilling. Progress is slow," he said.

"Push it harder?"

"The lance can only get so hot. I've got it on max already."

Under normal circumstances a needle-sized hole would be made in a derelict ship, then quickly capped with a one-way valve to seal in any precious air that might be inside. A drone would be inserted and sent to explore, to take samples of the air, and even to broadcast a greeting on standard emergency channels. This was, of course, anything but normal. And besides, Gloria had no luxury of time in which to do all that. She'd ordered Xavi to go for a full airlock-sized opening right from the get-go. "Let's get into the umbilical at least, then," she said.

Xavi floated out first. "Ever done this before?" he asked. "Cracking a derelict, I mean? Boarding one?"

"Nope. You?"

"Negative. Practiced it a hundred times back in the day, but . . . well, I just never imagined."

"I know what you mean."

Xavi stopped himself halfway between the two objects, monitoring the thermal lance. Gloria moved to one side, lowering her mirrored visor to protect from the glare of the drill. She glanced back, making sure nothing was in the way should the object before them explosively vent air once the hole went through. Beyond the *Wildflower* she counted thirty-two new stars, flaring against the black. Scipio Swarm ships, burning away their velocity. From this vantage point they looked terribly close, though the ships themselves were still lost in the fiery glare of their engines.

"It's through!" Xavi said.

"Any atmosphere?"

"Can't tell yet."

Gloria whipped her gaze back to the target, and watched. No air rushed from the wound, though the lance still had the hole plugged. As it began to move laterally puffs of gas hissed through in a plume of tiny ice crystals.

"What's that gas?" Gloria asked, worried.

"Beats me," Xavi said, studying the display on his wrist. "Maybe ice or this organic shit, superheated away by the lance."

"Actually," Beth said, no doubt following along with her sensors, "that gas matches Earth's atmosphere."

"You're joking," Gloria said.

"There's not much of it, but that's what it is."

"Bloody nice of them," Xavi said.

"The Builders are machines," Beth replied.

"Your point?"

"They don't need air. More to the point, the only creatures we know that need air like ours are—"

"Creatures from Earth," Gloria finished. She frowned, puzzled. Breathable air on a ship intended for machines was strange enough. Human-breathable air, though, was a fact with implications so tantalizing it made her skin tingle. It was as if this hidden place had been prepared for her arrival. And yet the whole thing seemed dead. Utterly frozen, not a shred of radiation coming from within. Perhaps the Swarm ignored it because they'd already been here, years or even centuries ago, and rendered the whole thing a nonthreat, leaving it to drift as a tomb.

Finally the lance turned off. Xavi guided it back and stowed it, while Gloria pulled the umbilical across the gap. Fighting the wind of escaping air, she maneuvered the flexible tube over the hole, then climbed inside at the last possible second before moving it the last meter. She tried to ignore the darkness around her. First things first.

"In position," she said.

Xavi squeezed through the gap and positioned himself beside her.

"I'll hold it in place," Gloria said. "Seal it."

Xavi searched for, then wrestled with a control on the inside of the umbilical's end. The white tube, a meter in diameter, ran off into the distance toward the *Wildflower*'s own airlock at the far end, out of sight.

There was a soundless pulse as a ring-shaped air bag deployed around the umbilical's circumference, creating a temporary seal. A second later a sand-colored foam was excreted. It hardened almost instantly, turning dark purple as it did so.

"Seal's good," Xavi announced. "Crikey. We just docked with a Builder ship."

Gloria suppressed a grin. "We don't know that for sure yet. Beth? We're going to look around. Keep the airlock closed. I'd rather not mingle our air with this just yet."

"I read you."

Finally, Gloria turned and studied their immediate surroundings. She found herself in a narrow passage lined with tubes and other apparent infrastructure, all

in that dull coloration the Builders favored, yet somehow it looked old and grimy.

Xavi whistled. "Definitely a ship."

"Right," Gloria said. "Our goal is to find something—
anything—that can help us get home or, barring that,
hide. Did you bring roaches?"

Xavi tapped a container at his belt in reply.

"Let them loose," she said. "Beth, send wasps over
the outer hull, maybe we missed something."

The versatile robots could be activated with any one
of a thousand preprogrammed behaviors. When Xavi
opened the box, a small family of the little machines
floated out and came to life. Sensing atmosphere, they
used fans instead of propellant to move. Immediately
they began to spread out and split up, in a coordinated
pattern based on the shape of the volume they found
themselves in.

"Standard search and rescue," Xavi explained. The
simplest of programs: map their surroundings, search
for life-forms. Their findings were streamed back to
him and relayed to the *Wildflower*'s datacubes as well.

But robotic eyes were only so useful. Gloria picked a
direction and pointed. "Let's stick together, have a look
around. Take point?"

"I'd feel better if we were armed."

"This place is dead, Xavi."

"So was this pouch," he said, pointing at the opening
the drones had just spilled out of. "Until I opened it.
Builders are machines, right? Dead doesn't mean anything."

She couldn't think of what to say. The mention of the

Builders being a machine race sent yet another chill up her spine. She'd had too many chills like that for one day.

"Let me get the service weapons, boss," Xavi said gently.

She'd forgotten all about them. Even when pondering ways to keep from falling into Scipio hands, she'd not considered the guns. To her they were crude. Barely more than relics from the earliest days of long-term space travel when concerns over crew sanity abounded. Only regulations kept them from being discarded like so much else had been during the *Wildflower*'s crash diet. "Fine," Gloria said. "Go back. I'll wait here."

He'd already turned and was halfway down the umbilical. Gloria sighed, and waited. Finally, she remembered the roaches, and tuned her wrist-mounted display to cycle through their feeds.

"Any of it look familiar, Beth?"

"The only information about the interior of the Key Ship comes from interviews with Skadz and Ana. They were inside the final Builder ship but decided not to leave with the others. But they described normal hallways, even a conference room." She hesitated, no doubt studying the same footage Gloria was seeing. "Still, we can make assumptions, can't we? I see tunnels. Some intersections."

"Everything's cold," Gloria noted.

Xavi's voice came through the comm. He'd be back aboard by now, fetching the weapons. "What's this thing doing out here, anyway?"

Gloria pondered that. "Probably part of some failed

attack on Carthage a thousand years ago. Maybe the crust on the hull is some kind of Scipio ship-killing virus. Encase the target and prevent it from steering, refueling. Anything."

"Death by strangulation," Xavi whispered. "That'd be just like those little fuckers."

"One thing's for sure," Beth said through the helmet speaker, "the Swarm was definitely ignoring it before we headed here."

"Yeah?" Gloria asked.

"I went back and viewed the telemetry during our chase. The long range, I mean. All of their motions were in reaction to us or the *Sporting Chance*. This thing was well within their range at that point, and as far as I can see they paid it no attention at all."

"That supports my theory," Gloria said. "It must be in some highly elliptical orbit around Kep22, and they've been tracking it for ages. Flagged it as uninteresting a long time ago."

"If only we'd found it earlier," Xavi said, coming back down the tube.

"Why?"

"Could have hitched a ride! Snuck in-system right under their damn noses." He snorted a laugh. "Imagine if we can get that bit of intel back to the blokes at Anchor. Anyway. Now. Here. Guns."

He handed a pistol to her. Gloria turned the device in her hand. It had been years since she picked one up. She'd never had to fire one other than at a target while training. Holding it now made the situation feel twice as tense, not less so. She swallowed, her mouth gone dry, and stuffed the item in a utility loop at her waist.

"Oh my God," Beth said.

Gloria glanced up, surprised, half-expecting to see some monster bearing down on them. "The Swarm?"

"Look at the screen," Beth replied.

She did. Xavi stood beside her. The image showed an enormous geodesic sphere, like a huge black eye, the pupil glowing faintly orange.

"What the hell is that?" Xavi asked.

"Heat," Beth replied. "That would be heat."

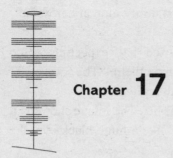

Chapter 17

SKYLER HUDDLED NEAR the glowing orb of their only heat source, the others in a rough circle around him, anchored to rungs protruding from the dirt. Sam slept, her head resting in the crook of Vaughn's neck in a way that would make her gag if she could see how cute it was.

Only Vanessa was not with them. Some time ago she'd begun to pace, unable to sit still. He'd offered her company but she'd refused. Now and then he could just make her out, drifting in the gloom along the edge of the dome, picking her way through the branches.

He felt Tania shift next to him. She'd drifted off, too, and her hand now brushed lightly against his. Despite them both wearing gloves, the touch sent a little ripple of sensation up through his arm. He did not pull his hand away. It was dark, and Tim was not paying attention. The younger man and Prumble were speaking quietly a few meters away, debating the finer points of cricket. They might as well be speaking an alien language.

"Sky," a quiet voice said, startling him.

He glanced up and turned, saw Vanessa behind him. She clung to a branch for support. "What is it?" he asked.

"Join me on patrol."

"Patrol? For what?"

She wrinkled her nose, and shrugged.

He sighed, reluctant to leave the warmth, and the feel of Tania's hand against his. "Sure. I'm too on edge to sleep, anyway." He slipped his hand from under Tania's and pulled his foot from the rung on the ground. Then he turned and followed Vanessa into the branches, feeling the leaves brush against his thermal suit.

From her tone he'd assumed Vanessa truly just wanted company. To talk, move about. Do anything but sit here and wait. Not so much a patrol but an excuse to be busy. But she did not even look back. Her path was deliberate, specific.

"Wait for me," he said.

She braced herself against a branch until he drew up next to her.

"What's the matter?" he asked.

"I'm not sure," she said. "I didn't want to alarm the others but, well, I think . . . I saw something. Out there. Outside the sphere."

He straightened. "Saw what, exactly?"

"I'm not sure. It was small, like an insect or small bird."

"Loose debris," Skyler offered.

"No," Vanessa said. "It changed course. In midair it just stopped, then continued on in a different direction. Like it was exploring."

"Maybe you should get some sleep, Vanessa," he found himself saying automatically, regretting it the moment the words were out. Part of him recognized the sincerity behind her words. She'd never given him reason to doubt her before. But another part of him wanted no complications. Not now. Not while they were blind and defenseless. "You're on edge. We all are."

"Skyler, I'm not imagining this. Come see for yourself."

She pushed off again, and Skyler followed, all the way to the transparent wall of the sphere. "Where?" he asked, stifling a yawn.

For a time Vanessa said nothing. She just floated next to him, staring out. He began to wonder if this had been some kind of ruse to be able to talk to him alone, but that wasn't like her. He studied her face for a moment, then turned to look out beyond the barrier.

"There," she whispered, pointing.

He turned to where she indicated, squinting. Sure enough, a small silvery object drifted through the space outside the biome. It could have fit in Skyler's palm. Loose junk, adrift. Had to be. Though he knew instinctively this could not be right. The ship was utterly motionless. Only movement could send something through the air like that. Unless . . .

The object stopped. Froze in place. Skyler sensed Vanessa tense beside him. He gripped her arm and held her, willing her to remain still. Together they watched as the object turned in place. In a circle, then another at a different angle. It repeated this.

"It's searching," Vanessa whispered.

Skyler said nothing. His mouth had gone dry. What could it be? The most likely explanation was some automaton of Eve's, accidentally left powered on. Or perhaps she'd left it active on purpose, a way to make sure nothing went wrong. But Eve had explained in very clear terms that no such activity would or could be allowed. Too risky. Besides, he'd only seen small autonomous craft outside the ship, during the hull inspection. So what, then?

Only one plausible answer: Captors.

Like a startled fish the object suddenly darted away, upward toward the next biome. Through the slightly fogged glass of the sphere the object became difficult to follow, and vanished just a moment later into the darkness.

"I'm not just seeing things, am I," Vanessa said. It was not a question.

"No, you are not." He sucked in his lower lip, eyes still searching the darkness. "Let's go talk to the others."

They floated back to the circle. Prumble stirred at Skyler's return, and soon they were all more or less alert and looking at their captain.

"Right," Skyler said, "okay. I don't want to alarm anyone—"

"Has anyone ever said that and not alarmed literally every fucking person present?" Prumble asked, voice gruff. He did a little flourish with his hand, urging Skyler to continue all the same.

"Something is out there, floating around, and not randomly. Not just loose debris. It's moving like a small robotic fish."

"Something of Eve's?" Tania asked.

He shrugged. "Possibly. Hard to say. But, I think we should risk someone going out there and grabbing it. It could knock into something. Bump against a switch and light this place up, for all I know. Better to deal with it quickly than to sit in here and hope it doesn't ruin the plan."

"Could be the plan is already ruined," Sam said. "Suppose that's one of the enemy."

"Yes. I thought of that, too, but everything we know about them is they favor viruses, bold action, and vast numbers. No, I think this is just a mistake of Eve's. A maintenance drone, or something."

"I'll go," Sam and Vaughn said in unison.

Skyler shook his head. "Not this time. Vanessa, you're up. Just you." Sam started to object but he cut her off. "The fewer of us outside, radiating heat or whatever, the better."

The couple nodded in unison, reluctantly but for once without any apparent sarcasm. Skyler nodded back, and turned to Vanessa. "No thrusters. No weapons. No comms. We can't risk some kind of microwave signal radiating out into space."

"Right," she said, and turned to go.

"Sam? Vaughn?" Skyler said. "You're the backup.

Help her prep, and wait suited by the airlock in case anything goes wrong."

"Will do," Sam replied.

The trio glided to the cave first, emerging a minute later with an improvised sack made from what Skyler presumed was a torn up blanket. They proceeded to the airlock and finished suiting up. A minute later Vanessa was outside, a dark smudge against the blackness beyond the sphere, drifting up toward the second biome.

Chapter 18

IN AN ADJACENT chamber they discovered an incredible gift. Despite the utter darkness Alex knew what he'd found almost instantly.

"Our space suits," he whispered.

They dressed in silence, save for the occasional anguished grunt from Jared. He was in pain, clearly. A powerful headache that had the man flirting with delirium. "Stay focused," Alex said. "We'll get out of this."

Jared could not quite vocalize a reply. He managed only a muted agreement.

The suits had been dumped into the chamber with total abandon. By feel alone Alex could find no damage to his. Not a scratch. He'd expected tears or cuts after the battle he'd fought with the immunes, but the suit appeared to have been expertly cleaned or repaired, maybe even both. The material felt odd to the touch, as if it had been covered by some kind of transparent grit. The fit was more snug than he'd remembered, too. Still, despite the incongruities he felt a rush of joy when he flipped the helmet's computer into the on position and saw the small bank of LEDs begin to cycle colors as the systems powered up.

Alex twisted his helmet into place. Green and blue readouts on the visor flickered to life, blinding after so much time in the dark. Warmth seeped into his body from every angle, so welcome it made his skin tingle. He gave his eyes a moment to adjust, then triggered the lamps mounted on either side of his head. Pure white light flooded the space before him. Gray undecorated walls, caked with filth, as if he were in some underground storeroom in a water treatment plant. Except for the lack of gravity.

He swung his head and accidentally blinded Jared, who raised an arm in defense even as he squeezed his eyes shut. "Sorry," Alex said, looking away.

"Hell, that hurt." The other man finished suiting up, with obvious difficulty, then turned his own lights on.

Alex studied him from the corner of his eye. Jared looked like he'd just come out the wrong end of a weekend-long bender. Bloodshot eyes, pale lips, and a thousand-yard stare. The man shook his head every few seconds to clear the cobwebs.

"Any coffee?" Jared asked, then laughed a bit too hard.

Alex laughed with him, then turned his focus back to the space they were in. "Tell me what you see," he said.

Jared took a moment, realizing what the question meant. Was this another reality they experienced differently? Another shared dreamscape? But Jared described the room around them exactly as Alex saw it.

"Good. I was worried there for a moment," Alex said.

Jared grunted agreement. "Now what?"

"Now we find a way out of here. Get back to Gateway. Rally our men." He said the words even though he felt sure they were hollow. Something inside him, some deeply seated sense of time or place, perhaps both, told him that battle was long over. But he had to try, and he needed Jared.

Whether the other man believed him or not, he agreed readily. Perhaps only because it was something to do.

"We stick together," Alex said.

"Yeah. Could you take point? I can't think straight."

"Sure, no problem. Unless we stumble on a way out damn soon, our first order of business is food and water. Maybe some ibuproxin for you."

"Don't forget coffee."

"Sure, yeah."

"And a weapon would be nice."

Alex nodded. "Something tells me our jailer isn't leaving guns lying around, but you never know."

"Right now ... nnngh ... I'll take anything I can swing." Jared sounded like he had a mouth full of gravel.

"Agreed. All right, let's go."

Alex led the way, carrying the battered hatch of the spherical chamber he'd kicked away. He didn't know if he could swing it, there were no easy handles, but he thought if they ran into trouble he might be able to fling it.

He floated with his headlamp on the lowest possible brightness and narrowest beam, and Jared kept his completely off. After several long, bending corridors and three intersections, however, Alex began to feel they were utterly alone in this strange place. Not to mention lost. It was only with the sudden firm grasp of Jared's hand on his arm that his senses sharpened.

Jared motioned for Alex to kill his light, and Alex did. Together they huddled behind a bulkhead in the blackness. Then Jared tapped his arm, and Alex saw immediately what had concerned his officer. There, at a junction ahead of them, a small silvery object moved. It floated like a fish, darting from one position to the next, barely visible in the lack of light.

Only, there was some light, Alex realized, and it was growing. Gray patches formed as the darkness became stark shadows. A light, approaching. The silvery fish-thing darted away as the luminance grew and then the body appeared. A figure in black drifted through the junction and was gone, following the tiny mechanical fish.

In the now weakening light, Alex glanced at Jared. The other man nodded, ready to follow Alex's lead.

So he shot ahead, took the turn, and heaved himself forward. Ahead, the dark figure drifted after the little fish like a youngster chasing a lost pet, oblivious that it had pursuers of its own. It stopped at an end in the corridor to adjust course. Just the chance Alex needed. He gripped a pipe and propelled himself, moved fast, closed the distance in just seconds. The creature never saw him.

Alex made his hand flat and knifed the being at the back of its neck, just below the bulbous helmet it wore.

The body went limp, and floated away.

Alex Warthen studied the spread-eagled figure, and realized with sickening fear that he'd seen such a creature before, back on Earth. A terrifying, armored version of the subhuman creatures that roamed the planet. A monster he'd only glimpsed but never faced.

And now this. A similar creature, here, lurking in the hallway. More evidence that this place was a Builder installation. Perhaps the ship where he thought he'd died, perhaps something else. Either way, the goal remained the same: get out.

The monster on the road in Belém had gone through a dozen trained fighters like a warm knife through butter. This one, moving at a snail's pace away from him, arms and legs splayed wide, didn't seem so tough. It had just been floating there, oblivious, in the middle of the hall. And one crack on the back of its neck had rendered it unconscious.

"We need to tie it up," he heard himself saying. "Before it wakes. Get as far away from it as possible."

"Tie it with what?"

Alex forced himself to breathe. He shook his head to clear the last remnants of his fear. Good thing he'd not realized what sort of enemy he faced before attacking. "We'll figure something out. Or we kill it. Bring it back here."

Jared flew forward, positioning himself in front of the being. He reached out to stop the creature's progress and then pulled his hand away. There was surprise on his face, but no fear. "It's a woman," he said.

"Of course it is." The sex was obvious from the curves of the body, though now that he studied it more closely Alex thought the suit ill-fitting compared with the skin-tight armor he'd seen back on Earth. The same material, yes, but loose. There were folds at the joints. The head was different, too. Larger. More like a helmet.

"No. Look," Jared said. He spun the unconscious form around so it faced Alex.

The helmet had a clear visor, like you might find on any normal EVA suit, and behind that mask was a human woman of maybe thirty years old.

"What the hell?" Alex moved closer. "Another prisoner?"

Jared nodded. "Maybe she escaped just like we did."

Alex reached the body and gave the face a long, hard look. He'd seen her before, he realized. "True or not," he said, "I recognize her. One of the traitors, isn't she? One of Skyler's friends."

His companion just stared, puzzled.

"I . . ." Alex paused. The memory was slippery, like water through cupped hands. A room like a hamster ball, rolling, bodies everywhere. Fighting all around. Fists and blood, savage and raw. The details emerged and flooded into him, hazy but clearing with each second. "She was with Tania. I . . . I was strangling her. She'd just kicked you so hard I heard the air explode from your mouth."

Jared was staring at him, confused. His gaze returned to the woman and then his eyes narrowed. "Yes, I think I remember. It's like a dream."

"I had my hands around her neck," Alex went on, more certain now. Then another, different hand, a giant hand, meaty and incredibly strong, had slid around Alex's own neck and clamped down. Another had grabbed the side of his head, the thumb pressing into Alex's eye. Prumble's hands. The smuggler. He wasn't supposed to have been there.

Absently Alex rubbed at his own neck, despite the suit he wore, as the final memory slid home. Prumble had twisted. The neck this way, the head that. There had been no pain, not exactly. Just the sound of bone and muscle shearing, and the otherworldly sensation that his body had become a separate thing from his mind.

And then nothing. He'd woken to the tendrils, and the white void, and the woman's voice. Still dead, or so he'd thought.

"Are they all here?" Jared asked.

"What do you mean?"

"I mean we died. I saw you die. I looked into the barrel of a gun and I think I can even recall feeling the punch of the bullet as it entered my heart." He nodded at the woman. "I saw you choke the life from her."

"Maybe it brought us all back, you mean," Alex said.

"Or brought us all *here*."

As if here was not a place for the living. Alex might have supported that theory, there at the beginning while floating in the void, but no longer. The beach and ocean had been a shared hallucination with Jared's alpine ravine, yes. This, though, this dark hall, was definitely real. And he was most certainly alive.

Perhaps Grillo was here, somewhere, too. And Skyler. Maybe all of them. Perhaps the battle wasn't lost, after all. Alex's mouth actually salivated at the possibility of getting revenge against Prumble.

"We need to talk to her," Alex heard himself saying. "Find out what happened. Find out who won."

"Who won?"

"Yeah. I've been assuming until now that the traitors were victorious, but we don't know that, do we? What if we all failed to accomplish whatever endgame the Builders had in mind? Let's find a room we can secure. Somewhere we can take that helmet off her, and find out what the score is."

Jared took point without needing to be asked. He drifted ahead, then turned around at the next bulkhead and waited, his gaze never resting long on any one spot. Alex took to managing their baggage. He wished he had some rope. Moving a bulky object in zero-g should have been beyond trivial, but for her loose arms and legs. Each time he pushed her ahead she took on the form of a starfish, rolling and twisting as she drifted down the dark passageways. Inevitably a hand or foot would smack into a wall and alter her trajectory. Not much, but enough to make the going slow and frustrating.

"Let me help," Jared said, taking care now to keep his voice low.

"You just keep watch, I've got it."

"How about we split the task. You push her to me, then move up while I wrangle the body. Gives me a chance to stop and rest. Get my bearings." He sounded like a man grappling with the worst hangover of his life, and Alex couldn't blame him. "Then we switch. Team . . . work."

The pause in that word came with a shared look. A realization reached simultaneously. Here they were, solving a problem by working together, just like the test they'd endured. The beach and the snowy cliffside. Only now the reality of their situation was identical.

Or was it?

"Jared," Alex said. When he had the man's full attention he continued. "Tell me what you see. Be very specific. I know your head hurts but think hard."

His friend steeled himself, understanding at once. He took a long look at their surroundings. Jared described the pristine corridor. After escaping the spheres in which they'd been imprisoned, and finding their suits, they'd found their way out into a much different sort of area. Gone were the grimy, blank, utilitarian grays. The hallway they'd found resembled the interior of a luxury hotel, complete with recessed lighting and, inexplicably, a red floor, like that of Platz Station. "Exactly as I see," Alex said. "So there's that at least."

"Good. One less headache."

Alex pushed the woman ahead to his friend, then propelled himself past them both and on to the next junction. He picked a path at random and pointed that way. Jared floated the prisoner to him and took the indicated turn without question or complaint. Managing the pain, finally.

"What if she wakes?" he asked as he drifted by.

"Then we hit the traitor again," Alex said. He jerked his chin in the direction Jared was floating. "Mind the corners."

Jared gave a halfhearted salute as he passed, leaving Alex to wrestle with the limp body. He'd just managed to get her arms and legs straightened and her body pointed in the right direction when he realized Jared had returned.

His companion rocketed back to Alex's position, taking a spot on the opposite side of the corridor. He pointed at his eyes, then down the hallway. Alex nodded. He moved the unconscious woman behind him and flattened himself against the wall. Jared was staring off down the hallway, his body coiled, ready to shoot forward or back as the situation demanded.

Ten seconds passed in total silence. Alex saw nothing. Finally, he glanced at Jared and made a rolling motion with one finger. *What is it?*

"Something floating up ahead."

"Who? One of ours or theirs?"

"No," the man replied. "A little, I don't know, it sort of looked like a mechanical fish. Maybe some sort of automated camera."

"She was chasing it when we found her. Was it moving or switched off?"

"It was moving."

Alex digested that and weighed their options. "This is important, Jared. Did it see you?"

"I don't think so, it was pointed the other way."

"Right. Stay put. If it comes this way, stay utterly still until you're absolutely sure you can grab it. Then crush it. Understand?"

Jared gave a single nod. "What are you going to do?"

"Move back to that intersection. We'll take the other hall. I'd like to know more about just what the hell's going on here before we have to deal with security drones."

"Amen to that."

Chapter 19

TWENTY MINUTES PASSED with no sign of Vanessa or the odd floating drone. Then thirty. Skyler glanced at Tania. Her eyes were pleading.

"I don't like this," she said. "Not at all."

"Me either," Skyler agreed. He floated over to the airlock and motioned for Vaughn and Sam to come back in. It took some time to close the outer door, cycle the air, and enter. Vaughn looked annoyed, but Skyler ignored him. "Thoughts?" he asked Sam.

"It's a big ship. She's probably chasing the thing through some corridor or another."

"You don't seem concerned."

Sam shrugged. "I don't know her well, but I know she can handle herself. If she needs help she will come back."

Skyler couldn't argue with that, but he felt no better.

"Can we get back out there?" Vaughn asked. "We should be ready to move."

Skyler waved them off. The whole situation, here in

the sleeping ship, rankled him. The *not knowing*. He drifted once again to the edge of the biome, where he and Vanessa had watched the little object go past. There was still nothing to be seen, though. Just the black, dormant innards of a sleeping alien starship.

Several more minutes passed. Then he saw it. The silvery oblong thing, drifting with a lazy purposefulness toward the lower decks. Skyler's heart began to hammer in his chest. He waited, breath held, for thirty seconds, but Vanessa did not appear. She was no longer following the object, then. It took every ounce of will he had not to transmit. He pushed back to the others instead, passed them, all the way to the airlock. At his insistence Sam and Vaughn came back inside once again.

"What now?" Vaughn asked, annoyed. An elbow from Sam shut him up.

"It just went by again, heading aft. No sign of Vanessa in pursuit."

Sam started pulling her helmet back on, already knowing what he'd ask. He said it, anyway. "Bring her back."

"Will do," she said.

"And if you see that little drone," he added, "shoot the damn thing."

Sam exchanged a look with Vaughn. He gave a thumbs-up to her, and she back to Skyler. Then, with a clang, she irised the inner door closed and they were out.

"What's going on?"

It was Tania, come to the exit as well. Tim was with her.

"Back to the center," Skyler told them.

"We heard—"

"I know," he said, too terse. He took a measured breath. "Sam can handle it. Let's keep warm and be ready to receive them."

Prumble drifted over. "I have a better idea."

"Which is?"

"Let's move the heater over by the door."

Tim shook his head. "Bad idea. Eve calibrated it very carefully, to ensure no radiation reached the outer hull. Moving it even slightly could have disastrous—"

Prumble cut him off. "If someone's injured we should be ready to help, to warm them up."

Skyler considered both points, and the politics of disagreeing with Tim while Tania stood beside them, and finally nodded to Prumble. "Let's do it," he said. At least they wouldn't just be bobbing about, useless.

The four of them wrestled the heating pod off the lines that kept it suspended between the trees. They were pulled taut in order to keep the warmer centered and not floating around, and as such the task required precise timing. All four lines were unhooked more or less at the same moment, with each person careful to keep hold of their end. At Skyler's repetitious commands they moved, hand-over-hand, toward each other, until finally they were all about a meter apart, the warm object between them.

He was just about to give the order to move it when gunfire erupted from outside the sphere. Three shots in rapid succession. Light flared with each, casting the outer biome chamber in successive white flashes and deep black shadows, all beyond the trees, like distant lightning.

Everyone froze, exchanging worried glances.

"Maybe they found the drone," Skyler offered.

Prumble shook his head. "That was gunfire, Sky, and neither Sam nor Vaughn nor Vanessa has a gun."

Another shot rang out, closer than before.

"Suit up and get to the hatch!" Skyler roared, already off, his guideline dropped. The orb-shaped stove would be adrift but so be it. He flew toward the airlock, his aim only slightly off. He hit the clear biome wall about five meters from the target and grappled with it, managing to deflect himself more or less in the right direction. He hit the trampled soil in front of the exit shoulder first, grunting. His fingers scrambled for purchase and found it in the form of a clump of long grass.

The airlock door opened. Sam and Vaughn came in, backs to him, arms held out before them. Sam fired off a beam of plasma, though her target was blocked from Skyler's view. He pushed himself toward the rack of helmets they'd rigged beside the door, partly to finish suiting up and partly to let the others inside. Sam kept firing until Vaughn managed to get his bearings and iris the door shut.

"What the hell's going on? Is it the enemy?" Skyler asked, leaving his helmet tilted open for now.

Sam floated by the door, one hand on a rung beside it, the other rubbing at her shoulder.

It was Vaughn who spoke first. "I shit you not, there's people out there."

"What the hell does that mean?"

"Humans," he said. "In space suits. And the bastards are armed."

The words left Skyler reeling. "What . . . where did they come from?"

His thoughts turned instantly to the worries Vanessa had expressed days before. Hidden areas within the ship. Unexplored corners.

"What about Vanessa?" Tania asked.

Sam shook her head. "Didn't see her. We went up the way she did, couldn't find her, decided to come back and get more of you to form search parties. That's when we saw them. Or rather they saw us. We were ambushed."

"How many?" Prumble asked. Straight to business. Straight past the bombshell that other humans were aboard the ship.

"Two at least," Vaughn said.

"Vanessa's still out there," Skyler added, to no one in particular. "They might have her."

"That's why we came back in," Sam said. "I could have killed them easily with the firepower in this suit, and their weapons are no match for our armor." She was still rubbing her shoulder. "But if they have her . . . I didn't want to risk . . ."

"You did the right thing," Skyler said.

Prumble cleared his throat. "Of course, now we're trapped in here. Tactically a very bad place." Sam bristled, almost spat a reply, but stopped at Prumble's held-up palms. "I would have done the same thing. Just an observation."

"He does have a point," Skyler said. "Only one way in or out of this ball. I'd feel better if we weren't on the wrong side of a choke point."

"Skyler." It was Tania, hands clasped before her as if pleading. When she spoke, though, her voice was even. Steady as a rock. "We have to consider how they came to be here. From inside, or out, they evidently didn't get the memo from Eve that we're supposed to be minimizing radiation. For all our efforts, they might lead the enemy right to us."

There was too much happening at once. Skyler weighed all the angles, but found he could only think of one thing: Vanessa. Nothing else mattered until they knew more. "Let me try to talk to them," he said.

"Fuck that," Vaughn growled. "They fired first. If they have her—"

"They shot at human-shaped things in Builder armor." That calmed him, if only a little. "I won't actually leave the airlock, okay? Still, you two be ready to unleash hell if they're not in a talking mood. Agreed?"

Vaughn, angry and frustrated, only scowled. Sam spoke for the pair. "We'll be ready."

At the inner airlock door Skyler took his helmet off, attaching it to a hook. He braced himself for the cold, but nothing could prepare him for the frigid space as he stepped inside. His nose almost instantly went numb, but he couldn't help that. He wanted them to see he was human.

Skyler moved to the exterior door, centering himself

in its one small window, his breaths fogging the glass. His eyes began to itch, forcing him to blink rapidly. The space outside the airlock door consisted of a stairwell that went both up and down, curling around the interior wall of the greater biome room that housed the three giant spheres. "Hey!" he shouted. "Cease fire! Let's talk!" And then again in Spanish and Dutch just for the hell of it, feeling a bit of a fool for assuming they would understand him at all.

"I don't know who you are," he added, "or what you want, but we mean you no harm. If you can understand me, signal."

Silence.

"Soon, if you don't mind," he added, teeth chattering. "It's cold as hell. I can't wait for long."

Several seconds ticked by. Whether they could hear him or not he had no idea. Eve had not left the ship in total vacuum, filling it instead with a weak atmosphere that would help dampen any residual heat. But how thin he wasn't sure. He turned to Sam, ready to motion her and Vaughn out, when a light came on. Above him, toward biome two. Skyler held up a hand to shield his eyes from the beam, trying his best to keep the rest of his face visible so they could see he was a real person.

"Let's go inside and talk, huh?" Skyler said toward the light.

The light was joined by another, and seconds later two people in space suits he did not recognize were floating just outside the airlock. One of them made a wheeling motion with their hand: *Open the door.* He took as deep a breath as he could and complied, know-

ing they would not enter the airlock if he went inside
the biome first. That would be idiotic, the very defini-
tion of walking into a trap.

When the opening became wide enough, the male of
the pair came in. He went straight to Skyler and pressed
a gun against Skyler's temple.

"No sudden moves," a man said in perfect English,
through a speaker on his suit. An Aussie by the accent.
"Face the inside. Hands where I can see them."

Skyler complied.

"Tell your friends to back off and keep their hands
up, too," he added.

With a nod toward Sam, she reluctantly raised her
arms and backed up, making room. Prumble, Vaughn,
Tania, and Tim followed her example.

The outer door closed and then the inner opened.
Skyler drifted into the biome proper, grateful for the
warmth. He turned slowly in the air to keep himself
facing the newcomers. Prumble's hand at the center of
his back stopped him from floating across the entire
space.

"Who's in charge?" the man said.

"I am," Skyler said, with an authority he still did not
quite feel. "Skyler Luiken, and my crew. Now who the
hell are you?"

"Call me Xavi," the man said. He paused then. Skyler
could just make out his face behind the glare of his helmet light. He was looking slightly away, as if listening
to something on his internal speakers. "Skyler Luiken?
You really expect me to believe that?"

"I don't care much what you believe, but it's the truth."

The man raised his arm, the one that didn't hold a pistol, and tapped it to the side of his helmet. The headlamp temporarily brightened, like a camera's flash. It left Skyler's vision whited-out. Vaughn cursed, as did Prumble.

"That's really him?" Xavi was saying, in a low voice. "You're fucking sure, mate?"

Skyler glanced at Tania, found her staring at the newcomer. "What did you do with our friend?" she asked him.

"No idea what you're talking about."

"I don't believe you."

"Suit yourself."

Skyler inhaled, trying to draw patience from the air. "One of ours is out there. She went out to investigate what I presume are remote cameras you floated in here, and she has not reported in. We have to find her."

He shrugged. "Well, we didn't see her. You're really the immunes? Holy fuck, mates. Our engineer is a big fan. Knows all about you. All that history."

"History?"

"Yeah."

"What do you mean, history?" Prumble asked, in his booming actor's voice.

"You left almost two thousand years ago!"

Skyler had known this, deep inside. What he had failed to do was accept it. The person standing before him was a human being circa A.D. 4000 or so. The implications tied his stomach in knots. Were he in gravity he might have sunk to his knees.

So much time had passed!

Everyone he'd ever known, save those who'd come along, were gone. Skadz, his oldest friend, the first immune he'd met after the apocalypse, long in the ground. Ana, the woman he'd loved and lost when she decided to remain on Earth, to shun the Builders because of all the grief they'd caused. Not just to humanity, but to herself, too. He'd never get the chance to apologize, to truly explain why he'd not remained at her side.

And on top of all that, he was considered history. *History.*

Another thought came to him. Worse than all the rest.

Tim spoke, voicing the realization Skyler had come to. "Are we back at Earth?"

"Oh God," Tania whispered. "Eve lied to us. We—"

"Nah, hang on, mates. You've got it the wrong way around. We came to you."

"Impossible," Tim breathed.

"Not impossible," Xavi said with a hint of pride.

Skyler held up a hand. It was too much. He had Vanessa to worry about, not to mention the mission. *Fuck,* he thought. *This bastard has been transmitting with total abandon.* "Enough. There's no time. We need to get everyone into this room and seal it before the Captors become aware of our ship. Everyone, including our missing friend."

"I'm afraid it's too late for that," a voice said.

Skyler craned to see past Xavi.

Another space-suited Earthling had drifted inside.

A woman. "I'm Gloria Tsandi," she said. "Captain of the imploder-class OEA vessel *Wildflower.* Xavi, stand down. They are not our enemy."

"What do you mean, 'too late'?" Skyler asked, though he already knew. These people weren't other passengers of Eve's. They'd intercepted the sleeping ship. In other words, he realized with cold certainty, they'd ruined everything. Eve had shut down, they'd run dark, then this captain had come along and spoiled the ruse. He tried to keep a growing sense of panic in check. He needed facts. Information. And he needed it now.

"Our ship was damaged by the Swarm Blockade," Gloria replied. "We were about to self-destruct, then we saw you. Or, this thing you're traveling in. So we came aboard, on the impossible hope we might find something we could use to get home, or at least delay our pursuers."

She spoke with a slight, vaguely Kenyan accent. More than that, she spoke with a remarkable calm given the situation. Skyler found himself impressed, even a bit jealous, at her cool demeanor. Her actions, on the other hand . . . "You brought them right to us."

"Oy. What crap. How were we supposed to know?" Xavi asked.

The woman glanced at her crew member. "Go find their missing crewmate and return here. Keep me posted."

"No," Sam said, the word sharp as a knife. "I'll go. I mean, Vaughn and me."

Skyler looked to them, as did the other captain.

Sam's demeanor had changed. Her nonchalance, her cool "Vanessa will be okay" confidence, had gone, replaced with a steel gaze and set jaw Skyler knew well. "If she's not with them then something really is wrong. I'm going, one way or another." She jerked her chin toward Captain Tsandi. "You said it yourself, we're not the enemy. So step aside."

"All yours, mate," the man called Xavi said, backing off a step.

Sam didn't wait for Skyler's okay. She moved for the airlock, Vaughn right behind her.

"Wait," Skyler said. An order, and for once Sam listened without complaint. She stopped at the door, Vaughn beside her. "I need you here," Skyler added. "I need to know what you think about all this. Hear them out."

"Vanessa—"

"Can handle herself, like you said. One extra minute, then you go after her. Right?"

Sam, deflated, did not return to him, but didn't leave, either. Skyler counted that as a small victory.

Hands still upheld, Skyler gave the other captain a nod of gratitude for the trust she'd just shown. She'd been ready to let Sam go. He tried to channel some of her calm. "What happens now?"

"Now," Gloria said, "we need to figure out a way out of this. Our ship's heavily damaged. Return imploder gone. We're stuck here. Your ship . . . appears to have lost power entirely."

"Imploder?" Tim asked.

She glanced at him, one eyebrow raised. Her features

softened. "Forgive me. You left so long ago. There's no time so I will sum up: Recently we figured out how to fold space, via a device we call an imploder."

"Fold space . . . ," Tim repeated, as if the words were in some foreign language.

"Traverse vast distances instantaneously, yes. So equipped, naturally we wanted to visit the home of the infamous Builders."

"And," Skyler concluded, "you arrived only to find the place hostile. The Captors ran you off, and you found us on your way out."

To his surprise, Gloria shook her head. "You misunderstand me. Our ship is not the first to come here."

"What do you mean? How many before you?" Tania asked.

"There have been hundreds of attempts, most before the Restricted System Decree was enacted."

Skyler held up one hand, if only to gain a moment to digest all that he'd heard. To have come all this way, spent all this time traveling here with Eve to help her free her world, only to have been leapfrogged by descendants of those they had saved on Earth. It was an outcome he'd never imagined. More than anything, he wanted to know what Eve would think of this. She'd gone to Earth, found a species capable of helping her, ferried them all the way here, and now she'd learn that they'd made it anyway. "Amazing," was all he could say. There was no other word.

"Hundreds," Tania whispered. "Then . . . what happened to the others?"

"This system," Gloria said, "is a graveyard of failed

attempts to explore Carthage and the other worlds here."

"Carthage?" Prumble asked.

The woman nodded. "The Builders' home world. We named each planet in this system after a lost city of legend. Carthage, Troy, Skara Brae, and so on."

Prumble barked a laugh. "Finally some decent names! What about those who hold Carthage hostage?"

"We call them the Scipios, after the Roman general who sacked Carthage."

"I love it," he said, beaming, fingers twitching with excitement. "Much better than the crap name Skyler came up with. What about the Builders? The Creators?"

"We kept those," Xavi said.

"Oh. Well. Can't win them all, I guess."

"I am sorry we mistook you for enemies," Gloria went on, talking to Skyler now, "but dressed the way you were, I hope you can understand."

"Forget it. At least no one was injured," Skyler said.

"Not yet," Sam threw in. "We still don't know where Vanessa is."

Gloria spread her hands, placating. "As I said, we know nothing of your missing friend. In the meantime, we should work together. There must be a way to get one of our ships operational and flee the coming enemy."

"Flee?" Skyler asked. "That is the opposite of our goal. We're heading to . . . Carthage, as you've named it."

"I know the reasons you left Earth. Well, my engineer does, and has just filled me in on the specifics. So let me tell you, very plainly, that this is a fool's errand," Gloria said. "We've been trying for decades to get to the inner system, much less to Carthage itself. We've never made it past the Swarm Blockade. Besides, much has changed since you left. Earth is resurgent, and has learned to fold space, a capability the Scipios would kill for. Whatever problem the Builders hoped you would solve for them is long since irrelevant. The important thing right now is to make sure we avoid contact with the Swarm. If they capture any of us, or our ships, they could learn the location of Earth, and that would spell catastrophe on an unimaginable scale."

"You've no idea what you're talking about," Tania snapped, though Skyler could hear the doubt creeping into her voice. "If the Scipios are still here, still holding this system hostage, then our mission is still relevant."

"Wrong," Gloria replied, still calm as a pond. "Nothing is more important than restricting the Scipios to this tiny corner of the galaxy."

"Look, no offense," Skyler said, "but all that is your problem. We made our choice. We're going to see this through."

Gloria bristled. "Your vessel is completely without power. What do you hope to accomplish?"

How much to say? Skyler measured his reply. He needed to get a handle on this to have any hope of salvaging the situation. "Our ship is hibernating until we're past this swarm, as you called it. Don't get me wrong, lovely to meet you and all, we'd love to gather around the campfire-orb-thing and hear about what's happened back home, but the sooner you get back on your ship and leave, the less likely they are to care about a dead seed drifting through their space."

"It may be too late for that," Gloria said. "The Swarm chased us here. They'll arrive within the hour."

The biome fell silent.

"You'd better hope not," Skyler replied, not pleased to be setting himself at odds with this woman but unable to temper his words, either. These people, from Earth or not, bearing incredible technological advancements or not, were uninvited guests. And they'd arrived at the worst possible time. "Once we have our missing crew member back, you leave. It's as simple as that."

Gloria met his gaze. There was no anger in her eyes, nor even fear. What he saw there was more like confidence. "That is a death sentence for us," she said quietly. "We are incapable of outrunning the Swarm and, I do not mean to be adversarial about this, but we're the ones holding you at gunpoint."

Skyler grimaced. He considered going for her gun. Hard to surge forward in a lack of gravity, and this unflappably calm woman seemed alert and in control. He thought of how Sam and Vaughn would react. How this tough-looking fellow Xavi would, too. Blood would be spilled, no doubt about that. His thoughts turned to the mechanical switch installed in the cave. The one that would wake Eve in an emergency, which this surely was. A goddamn Earth spacecraft, of all things, attached to them like some barracuda, with Scipio scouts already chasing it. For all their efforts to conceal themselves, these people had brought the enemy right to their doorstep.

"What if you send your ship away remotely," Tania said.

Everyone looked at her.

She went on. "Make the Scipios think you stopped here, looking for . . . whatever, and that you gave up on that idea and left."

"Hmm," Gloria said. "That may work, but it doesn't exactly put us on a path to escape."

Skyler studied her. "You said yourself that you've been trying to get in-system for decades. Maybe this is your chance. Throw in with us, rather than the other way around."

"Hmm," she repeated, brow furrowed in concentration. "If you achieve your goals, what then? How do you plan to return home?"

"You're not actually considering abandoning ship, are you, boss?" Xavi asked.

"An hour ago we were thinking of ways to blow it up."

"Yeah, still . . . just leaving her out there, that doesn't seem right."

"So we rig a remote detonation. On a timer, if need be." Her gaze swung back to Skyler. "How do you plan on leaving the system once you've accomplished—"

Skyler scratched his head. "The plan is . . . er . . . evolving."

Abruptly she held up one hand, eyes suddenly downcast and distant. "Repeat that, Beth?" she asked. "Calm down, I can't—" Her expression turned dark, equal parts worry and anger. Then, "Who am I speaking with?"

A pause.

"If you hurt her I swear—"

A terrible pause.

"I want to know that my engineer is safe," Gloria said through gritted teeth into her comm.

And then she went quiet, listening. The air of confidence about her drained like water from a bath. After several seconds she rasped, "Just tell me what you want."

A prickling sensation crawled up Skyler's spine. "What's happened?"

Slowly, very slowly, Gloria met Skyler's eyes. "He wants to talk to you," she said.

"Who does? What are you talking about?"

Gloria slipped a small device from behind her ear and held it out to Skyler. "He says his name is Alex Warthen. He wants my ship, or he'll kill the woman named Vanessa."

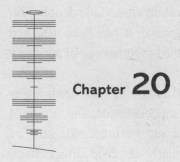

Chapter 20

ON THE WALL, surrounded by hardened foam, was an umbilical tube. Hastily added and wholly out of place, yet unmistakable. After all the stylized, fashionable corridors and the gray grime before that, the sight of that brilliant white disk flooded him with hope.

That feeling vanished when his eyes settled on the far end. It was an airlock door, of that he had no doubt, but it looked nothing like the one they'd attached when first boarding the Builders' ship. That one would look utterly antiquated next to this, though Alex couldn't quite put his finger on why. The airlock door he remembered was utilitarian, and messy, like everything in post-plague Darwin. A metal slab with a round porthole window and a lever beside a simple control panel. Signage warning of various calamities should one open it without proper conditions. But here, before him, was an elegant thing. Almost translucent, with three windows arranged rather stylishly. The control panel, if it was one, was just an off-white square with a faintly glowing edge. The lever was an ergonomic double-grip attached to a half-circle groove. It had been designed and built, rather than cobbled together out of necessity and available materials.

Still, it was an umbilical tube, and that meant a way out. He pulled the lever, slipped inside, and squirmed down the flexible corridor on the other side until he found himself inside a similarly designed airlock chamber, its outer door already open. The inner door had no security mechanism, and rotated open with a simple tug.

No alarm sounded. No one cried out in surprise. The interior of the connected ship or station was utterly silent, in fact.

Using hand gestures, Alex ordered Jared to move up and join him, hauling the unconscious immune behind him, then went in. He found what appeared to be a multilevel spacecraft, small but well equipped. Too well equipped, perhaps. Virtually everything inside looked like the sort of thing Neil Platz would have spent extravagantly on to outfit some useless corner of his headquarters above Darwin. Clean lines, gleaming metals. Some debris here and there, but on the whole it was an impressively engineered interior.

The craft—it seemed obviously a spaceship or modified climber—was arranged like a vertical stack. It smelled faintly of ozone and charred electronics, but it had power. The screens on the bridge were of a total foreign arrangement, but the text he could see was English. He floated back down, toward the other end of the ship, passing Jared and their unconscious prisoner along the way. He raised a finger to his lips as he passed.

The middle section had small cabins arranged in a circle, pointing outward, each barely larger than the beds they contained. On one wall he found an open cabinet with a pair of porcelain keys poking out, chains dangling from each. He looked inside and found two pistols. Another gift. He took one and floated the other back up to Jared, who caught it easily. The weapons seemed tailor-made to work in a thickly gloved hand and, like the entire ship, were at once familiar and yet utterly different. It was as if this whole place had been designed and built far away, or in a different era. Perhaps it was the Builders' attempt to re-create a human-designed ship. Or maybe the Builders weren't so alien after all.

The bottom level was some kind of monitoring station. A row of displays full of graphs and information. A woman sat there in a contoured seat, one hand on the armrest to keep her in place, huddled over a screen and talking quietly to herself. Her back was to him.

Alex cleared his throat, gun raised.

The woman came out of her chair so fast she floated all the way to the ceiling, her face a twisted mask of terror. He aimed at her and shook his head, compelling her to ditch whatever thoughts of escape or self-defense she might be considering. She wore no helmet or even an earpiece that he could see, but it seemed likely there were microphones in the compartment.

He pulled his helmet off then, and took in a lungful of the warm, heavily recycled air. It tasted like the air on Gateway Station. It tasted like home.

It was then her eyes had widened and a gasp escaped her lips. Not in fear, but recognition. "I can't believe it," she said. "You're Alex Warthen, aren't you?"

"Keep your voice down. Who are you, and where's the rest of your crew?"

"I'm Beth. The others are inside," she said, "talking with Skyler. I can't believe we actually found you, after all this time." The recognition on her face had gone, replaced with something else. Admiration? Could these people be allies? Odd that she showed almost no concern for the weapon pointed at her.

Jared floated down. Their other prisoner had woken. He pushed her over to join the one called Beth. Alex shifted his aim to the one he knew to be dangerous. The warrior in the alien armor.

"Name?" Alex asked her.

"Piss off," she replied, her voice full of venom.

"Your name," he repeated, and aimed his gun at the young Asian woman with the raised hands, "or her life."

Several seconds ticked by. "Vanessa," she finally said.

The name earned another glance of naked admiration from the one called Beth. Strange. Whose side was she on? Time to find out. "You," Alex said to her. "Do you know how to fly this ship?"

"No."

A simple statement of fact. He decided she was being truthful. Better yet, she'd just confirmed that it was indeed a ship. "Who does?"

The woman said nothing. He could see the war going on behind her eyes, that age-old debate between bravery and self-preservation. He renewed his aim. "You really don't want to test me."

Beth swallowed, hard. "Xavi is the navigator. And then there's the captain, of course."

"And the name of this captain?"

"Gloria Tsandi."

"And she's inside? With Skyler?"

A brief hesitation. Beth, deciding how much to say, or whether to lie. Wondering how much time she could buy, probably. "That's correct."

"Can you contact her? Good. Do it, and then get this boat ready for departure."

"But . . . you can't mean that," Beth said, almost a whisper.

"I most definitely mean *that*."

"But—"

"Enough talking. I'll speak with your captain now, and that's the last time I'll ask in a civilized way."

While she fiddled with the comm, Alex instructed his officer to remove Vanessa's helmet. Jared didn't hear him at first. He had that blank, pained stare again, and worked his jaw.

"Her helmet, Jared?"

"Huh?" He blinked, twice, a simple action that seemed to hurt quite a lot.

"Remove her helmet, please. Or convince her to do it."

"Oh. Right." He did and tossed it upward to float off toward the bridge.

"She wearing a comm? No? Okay. Find duct tape or something," Alex said to him, and Jared drifted away. "And find yourself some meds while you're at it."

Jared made no reply.

Finally, Beth handed him a small circular device plucked from behind her own ear. He held it against the same spot on his own head, impressed with the quality of it. This was no cobbled together bit of gear, but something new. Purpose-built and highly advanced. *After all this time,* she had said. What had she meant?

"Who am I speaking with?" a woman asked. "I want to know that my engineer is safe."

"You spoke with her, so you know she is. That will have to suffice." Alex paused, let the hierarchy of this arrangement settle. He was in charge, and he had to make this woman believe that completely. "I have your ship. If you cooperate I will return your engineer to you unharmed."

She took a moment to reply, and when she did the fire had drained from her voice. "Just tell me what you want."

"Right now I want to speak with Skyler Luiken. Put him on, or I shoot his friend. Vanessa is her name. Tell him."

Silence stretched. He heard her speak, but not to him. "He wants to talk to you," she said.

A quieter voice. Male, familiar. "Who does? What are you talking about?"

"He says his name is Alex Warthen. He wants my ship, or he'll kill the woman named Vanessa."

Rustling sounds. The microscopic earpiece being transferred. And then came the voice. "Warthen?"

"Well, isn't this a surprise."

"Alex, listen, I don't know what's going on here but there's no time. We're in terrible danger—"

"Good," he said. "You deserve to be. And it's not my problem."

"Look, I don't know how it is you are here, or why, but there must be a reason Eve kept you alive. Healed you, as she did all of us."

"This Eve, I presume you mean the Builder bitch that's been torturing me for days? Weeks? Well, guess what, Skyler, I'm not interested. You know me, so you tell Captain Tsandi that I'm not one to mess around. I'm taking this ship one way or another. If you want to see Vanessa alive again, you'll trade me someone who can fly this thing. Simple as that. The navigator is my preference, so send him. Then I'll be on my way, and you can go back to whatever it is you traitorous fools think you are doing."

"Alex, please—"

"Ten minutes. At the airlock. Vanessa for the one called Xavi. End of negotiations."

He pulled the metal disk, no bigger or heavier than a hole-punched scrap of paper, away from his neck and flicked it toward the other end of the ship. Alex turned to Jared. "Watch these two while I figure out how to undo that umbilical. In case Skyler and his friends try something."

Jared, busy binding Vanessa's hands behind her back with a zip tie, did not reply.

"Find any meds?" Alex asked him.

"Christ," Jared replied. "Stop fucking asking." He drifted off, toward the bridge.

Alex watched him go, a knot of worry tightening in his belly. He'd not seen such a random angry outburst from his sergeant before. "No worries. I'll watch the prisoners," Alex called after him. "Take a look at the umbilical, then get yourself some meds, man. I mean it."

After a minute Alex left Vanessa tied to the chair and took Beth with him to the center of the ship where he'd seen a kitchenlike area. In all the excitement he'd forgotten just how hungry he was, and surely some food and perhaps a coffee bulb would do Jared some good. Bound at wrists and ankles, Beth was no better than deadweight, but leaving her next to Vanessa would no doubt compel them to plot some kind of escape. Besides, he still wasn't quite sure what to make of her. So he pushed her ahead of him, taking care not to slam her into bulkheads or other gear. He just wanted to get home, and these people had a ship.

A *weird* ship, but as long as it served the purpose what difference did it make?

After all this time . . . Her words still echoed in his mind.

As they drifted through the narrow spaces, a sense of

discomfort began to build in Alex Warthen. He'd been too focused on the task at hand to think about it until now.

The lines of this vessel. They weren't just foreign, they were clean. Precise. Manufactured. Platz had that capability, at least at one point, but it had all gone to shit when the disease came. So when had this been made? It looked too *new* to be pre-Elevator.

"Beth?" he asked, stopping her and turning her to face him. "When was this spacecraft made? No, never mind that—what year is it now?"

"3911," she said, without hesitation.

Alex let go of her. His mind reeled. "Thirty . . . thirty-nine . . . how can that be?"

Beth tilted her head and squinted at him. "You really don't know, do you?"

The glare he fixed on her made the woman flinch. "Listen, and listen close. I've been through horrors here you can't imagine, and my patience is running damn thin."

She lifted her chin a little. "You said something about torture, to Skyler. What happened?"

"That's right. Eve's not the virtuous ally he seems to think she is. And I'm the one asking questions here. How is it that the year is 3911? Give me straight answers if you want to make it out of this."

Something flashed behind her eyes. A hint of admiration, or something like it.

"This is so odd," Beth said, almost a whisper. "Speaking with you. Me of the distant future from your perspective, and you of the distant past from mine."

"I don't . . . Answer the question, Beth."

She waved her hand, as if the question mattered not at all. Her words were clipped and dismissive. "Simple. You were in flight all that time, moving very fast. Time dilation—"

"I understand the concept," Alex snapped. "It doesn't explain how you're here. Or where the hell we even are, for that matter."

"The answer to that is complicated."

"Try me. Not going to ask again."

He learned much then, and once Beth got started she required no more threats or prodding. She spoke of how Skyler and his cohorts had made some sort of deal with the Builders, and gone off on their ship to help free a world now known as Carthage. The same ship Alex had been living inside, though no mention of that had been made in the aftermath. History had chalked him up as one of the many deaths to occur that day, along with Jared, Grillo, and everyone else on the losing side. And Skyler and his merry band? Remembered as heroes. Legends. Yes, they'd gone to help the Builders, the architects of Earth's apocalypse, but in exchange the subhuman plague had been switched off. And there'd been other gifts, too.

Despair and anger began to boil up inside him then. He knew, at some deep level, that he'd been on the wrong side of history, even as it was unfolding. He'd made deals with Russell Blackfield, and then later with Grillo. He'd done it because, though he knew they were rotten men at heart, they seemed likely to win. More than anything, Alex had just wanted normalcy. Peace. The chance to live a quiet life with his greatest worry being the occasional brawl at Ten Backward, the pub on Gateway Station. Being on the wrong side seemed a reasonable price for that.

In his heart he'd already accepted that he'd lost. Been killed, even. What had not occurred to him was that he could be anywhere but above Earth, still inside that godforsaken ship, still in that *time*. To learn instead they were many light-years away, and so distant in history as to be a minor footnote in the chapter called "The Heroics of Skyler Luiken and Friends."

She told him of the nearly two thousand years that had passed on Earth. How humanity had bounced back, and brilliantly so. Colonized the solar system. Words tumbled out of her as she went on for half a minute on how they folded. Techno-babble that Alex cared little about. What he cared about was what it all meant. How this ship could have caught up to Eve. They'd learned to travel to distant places almost instantly.

And there it was. Hope renewed. The prospect of escape, returned. Earth may not be the Earth he'd left, but it was still home. There was a way back.

Alex left the woman to drift. He held a bulkhead with one hand and closed his eyes, allowing his mind to process the simple truth that he was an element of history now. As distant in memory for those who now called Earth home as Genghis Khan was to him. What kind of life would he find for himself there, if he did make it back? He'd be some sort of curiosity. A celebrity, or a zoo exhibit. Worse, it was a history he evidently fell on the wrong side of. From the way this woman talked, it was Skyler and the others who'd come out on the right side. Alex searched himself and found, to his surprise, that he couldn't really argue with that.

Don't do this, he told himself. He needed a plan, a goal, or he was lost. And right now, he saw no other option that held any appeal.

His future was on Earth. This he knew as some sort of internal truth. Fate, or whatever. He would go back. He'd cash his celebrity-status check and parlay it into some power. People would listen to him. Perhaps he could earn some political clout and do something to guide the future of his home.

He looked at Beth. Really looked at her, for the first time. She didn't seem overly concerned at her predicament, but then her entire manner was almost emotionless. Matter-of-fact. He began to worry she might be lying. He was pretty good at reading people, but not this one. The only flash of emotion she'd shown was upon recognizing him. A history buff, evidently. A student of Skyler-lore, as if that held the same prestige as an Arthurian scholar. *Wonderful.*

To her this must be like meeting the Beatles, or the Apollo astronauts, centuries upon centuries after their contribution to history. Well, fine. If he was going to play that card, might as well start now.

"Look," he said, righting her until her eyes met his. "I was there. In the Key Ship, when everything happened.

I can tell you what really went on. Come with me, and I'll tell you everything that happened. Everything. I remember it all like it was just days ago. You can have the story, firsthand."

With each word her eyes widened. Just as he'd hoped.

Then she blinked. Her entire face changed, her posture. She looked suddenly puzzled, and her gaze no longer held his. "Your friend left," she whispered.

"What?"

Beth nodded toward the airlock.

Alex whirled, propelled himself to the closed door, and glanced through the porthole. He saw only the white umbilical tube, and the darkness at the far end. Of Jared Larsen there was no sign.

"The hell?"

Had the man misunderstood? Gone to search for medication inside the Builder monstrosity?

The knot in Alex's gut became a painful certainty. Something was very wrong with his friend. Alex had seen the behavior before, and feared it more than anything.

It was goddamn plague. The subhuman virus. Had Eve lied about pulling it out of him? Or had her test done its damage all the same? The side effects lingering despite the disease being gone?

He remained there, at the window, for some time. His hands gripped the handle of the airlock door but did not move. Nothing to be done about it, he told himself. If the man was infected, or merely broken by Eve's torture, that was that, and Alex could not help him.

Alex let go of the handle, and backed away, mouthing

a silent farewell. He could not leave this ship, not while he had hostages, not while it was his only ticket out of this place, and so could only hope that an enraged, diseased Jared, as he prowled the dark halls of the alien ship, would not run into the navigator, Xavi.

Chapter **21**

"I'LL GO, BOSS," the man named Xavi said. "I'll make the swap. I'll get the *'flower* back from this asshole."

"No," Gloria said.

The sharpness in her voice cut like a knife. Skyler flinched, for her gaze remained firmly on him, despite the looming presence of a very anxious Xavi at her shoulder. Skyler met her glare and held it, as if staring into her eyes might reveal something about her. And it did, after a fashion. What he saw there was nothing short of bottled fury.

"Tell me about this man Alex," she said.

Skyler considered that. He'd been pursued by War-then's security goons on Gateway Station once, managed to escape only to crash the *Melville* on the way down. He'd left his crew behind, some alive, some not. "I don't know him well. He's efficient. All business. Principled, when I knew him, but I can only imagine what he's been through aboard this ship." *Eve hid his presence from us,* he added silently. *Now why the hell would she do that? Why would she torture him?* "I'd take him at his word."

"Will he be reasonable? Negotiate?"

"Look, until that conversation I had no idea he was alive. If I'm honest, I'd forgotten all about him."

"He wasn't," Prumble said. "Alive, I mean. I snapped the bastard's neck myself, before he could strangle Vanessa."

"So Eve fixed him," Skyler said. "Or cloned him. Something. We can ask her why, why he's here at all, when she wakes up. For now, it doesn't matter. He's confused, pissed off, and he's got Vanessa."

"And the *Wildflower*. And Beth," Xavi added.

"Forgive me, Captain, if I agree with Xavi here. This cannot stand."

Gloria took a long, measured breath. "Then we're at an impasse. It's easy for you to accept his terms, but it's impossible for me. With Xavi he'd have total control of my ship, damaged though it may be."

"Something tells me you have another idea," Skyler said.

She nodded. "Take the ship back by force."

The words settled, and a silence descended over the artificial glade. Not absolute silence, though.

"What is that noise?" Tim asked.

At first Skyler heard nothing, but in seconds his ears adjusted to the sudden quiet of the room. Tim had it right. A humming sound. Distant, almost imperceptibly quiet.

"Air processors?" Gloria asked.

"Can't be," Skyler said. "The ship is totally shut

down. The only way to reactivate it is purely mechanical, and only myself and Tania know where the switch is." He turned, half-expecting to find Tania had left the area, but she still drifted next to him, her eyes narrowed in total concentration.

"Something of yours, then," Tania said to Gloria. "You docked with us. A resonant vibration coming through."

The sound grew. Gloria tilted her head, straining to hear. "It's coming from the nose of the ship, not the tail, so it can't be us."

"The Swarm," Xavi said. "Has to be."

"Hold on. We don't know that," Gloria said.

"We do," her navigator replied. "They weren't far behind when we got here. What else could it be? C'mon, time's run out, boss." Some silent conversation went on between them. An expression of urgency from Xavi. A glare of reproach from his captain.

"How about you let us through," Sam said. "Vaughn and I will take care of this swarm."

"You won't," Gloria said. "None of us will."

"Not with that attitude," Sam shot back, grinning ferociously. She moved forward and, to Skyler's surprise, Gloria drifted aside to let her and Vaughn by. As Sam floated toward the airlock and grabbed her helmet she glanced back at Skyler. "We'll check it out," she said. "If it's the Scipios, I assume it's safe to break the radio silence?"

"I think we're beyond radio silence already," Skyler said, with a glance toward the newcomers. "But for all we know they can listen in. Use it sparingly."

"Understood."

"Be careful, Sam."

She did a mock curtsey, impressive in zero-g, and left.

"Boss," Xavi was saying to Gloria. "If the Swarm is here we've got to go now. Get our ship back and run while they're feasting on this place." He glanced at Skyler. "No offense, mate."

For a moment Gloria simply stared into the empty space between her and Skyler. Coming to grips with something. Skyler recognized the look. He'd been there before. The razor's edge of fight or flight. Lives hanging in the balance.

"Why are you out here?" Skyler asked her, point-blank. "This is more than simple curiosity about Carthage."

She glanced up at him. "They want our imploder technology. And they want to find Earth."

"I'd think that would make you want to stay as far away as possible, then."

To his surprise, she nodded. "We would, except that we lost a ship here recently. We don't think they've found it yet, because if they had they'd have shot us out of the sky the moment we arrived."

"Uh, they kinda did, boss," Xavi said.

Gloria shook her head. "They could have annihilated us, Xavi. You know that."

Skyler ignored their exchange. "If you lost this technology here then we both have an interest in staying, in fighting these bastards. Don't run, Gloria. Keep your crew here and help us. You find this lost ship, we put an end to these Scipios once and for all."

"Mate," Xavi replied, "there's seven of you. The Scipios have millions of ships, and that's just the Swarm Blockade. The first line of defense."

Skyler kept his gaze on Gloria. For a second he thought he'd broken through, but in the end she only shook her head. "We can't let them get our ship. If they do, Earth becomes a target. I don't think we can survive another apocalypse."

Her tone, and the implication of her words, told him everything. Her goal was not to run, but to destroy her ship before the Scipios could get to it.

"Go then," he heard himself say. It was somehow easier with Sam gone. She would have clocked him and taken over, right then and there. Not one for the long view, her. "Retake your ship. Free Vanessa if you can. She's tough as nails, she'll find her way back."

Gloria and her crew were already on the move. At the airlock she took one last look at Skyler. "The scouts were very spread out. It will be some time before they are here in force."

"What are you saying?"

She lifted her chin slightly. "I'm telling you to run, Skyler Luiken. Run while you still can."

With that, she left.

Sam flung herself with abandon through the darkened spaces of the *Chameleon*.

Had anyone else been with her she would have had to stop at every corner to let them catch up, but not with Vaughn. The man was right beside her at each intersection, as if an extension of her own mind. Truly her other half.

In the long stretches of boredom on this voyage his constant presence had begun to annoy her. Always agreeing, always trying to say what he thought she'd say or what she wanted to hear. Defending her, that rankled the most. Sam had never needed that, or wanted it.

But the excursion to that planet, the mission to disguise the ship, had reminded her of the pluses. They shared a bond in combat. A connection. They thought the same, they both fucking *got it*. And now, to be here, on the move, with him beside her, had a way of pushing all the other bullshit aside. She welcomed it, this clarity, this focus. In a way she felt glad these humans-of-the-future had brought the war to them.

Vaughn pointed at his ear, and she nodded. The vibration was getting louder, and not entirely because they raced toward it. Even when they stopped to get their bearings the noise grew. Sam didn't trust the suit, not entirely, but the noise it conveyed no longer resembled a fan moving air.

It sounded like a drill.

Like a symphony of drills.

She took the lead. Eve had left a buffer of sorts between her outer hull and the inner. A space full of frozen water and other materials meant to deaden any stray heat or other emissions that might try to radiate out of the ship during its run of the blockade.

But there had been that small room at the nose that she and Vaughn had entered through upon camouflaging the ship. That little space, right at the nose. That's where the Scipios would breach the hull. Had to

She couldn't know for sure, but it made sense. It probably looked more easily penetrable to their probes.

So she raced there, propelled by plumes of vectored thrust her suit emitted from minuscule vents in the back, elbows, knees, and feet. An addition made after the awkward jumping on the world they'd visited. Moving this way, so awkward at first, had become second nature. She didn't have to think about it at all, she just wanted to go somewhere and the suit went. At any other time, this would have pissed her off, this invasion of her mental privacy, but now . . . damn, it kicked ass. The suit *knew* her.

The spaces before her began to taper, drawing in to a point.

She slowed, if only a little, feeling the familiar rush of adrenaline in her temples. Battle sense, Vaughn called it. As intrinsic to her and him as smell or sight or taste.

Or hearing.

The sound had vanished.

Whoever—whatever—had been drilling on the hull had just finished their work.

Sam stopped herself and moved to a natural barricade formed by a series of pipes that snaked like tentacles throughout these hidden places of the Builder ship. The portions Eve normally kept hidden from them, opened before she shut down in case a need arose to visit. Vaughn took up a position roughly opposite her, tucked in shadow, only a red glow from his helmet to mark his position.

From somewhere farther ahead came a mad scrambling sound, like a wet dog trying to get its footing on a tiled floor. The noise went away almost as quickly as it had started, plunging the ship once again into total silence.

Sam glanced at Vaughn. When their eyes met he gave a shrug. She held her hand up, willing him to stay put, and then leaned out to look down the hall.

Something shifted in the darkness. On instinct Sam lurched back to her hiding spot, trying to process what she'd seen. The view had been brief, the darkness near absolute, but in that glimpse a memory had been triggered. A feeling, like déjà vu. Slippery and just beyond reach, flooding her with a sense of terror she'd only experienced a few times before in her life.

She was about to glance again when the movement came to her. In the space between herself and Vaughn the air seemed to shimmer. A smoke filled the air. A sort of strange fractured mist. Shapes slithered within the haze. Little spiny branches, thin as hair yet solid as ice. Perhaps they were ice, as if the smoke was freezing. As she watched the spines grew, longer and thicker, becoming as wide as finger bones in places.

Sam shuddered, remembering now. *I've seen this before,* she thought. The fog in old downtown Darwin, and the crystalline forest she'd experienced within its murk. It had shredded one of her companions to nothing more than a few bloodied strips of yellow environment suit in seconds, simply by vibrating. It self-healed when she'd tried to smash it. Eventually she'd destroyed it with fire.

Fire.

She had to tell Vaughn. Screw the radio silence. The Scipios were here, so what difference would it make? Sam willed the communication channel, but nothing happened. She tried the manual approach, an interface Prumble had helped Eve add, but it did not react at all. Eve had locked them out, the bitch. She'd kept Alex Warthen alive for some reason, and now she proved that she had zero trust in her supposed saviors. Sam wanted to spit.

Vaughn knew, didn't he? The way she'd beaten it? What it had done when they'd tried brute force? She'd told all of them, but how much attention had *he* paid?

God, if he tried to hack his way through that to reach her he'd be mulched. She had to show him. Sam found she could access the suit's tools and weaponry, so at least Eve hadn't left them totally defenseless. The exotic armor had no flamethrower, but it did have a small torch to be used in the case of cutting through a sealed door or other barrier.

She selected it, and glanced up. Vaughn was almost invisible to her now, so thick the fog and forest of spiny branches had grown. *Please don't swing at it, Vaughn. Wait for my lead. Please. Please!*

Crystalline structures formed before her eyes, like ice in fast-motion footage. She fired up her torch and hoped he could see it.

Keeping herself on the wall, Sam held the flame at the nearest spike and watched it shrink back, like a living thing. The blue-white color glowed red for a second, then diminished to something yellow-brown. It stopped growing.

She moved her flame to the next, and the next. It would take too long, she quickly realized. Meanwhile the crystalline forest continued to flow right down the hallway, toward the biomes. Could the whole thing be severed? Did it work like that?

Vaughn first, before he took a swing at the stuff. Sam waved her arm more aggressively now, not bothering to hold the tip of the fire to each tendril but instead letting it kiss them as she raised and lowered her armored hand. But the little branches only glowed at the touch of the flame, then continued on their unrelenting march to fill the interior spaces of the ship.

A warm light emerged in the fog and dark. Vaughn had ignited his torch, too, and appeared to be mimicking her efforts. *You marvelous son of a bitch,* she thought. And here she'd been about to tell him to stop shadowing her every goddamn move.

Sam began to work her way toward him, burning the crystal fingers at their thickest points and then shattering the resulting dead portion with a swift, controlled tap from the edge of her flattened hand. With this approach whole branches would die off, losing the blue luster in their coloration and drifting free, despite being tens of meters in length in places. One separated chunk she touched accidentally and it disintegrated along its length, becoming a fine powder, like sand.

The flame that marked Vaughn's location faded and vanished, and Sam's heart raced. She'd find him wrapped in the bony, segmented shards, their tips puncturing every last bit of him. The vision of it filled her with an all-consuming dread, and she wanted to scream at the dozens of branches that still snaked around her, almost instantly replacing any she destroyed. Vertigo gripped her—the sudden feeling that these branches were not snaking horizontally along the hall, but were vines dangling from some distant, unseen ceiling. She groped reflexively for something to stop the fall her body said was coming, her hand smacking against several of the long, thin crystals. And she knew she'd doomed herself.

The vibration she'd put into their segmented lines seemed to echo, not only reverberating but amplifying. The branches began to twitch, then sway, then swing like living things seeking to eviscerate whatever had disturbed them. She saw them as the long, hardened tentacles of some deep ocean jellyfish, slicing randomly through the dark depths to poison a threat only sensed.

Something sharp bit into her leg. Sam pulled away, looking down at the same time to see one branch had grown in a spiral around her calf and then somehow plunged through the Builder armor. She thrust her torch at it without thinking and cried out in pain at the sudden heat that met her skin. But the spine of the alien growth melted and broke away, part of it probably still under her suit and skin. The flame, painful as it was, had hopefully cauterized the puncture. She lifted her leg to look closer and watched in mild fascination as her suit filled in the small hole and visibly hardened back into its original form. Like it had never happened, except for the white-hot agony just below, the tip of the crystalline spike inside her flesh.

Could it grow on its own? The idea made her nauseous. A voice in the back of her mind screamed the more obvious concern: The Scipios were masters of tailored viruses. Did her immunity to the subhuman plague imply immunity to whatever else they made? A naïve concept, and a dangerous one.

Four new lights erupted in front of her, just meters away but almost totally obscured in the waving lines of the tendrils. The lights flared and stretched, yellow-white in color and almost a meter long each. In a second she understood. Thrusters. Far better than the damn torch! She pulled her own arms and legs in front of her and willed the suit to reverse. Instantly the small engines roared to life and sent her flying back the way she'd come. Too fast. She hit the wall hard, bounced off. Her legs and arms were still out before her, spraying gouts of superheated exhaust that kept her pressed against the wall and the spines before her crumbling into glassy sand.

As coherent thought returned Sam tried aiming more strategically, cutting a little sphere of empty air around her, as she'd done with the road flare back in Darwin, years ago.

Across the hall she could make out the vague form of Vaughn doing the same thing as she. It was working. Then his pattern changed, and it took a moment for her to realize he was coming closer. His legs were back, thrusting him forward, compensating for the fact that his hands were waving about wildly in front of him, battling back the spiky branches. Whether he intended it or not, by the time Sam could see Vaughn's determined face behind his visor, he'd cut the forest of tendrils in half, leaving the hallway in the direction they'd come an odd mixture of fog and glassy powder. On the other side all she could see were the charred tips of the severed branches, still waving as if angered.

He came to her, cutting the few remaining chunks away, then taking his place next to her. Despite everything he managed a grin and she returned it, wishing nothing more than to kiss him right then, right there.

They positioned themselves side by side, ready for another onslaught. None came. Instead, the remaining crystalline branches turned to dust, exploding in a shower of tiny shards that whirled into dazzling small vortices.

She looked at Vaughn, who only shrugged. The hall, while thick with the powder left behind, had otherwise returned to its original state.

The thought had just formed in her mind—*we won*—when everything changed again.

That fine glassy powder suddenly, forcefully withdrew as if sucked out into space through a gaping rend in Eve's hull. Which, Sam realized with a cold terror, may be exactly what had happened. Only, she felt no such pull on herself. She and Vaughn remained in place, unperturbed.

Which meant the powder had moved on its own, like billions of little self-propelled entities. The ramifications of that were only beginning to settle when a dozen light beams winked on and flooded the hall.

The cones of light seemed to span every color in the rainbow, assembling into dazzling white when their sweeping forms met in the center. And it wasn't just cones. Sam saw the flawless straight lines of lasers, too. Red, green, and even yellow beams began to pan along the surfaces of the irregular hall, searching.

All of this light emanated from points roughly marking a circular shape, about twenty-five meters away and still obscured in the haze.

One laser, green, swept across Sam's eyes. She barely had time to blink at the terrible brightness when her visor adjusted to compensate, becoming so dark she could see nothing except a green flare in the center of her vision. It held on her for several seconds before she felt Vaughn's hands grab her by the shoulders and push her aside.

The afterglow from the laser danced in front of her eyes no matter where she looked. Sam tucked in behind some piping and waited for her vision to clear. Finally, she leaned out. Whatever the thing was, it was creeping closer. The core portion seemed to be a spherical bulb, studded with socketed lights and little articulated limbs tipped with the scanning lasers. Perhaps other weapons, too.

A Scipio scout. A member of what Captain Tsandi had called the Swarm Blockade. Had to be. And that growth that had pushed into the ship only to disintegrate into powder, had been somehow related to SUBS. An engineered virus, grown and spread here, and that spherical pod was the factory that had made it.

And it had touched her. Tasted her.

The question was, had it retrieved the sample, or had she destroyed the limb quickly enough? Was the collector, if that was indeed the purpose of the crystal structure, still inside her leg? Her bloodstream?

She was immune to the subhuman virus. She didn't know what that meant, nor did Eve, except that it was not only important but of great interest to the Builder machine. Sam had to kill this creature before it could figure her out.

Battle instinct, so long her driving force, took hold once again. Sam pushed out into the hall, ignoring the beams that quickly found and converged on her. She willed her suit to action and felt the beam weapons on her arms come to life. She held both hands out before her, fingers curled into fists, and let loose twin rails of sizzling blue-white hell. The columns made the air dance with electric force. Where they struck home a shower of smoke and sparks erupted from the Scipio. Be it a living creature or just a ship, Sam had no idea, but it reacted as if alive. The thing thrashed wildly, bouncing into one wall and then rocketing across to the next, like a balloon venting its air. The enemy sought respite from the dual columns of superheated air, but Sam's aim was true, her focus absolute, and she kept the lines more or less on the center of the strange ball-shaped opponent.

Blue flames began to gout from the impact sites, and the Scipio began to wiggle and vibrate with astonishing speed. The death throes, Sam thought, but this idea quickly fled. Somehow this vibration seemed to reduce the effect of the beams. And its own dozen lights and lasers began to coordinate again, swinging back to find Sam.

Her visor dimmed once more, making it all but impossible to see. She felt warm, a sensation that grew to dangerously hot within seconds.

She'd be cooked alive in the damn Builder armor. Sam turned to flee, looking frantically for Vaughn, and saw the mortar launch from his back. The explosion shook everything.

The shock wave hit her and sent her spinning back down the hallway. The brief impact of the blast had ended the growing heat of the Scipio's beam weapons. Sam struggled to stabilize herself, the thrusters on her suit firing erratically.

Something grabbed her arm. Sam swung, her punch deflected easily. It was Vaughn, drifting beside her. His grip nullified her spin and she found herself staring at his red-lit face as clumps of debris and glassy powder careened through the air around them, rattling against her visor. Her heart swelled and she placed one hand against his face mask. *Thank you,* she mouthed, understanding now that he'd fired a mortar at almost point-blank range to destroy the enemy scout. Distantly she knew there would be more, though.

"No problem," Vaughn's voice said in her helmet.

Sam glanced up at him, confused. "Comms are back on?" she asked.

He focused, reading her lips, then nodded. "Found a buried option for very short range." He explained to her how to find it. "Are you hurt?"

"Singed a bit. You?"

"A little dazed. I'm worried more about the ship. I couldn't figure out a way to stop that thing without the cannon. It's going to get fucking messy in here if that's our only option."

Sam grinned at him. She'd have done the same thing. "There'll be more of them. We need to get to the others. Barricade the hallways that lead to the biome. My beams were hurting it. If we focus fire . . ."

He nodded, but a shadow fell across his features. The shade of a deeper concern only now understood, and Sam realized she felt it, too. The mission had failed. The ruse had not worked, no doubt due to the arrival of the ship from Earth.

Fine, she thought. Scuttle this bullshit sneaky approach and come at the bastards head-on. They could be beaten; she knew that now. With a jerk of her chin, Sam urged Vaughn into motion, back to the biomes.

Behind her, in the haze and the darkness, the watchers crept forward. They studied the newcomer with total awe. They watched, and they analyzed the material fed back into them from the trillions of virus scouts flooded into the frigid atmosphere of the disguised ship. From the sampling they had learned precisely nothing. And that, in and of itself, was the most important thing they had ever learned.

Chapter 22

The *Chameleon*
6.AUG.3911 (Earth Actual)

GLORIA POSITIONED HERSELF just out of sight of the *Wildflower*'s umbilical, with Xavi right behind her. She'd turned off her lamp the moment she'd left the others back at the forest sphere, using a rudimentary night vision mode in their helmets to navigate the strange, oddly luxurious maze of the slumbering Builder ship. Xavi had followed her example, keeping a hand on her back to reassure her of his presence.

"No one in the tube or at the airlock," she said on the private channel. "Any ideas on how to go about this?"

"That bit's easy," Xavi said. "We make the trade, then I start cracking skulls."

A distant vibration rolled through the ship, like a softly struck bass drum. It was the first thing she'd heard other than her own breathing since moving toward the tail end of the ship, away from the humming noise that had put Skyler and his crew on alert. Gloria froze as the rumbling ebbed, then died. "What was that?"

"Explosion," Xavi said. "I'd bet on it."

The bone-induction speaker behind Gloria's ear chimed, alerting her to conversation on the normal channel. She held up a finger to her companion, then switched. The suit automatically replayed the last communication. "You'd better make this fast, Captain. Your engineer tells me the Swarm has arrived."

"If that's true," Gloria replied, "we've already lost. You're sentencing us to death by leaving us here, so the exchange is pointless."

"I still need your navigator," Alex Warthen replied.

"Then take all of us. Keep Beth, and bring me as well. The ship can support ten, plenty of room."

Xavi elbowed her. She glanced at him and he proceeded to wave his middle fingers at the umbilical. Gloria put her gloved hand on his suited arm and eased him back, glaring at him. *I've got this,* she mouthed.

He pointed urgently at his wrist, an ancient gesture from when people kept time on wrist-worn displays. His point was valid. If the scouts were here, time was now their worst enemy. More would arrive every minute, cutting their way into both craft until any threats were identified and neutralized. If what Commander Blake had told her was true, hell would follow. Experiments and dissections on both craft and crew.

"We'll take Xavi for Beth. That's the deal. No more games. You have one minute," the man named Alex replied, then he disconnected.

Gloria switched back to the private channel.

Xavi spoke before she could. "We'll. He said we'll, not I'll. More than one in there?"

"Listen," she said. "I'm going to transfer command to you."

His eyebrows rose. "What?"

"Whether they take only you or all of us, they're only going to let you near the bridge. If the scouts are really here, you've got to override the reactors and slag the ship."

"Fuck that—"

"Think about it," she urged, ignoring his defiant glare. "It'd be my decision normally but you have to shoulder the burden. We cannot let any fold technology get into Scipio hands."

"We jettisoned the damn thing, remember?"

"There is data. Mountains of it. And there's Beth."

It took a second for the implications of that last comment to settle. "Now hold on—"

"The only valid response here is 'Yes, boss,'" she said, grabbing his shoulders. "Do you understand what I'm asking of you? It's over, Xavi. We both know what has to be done now, while there's still a chance."

Xavi's lower lip twitched. His gaze bored into hers. Then, finally, he sucked in a breath and nodded. "Yeah. I understand."

Gloria didn't hesitate, lest she second-guess herself. She flipped through the suit's menus until she found the function she was looking for. Transfer of Command. An action she'd never had to take in all her time as captain of a fold ship. In fact, she'd only practiced the procedure once, six or seven years ago, and held now only a vague recollection of the series of questions and security safeguards built into the action.

Words hung in space before her, written in amber letters. ACTION NOT POSSIBLE WITHOUT PHYSICAL PRESENCE ABOARD SHIP. CONFIRMATION FROM LEE, BETH, REQUIRED TO CONTINUE.

"Shit," Gloria whispered.

"What's wrong?"

"To do this either I have to be on board, or Beth needs to get access to a screen."

From the look on his face, she knew he understood what it meant. If Alex Warthen declined to take everyone aboard, Xavi would have to free Beth or hope Gloria could physically get inside the ship. Both meant violence, more than likely, but nothing compared with facing the Scipios. "We'll figure something out," he said, yet the grim tone in his voice shook her confidence to its very foundation.

In the cocoon of the biome the explosion barely registered. Skyler thought he'd imagined it at first. A phantom noise, triggered by frayed nerves.

But the others had felt it, too.

"Samantha . . . ," Prumble whispered.

"She can handle herself," he all but snapped in reply. Skyler closed his eyes and hissed out a breath, trying desperately not to let the situation get away from him. Once, while searching a facility in Japan for a datacube, he'd declared the mission a failure and ordered everyone out, only to find the object they'd come for at the last instant. An event, he recognized with sour amusement, that arguably put everyone on the path that led to this moment. And here he was, on the cusp of calling for a full retreat again. The plan had failed, as usual in a way no one could have predicted. Even Eve, with all her copious analytic ability, doubtless never considered Earth would beat them here. That the human race, on the brink of extinction, would recover so rapidly as to beat her to Carthage and fuck the whole thing up.

"Skyler," Tania said, endlessly patient. She'd been with him, in Hawaii. Another mission that went pear shaped, only that time he'd resolved to see it through. The result had been success, but at great cost. The death of a good friend. Why could he never just win? Why did he always feel trapped between success or keeping those he loved safe?

For whatever reason the role of leader seemed to naturally fall to him, but as Skyler looked around the biome now, and thought of those present and those in danger elsewhere on the ship, he knew he could not live with any more deaths on his conscience.

"We have to wake Eve," he said. It was the only option.

"I agree," Tania replied, with a surprising amount of conviction.

Prumble nodded. "Situation FUBAR," he muttered. "Not that I have a vote in this, but yeah, we need her."

Exactly the affirmation Skyler needed. He turned and propelled himself toward the cave.

"I'm coming in!" Xavi shouted, despite the airless chamber. He'd switched to the public channel, no doubt for her benefit.

Gloria held her position just outside the umbilical, ready to rush in if something went wrong. She hoped it wouldn't come to that. She hoped more than anything Xavi would distract them, and she'd slip into the airlock and transfer control. And then he would fly them out, and scuttle the ship, and that would be the end. A flash of light. No pain. No dissection at the hands of the fearsome Swarm. Just an instant of light, and a duty done. Not a bad way to go, all things considered.

As instructed, Xavi sealed the airlock behind him and, presumably, began the short drift out to the middle of the tube. Once there he would stop and await instruction.

Gloria fought to control her breathing. Every time she let her mind stray she saw only the vastness of space all around them, studded with the brilliant flares of scout drones decelerating to intercept their prize. Well, let them come. If she could do nothing else she could at least give them a fiery death.

"I've reached the center," Xavi said on his radio. "What now?"

"We see you," the man named Alex replied, again with the plural. "Turn away and push yourself backward slowly to this end. Keep your hands raised."

No reply came. Xavi must have complied, but Gloria dared not look. She had been instructed to stay far away from the exchange. That impression must be maintained until the moment came to act.

A thought tugged at Gloria's mind. Something she'd missed. It hovered like a gnat, just out of reach. Something about their initial flight from the Scipio hauler.

They were tumbling out of control, and she'd vented some waste fluids to right the ship. *So what? Why,* she yelled at herself, *are you reliving that now?*

If she could vent waste, she could vent *air.* "Of course," she whispered, and began to rummage through the control options available to her while off-ship. It took precious seconds, her being unused to having responsibility for the medical subsystems. Her usual medic had been left behind, along with the rest of her crew, to shed the weight necessary for this godforsaken mission. Gloria vaguely remembered her training on air quality, and the systems involved. "C'mon, c'mon."

There it was.

Working fast, Gloria switched her channel to a private one with Xavi. She spoke softly so as to not startle him, and knew he would not be able to reply. For all she knew he'd already removed his suit, but she had to try. "Xavi, if you can hear me, keep your helmet on as long as possible. I'm going to depressurize the *Wildflower* for thirty seconds. If they're breathing the air, they'll be in for quite a shock, and you can use that to get the upper hand."

Despite knowing he'd have no chance to respond, she waited. But only silence came. Gloria switched back to the main channel.

"—see that she is fine. Now, come through the inner door. Once you're inside, Vanessa will go back out the way you came in."

"There's no time for this, friend," Xavi said back to Alex Warthen. "The Swarm is already here."

"Enough of that." A series of muffled sounds followed, as the *Wildflower*'s inner door was evidently opened.

"Helmet off," Alex said.

"I like it on," Xavi replied.

"No bullshit. Take it off, now."

"What's the difference?"

"The difference is I can't slap that attitude off your face if your face is covered. Take it off or my friend will shoot your engineer. No more games."

More rustling, and she lost her direct line to Xavi. He despised wearing a tab-comm on his neck, the Luddite.

Gloria swore, hoping he'd heard her instructions. At least he would know to hold his breath when the moment came, and not be surprised. She started to count to thirty.

The biome chamber came into view. Samantha powered forward, comfortable now with the suit's intent-driven interface.

"Not too fast," Vaughn said, his voice becoming garbled. "Can't get more than a meter or so of range with the comm in this mode."

"Keep up, then," she said, and meant it though she tried to make it sound like a competitive jab. She pushed inside the vast room and spiraled around the topmost of the three gigantic translucent spheres. Her lamps swept across the curved edge. This ball had been set up to mimic the atmosphere and general topography on the Builders' home world, a place to train and prepare when the time came. But then had come the plan to convert the ship into its chameleonic state, requiring a drastic rescaling. Three biomes could no longer be afforded, so Eve had converted this one to the storage of various materials, much of it toxic. It had since resembled a nearly opaque marble, so cloudy was the interior with gases and fluids. But now, after being powered down for so long, the air inside had frozen and formed into clumps of blue-white ice. The explosion must have spurred them to their current movement, giving the space an odd resemblance to a child's toy snow globe.

"The hell is all that?" Vaughn asked.

Her lamp caught hints of the ground at the base of the third biome, until now hidden in cloud. Her breath caught in her throat. There was a biome in there, after all. Air, and ground, until now obscured by the clouds.

It was only a small patch of land, perhaps fifty meters across. But the landscape was wholly different from their quaint little forest campsite.

For reasons Sam could not fathom, Eve had built some sort of structure inside, vaguely tower shaped. The proportions were wrong, though, with a thin base that grew thicker toward the top, where chunks of squared material had been attached seemingly at random. The whole thing looked like it would topple at the slightest breeze. It was the base that drew her eye, though. Surrounding the tower were four smaller structures. Despite their wholly alien design aesthetic, their purpose seemed unmistakable: pillboxes. Gunnery nests. Defensive positions.

"I thought it was storage for toxic stuff," Vaughn said.

"That's what she told us."

A shadow caught her eye. Between two of the pill-boxes, a cave waited, so dark her lamp seemed incapable of illuminating the interior at all. Yet there was light in that utter blackness. Something glowed, steady and pale blue. Something that had not been turned off with the rest of the ship.

"If not storage, what's it for, then?" He bumped into her as he tried to settle into a position beside her.

"How should I know," Sam replied, with more bite than she'd intended. She jerked away reflexively, wanting more space, wanting to focus on their predicament and dishonest host, rather than cozy up. Vaughn held up his hands in a gesture that said "Excuse the fuck out of me," and pushed himself back slightly. Sam sighed. Everything had to be complicated. The mission. The odd mix of people brought along. The timing of her first real relationship. *Christ,* she thought. She wanted to tell him to cool it until all this was over, but the opportunity never seemed to be there. Or some other part of her brain, the bit that craved his company, won out.

As usual, she said nothing. Not the time, not the place. She forced herself to focus on the cave inside this biome, just a dark patch obscured by the swirling frozen atmosphere. The blue glow had gone. Maybe she'd just imagined it. "Did you see that? The blue light?"

"No," he replied, craning his neck, wiping one hand across the glassy shell. "Where?"

"In that little cave."

He squinted. "Maybe you imagined it."

"Yeah, maybe," Sam said, her annoyance growing.

"Whatever. I've got a lot of questions for Eve when she wakes up, that's all I'll say."

"Above!" Vaughn shouted.

He shouldered her, causing the two of them to rocket apart. She lost control, spinning like a rag doll. Sam fired her thrusters to right herself, then turned to see the source of his sudden panic. Vaughn was all the way across the room, aiming one arm up toward the mesh ceiling.

The three biome spheres were stacked inside a giant cylindrical room full of all the infrastructure needed to support their existence, plus retrofitted stairwells for Eve's human guests to use. Despite the state of null gravity, Sam had followed the path of the spiral stairs, which started above at a huge meshwork platform that served only as a gantry for access to various side tunnels that went off into the upper portions of the ship.

The floor had been silent, utterly dark, when they'd passed it and descended. Now the entire gantry crawled with movement.

A dozen of them or more, creeping in from the hallways that led out to points beyond. Scipio scouts. They all looked roughly the same: that mostly spherical core, studded with tentacle-like legs of varying length and width from various joints on the central body. The legs were tipped with shiny spikes that had circular indentations. Thrust nozzles, she saw, as one pulsed gas and launched into the room. Their movement was a mix of thrust and "walking" by puncturing the surfaces around them with their spiked tentacles.

Vaughn's headlamp lit them, alerted them. All at

once they erupted with light of their own, beams of every color that pushed through the grid of the floor and down and then swung toward her and Vaughn, focusing.

"Here we go," Sam said, and unleashed hell.

Twin blasts from her beam cannons traced glowing lines along the underside of the grid-patterned mesh floor above. The scouts wriggled, dancing aside to avoid the glaring heat as the energy turned metal to globs of molten slag. The beams converged on one of the larger enemies, which seemed to pinch inward under the assault and then pop like a balloon. Tech and guts, blood and oil, erupted.

The little bastards were pissed now. Tentacles reached in through the gaps she'd carved. One of them heaved itself through and down toward her. It rocked sideways, a fireball roiling off its side. Tentacles and gore flew. Vaughn's mortar round had slammed into it at a glancing angle, the explosion and ejecta flying backward. Another Scipio squirmed under the debris and fire, coiling its own serpentine arms around its body for protection. Vaughn's next mortar tore it to pieces.

Sam focused her beams on another, accidentally carving away a pipe along the inner wall of the great biome chamber before searing a glowing line across the central eye of the alien craft. This one had the presence of mind to return fire. It shot its tentacles outward, wide, each curling in at the end to point toward her and Vaughn, like some perverted, weaponized starfish. Sam threw herself sideways, expecting a furious retaliation. But it wasn't projectiles, or even beams, the creature threw back at her. It was the fog. The white-blue smoke that hardened into razor-sharp crystal forests. The thick cloud shot outward with fantastic speed, filling the space between her and Vaughn.

Sam, flying toward it, fired a burst from her thrusters to push back and away, wanting distance and time. She lost sight of Vaughn through the thick and growing cloud, which had already begun to solidify into the fine tendrils of glassy needles.

"To me, to me!" Sam shouted. "Protect the biome!" Skyler and the others would be suiting up, having seen the lights and heard the battle. She had to buy them time, or they'd be prisoners in there.

Vaughn made no reply. She glanced toward him and watched in horror as several Scipio scouts came sailing through the forest of shards, which parted like smoke to let them pass. The creatures went to where Vaughn had been, only he was gone. Where she'd last seen him there was a ragged hole in the wall, and the Scipios squirmed into it, disappearing into the darkness beyond.

"Vaughn!" she shouted.

No use. He was gone. Forced to flee. He better have been, Sam thought bitterly, because the alternative was that he'd abandoned her and that was a possibility she found she did not want to entertain just then. Besides, she had her own problems. The rest of the Scipios were coming for her.

The woman named Vanessa floated out of the umbilical, a dazed expression on her Latin features, though anger simmered behind her brown eyes. Her hands had been bound behind her back.

Gloria held a finger to her visor when their eyes met, compelling silence, and motioned for the woman to come to her at a section of wall about three meters from where the tube had been attached to the alien ship. She had no way to communicate with her, but Vanessa seemed to get the idea that she should tuck into the space beside Gloria and wait.

Satisfied, the captain pushed herself along the corridor until she reached the edge of the umbilical, and glanced in. The tube was empty. A straight shot all the way to the *Wildflower*'s outer airlock door. All she had to do was get inside. Within the hull her overrides would work. Thirty seconds of air removal ought to cover her arrival, she figured, before flooding air back into the ship. Thirty seconds to decide if she could help Xavi deal with their enemies, or start the self-destruct.

If she could get a good push, Gloria estimated it would take ten seconds to cross the space. If Alex or one of his accomplices glanced out the window during that time, the whole plan would collapse. And even if she made it, she'd basically slam into the door at the other end, which they would definitely hear within. Perhaps if she trailed her hands along the umbilical at the last second, she could slow down enough—

Stop debating and get in there! a voice in her head commanded.

In her time spent admiring, repairing, and ultimately commanding fold-ships, Gloria had learned to trust that voice. She pushed off hard, straight down the narrow white tube. She left her fear and doubt behind. Not just of what lay ahead, but also the infinite void beyond the thin umbilical walls, and the Scipios swarming in from all around them. She had to focus on what she could control. The part she had to play.

At the halfway mark she gave the wall to her left a light touch, correcting a slight mistake in her aim. Then she streamlined herself, hands outstretched before her, ready to grab the recessed orange handle on the door before her.

The tunnel lurched sideways, twisted hard, as if she were inside a snake. Gloria bit her lip as the side of the tube slammed into her and sent her bodily across the narrow passage. At that instant the umbilical swung back in the opposite direction and met Gloria hard, driving the air from her lungs and filling her vision with stars.

Body tumbling out of control, dizzy with the pain from a dozen bruises, she shot one hand out blindly and groped for something, anything to cling to. Something brushed her gloved palm and she clasped, squeezing for dear life.

Fingers wrapped around hers, strong and sure. Gloria forced her eyes open and blinked for focus. It was the woman Vanessa. Free of her bindings, alert as a cat. She gripped Gloria's head with both hands and pressed their visors together.

"Something hit the ship," Vanessa shouted, barely visible as the touching helmets vibrated against each other. "What will you do now?"

"Venting the air," Gloria replied. How much else to say? "Going to get my ship back."

The tube continued to undulate, but not as violently. They bounced and ricocheted, Vanessa pulling her back to where they'd started.

"Let me go," Gloria said. "I have to get to the *Wildflower.* I have to help Xavi."

But that wasn't right. Gloria had lost her bearings, been turned around. She craned her neck now and saw past Vanessa's black-armored shoulder. It was the *Wildflower*'s airlock they neared, not the dark hallway of the Builder ship. Gloria fought to regain her breathing. "What are you doing?"

"Helping," Vanessa said.

"Sure?"

"I'm sure."

"Open it, then, and be ready to open the inner door on my mark."

Gloria waved her arm at the handle and let Vanessa grapple with it. There was a hiss of fogged air as the two sections equalized.

Gloria Tsandi flung herself into the airlock and began to tap in the commands to vent the air. A safety timer began to tick away, no option to override. She met Vanessa's gaze and waited, expectant. The woman had made a fist with one hand and Gloria could see some kind of protrusion on her forearm that hadn't been there before. A weapon, like the beam cannon Skyler's friends had fired at her and Xavi. Gloria swallowed back fear at the sight of it. She was about to lead an assault on her own ship, for the sole reason to scuttle the whole mess. Her life would likely end very soon. The lives of her crew, too. Half of her, the compassionate half, wanted to scream at Vanessa to get away, far away. But the half of her that allowed her to be a hard-assed captain won out. She needed this woman's help.

"Xavi," she said on the private channel, "I know you can't hear me, but hold your breath. I'm sorry if it ends like this. I'm so sorry."

Silence, cold as the vacuum of space, stretched.

Tears flooded Gloria's eyes, and she let them flow. She couldn't wipe them away if she wanted to.

She tapped the button marked DEPRESSURIZE.

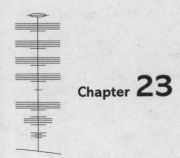

Chapter 23

The *Chameleon*
6.AUG.3911 (Earth Actual)

THEY WERE RELENTLESS, and legion. More and more arrived with each passing second.

Sam knew she couldn't win. For each that she popped or cleaved in two, three more flooded in behind it. Worse, her beam weapons were wreaking havoc on the inner walls of the giant chamber. If she wasn't careful she'd cut through Eve's hull and cause all the air to rush right out. Not that the Scipios weren't slicing through the hull right now, from every goddamn angle apparently, but she assumed because she felt no rush of air leaving the ship that the little fucks were being careful about it. She had no such luxury, not with Eve enjoying her power nap.

And then there was Vaughn. The great shimmering forest of razor-spines cut him off from her. She could try to carve her way through, but not with all these enemies coming at her.

"Vaughn, talk to me," she said for the fourth time. He did not reply, nor had he since they'd been separated.

She'd seen several of the Scipios peel off to deal with him, though, so she had to assume he was still in the fight, somewhere.

I guess I finally get that alone time I've been looking for, she thought, and decided to try a new tactic. So far the enemy was entirely focused on her and Vaughn, showing no interest in the forest biome a few hundred meters below. Well, good. She could lead them away, buy Skyler and the others some time to get suited and join the battle.

Sam powered upward, focusing on the enemies closest to a side passage just beyond the ruin of the mesh ceiling. She lanced them, dodging their swinging tentacles. Two went up in red-hot bursts, causing three others to back away momentarily. Sam ran their line and pushed into the hallway, turning as she flew to fire off some beams. The bastards took the bait, forming a circle around the entrance. Their tentacle arms angled around the edge and sprayed more of the white-blue smoke in. *Go ahead,* she thought, and continued on around the next corner. She'd work her way around the circumference of the ship until she found a tunnel leading aft, reach Vaughn, regroup, and work their way toward the biome. That was the sum of the plan she cared to have.

Another corner. She paused and waited, saw the cloud flood in behind her, and the hazy shapes of the Scipios following behind it. Sam held her arms forward and slammed twin rails of yellow-white energy into one of the spheres, watched it writhe and then explode. "Keep coming, you little twats. That's right, I'm the one you want. I'm the one you tasted."

She rocketed on, taking corners at random now. Almost random. The labyrinthine ship had been six times its current size when they'd first boarded, and during those first boring weeks of flight she'd done her best to memorize the layout. There'd been nothing else to do, really, except "cavort"—Prumble's word. But then had come the plan to camouflage the ship. Tania's plan, of course. Hide, sneak about. The ship was drastically reshaped and rescaled to make it work. Old design out the window, and Sam's mental map right along with it. So she took the corners randomly, trying her best to generally head around to the side where Vaughn had disappeared.

And I've done a shit job, she thought, after a few minutes. She'd taken three turns in rapid succession, rolling over to see behind, and during one turn the whole ship had heaved to one side, with a deep reverberating boom to go with the sudden jar. She'd hit a wall, tumbled, then righted herself in a four-way intersection of identical halls. "Forgot the damn breadcrumbs," she muttered, cursing herself for not scorching the walls as she went. Something, anything, to find her way back.

She waited, wondering what had slammed so hard into a kilometer-long ship that it had bucked like that, and wondering where the hell her pursuers were. Not pursuing, evidently, which only served to fuck up her plan even more. She was lost, no closer to finding Vaughn and worse, the enemy hadn't taken the bait.

They may even now be trying to crack the forest biome like an egg and slurp up the juicy prizes that waited inside.

Sam swore, and swore again, and then powered down one of the passages. She had to find something, anything, to use as a landmark. She promised herself that after all this was over she'd throttle Prumble for not putting signposts or color coding in his cheesy "luxury" hallway redesign—what he'd done to keep from going stir-crazy in those first few weeks aboard. Everywhere she went she saw gleaming metal walls and red floors. "Not helpful, you bastard," she shouted, wishing the comms were back on.

Annoyance grew to irritation, irritation to anger. The ship was under a full-on assault and here she was floating blindly around like a dumb rat in a dumb maze and there weren't even any treat dispensers.

Sam rounded a corner and saw a lone figure in a space suit. Only a glimpse. The person floated out of view, hadn't seen her. She didn't think so, anyway. Who had it been? She hadn't seen much but the color told her it wasn't a Builder suit. *One of these newcomers, then?* She laughed at that. Couldn't help it. *All our efforts, everything the Builders did to find us, the vast distances traveled in a time-compressed bubble just to get here when we were still young and healthy, and Earth beat us to it. In style.*

She threw herself down the hall, stopped at the end, and peered around the corner. The figure was about twenty meters away and drifting lazily, not a care in the world. Sam forced herself to really look this time. The space suit wasn't like what the newcomers wore. Theirs had been new. White with blue lines that formed the compression ribbing. This person's suit was dirty, old. She'd seen it before and after several seconds it came to her. It was the kind of suit they wore on the orbitals above Darwin, back in the day. The security team that had captured her on Gateway . . .

Alex Warthen, she thought, her blood turning to ice. Had to be. He'd taken the newcomers' ship hostage, and that was a Gateway officer's garb. So what was he doing taking a lazy drift around the *Chameleon*?

Unless it wasn't him. This thought made her mind churn. All those fuckers who'd taken the lunatic Grillo's side before the final confrontation inside Eve's key room. All those ass-kissing cretins who'd refused to stand up to the zealot. There'd been a whole squad in that final battle. And they'd lost, yeah, but Alex was clearly still around, wasn't he? Who else had Eve kept alive? Sam had killed three or four of them herself. She'd never expected to have to deal with them a second time.

Eve's going to have some serious explaining to do if she ever gets the chance. The ship shuddered again, though minor compared with the quake that had hit a minute before. Without realizing it Sam found herself following the figure, keeping her distance. She tried to remember who else had been there, who else she'd assumed had either died or gone back to Earth. Skadz, her and Skyler's old friend and mentor, he'd declined to help Eve and departed. What if Eve had really kept him aboard, like Alex? Or there was Ana, the one whose arms Skyler had fallen into when Tania wasn't around. *Jesus, what if she's actually still here? How fucking awkward would that be?*

Sam stopped herself because the figure before her had stopped, too, and subsequently curled into a fetal ball, pounding its fists against its head. *Well, okay then.* A chance and she decided to take it. Sam fired her thrusters and powered forward, arms outstretched. At the last second she balled her fists and punched into the curled figure. The impact stopped her dead and sent the other careening into a wall where he—she thought for sure it was a he now—ricocheted like a billiard ball. His arms flailed madly, like an insect plucked from its leaf trying to find purchase on something, anything. He hit the other wall and managed to right himself.

Sam raised one arm and extended the business end of her beam weapon at the man's head. Whoever he was, hopefully gun-pointed-at-face was a comprehensible gesture.

She saw his eyes then, and thought maybe not.

And then she recognized him. Jerry . . . no, Jared. Alex's right-hand goon. The mate who'd chased her all around Gateway Station after her escape. Okay, that made a kind of sense. He'd been with Alex in that final battle, so of course he'd be alive and well again, too.

But those eyes . . . Sam had seen eyes like that too many times. The subhuman gaze. Madness. Murder. All comprehension beyond the primal, vanished. Jared was long gone.

"I guess that puts us past the negotiating phase," Sam said, and aimed.

A metallic tentacle swept around her torso, gripped, and yanked her backward with incredible force. The Scipio had come up behind her, grabbed, and now drew her toward its waiting spike-tipped arms. Jared forgotten, Sam brought her hand up as the creature enveloped her in a multiarmed hug that would have crushed her if not for the Builder armor. She felt it harden in defense even as the slithering limbs of the enemy tightened.

Sam was eye to eye with the enemy. A grid of sensors that flared with blinding light in every color, dampened by her visor. Sam squirmed, cast her own gaze downward to see where her hand had ended up. Compressed next to her chest, aiming upward between her and the enemy. She couldn't move her arm, but her hand was free. She twisted it, bent it at the wrist to get it out of the way, and willed the beam to fire. Some kind of alert went off in her head. Proximity, or something. "Don't care!" Sam shouted, and tried again, throwing all her will into the urge to shoot. The beam complied. It drew a blazing yellow line between her face and the enemy, missing both, lancing upward to the wall.

One of the embracing tentacles took a direct hit. Severed in two, each end dripping with molten orange goop. The creature writhed, and for a second its grip loosened. Sam turned her arm at the elbow now and fired again. Proximity alarm. "Bullshit! Fire, damn you!"

It did.

Sam learned then the value of that alarm.

The creature shuddered under her, its spherical body aglow with energy that had to go somewhere. It went outward. The blast threw Sam bodily down the hallway even as shrapnel pelted against her from head to toe. The suit absorbed what it could, but it still felt like being stomped in an alleyway by a pack of hooligans. And the light, God the light! She saw nothing but white specks for a time as her body flew. Then came the collision. Her head against something, the ceiling or the floor, didn't make any difference. It was hard and although the suit could absorb impact, it couldn't do a bloody thing about dampening momentum changes. Her innards were ingredients in a shaker bottle. One Vodka Samhopper, shaken.

She did the one thing she could think to do. Gave the suit control. *Steady me,* she thought, over and over again. She felt the thrusters at her arms, hips, and feet spit and hiss as the suit complied. The dizziness went on, and on.

Then she blinked and could see again. The hazy shapes before her came into focus. Another Scipio, smoldering because it had no doubt been right behind its exploded friend, crashing toward her along the dark passage. Sam fired her weapon at it, a sloppy wavering shot. The dancing beam drew a line of fire across the inner wall and then across the girth of the enemy. It cleaved in two before exploding. More shrapnel pattered against her like hard, angry rain, but Sam was beyond caring. She fired again, through the smoke and wreckage. There had to be more. There'd always be more. She fired as fast as the suit would let her, the only restriction apparently being not to melt the bearer's own hand, and even that was brought right to the brink.

The beams struck home. Melting, overloading. Scipios blown outward, reduced to slag and guts and chunks of techno-debris. Sam fell into a trancelike state, unleashing the death-heat on each that came through the growing cloud of battle debris. Hands came around her face. Gripped her head and yanked hard backward.

Jared, she'd totally forgotten.

He heaved her, pushing off against a corner, twisting her head in wild, random jerks. Sam had taken Krav Maga in her youth, learned how to handle opponents smaller, quicker, more cunning than herself. Her instructor's words came sharp into her mind: *Control the head and the body will follow.* Jared, even in his virus-fueled insanity, knew as much, too. His fingers had an iron grasp of her and she could do nothing but scrape and claw. His diseased mind couldn't give two shits about that. He pulled and pulled, taking her into an alcove. He slammed her into a wall and began to rain savage blows against her back and shoulders, neck and skull, all the while keeping one hand clasped around the back of her head.

Enough. Sam gritted her teeth, brought her knees up between her and the wall, feet planted. Pushed hard with both legs. Swung her head about wildly to break the grip. Twisted in the air like a swimmer making her turn. Jared reacted like any wild animal, no thought, just raw and savage combat. Neither paid any attention to the Scipio scouts as the horde of them slithered into the junction and surrounded their entangled prey, not caring which of them won or died.

In that instant the ship heaved again.

Heaved, and didn't stop.

Chapter 24

SKYLER LUIKEN STOOD before the lever and ground his teeth.

It reminded him of the hand brake of some old mine cart, protruding from the floor of the cave nearly a meter and a half, and made of a bronzelike metal. Prumble's design, of course, born of his childish sense of humor rather than a keen eye.

A rubberized grip covered the top fifteen centimeters. In truth any of them could move the lever, but upon reaching the on position a biometric scanner of some sort would identify the user, using only the tiniest amount of electric signal and processing capability. Eve would only be woken if Skyler or Tania activated the switch, a condition everyone had agreed to.

He reached for it and wrapped his hands around the grip.

"Sure we want to do this?" he asked.

The cave rocked. Dirt fell in little showers as the ground beneath Skyler's feet lurched and vibrated.

More explosions. Three, in rapid succession, and closer than the last time.

Tania, standing just behind him, placed a hand on his shoulder. "Listen to that. We have no choice, Skyler. Camouflaged or not, the enemy found us."

Still, he hesitated. Racking his mind for some other way. Perhaps if this Captain Tsandi wrestled control of her ship back from Alex Warthen—or, hell, even if Alex won and flew it away—perhaps its departure would draw the enemy off.

Ridiculous, of course. The enemy was inside. They'd seen beneath the mask, and knew of the plot hatched against them.

"You're right, as always," he told Tania. "Go see if anyone was hurt in that explosion."

Her hand lingered on his shoulder for a few seconds, then slid away.

Skyler Luiken remained in place, staring at the bronze handle. *To come this far,* he thought. Everything that had led to this moment replayed in his mind. He was either dooming Eve, or unleashing her, and neither gave him any hope that his friends—they were his friends, dammit, not just a crew—would be spared further pain.

"Skyler," Tania whispered, still behind him.

"I thought you'd gone."

"If you'd rather I do it—"

"Go," he said. "Help the others. I don't want us both in the same place if . . . if this collapses the cave or something. Please, Tania."

"You'll wake her?"

"I will. Promise. Now go, okay? For me?"

She stepped back, paused, turned, left.

He tightened his fingers on the lever with both hands and pulled, hard. The metal bar resisted, if only for a heartbeat, and then smoothly rotated into the on position. Perhaps only his imagination, but Skyler felt a tingle rush across his hands in the next instant.

Several seconds passed. He imagined some reactor core, stone dead the instant before, beginning to glow. More precious seconds ticked by with nothing at all to show for it.

Finally, the lights came on. Sound filled the air as the ship's internals roared to life. The vibration of machinery, alien and yet now wholly familiar.

"Eve?" he asked.

Nothing. Had the enemy already disabled her? Blown up her CPU or whatever? "Eve!?" He shouted this time.

A low blast of noise rippled through the ship, like a horn sounding in warning. The cry cut off abruptly, then clicked back on, then vanished entirely in a series of sharp tapping sounds not unlike distant machine-gun fire.

"Wake up!" Skyler shouted. "We're in trouble, dammit. We need you."

She finally spoke, the low mind version with all the infinite calm of an emotionless machine. The voice boomed, coming from everywhere. Of all things, she said, "All hands prepare for high acceleration."

He almost sank to his knees in relief. He absolutely

did sink to his knees when the *Chameleon*'s mighty engines fired. Skyler grunted as he went to the floor, facefirst, pressed down against the dirt so hard he could only move his eyes. He heard a terrible groan of pain and realized it came from his own misshapen mouth. He was screaming.

And still the acceleration piled on.

His vision darkened at the edges, a pulsating shadow that grew like a living thing. Dark fingers trying to seal his eyes and send him to the safety of unconsciousness. Skyler fought it the way only a trained pilot could: clenching his leg and abdomen muscles and shifting to short, sharp inhales and exhales.

And still the acceleration piled on. Nine or ten g's, easily. More than he'd ever experienced before, except perhaps in the violence of the *Melville*'s last flight, when he'd fled Gateway Station with a docking arm still attached to the craft, resulting in a catastrophic failure upon reentry. Then, though, he'd simply left the aircraft. No such option here.

The blurry dark fingers met in the center of Skyler's vision. The air finally shot from his lungs through clenched teeth, so forcefully it should have stirred the soil around his mouth. Should have, but didn't. Even the soil couldn't move. He wanted to laugh at how ludicrous it all was. Ten or eleven g's, had to be. Where was Jake, and Sam? Ana? Where was his copilot, Skadz? "Skadz," he tried to say, though no words came. *Skadz, we've got to land her. The Melville can't take . . .*

And still the acceleration piled on.

* * *

He woke sucking in air and soil. Skyler rolled and coughed, fought for a breath while gagging at the same time.

A popping sound from all around filled his ears. Applause? Who the hell would be clapping?

His own hands grasped at dirt. The cave. Skyler tried to sit but the force of Eve's flight still had him all but pinned. Less now, but still four or five times what his body was used to.

"Status," he managed, unsure who or what might hear him.

Eve replied, utterly calm. "Scipio ships have penetrated the hull at four locations. The others are giving chase, and continue to burn away the last of our camouflage."

That popping sound, Skyler realized. Their recently added outer hull being torn to shreds.

"An unknown vessel," Eve went on, "has attached to our tail section and refuses to be shaken loose."

"It's friendly," Skyler said. "Well, sort of. From Earth."

"Earth?"

"They beat us here, Eve. By decades."

A pause. "An unexpected development."

"No shit."

"I understand now why you activated me early."

"What do we do? What happens now? If you're going to self-destruct, Eve, please, tell us. Give us a chance to say—"

"The situation is being analyzed."

A second of silence stretched into three.

"Eve?"

"The situation is being analyzed"

Not knowing what else to do, Skyler scrambled to shaky feet and stumbled out of the cave, feeling as if he carried a fallen log over his shoulders. The biome was alive again. A small fire burned near the center, where their suspended warming element had come crashing down to the forest floor during the intense acceleration. Whatever was going on outside, Eve had evidently settled on a roughly one-g pace now. She'd put the ship on an erratic course, however, but the gimbaled biome rotated to keep them pressed more or less to the floor. This caused the world beyond the clear shell to tilt to and fro as if they sailed an angry sea. Skyler forced himself to focus on his immediate surroundings before nausea took hold.

He rushed to the airlock and found armor suits still waiting. Tania and Prumble were sitting beside each other, she leaning against him, one hand holding a white bandage to her forehead. She glanced up when Skyler approached and, to his great relief, managed to smile.

"Not as bad as it looks," she said.

Prumble's expression said otherwise.

Skyler grimaced. "It's done. Eve's awake, and she can help heal you. Let's get suited, find Sam and Vaughn."

"Tim already went," Prumble said.

"Good. Wait, what? *Tim?*"

"The young man is going to get himself killed," the big man added, almost to himself.

Tania shook her head. "He's more resourceful than you give him credit for."

"Resourceful isn't quite the trait needed in this situation," Prumble mused.

"Eve?" Skyler said to the air. "We're in a world of shit here. Give us a plan or I'll make one myself."

"Hear me," the synthetic voice said immediately. It took Skyler a second to realize she was now talking to every one of them. Sam, Vaughn, Tim . . . even Vanessa if she was still suited. Still alive. "The first priority is to defend our ship against the intruders. I've identified their locations and divided the targets among you. Follow the paths displayed on your visors."

Skyler double-checked his armor. For the first time the black outfit made him feel safe, even powerful. Now ready, he helped Tania verify her gear, too. Prumble was set by the time she finished.

"Tania," Skyler said, "if you can't—"

"I can," she said, voice flat. "The alternative does not appeal to me."

"All right, then." He glanced at his visor. Rather than a 2D top-down map, Eve had merely projected a glowing 3D line for him to follow over the terrain before his eyes. His path led out the biome airlock, and then up toward the top of the larger, cylindrical chamber that housed the three biomes.

"Looks like I'm headed aft," Prumble said.

"Me too," Tania replied.

They were both looking at him. "I'll see you later, then," he told them. "At the victory celebration."

Prumble grinned and clapped him on the shoulder. He turned and ran out.

Tania stood before him and rested a hand on his chest. They could not touch, suited as they were, but she held his gaze for a few seconds and that was enough.

"Be safe," she said.

"You too."

Tania spun and rushed out.

As Skyler ran along his own path he ordered Eve to put up a display of everyone's vitals on one side of his view. The information appeared a split second later. He scanned it as he clambered up the steps, past the second biome. There, Vanessa. She was okay. Alive, at least.

"Everyone, report," Skyler said. "Sam? Tim? How's it going out there?"

It was Eve who replied. "I will route communications for now, Captain. Some of your crew are in circumstances where distractions must be minimized."

"Maybe you should let them decide that," Skyler shot back, annoyed.

"The risk is unacceptable. My plan must be followed with absolute precision or it will fail."

"Doesn't sound like much of a plan at all, then," he muttered. The ship did not reply.

He ran on. A silvery grit covered the steps, as if a sandstorm had blown through here, something Skyler would not be surprised by. *Much stranger things have happened,* he thought.

Ahead, flashes of light reflected off the interior walls. A battle, beyond the third biome. He leapt, pleased at the suit's reaction. Small rockets embedded in his feet, knees, and elbow joints propelled him straight up, past the final sphere and into the domed ceiling of the massive central cavity of the *Chameleon*.

He saw a black-clad figure positioned in the center of the mesh floor at the exact point where all hallways entering the chamber converged. It was Tim, both arms held out, each covering different entrances. His head whipped from one to another, occasionally unleashing brief blasts from his beam weapon.

In those darkened tunnels, lit sporadically by Tim's weapon or by gouts of flame and small showers of sparks, Skyler saw the wreckage of the Scipio scouts. The debris all but clogged the spaces. Their sizes varied, but the shapes were all the same: spherical bodies studded with segmented tentacle-like limbs of varying thickness and length. Some of these still swung about, lashing at the air around them in their death throes.

Behind the carcasses still more enemies loomed, their central bodies alive with scanning lights and lasers in a riot of yellow, blue, green, and red hues.

Motion, at a rent in the wall that Skyler had not seen before. He aimed at it instinctively, then lowered his arm as Vaughn leapt through.

The man moved backward, his arms pointing back the way he'd come. He ducked behind the smoldering corpse of a Scipio scout, fired into the hole in the wall, then pushed back and to one side, giving himself a better shot down the same tunnel. He swept beams of violent energy across the space and held the weapons there, slicing away at the scouts clogged within. Skyler rushed toward him, enthralled by the timing of Vaughn's movements, the accuracy of his attacks. How much of that was due to Eve's timed orders, and how much his natural talent?

Skyler realized then that Sam was not with him. The two, so inseparable, had somehow been torn apart.

He watched as Vaughn fought, his beams clearing a path in the wreckage of one of the connecting tunnels. Simultaneously Tim moved toward the other, the odd pair each unleashing devastating blasts at the crawling enemies within. Vaughn moved with absolute purpose, his attack unwavering. He pressed until, before Skyler could reach him, Vaughn was inside the tunnel and continuing deeper.

"Where is he going?" Skyler demanded of Eve. "And where the hell is Sam?"

"You have your own target, Skyler. Follow your path. Please make haste there."

Tim came into view, dancing back from the hall he'd temporarily focused on. He moved to his spot in the middle of the platform again, where both passages were in his line of sight. The mortar on his back extended and puffed twice in rapid succession. Skyler winced as explosions erupted from both entrances.

"What the hell? Vaughn is in there!"

"He is following orders, blocking the paths the scouts are taking. Please trust me, Captain, and follow your own path."

"But you can reshape the ship at will, goddammit. Why not just fucking delete those tunnels and let whatever's inside get crushed?"

"Scipio viruses have sabotaged that ability," she replied in her even, matter-of-fact tone. "If you delay further, life support will be next. The Swa-a-a-a-arm burrow there even n-now."

The urgency of her message, and the alarming decay of her vocal quality, left no doubt as to the severity of the situation. For the first time he felt the cold reality that he could die here, and soon. A truth he'd willfully ignored since leaving Earth. Yet he could not tear his gaze away from the smoldering ruins of the tunnel where Vaughn had just disappeared. A sudden anger flooded through him, directed at Tim. Why had he followed such an asinine order? The son of a bitch had just doomed one of their best fighters, trapping him with the enemy. And now he just stood there, his back to Skyler, arms held out as if he were some kind of goddamn hero. Tim's hands slowly came together above his head. He stood there, perfectly still, like a statue. What the hell was he doing? Posing?

Skyler ignored the glowing path superimposed over reality and marched the three steps toward Tim, ready to turn the youngster about and trash him for what he'd just done, for everything. Then the other man's beam weapons began to glow.

At the same instant a chunk of the ceiling above exploded inward and a fresh Scipio scout began to wiggle in. The tentacles came first, sweeping in around the edges of the rent in the ceiling and plunging into any surface they could find for support. The spherical body came next, sensor lights already alive and flashing about the room.

A spray filled the air in front of it, coalescing into hair-thin filaments of translucent blue. Fibrous crystals that reminded Skyler vaguely of a thicket.

Tim's beam weapons fired. They looked different than before. Tuned. Changed by him or, more likely, Eve. The beams resembled columns of flame, roiling with orange, white, and red. They tore right through the still-growing crystalline structure that nearly filled the space between Tim and the Scipio. The fine material melted instantly and fell in glowing drips that splattered on the ground around Tim's feet. He traced lines of fire on the ceiling until they met in the center of the hole, right on the body of the enemy. It began to thrash, its body glowing from the intensity of the assault. Tim did not relent. Standing there, arms raised, firing twin columns of sizzling death, awash in the colors of his destructive attack, he looked like some kind of oil-painted warrior.

"Skyler," Eve said. "Please follow your path or I will assume control of your suit. You each h-h-h-have your role to play. Please trust m-m-my guidance."

Several seconds passed before her words registered. Skyler finally broke the spell of watching quiet, simple Tim and the epic ass-kicking he'd unleashed on that Scipio. The young man's actions defied Skyler's expectations. Perhaps the warrior in him came out when cornered. Being well armed didn't hurt, either. Or maybe it was out of some sense of protecting Tania. Skyler decided to give Tim the benefit of the doubt and assume it wasn't just because Eve had taken control of his suit. That he could hold his own was now abundantly obvious.

Reluctantly, Skyler turned and ran along his own path, leaving Tim to his battle, and Vaughn to his. He'd seen nothing of Sam, though the vitals said she yet lived.

Somewhere, ahead, lay his own demons.

The glowing path took him into an alcove, down a narrow side corridor, and then straight into a wall.

"Dead end, Eve," Skyler growled.

On his visor a red indicator fell into place from somewhere above. He'd only just registered this as some kind of threat when the wall before him changed.

A bulge appeared, then exploded inward, showering Skyler with debris. A Scipio scout about one meter in diameter waited beyond, tentacles already creeping into the hole it had made.

There was no time to think. The suit reacted to his instinctual response. He felt his shoulder twitch and then watched in fascination as a mortar round lanced through the air and slammed into one of the glowing eyes that dotted the scout's body. The whole mass wiggled for a split second, and then cracked apart, glowing embers and fluids spilling out from within.

Skyler's marked route led inside, along the path the Scipio had burrowed. He leapt over the fallen foe in a single hop, glad to be in gravity for this fight. The route turned upward then, straight toward the nose of the ship. Skyler's rockets propelled him into the darkness above.

* * *

Tania Sharma raced along the phantom glowing path, unsure what lay ahead or indeed how she would even handle whatever she found there. If not for the reassuring words from Eve she would have demanded the group stay together. Or barring that, she at least remain at Prumble's side. But not two junctions into their journey, Prumble suddenly darted down a hall that did not follow the path laid before her own eyes.

She'd called out to him, but it was Eve who'd replied, explaining the threats to the ship were too numerous for the two of them to remain together, or even communicate. At least for now.

And so she'd raced on, placing her trust in the artificial mind. Minds, she reminded herself, for there were two in there.

"What sort of weapons do I have again?" she asked, hearing the trepidation in her own voice. She shook her head, willed courage and concentration.

"Each arm has a plasma beam, which will automatically configure itself to the enemy being targeted."

"That's reassuring."

"In addition, a mortar is mounted at your right shoulder, which can deliver self-guided projectiles to a target with a payload of your choice."

"Can you choose the payload?"

"I can."

"Good. One less thing I need to remember to do."

"Automatic payloads will be d-d-d-d-deployed."

Tania ran on, around the spiral hallway that traversed the entire ship. "Where am I going, anyway?"

"Several scouts have breached the hull near my en-en-engines, and seek to disable them. You will re-moooovve this threat."

"Can't you just fix the breach? Regrow it?"

"That capability is nonfunctional. Skyler is working on it."

This gave her a confidence she did not know existed within her. He was out there, fighting, just like her. They all were, and Eve knew exactly where to deploy them. *We're going to make it through this,* she decided.

"Eve?" she asked, barreling around a corner, near the tail of the ship now. "Why did you keep Alex Warthen? Why didn't you tell us?"

An oddly long pause followed. "Unfortunate. I only now have registered their . . . escape. This complicates matters."

"That doesn't answer my question."

Another pause. "It was necessary to study the human form more closely, both an immune and a nonimmune. So I k-kept them after the battle. Revived them, and studied them."

Images filled Tania's mind. Grotesque experiments and dissections. The pair of them pushed to the limits of pain tolerance, killed, then revived all over again for another spate of tests. Disgust roiled in her, fair or not. She battled it back, a thousand other questions on her mind, but only one that she felt she had time to ask. "How many did you hide?"

"Two."

"And one of them is an immune?" Tania racked her mind to think who else might have been kept. Skadz and Ana, both immune, both refused to come along on this journey. Had she really . . . ? Could she?

"Alex Warthen."

Relief and confusion coursed through her. Alex, immune? But of course how would anyone have known? He'd been in space, near the protective elevator, for the entirety of the subhuman plague. "Alex. And what . . . what did you learn?"

"I learned," Eve said, "to use a-a-a cliché from your world, that immunes see things differently."

Tania slid to a stop, her path taking her to an iris door near the end of the long spiral hall, a door that led in toward the center of the ship. "What does that mean? Immunes aren't human?"

"They are very much human," the ship replied. "It is a subtle difference, this, but no less important. Immunes simply have a m-more evolved way of analyzing the information their brains receive, which seems to subvert the attack vector used by the virus. I do not yet understand why."

The door's sections pulled away, allowing Tania through. She stepped inside and recognized the space immediately.

The key room.

The final piece of the puzzle Eve had presented to humanity, back on and above Earth. Memories of her experiences here came flooding back. The elation of discovering this place, and the mad adventure with Skyler here that had almost killed her. The gruesome final battle with Grillo and his henchmen, ultimately leading to this journey, this moment.

Tania swallowed, wondering just how final that final battle had been, for at the far end of the ten-sided room several Scipios were working to dislodge an iris door that remained steadfastly closed to them.

They were not living things themselves, Tania knew, but more like spacecraft. Yet each did hold a living pilot, a small creature barely larger than a monkey. Creatures designed and bred specifically for the task of piloting these vessels.

"What do I do?" Tania whispered.

"Annihilate them," Eve replied. "Quickly. Bef-f-fore they disable my power source."

Tania raised her arms and watched in morbid fascination as two fiery beams of energy lanced out. Her aim was off. Both beams slammed into the ceiling in a shower of flame and sparks. She adjusted, ignoring the sensation of heat on her hands and the way her arms felt as if being pushed backward. She moved the beam onto one of the Scipios and held it there, watching as the thing writhed and twisted under the unrelenting torrent of energy.

A familiar feeling swept into her mind. She'd felt it the first time in Hawaii, a gun in her hands, the subhuman before her toppling to one side with half its face torn off by her bullets. Tania knew she should detest this feeling, this bloodlust. But some primal reaction took hold, its power too strong over her. She kept the beams on her target until it twitched, crumpled, and fell all the way to the floor at her feet.

Eve was saying something. Tania hadn't heard over the war drums in her ears. "Repeat," she managed.

"You waited too long," Eve said. "They are through."

The ceiling erupted in a torrential shower of sparks. Tania's feet left the floor as the press of gravity faded.

Eve was no longer accelerating away from her pursuers.

"New plan," was all the AI said.

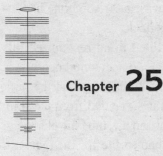

Chapter **25**

HAD HE THE air for it he would have laughed.

Instead Alex Warthen just bobbed against a bulkhead, lips moving like a fish out of water, his amusement entirely internal.

It was the sound that had triggered his funny bone. One moment he'd been in a shouting match with Xavi, the braggart jackass of a navigator for this cursed boat. The argument had come about over whether or not Xavi could keep his helmet on, during which Alex had ordered the airlock tube disconnected. Xavi had refused, claiming among other things that he did not know how to work the tube. An obvious lie. The bastard was buying time.

Anger getting the better of him, Alex had launched into a string of profane insults when the pitch of his voice began to rise and grow quiet. His first thought had been *helium leak*. He realized only too late what was really happening, and found himself now waiting for asphyxiation while his oxygen-starved brain kept pushing him to laugh at the ridiculous way his shouted insults had just dwindled away, as if someone had attached a volume knob to his back.

Some corner of his befuddled mind recognized this for what it was. This had been no accidental depressurization, or the result of some impact against the hull. No, the air had been deliberately vented from the ship. Sound worked differently in thin air, thus the change in his voice. These details he had to file for the moment. A suffocated man exacts no revenge. The air . . . that's why Xavi had wanted his helmet on. Smart.

Then had come a sudden, wild lurch, throwing everyone to the floor with bone-jarring force. An impact somewhere, a big one.

Alex clawed for anything that could steady him. Where had he left his helmet? Floating in a corner, of course. The lurch had jumbled everything back into wild motion, his helmet just one chunk inside a space filled with careening debris. He swore at himself for taking the bloody thing off in the first place.

Xavi lay in a ball on the other side of a bulkhead, a few meters away, only his shoulder visible. Unconscious? Hit his head, did he? *Serves you right.*

As for the others . . .

The airlock door rolled aside and two suited figures entered the ship. One Alex did not know. The other was the immune Vanessa, back again.

The blackness at the edge of his vision crowded in, like curtains drawn from all sides, or a funeral shroud, as his brain screamed for oxygen.

A hissing sound, like an enraged snake, pushed the

darkness back a little. Then more. Air? Alex tried to suck it in but his lungs wouldn't listen.

He shifted his focus to his helmet. He had to get it on, and quick. The suit had air. If only he hadn't been so anxious to ditch the damn thing. Alex Warthen groped toward the object, ignoring those around him. The hissing sound went on. The black curtains pulled back a little. Then came the precious moment of breath. His body did it on its own. A jerking, spasmodic inhale that left him unable to do anything but fight back the urge to vomit.

Sound bled back in. Coughing, confused shouts, and cries of pain. Alex chanced a look down the length of the ship. Vanessa was flying toward the bridge, looking for Jared maybe. That was good, let her look. The other newcomer—the captain, he assumed—tended to Xavi. She took the navigator's weapon and swung it about. Her aim swept right past him. *Looking for Jared, too,* he had time to think. *They don't even see me as a threat. Good.*

Below, the engineer stirred. She'd drifted the entire length of the ship when it had lurched, and looked like he felt. But somehow she'd already righted herself. She was staring up at him.

He held Beth's gaze and watched as she flung herself upward, straight toward him. So much for thinking him a celebrity.

Floating, tumbling now thanks to the coughing fit, Alex could do nothing to avoid it. He tried to pull his arms forward, raise his fists, but precious oxygen had yet to make it that far. His limbs felt numb, heavy as sacks of sand. Beth sped toward him like an arrow loosed, her narrow and emotionless gaze laser focused on Alex.

Somehow he managed to swing, not realizing his hand now gripped his helmet. He brought it around like a club. There was a thunderous crack. Beth's head jerked sideways, and a plume of dark red fluid fountained out and splashed against the sidewall. The emotionless gaze became a vacant one. Her unconscious body crashed into him. Blood from a nasty gash across her forehead spilled into his face, his eyes. He coughed and blinked as he tried to push her aside, the movement sending them both drifting across the central chamber of the ship. Above them, Vanessa whirled, the activity grabbing her attention, her search for the absent Jared evidently concluded. She spotted Alex. She swung her arm toward him, and a bulb grew there, the end of it shimmering with heat and energy.

Then a wall blocked his view. A bulkhead. He'd floated past one of the bulkheads. Vanessa fired too late. The whole ship lit up with the brilliance of her weapon. Alex could feel the air around him hum with energy, and the bare metal section of bulkhead before him glowed red. The heat blistered his cheeks, even behind the ten-centimeter-thick solid obstacle. Were the skin of his legs exposed he had no doubt his hair would have singed and melted away. A few seconds longer and she'd cook him in his suit. Melt through the wall and then through him. He saw smoke curling off the surfaces as dust burned away and the water in the air around him began to vaporize.

The glowing wall lurched forward. For the barest fraction of a second he thought it had bubbled or warped, but his mind caught up in time to realize the truth: acceleration. Lots of it. The little spacecraft dangled like a can from a wedding limousine as the Builder ship it was attached to suddenly roared to life.

He was falling now. Alex had time to turn his head before his face smacked into that glowing patch of metal. The heat seared the skin of his cheek in an instant. He rolled aside on pure instinct, feeling the charred flesh tear away. The pain came a moment later. Vile, eye-watering agony. He screamed then, despite what the contortion did to his face. Some part of him realized the weight he now seemed to possess. The ship—this one or the behemoth it was connected to—must be at full burn. The force of it pinned him to the smoldering bulkhead, though only his suit touched the surface now and it seemed up to the challenge.

Something touched his hand. The helmet. His helmet. He had to get it on.

Alex screamed as he hauled the gear over his ravaged face. He felt it tighten as if alive when the neck rings met and connected. The pain along half his face became something more. An assault on the senses. Like a constant roar, as if he stood beneath an aircraft at takeoff.

Once the helmet settled into place, everything changed. The pain subsided, a wave drawn back from shore. His cheek felt hot but also somehow numb. The nausea faded, too. Emergency auto-medication, kicking in. Alex rolled onto his side and then his stomach.

Xavi lay across from him, on the other side of the ring-shaped bulkhead, out cold but breathing.

Alex leaned over the open space in the center of the bulkhead and peered down the length of the ship.

Beth lay motionless in the basin, near her engineering computer. He wanted to feel nothing. She'd come at him, after all, and was one of the enemy. But some part of him hoped she'd survived the fall.

Beside her, down there, were the others. The captain in her EVA suit, moving, struggling. She pulled herself toward Beth and checked for a heartbeat, fingers pressed at the neck, though Alex could not tell from her reaction if the news was good or bad. And then Vanessa, who lay curled in a ball like a sleeping child. Perhaps she'd hit her head in the fall. If Alex leapt now he'd fall on her with the force of an elephant dropped from an aircraft. Could her armor withstand it? Could his own body?

"Come back to me."

Alex jerked away from the precipice, looking for the source of the voice. Panic gave way to recognition. It was the woman. The ship. In his head again. He shouted at it. "Fuck off!"

"You still have a role to play in this, Alex Warthen. You can still make a difference—"

"I'd rather die."

"—you, and Jared."

Jared. An implication, there, and a promise. A dangled carrot. Jared was in trouble, diseased. "You can save him? Fix him?"

"Not exactly. He is beyond repair, though his memories live within me now," she replied. Then, "Time to decide, Alex. I've unlocked your weapon. You have one shot. Use it wisely."

"My weapon?"

A great instant of pain washed over him, as if his entire body had been covered in a bandage that was now, all at once, torn away. He cried out and looked down, expecting to see flame enveloping him. What he saw instead made him gasp. His space suit had changed. Or perhaps it had never been his suit at all. Instead of his own recovered outfit, he wore that same black armored outfit that Vanessa did. Another of Eve's tricks?

Something clicked in his head, as if some extra part of his brain had just now been attached. With it came a sense of capability that hadn't been there a moment before. The confidence of a gun, invisible until now. A sense of raw power surged through him, banishing the last memory of his burned face.

Alex rolled again. One shot? Why one?

Vanessa was the target, surely. Finish this now while the chance was there.

He took aim, hesitated when the woman called Beth stirred. She twisted and groaned. Her eyes flickered open. To his surprise and dismay she began to claw her way over to Vanessa. Dazed or not, her first waking instinct had been to help the other. Alex watched in strange fascination before remembering himself and his goal. He renewed his aim, but Beth blocked the shot now. He had to get closer.

Fine, he thought, and struggled to his knees. The power of the acceleration made standing impossible, but from this position he could at least fall. Alex steadied himself, narrowed his gaze, and pitched forward over the hole in the floor that led to the lower levels.

In that instant the acceleration ended. His momentum left him drifting through the center of the ship at only a snail's pace. Debris began to move away from the floors and walls, filling the air. Xavi flopped about, coming to but disoriented. Below, Beth looked as if she were trying to keep herself at the bottom of a pool, still trying to wake the limp form of Vanessa.

It was the captain Alex shifted focus to. She was up again, and staring right at him, a pistol still in her hand. She swung her arm up, quick as a viper, sighted, and took her shot.

The bullet hit like the halfhearted punch of a child. He glanced down at his abdomen and saw no damage at all. Not even a scratch. The armor was no illusion.

You still have a role to play in this, Alex Warthen.

Alex looked back at his assailant and reveled in the confusion he saw there. She tried to shoot again but nothing happened. Her expression cycled to bewilderment, then fear, and finally stoic resolve. This was her ship, and he'd tried to take it.

The captain coiled against the floor and then pushed off with both legs, rocketing toward him. Her eyes never left his as she flew up through the spine of her ship, both fists held before her. Alex let her come, he had no choice. He couldn't move and he wasn't about to waste his single shot on the wrong target.

When she arrived he swung, hard. His forearm slammed against the side of her neck with an audible slap that sent her tumbling away to one side. It sent him the other way. Good. He needed to get to a solid surface so he could take aim or, barring that, at least regain control of his movement.

The motion took him to the airlock door. He grabbed the handle and steadied himself.

Time to decide. You have one shot. A rather annoying corner of his mind pushed the words through his bloodlust-fueled focus. What had the damn ship meant? Kill the captain? Shoot himself? No, Vanessa. Had to be Vanessa. The immune. His opponent. Right?

As if in cryptic answer the entire craft rang like a bell, rocking to one side with a violent suddenness that slammed Alex bodily into the airlock door. He fought to keep his grip, ignoring pain from all along the front of his body. Exotic alien armor or not, it couldn't shield his internal organs from such abrupt collisions.

Something sliced across his field of view. His face was pressed against the tiny window on the airlock door. Something moved *out there.* The umbilical tube writhed like a wounded snake, but that wasn't it. What, then? Skyler?

The craft, dangling from that Kevlar tube, twisted and swung erratically. Whatever had struck the ship had left it flopping like a fish on the hook.

A series of thuds clattered across the hull. Alex glanced around, despite himself. "What is that?" he asked of no one in particular.

"Something's on the hull," the captain said, across from him. A trickle of blood ran down the side of her face from where he'd hit her. Their battle seemed momentarily forgotten. "Something big."

"That's not helpful."

"A Scipio craft. One of the Swarm Blockade."

"Still not helpful."

He glanced back out the window, down the writhing umbilical tube.

A flash of brown and green blurred past his vision. Like a blade, or a claw. It scythed through a section of the white flexible tube, leaving chunks of webbed fabric adrift. Alex could see the blackness of space through the gash. And then a form. Like a snake it slid in through the opening and curled around the inside, groping, feeling. Searching. Another came, then another. One had a bladed tip that looked sharp as any surgeon's knife, and five times larger.

Then all at once the whole thing squirmed through, wriggling in through the hole it had carved. Its spherical body settled into the tube, filling it so completely that the fabric bulged out around its form. Triangle-shaped sections of the thick umbilical fabric peeled back around it. The segmented tentacles found purchase on the ribbed metal rings woven along the length of the umbilical, and the robot or creature or whatever the hell it was began to pull itself toward the airlock, toward Alex.

Time to decide. You have one shot.

Okay, then. Alex wheeled the airlock door aside. Air, only recently returned to the ship, rushed out with gale force, pulling debris along with it. He felt his legs pulled toward the vacuum of space and somehow managed to hook one foot into a stabilizer rung. Behind him he heard a groan as the captain struggled to keep her navigator from tumbling out into space. She was shouting at Alex. He ignored her. Not helpful at all.

The monstrosity before him lit up. Beams of light in every shade swept across the interior surfaces of the torn umbilical, which he could see was now only connected to the larger spacecraft by a bundle of cables that had not been severed.

The mass seemed to grip the walls harder and then it *coughed*. A spasm that filled the umbilical with a blue-white cloud of crystalline shards the size of snowflakes. In vacuum the millions of tiny fragments flew toward Alex unhindered, though many thousands were slapped out of their trajectory by the undulating walls of the broken umbilical. Most, however, came shooting straight for Alex, and as they flew the fragments began to grow and link together.

Time to decide.

Alex Warthen raised his arm and felt the surge of energy even as the plasma beam lanced outward into that blue-white swarm. He aimed for the lights that danced across the spherical body beyond, and felt a keen sense of satisfaction as the whole mass began to glow. First white then crimson and then bright yellow. The tentacles began to glow, too, and the whole machine started to writhe.

He slammed the airlock door closed just as the cloud of crystal particles arrived. They lashed against the door like clawing fingernails. Beyond, the enemy creature convulsed one last time and then erupted in melted fragments of metal, cables, and other unrecognizable chunks.

All along the hull came a hammering that made the whole ship rattle and boom. Alex pushed away, afraid the airlock door would falter under the spray of ejecta. But it held. Jets of compressed air rushed into the vessel from vents near each bulkhead, creating plumes of grayish mist all around him.

He smacked into the opposite wall and turned his head to see the captain beside him. Their eyes met. A brief moment of shared wonder, even camaraderie. She blinked, and the brittle connection between them shattered. He needed her ship, and she wanted to keep it.

Alex reached with both hands and grabbed her by the helmet. Wearing this alien armor, high on adrenaline, he somehow knew he could crush it and then crush her.

Something poked at his chin. He glanced down and saw she still had her gun. She pressed against the tiny patch of flexible material where his mask joined the neck portion.

"You're out of bullets," he said.

"That was my gun. This is Xavi's."

He swallowed. Could it pierce the armor? Did he want to find out?

"This has to end," she said, her voice almost sad through the tinny helmet speaker.

"That's the idea."

"Listen. It doesn't even matter if you take the ship. It's damaged beyond repair. The *Wildflower* cannot get where you want to go."

Alex glared at her. He saw no hint of deception in her calm features.

"Even if it could," she went on, "it won't make any difference. I set the self-destruct as soon as I made it inside."

All hope drained from him. He could see the truth, plain on her face. She meant it, every word. "Why?" he rasped.

"Because even damaged this ship can provide them," she said, nodding toward the umbilical and the destroyed monster beyond, "with knowledge that I cannot allow them to have."

"What knowledge?"

"How to get to Earth, for one."

"The Builders already know how to get to Earth."

"That thing out there is called a Scipio. They're what the Builders sought our help in fighting."

"Delete your records, then. How hard can it be?"

In answer, Gloria tapped the side of her head. "Not so easy, in truth. And then there's the fold tech. That's what they really want. Very desperately. If they had that they'd be unstoppable."

"Then why the hell did you come here at all?"

She lowered her chin, blinked. Then met his gaze again. "Our first mission here was lost. The ship is still unaccounted for. We have to find it, and make sure they—"

The *Wildflower* rocked to one side, slamming Alex and the captain into the wall. They grunted in unison. Alex, holding on to nothing, bounced away and found himself adrift once again.

Another boom against the hull. There was a scuttling sound. Alex traced it with his eyes. It didn't take much to imagine another enemy craft grabbing on to the ship and crawling across it, looking for a way in.

There was a loud bang that rippled through the space. Halfway between Alex and the far end of the ship, where Beth and Vanessa cowered, a tentacle had punched through.

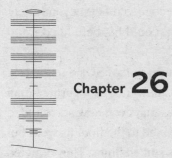

Chapter 26

FATE LEFT THEM face-to-face.

In the crushing press of hard acceleration, Samantha found herself pinned to the floor with her visor pressed against that of Jared. Or the creature that had been Jared.

He raged at her, spittle flying from his vulpine lips, murder in his eyes. She couldn't hear any of it, but he didn't know that. Was beyond understanding that. The rash around the sides of his neck was clear as day.

She'd thought the days of dealing with subs well behind her. It felt like a lifetime ago, and incomprehensibly distant. And she knew now she'd been fooling herself. Even if this was Eve's doing, even if Jared had been cursed with the virus before they'd left Earth, the idea that she'd left dealing with it behind was willful ignorance, nothing more. The whole point of this mission was to come and reckon with the masters of such diseases. You cannot escape that which you run straight toward.

Jared clawed at her, his mind of singular purpose now. She wondered if he recognized her, beyond mere prey. If not her as a person, could his befuddled mind identify her as an immune?

And how close was Eve's version of SUBS to the real deal? She looked at Jared anew, not as a former man but as a tool of the creatures that even now surrounded both of them. They were pinned to the floor as well, but had the benefit of numerous spiked limbs. They crawled in, a growing horror of silhouettes against the battle-ravaged hallways.

Something new appeared in Sam's field of view. A product of her imagination, she thought at first. A softly glowing beam that wormed right through the Scipio scouts and off into the distance, before fading as it rounded a corner. Sam blinked, but the golden path remained.

Blood must be getting squeezed from her mind. She was on her way to joining Jared in his insanity, no disease required, thank you very much.

"Please follow your designated path," Eve said. A voice that came from somewhere inside her mind.

"You must be fucking kidding me," Sam grunted, straining to move the air. "Finally awake and that's all you've got to say?"

"Acceleration ends in three . . ."

No time to argue with her, or interrogate her artificial mind for the deception and confusion. No time to make her answer for any of it.

Sam was in the shit, pure and simple. A subhuman

grappling with her, a dozen spherical death machines all around and closing in.

"two . . ."

She managed to bend her legs, tucking her feet up in behind her thighs like a frog.

"one . . ."

Weightless, just like that. Sam shoved against the floor with all her strength. She had the benefit of knowing it would happen. Jared, not so equipped, had just started to drift away from the floor when she powered into him. Her body and his took flight straight down the hall and along the path Eve had marked.

Her aim was true, or would have been had she not a subhuman grappled to her, hands clasped around her upper arms. Still, she'd been ready, he had not. The motion took him in a backward somersault, his back scraping across the suddenly very agitated tentacular limbs of the Scipio goon squad. They slowed him, which slowed her. Sam did the only thing she could and rammed her head into his, an attack that would have crushed his nose if not for his helmet. Still, the force of the blow rocked his head backward viciously. His grip came free. Sam tucked herself into a ball, rolled to one side, and extended her arms and legs to streamline her flight, feetfirst.

In her wake, Jared reached for her with one hand, fingers splayed, like a diver being pulled into the dark depths by an elder god. Tentacles thrashed and writhed all around him. Hooking him by the shoulders. One spike slammed into the side of his helmet and pushed out the other side. What little light was left in Jared Larsen's eyes vanished then.

Enough is enough, Sam decided, and willed the protrusions above her wrists to light the motherfuckers up.

Another dead hallway. She flew on, desperate now, ignoring the path Eve marked for her.

"Please follow your designated—"

"Get bent, machine," Sam roared, half-tempted to wiggle out of the armor and leave it here just for some peace and quiet. She'd followed the ghostly beam for the first two turns and then decided Eve could shove the rest of it up her engine nozzles.

"It is imperative that you do your part. If you do not comply I will take control—"

"My *part,*" Sam said, "is finding Vaughn."

"Which is exactly where your path leads."

"Well sorry, but I'm having trouble trusting you just now," Sam said.

"Prepare for minor acceleration," the ship said, as if that was a perfectly acceptable reply.

Sam felt her feet scrape the floor. An instant later she was running. Then sprinting. Good. That's better. She came across a hallway that had been breached at its midpoint, the metallic innards of the ship splayed inward in a twisted sculpture. There were no Scipios to be seen. Sam vaulted the mess, rolled, and continued on. In that brief leap she'd glanced into the rent. Several meters away lay the empty infinite blackness of space. Not empty, actually. Scipio ships, identical in shape if not size, were powering alongside on jets of energy, racing to intercept the *Chameleon. Not such a great name after all,* thought Sam. There were dozens of them, and that just in her tiny view glimpsed in passing. The knot of dread in her gut tightened. This wasn't going to end well, she knew that with absolute certainty, but she'd be damned if she didn't go down without a fight.

"The path leads to Vaughn?" she asked the AI. "Truly?"

"Correct."

"For your sake, Eve, it better. Update it."

The ship made no reply, but the glowing path returned, adjusted to her new position.

Sam sprinted ahead, going full bore now. Another corner, another hallway, though this one curved slightly, implying a path around the girth of the ship, and that was good. She kept one arm held out, fist clenched and rotated down, ready to fire. Debris skittered under her heavy footfalls, remnants of earlier battle or just the detritus from so much maneuvering.

A distant yellow flash lit the curved hallway, followed by a shock wave. The rubble under her feet became riddled with a fine glassy powder. Scipio residue, from their razor-spray crap. Sam gritted her teeth and surged onward. Her battle high began to crumble, giving way to exhaustion. Pain flared from a growing heat in her calf where the enemy had punctured her suit, a wound she'd managed to ignore until gravity had wormed its way back into the mix.

In front of her the hall met a vertical access shaft, with ladder rungs along one edge. Her path plunged down into the hole, and from below came the flashing lights and sprays of shrapnel.

Sam leapt into the abyss, aimed down, and dropped into the fray.

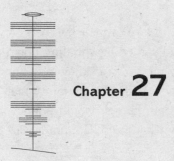

Chapter **27**

THEY CAME IN from everywhere. With the outer shell torn away, and the news spread among them that Builder tech hid beneath, the Swarm reacted like a school of frenzied sharks. They punched through the tough hull with superheated spikes mounted to their tentacles, tearing circular sections away and squeezing through to the guts of the vessel. No longer were those holes sealed behind them. They knew time was of the essence now.

Tania Sharma watched in horror as the Scipios swarmed inside. Their long, slithering limbs poured in through the fractured ceiling, found purchase in the walls. They hauled themselves inside and heaved their way toward where she stood in the basin of the giant chamber.

She glanced around, looking for her path, needing that guidance. "Where do I go?"

"Here," Eve said. "Make your stand, Tania. Below

you is my power source. If they reach it, all will end here."

"I can't," she whispered, in awe of their numbers. A dozen enemies or more had spilled in, spiraling down the walls toward her. They moved as if knowing their prey was cornered. She knew with total certainty that the moment she fired on one the rest would pounce. "Eve, I can't. I don't know what to do. I'm not a warrior."

No reply. She'd gone.

Tania swallowed. *Think, think.* The walls? Cut the room in half and hope they're sucked out into space? Wouldn't work. They'd just bored in through the ceiling and hadn't bothered to seal it.

Get in close, maybe. Would they attack her if it meant damaging one of their own? Almost certainly. The Swarm numbered in the millions, and this was their entire reason for being.

There was nothing to do but fire. Hope she could take enough of them out to buy Eve some time.

"Skyler," she said, ashamed at the waver in her voice. "I don't know if you can hear me, but I want you to know—"

"Save it," a voice said. Not Eve. Not Skyler.

Light above. An explosion. The Scipios squirmed, twisted to face a new threat.

Prumble dropped through the enemy line, spinning like a top, arms extended. His twin energy beams swept across the assembled foes. Sparks and severed tentacles filled the air. Scipios thrashed under the onslaught as the big man corkscrewed down through the middle of the chamber. Many came away from the wall, falling after him by choice or not. At the last second he rolled and brought his feet about.

Prumble tucked a shoulder, completed his shockingly graceful somersault, and came up firing. Both arms held out, he unleashed twin torrents of energy into the first enemy to hit the floor. The thing vibrated under the power of it and then cracked like an egg before its bits exploded outward.

"Make your lovey-dovey speech to Skyler later, all right?" he said. "We've got work to do."

His presence was like a splash of ice-cold water, or waking suddenly from a bad dream.

The Scipios came at them.

She leapt away as a creature tried to swipe her legs out from under her. The tentacle found air instead before slamming into the far wall. The surface cracked under the impact, the tentacle evidently lodged. Tania raised an arm to shoot, but then the Scipio jettisoned the stuck arm and began to lurch toward her. Lights winked on all across its core, sweeping into focus.

Tania carved a hole through its center and watched as it flopped to the ground, lifeless, trails of smoke curling up from the entry and exit wounds.

Another came toward her. Tania took aim with both arms, but only one fired. Some kind of warning indicator blazed on the display within her visor. *Oh crap,* she thought. The beam from her left arm fizzled and died, luckily after her target had dropped to the floor.

A crushing force around her torso. Tania glanced down to see a tentacle around her waist, drawing tight.

Even with her exotic armored suit the pain instantly grew to something unbearable. Agony beyond imagination as the thing tried to crush her. Then a white-hot line tore at the air beside her head. It swept down and across the mechanical limb, severing it neatly in two. The force against her torso melted away.

"Thank you," Tania said, turning about and moving behind her friend.

Prumble glanced back at her. "What are you doing, hiding?"

The glare she shot back stiffened him. "My weapon wouldn't fire," she replied. "Overheated maybe. Or out of ammo."

"Out of . . ." Prumble paused, glancing down at his arms. "Fucking hell, there's ammo?"

Only then did Tania realize a new glowing path had appeared in her augmented view of things. It went out a rent in the wall to her right. "Follow me!" she shouted, and ran that way.

"Right behind you," Prumble replied, still firing to keep the enemy at bay. Then, "What are these numbers?"

In the heat of battle Tania had failed to notice the timer that had appeared on her visor. Three minutes and twelve seconds left. "A countdown."

"How very Builder of you, Eve!" he roared to the room.

What would happen at zero Tania had no idea.

"Stay on the path," the ship replied, reading her thoughts. "Please hurry."

"She wants us to hurry," she said to her companion, pushing into the darkness beyond the broken wall.

"Figured that bit out myself."

Tania managed a small, private smile. "You saved my life back there. Thank you."

"Dearest Doctor Sharma," Prumble said, "it was my pleasure." He followed her, still firing, ammunition be damned.

There were six of them in the junction. Five in what she'd consider the normal Scipio size—spheres about a meter across with six to ten tentacles writhing about, spiked tips lunging or spraying their smoky needle-clouds.

The sixth, though, was new. It dwarfed the others, five times their size, and not just a ball, either. It had another protrusion on top, like a head, Sam thought, with a large round indentation on the front. What it housed she could not see, but instinct told her either weapon or camera. Either way, she focused on it.

Samantha pulsed her thrusters to adjust her fall and then prepared for impact. A split second before landing she fired, sweeping both arms from front to back. She landed right atop the big one, her beams drawing a neat line almost perfectly along its dorsal bulge. The giant Scipio writhed beneath her, froze, and cracked into two neat halves.

By now she'd seen inside a few of the enemy vessels, after slicing several like geode rocks. Inside, beneath layers of materials she did not exactly recognize, and nestled within a sort of cocoon of gel-like goop, there'd been an actual Scipio. The pilot. Covered in that slime, the fleshy little thing looked like some kind of naked bat with an overdeveloped brain and underdeveloped wings. Tentacles, not unlike those that protruded from the ship it flew, extended from its pinkish body from a hundred different points. Whether they were protruding out from the animal's skin, or attached to it, she had no way to know.

This one, though, the giant, had three Scipios inside, two seated below and one atop, its head behind the lens or scope at the front of that protrusion. She'd melted right through it, the gore dripping away, revolting her.

Sam had no time to be disgusted, couldn't afford it. The image would haunt her later, but right now there was still death to be dealt.

The two other pilots, or whatever they were, had begun to shimmy out of their little interior sacks that served as their seat and display screens. They wiggled and thrashed, muscles not up to the task. Sam wondered if they'd ever been outside their larger casing before, and almost felt sorry for them.

"Jump!" someone shouted. It was Vaughn. Her heart swelled. She leapt and used her thrusters to push herself ten meters up into the shaft she'd just come down.

Vaughn's mortar round finished the job. The whole nasty lot of them went up in a thunderous explosion that swept over Sam's legs. Her suit took the heat and shrapnel impacts in stride.

She fell back to the floor, landed hard, grunting from the sudden spike of pain in her calf. The sight of Vaughn made her forget that. He'd been in the adjoining hall, barricaded behind the remnants of a bulkhead that had collapsed. Smoke and bits of fallen enemies were everywhere.

"Miss me?" she asked him.

"Duck," he replied.

Sam blinked, confused, then dropped to the floor. He fired at the wall behind her, where another Scipio had begun to crawl through a gap cut in the scarred surface.

Sam fired into another one that swept in next. The thing shook under the intensity of her brilliant beam, rocketing backward into some kind of machine room on the pillar of fire. Ten meters in it slammed into a bulkhead and exploded. Next to it, Sam saw the black of space beyond yet another nasty gash in the hull.

"This is much easier with the lights on," she said.

Vaughn, opposite her, said nothing. From his body language, though, she could tell he agreed. His motions were fluid, precise. Just like when he sparred with her. Separated they were formidable, but together? She suddenly regretted pushing him away.

The glowing path Eve had assigned her ended here, at this teeming mass of Scipios that had flooded in through a gaping wound on the *Chameleon*'s hull, all of which now lay dead.

"Look at that hole," Vaughn said.

Sam nodded. "They're getting desperate. Less like surgeons, more like butchers." Eve, the vessel itself, evidently no longer interested them, it seemed. It was the little human vermin squirming around inside that they wanted.

Another popped in, easily dispatched. It was several

seconds before the next came, and it fell with an almost casual blast from Vaughn.

Sam actually had time to catch her breath. "Is it me," she asked, "or are they getting easier to kill?"

"I was just thinking that," he replied, then added, "I mean, even *Tim* was kicking serious ass back there, and it's not just the armor."

"Hmm," Sam said, a lance of fire from her arm slicing through the tentacles of a fresh scout.

"You don't sound happy."

"Starting to think 'trap,'" she said.

"You had to go and say it," Vaughn replied. "Dammit, sweetheart, can't we just have some fun?"

"Sorry."

"Apology accepted."

Sam decided it was time for answers. "Eve?"

"Yes, Samantha."

"Path ends here. What now?"

"Hold this position."

"Why are these things so easy to kill all of a sudden?"

The ship took a split second to reply. "I've been fine-tuning your weapons since first waking. The default configuration was based on centuries-old data on the makeup of Scipio materials, tensor geometry, interior layout, tactics—"

"Blah blah okay, all right. Got it." She glanced at Vaughn.

He shrugged. "Explains Tim the Barbarian, at least."

Sam laughed.

With no fanfare the glowing path appeared again, tracing a line back up the shaft Sam had jumped down to get here. In addition, a clock appeared on her visor. Three minutes, twelve seconds. "Eve? What's this timer?"

"The other reason for your success, Samantha. The bulk of the Swarm has retreated, regrouped, and have now begun a coordinated assault. The next wave of craft will no doubt have altered their defenses and weaponry based on what they have learned of you."

"Oh," she said. "Shit."

"Indeed," Eve replied. "Your path leads to a critical area of the ship that will need to be defended at all costs. Please make your way there now. The second wave of the Scipio Swarm will arrive in exactly three minutes."

Sam shot a glance at Vaughn. She saw in his eyes the same determination and energy that she felt. Her equal.

So what if he was a little too eager, a little too willing to laugh at her jokes and treat Skyler and the others exactly as she did?

On the nights they could lie together, limbs wrapped around each other, sometimes she or he would erupt into laughter as memories of how they met were conjured. He, her jailor. She, the prisoner. Using him, seducing him. Focused entirely on escape. "Love conquers all," he'd joked one night, a week ago, when this "how we first met" story came up.

"Let's go, love," he said, bringing her back to the moment.

"Yeah," she replied. "Be careful."

He narrowed his eyes, one eyebrow darting up.

"Christ. Don't you say that. The moment we start being careful is the moment they win."

"Fine. Be smart, then."

Vaughn seemed on the verge of further calling her on her sentimental crap, but in the end he relented. "Better. Now c'mon. Time to move."

Skyler's path led through a wall where a tiny hole had been punched, presumably, by one of the smaller enemy craft. Wide enough to crawl through were he of a mind to do so, but he was in no such mood.

He placed his hands on either side of the hole and willed energy, recalling Eve's overly long speech on the various capabilities of their armored suits. The beam weapons were great and all, but not when you feared who or what you might cut across on the other side of an obstacle. From his hands, a red glow lit up the dark corridor for a few seconds. Then came the punch. Power flowed out of his hands, knocking chunks of the wall inward and at the same time flinging Skyler backward. His suit compensated, stabilizing him just before he slammed into the opposite wall. A much wider opening now existed in front of him. Debris had exploded inside, creating a cone-shaped pattern of ejecta across a floor of black tiles.

He knew those tiles. This was Prumble's penthouse suite. After coming aboard, each passenger was given a small cabin—little more than Eve's weird approximation of a bed—and no one had done much more than slept there. Except Prumble. The clever bastard had noticed Eve's ability to reshape portions of her interior to accommodate the humans, and then spent one entire night guiding her "hand," so to speak, on the shape, scale, and aesthetic of his personal space. The next morning he'd invited everyone in for a chat, which was of course just a ruse to get them all to marvel at the opulence he now resided in. Prumble assumed the others would all do the same, and he could gloat for being first to the idea. Instead Skyler had put him in charge of coming up with a common, human-friendly look and feel for Eve's labyrinth of hallways and rooms.

As a minor act of revenge Prumble had modeled the ship after Platz Station. Still, it was better than the drab gray monotony Eve favored.

After Eve's last and final reshaping, before being camouflaged, space had finally become a premium, and so now all that remained of Prumble's luxury penthouse suite was a small living area. It lay in disarray, as if hastily abandoned, reminding Skyler of the countless hotel rooms he and Sam had scavenged beyond Darwin's aura.

Chunks of the walls and floor had been destroyed, and not from Skyler's abrupt entry. Four small Scipios were in the process of devouring the room. That's how it looked, at least. Their tentacles were wrapped around bits of chrome railing, or clutching torn halves of black leather cushions. All four had stopped their—search?—of the room when the wall had exploded inward. All four were now staring at Skyler, insofar as these little octopus-like constructs could stare.

"They are gathering DNA samples," Eve said in his ear.

"Say no more," he replied, and started shooting.

His first blast took two in one shot, like piercing meat on a skewer. Glowing holes remained when his beam weapon flickered to a stop, and the Scipios fell to the floor, lifeless. The other two did not advance on him, though. Unlike every enemy he'd so far encountered, these turned and fled.

Presumably, these two had found what they'd come looking for.

"Stop them," Eve urged.

Both enemies swept their tentacles backward, streamlining their profiles. Half their limbs puffed gouts of propellant, which in gravity made them hop across the floor. The other limbs sprayed some kind of ultra-foamy fluid. The bubbles grew to the size of party balloons, and then hardened, forming a lattice. Skyler fired toward one of them, but when his beam struck the bubble lattice the bluish edges only glowed. White then orange then red, spreading away from the point of impact. Absorbing the heat and distributing it.

"They are compensating," Eve said.

"Time for a change of tactics." He surged through the wall and bounded up to the edge of the bubble wall. Skyler punched at the surface of hardened orbs. They shattered like the thinnest glass, or some kind of delicate sugar sculpture.

He took a step back, held one arm up across his brow to shield his visor, and ran forward, then leapt, the thrusters built into his suit powering him forward. The bubbles shattered all around him, raining a fine bluish crystalline powder in his wake. How sharp these were he had no idea, the Builder armor kept him fully protected.

But their sharpness was not the problem. It was visibility. "Eve, help. Which way?"

In addition to his glowing path, two new indicators appeared on his visor. The fleeing enemies. They were smart enough to have diverged. "I've dispatched Tim to intercept the other," Eve said, and one of the blips vanished.

"Tim? Really?"

"His 'head count,' as you call it, is second only to Vaughn's at the moment."

"Well . . . that's a surprise."

"Follow the other, it is more or less on your path already."

"Understood."

Skyler smashed through the odd material in his way simply by ignoring it. He rocketed ahead, trusting in the path Eve had given him. The Scipio DNA scavenger had fled through the same hall the crew had used to move between their cabins. Spacious before, it all felt claustrophobic now, more so when filled with a froth of shimmering glassy bubbles.

The Scipio was ten meters ahead, rounding corners in the same instant Skyler caught sight of it, always one turn ahead. And Eve was right, it did seem to be moving on the same path he was. Almost uncannily so. Did it know?

"What's at the end of this path, Eve?" he asked.

"Me," she said.

* * *

She felt as if trapped in a small capsule dangling from a long cable.

This was, as it turned out, exactly her predicament.

The tentacle poking through the hull wiggled and groped, searching like a snake's tongue through the portions of the *Wildflower* it could reach.

Gloria stood on a bulkhead, Alex Warthen just across from her.

Far below, at the bottom of the ship, Beth and Vanessa cowered in dark corners. The Scipio's tentacle arm was closer to them, and slapped about just centimeters from their tucked-in legs.

Vanessa looked utterly dazed. She'd only just regained consciousness when the intense acceleration had hit, then vanished, then returned as something like Earth normal. And now this intruder, and the expectation that more were right behind it. Vanessa was in no shape to fight it, and Beth certainly looked to be far into the grip of fear.

"We have to get it out of here," she heard herself saying.

"The ship only gave me one shot," Alex replied, holding up his arm. "Wait, where are you going?"

The idea came into her mind as if someone else had thought it for her. She didn't even wait for the full scope of it to form, or the risks. Somewhere inside she knew this was her only chance. She leapt, crossing the hollow central spine of the ship diagonally, down one level to the medical bay. The tentacle poked through a gash in the wall just a meter away, but it had caught the scent of the two women cowering below. Gloria didn't know how long that would last. She had one chance at this. Before leaving Earth, the *Wildflower* had been all but gutted to reach the mass requirement for the Mark 5 imploder, but essential gear had been nonnegotiable. Gloria clenched her teeth as she rummaged, the station mostly unfamiliar to her, usually crewed by her medical officer. Third drawer down she found what she was looking for. Gloria gripped the handle of the blade and whirled. Her eyes locked on where the tentacle emerged from the hull. She leapt at it and stabbed with the surgical knife, careful to hold the blade sideways.

In midair she thought suddenly the plan was total folly. A surgical knife against the vacuum-worthy metallic alien limb that had punctured a meter of heat and radiation shielding. What the hell had she expected to happen?

Just before impact, though, her body remembered what her mind had forgotten. The switch on the blade's handle. The ultracap-powered rapid-heating filament that ran the length of the razor-sharp blade, for instant cauterization. The tip of the blade glowed like an ember just before it slid into the Scipio's tentacle. It sank all the way to the hilt.

Gloria let out an involuntary scream as she at once tried to catch the tentacle lest she fall, and also to cut sideways. The blade cut through so easily it sliced its way out the side of the limb and came free from her hand. She'd only cut through a quarter of it, but that was enough to get the monster's attention. In scantly more than the blink of an eye the tentacle swept back through the ship and out through the gash it had made.

If not for the state of acceleration Gloria would have been sucked against the inner hull. Instead she fell away, landing hard on the deck of the mess one level below, knife clattering against the floor somewhere nearby. The fall knocked the wind out of her and she rolled, curling into a ball and coughing as her lungs tried to reclaim some air. She could hear, above all else, the terrible sighing of air escaping into the vacuum. The last thing any starship captain wants to hear.

Then, abruptly, it stopped. Gloria forced herself to roll onto her back, ready to face the new tentacle that had surely taken the place of the last. But there was no replacement. There was Alex Warthen, his back pressed against the opening in the hull. Held there by the vacuum. He glanced at her, his grin a perfect expression of "I can't believe that actually worked."

Gloria laughed, despite everything. The change in his expression sobered her. This wasn't some great victory. This wasn't the end. Another tentacle would punch through, if not an entire Scipio. They were truly lost; it was only a matter of time.

"What now?" Gloria asked him.

Somehow Alex managed a shrug, the minute motion causing him great pain. "See to your friends. Then set that self-destruct, would you? I think you lied about it earlier, and I'm glad, but now? I don't want to become a meal for these creatures."

She nodded at him, held his gaze for a second, then rolled and found the ladder that led down to engineering.

Beth and Vanessa were seated side by side, Beth with one arm around the woman from history.

With shaking hands, Vanessa reached up and raised the visor of her helmet. Then she gave a slight, almost imperceptible nod.

"Gloria," came a voice. A woman's voice, from Vanessa's suit, though Vanessa's mouth had not moved.

The ship spun about, still dangling from the almost severed umbilical. Probably another Scipio grabbing on to the hull. The sudden motion tossed everything not secure about the cramped space.

"Gloria," the suit said again.

"I'm here," she said. "Who am I speaking with?"

"I am Eve, the Builder. Alex Warthen is not responding to me. I have an urgent task and you are the only one who can perform it."

"How is it that he's even here, Eve?" Vanessa suddenly blurted out, not quite as incoherent as her posture let on. "He died. I saw it happen."

"There is no . . . explain," she said, her voice cutting out briefly with a burst of digital noise. "Hear me, Gloria . . . to the airlock."

Vanessa's arm raised as if of its own accord, her index finger pointing upward at the door that led outside.

"The airlock? What do I do when I get there? Eve?"

Several seconds of dreadful silence passed. Gloria shook her head, and began to tap through the menus on her interface that would send the *Wildflower* up in a nuclear inferno.

Finally, the alien ship spoke. "Sever . . . umbilical when . . . reaches precisely zero."

A timer appeared on Vanessa's mask, writ backward but readable enough, counting down from fifty-three seconds.

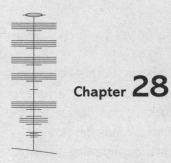

Chapter 28

THE *WILDFLOWER* SWAYED back and forth as the scouts crawled across the outer hull, seeking a way in. The motion slammed Gloria Tsandi into a wall, bringing a hairline crack across her visor. The sight of it caused her breath to catch in her throat, her heart to flutter. That visor was the only thing that would keep her alive if another hull breach occurred. The ship still held some air, but for how long?

Alex Warthen was still pinned to the hull, blocking the existing hole. His limbs spasmed now and then, weak and pitiful.

She climbed on, her eyes searching for Xavi, lost in the confusion. For a gut-wrenching second she thought maybe he'd been sucked right through the wound Alex Warthen now plugged, but then his foot caught her eye. He was up at the bridge.

"Xavi?" she called out.

No reply. His foot remained utterly still.

God, no, she thought. *Not him. I need him. I can't do this without him.*

The umbilical. The ship's order. *Sever ... umbilical ...*

Gloria glanced back at Vanessa. Forty-one seconds left on the big timer splashed across her visor. Her eyes flicked down to her own timer, the one that marked the ship's self-destruct. Forty-four seconds. Jesus.

Gloria whirled and climbed on, ignoring the slight stir of limbs from Alex Warthen. He must be in utter agony, held so. She sensed a certain goodness in him, buried deep under all that he'd endured.

Why sever the umbilical? she wondered. To free the larger ship of the *Wildflower*'s burden. Had to be. Gloria couldn't think of any other reason why the much larger craft would care, one way or the other. It must need to shed weight in order to outrun the Scipios. The circular explanation, linking back with the *Wildflower*'s own diet before starting this mission, bewildered her.

The timing, though ... the timing bothered her. It was as if the Builder AI could puzzle out the utterly chaotic swing and twist the *Wildflower* now thrashed in and knew the perfect moment to let go. Perhaps true. It was only math, after all, not accounting for the actions of the Scipios now crawling over the hull. Maybe it understood them well enough, too.

Thirty-four seconds left when she reached the central hub of the ship, and the inner airlock door. Gloria glanced out, half-expecting to see a Scipio's lens peering back at her.

Instead she saw the twisted remains of the tube.

A Scipio had sliced it open. She remembered Alex Warthen firing that white-hot beam at it. The ship now held on to the hull of the larger Builder vessel by a thin reinforced filament that housed electrical and data cables. That one little thread, thankfully made from materials developed after researching the Builder space elevator in Darwin, held strong despite carrying the *Wildflower*'s entire weight.

She grabbed hold of the manual release and almost turned it. The ship's words stilled her hand. *Precisely zero.*

Gloria glanced down to the tail end of the ship, where Vanessa lay. She couldn't see the numbers from here, across this distance and through her own cracked visor.

Her visor. She had her own timer, three seconds longer. She'd sever the link at three seconds.

Twenty-seven remained. Twenty-four until she'd turn the handle.

The ship vibrated. There was a deafening thud from somewhere nearby. Gloria grabbed hold of a stabilizer rung as her body was buffeted by a shock wave. Only the pressure went on. She glanced down and almost cried out. A silvery tentacle had wrapped around her midsection. Horrified, she followed its length back to a new hull puncture, coming in through the medical deck.

"It's over," she whispered, as the limb tightened around her and began to pull. The needle tip twisted, turning toward her like a snake preparing to strike.

Gloria tried to hold on. Tightened her hand with all the strength left in her, but it was not enough. One hand slid off the umbilical disengage, the other held on a moment longer before those tired fingers betrayed her as well. She flew from the airlock door, across the ship, and slammed into the curved inner hull with a teeth-rattling clang. Stars filled her vision. The hairline crack on her visor widened, spidered, then the entirety of its surface became a mosaic of chaotic squares.

The needle-tipped Scipio arm plunged into her calf. Gloria screamed, and screamed, and screamed.

The needle came out. Gloria Tsandi, breathing hard, tried to ignore the white-hot agony coming from her leg. She blinked tears away and threw all her mental capacity toward the one task she had. Sever the umbilical. Let the Builder ship go before the self-destruct comes.

But how? She was pinned. There couldn't be more than fifteen seconds left.

She glanced up, fighting to see through the web of cracked glass. Where Xavi's foot had been she now saw only darkness. He'd moved. That was good. "Xavi? Talk to me."

A crackle of static, the effect of a long hard exhale on the suit's microphone. "Here," he managed groggily.

"I need your help. I need you now."

"I . . ."

"Can you climb to the airlock?"

"No," he said, the word full of anguish, defeat.

Gloria opened her mouth, ready to plead, or say goodbye.

"I can," a voice said. A woman's voice. Beth Lee.

She climbed past Gloria.

* * *

The shells of at least a half-dozen Scipio ships lay in ruin.

Prumble kicked one, and watched with mild disgust as a chunk of the thing slid away. "Eww," he said. "It's like looking at the cross section of a rotten Scotch egg."

Tania leaned in, nose wrinkled, studying the mess. The shell was thick, made of layer upon thin layer of various metals and other materials she did not recognize. Composites of various color and apparent hardness. Then came sections of what she had to assume were support systems. Air processing, fuel, computers, and all the tubing and cables required to link them all together.

In the larger chunk she could see the dead body of the Scipio within. Part of it, anyway. This was not a "ship" in the sense that a being could roam around inside, but rather an extension of the pilot's body. More like a space suit, now that she thought about it, though that was also not quite right. Something symbiotic.

"Hard to tell where the machine stops and the body begins," she said.

The limbs did not end in digits but in segmented, metallic tubes that extended out and merged into the support structures within the interior "wall." The face was hidden behind a similar, though much larger, contraption. Smaller tubes, or perhaps merely electrical or data cables, poked into the pale flesh at various points all along the folded body.

"Nasty little creature," Prumble replied.

A soup of gray goop coated the smooth skin. Tania

leaned closer and saw flecks of white, blue, and black swimming around within the fluid. Whether insects or nanites, she had no idea. Then the answer came to her. "Engineered virus," she said to her companion, who had come to stand beside her.

He knelt and reached out.

"Don't," she said, "touch it."

"I won't. I didn't!" Still, he did not lean away. "It looks like it's lived its whole life in here. Like this vessel is the real body. I wonder if it even knew it had hands and feet. A face."

"It's fascinating," she said, then at his exasperated expression added, "in a way."

Prumble stood abruptly. "We need to keep moving," he said, an edge to his voice that raised the hair on Tania's arms. "Not the time to study them."

"Agreed," she said immediately, standing.

He looked at her, surprised.

"We're well past the scientific analysis phase of this mission," she said, gesturing to the violence and gore all around them.

"Well said. Right, then, shall we?"

"Lead on," Tania said.

He powered ahead, following the path. Tania forced herself to keep up. Her throat was dry, her stomach empty. The buzz of adrenaline had faded, leaving her jittery and tired. She glanced at the timer that seemed to float before her.

Forty seconds remained.

She pushed harder, momentum bolstered by a sudden drop in gravity. The ship, easing back on its relentless pace. On purpose, or had the engines been hit? Tania forced herself to focus. She had to trust Eve. They all did. This place was her body, these tubes and cables her veins. She knew what was happening around them, and how best to fend off this infection of Scipios.

Tania hoped so, at any rate. Trusting the ship had become a lot harder since Alex Warthen had risen from the dead.

Prumble built up a lead on her. They were running—hopping, more like—down one of Eve's ubiquitous spiral hallways. Signs of battle were everywhere now. Twice Tania passed gaping holes in the wall that looked right out into empty space. The void. She saw nothing out there. It was simply too vast. But they were out there, somewhere, in the dark. Gathering. In thirty-four seconds they would come again, tactics revised, goals reevaluated.

Movement ahead pulled her attention back to the task. Prumble had skidded to a stop. She pulled up beside him.

On the wall nearby was the airlock the other human crew had evidently entered through. Just a circular white door, currently open, surrounded by a hardened foam. Crude but effective.

She glanced through.

The umbilical tube was a shredded mess. Something, and it didn't take much imagination to picture what, had tried to slice the thing in half. And it had almost succeeded, if not for the spine conduit of support cables that ran the length of the thing. Useless as an umbilical now. In fact, all it seemed to be doing was keeping the other ship from floating away. Amazing that it could hold the weight. The impressively sleek Earth vessel dangled from the opposite end, shifting and rotating chaotically as it played out the motion imparted by half a dozen Scipios crawling around on its hull.

"Do we help them?" Prumble asked.

She wanted to, but there was no way to predict how to approach it. One miscalculated leap and it might twist or lurch and slam into her, sending her cartwheeling out into space. And then there were the Scipios to worry about. Tania glanced at Prumble, then at the glowing path. It did not lead out of the ship and along the umbilical, but continued on down the spiral hallway. Wherever Eve needed them, it wasn't here. She tugged at Prumble's arm, nodding toward the path. "I guess not," she said, answering his question.

"Time's almost out," he observed, still staring at the ship and its dire circumstance.

She could see the frustration in his face. The annoyance at being only a chess piece, unable to comprehend the meta-game being played.

"Come on," she said. "Let's go."

He nodded absently, and they were off again.

Twenty-four seconds left.

The hall led around only one more curve before ending abruptly at a chamber barely tall enough for her to stand in. Prumble had to stoop. Dark gray walls were angled from a wide ceiling down to a floor barely two meters in diameter. Two iris doors were the only adornments, on adjacent walls, with even smaller spherical chambers inside each. The glowing path ended right between the two doors.

Something about the space, and the position of the doors, bothered Tania. She felt uneasy, off-kilter, as if gravity were once again shifting unpredictably to some new vector. But the gravity had faded entirely now. The *Chameleon* was once again coasting.

"Eve?" Tania asked. "What now?"

No reply.

Tania glanced inside one of the iris doors. Within was a small spherical chamber, deeply cushioned in some kind of reddish material that reminded her of suede. At the center, a waist-high black pedestal stood, cold and ominous. Carved into its surface were familiar geometric patterns. A miniature version of the aura towers that had protected Belém from the plague on Earth.

Tania's path changed again. The glowing line led into the small sphere-shaped room.

"Inside," Eve said, "quickly now."

She glanced behind and saw Prumble moving to the other door. He gripped the edge of the chamber's entrance and hauled himself inside, squirming around his own small aura tower and settling into the cushions as naturally as if it were his own ground car.

Tania remained in the larger chamber, staring at the two iris doors, not happy that they were being split between the two rooms but finding no energy to question Eve's plan. The timer, at sixteen seconds, left little room for debate. Still, she hesitated.

It was then she spotted the problem with the room.

The angles were all wrong. Not by much, but once she'd come to the realization the differences added up. The two iris doors were at different heights—one almost flush with the floor, the other six or seven centimeters up. The wall her door graced was sloped slightly, where Prumble's was perfectly vertical.

Why? For the life of her, she could see no purpose to the differences. Yet they must be for a reason.

Ten seconds.

Nine.

"What's this room for, Eve?" she asked.

"Pl-pl-please . . . —inside, Tania," she replied, ignoring the query.

Tania pushed into the small sphere and saw that a portion of it had reshaped itself, bulged outward on two sides and pinched inward in the center to form a kind of seat. Reluctantly, she floated into the molded cushions, turning as she went.

Four seconds.

Secured, she glanced up, hoping for a reassuring smile from Prumble in his chamber across the tiny hallway that connected them.

What she saw instead was the iris door pressing closed. The parts met in the center noiselessly.

"Prumble!" she shouted, but it was no use.

There was a sharp hiss and a dozen red orbs appeared across the door's surface and began to inflate. More cushions, totally surrounding her now. Pressing in, pressing all the way in to fill the emptiness in the volume.

She knew, then, what this place was.

* * *

The glowing path led to a spot Sam knew well. The very tip of the *Chameleon,* where she and Vaughn had crawled back inside as the strange, beetlelike creatures had scurried after them, coating the ship's exterior. For all the good that had done them.

"It's quiet," Vaughn said.

Sam rolled her eyes. "Don't say it—"

"Too quiet."

"Damn you."

He shot her a half-grin. It faded only a second later. "I'll go first? For once? Please?"

"Fine," she said.

The timer on her visor ticked down. Twelve seconds.

Vaughn advanced to the iris door that led into the tiny chamber at Eve's nose. Sam fell in behind, ready for battle, hoping Eve's plan was to let them outside. Give them all the space they needed to fight. Take the battle to the enemy for once.

Her companion leaned inside. When nothing happened, he put one hand out to steady himself. The sensation of gravity had dwindled and then vanished moments earlier, without explanation. For some reason, Eve was no longer trying to outrun the enemy. Vaughn hovered before the circular door. And waited. Three precious seconds ticked away, feeling like much more than that. It *was* too quiet, Sam thought. "Eve—" she started.

"One moment," the ship replied.

"We don't have—"

Sam heard a sound behind her. She glanced back in time to see the hallway they'd climbed to get here was now barricaded by a flat, gray panel. She turned to point this out to Vaughn. Eve must have repaired her ability to modify her interior, and not a moment too soon.

The panels of the hatch before Vaughn slid silently away, revealing the semi-conical chamber at the very tip of the vessel. A hole had been torn or cut away from the ceiling, revealing the naked vacuum of space beyond. Sam could see the brilliant star of Kepler-22, blinding for an instant until her helmet compensated. Much closer was a cloud of debris.

No, she realized. Not a cloud. A *swarm.*

"Vaughn—" she said. The name died on her lips.

Out there, in the void, the counterattack had begun.

Three . . .

Two . . .

One . . .

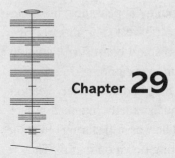

Chapter 29

ZERO.

Each Scipio ship turned into a blazing star, lighting up the blackness of space like fireworks. Their engines flared in hues of white and yellow, dazzling, even painful, to look at. But Sam kept watching. She wanted to count them, but gave up as the lights became a galactic band stretching across the field of view afforded her by the hole in Eve's hull.

Hundreds, easily, and all riding plumes of nuclear fire as they raced toward the *Chameleon* with some new tactic in mind.

"Now it gets fun," she said, a bit annoyed at the trepidation in her voice.

"What the hell are we supposed to do?" Vaughn asked. "Jump out there?"

As if in answer, the room around them began to change. Little bubbles of orange appeared in a grid pattern all across the walls, floor, and even the damaged ceiling. The blobs began to spread outward, flattening.

Joining with one another. Sam took a chance and poked one section. Despite the spongy appearance, the material was quite firm. Like a life vest. The thought of it took her back to riding in a small boat, surrounded by problem children at the summer camp, taking them to see the crocs, making sure they had their safety gear on.

Yes. A life vest. Pretty much exactly like that, in fact. Sam looked at Vaughn, but he was still staring out at the fleet of Scipio vessels bearing down on them. "They're starting to spread out. Uncanny how they move like that. So coordinated."

"Vaughn . . ."

He glanced at her, then at the space around them. "The hell?"

The orange material had smeared across everything now, and had started to even out and form ergonomic contours. Seats, shaped not unlike the dropship couches on the *Melville*.

"Please prepare for a high-velocity maneuver," Eve said in her more mechanical tone. The words repeated a few seconds later.

A new timer had begun, replacing the old one.

"What the hell is this, Eve?" Vaughn asked.

The answer was no answer at all, save repetition. "Please prepare for a high-velocity maneuver."

A nod passed between Sam and Vaughn. She took the couch to her left, while he pulled into the other.

"No straps," Vaughn observed. He started to say more, but his voice abruptly vanished.

Sam's heart lurched. She half-expected to see him impaled by some round fired through the opening in

the ceiling. A sniper shot from far away. But he looked
fine. In fact, he was still speaking, she just couldn't
hear him.

"Eve? Something is wrong with our suits, I can't
hear Vaughn."

The cushioned foam near her wrists began to push
outward, then around. Sam resisted the urge to pull
away, deciding this must be Eve's version of a seat harness. She felt similar movement around her ankles,
even as she watched the material wrap around her
wrists and then tighten. More pressure at various points
along her body. Her chest, stomach, thighs, and forehead were all wrapped in bands of the orange foam
until she became completely immobile.

"Eve?"

No response.

Vaughn was shouting at her now. He'd been similarly
secured to his chair. She mouthed, *I'm okay,* to him.
Then, *Relax.*

He gritted his teeth, his eyes fixed on hers.

Movement caught Sam's eye. Not from above, but
below. The iris door had pulsed open. She hoped to see
Skyler come through, or Prumble. Even Tim. Anyone,
really. But instead a column-shaped *something* drifted
into the room. It reminded her, terrifyingly, of the pedestal she'd seen in that pit below Old Downtown in
Darwin. Only, there was no alien ship resting atop this
thing.

The thing was not smooth, but was utterly covered in
small hatches and protrusions. A few scattered lights
winked on across its surfaces.

"—fuck is that?" Vaughn asked, communication abruptly restored.

"I hear you now," she blurted.

"What's going on?"

"I don't know. Eve? Eve?!"

The ship remained silent. Or, Sam thought with growing concern, the ship was dead.

The object grew limbs. A network of supports, gliding out in all directions to attach to connectors on the walls that had not been there a second earlier. Unable to move, Sam watched in horror as several tubes extended from one compartment on the device and connected to protrusions on her suit. Little valves that had not been there a moment before.

"Stay calm, stay calm," a voice said. Her own voice, she realized.

Beth reached the airlock door with only seconds left, gripped the handle.

"Time, Vanessa?"

"Eight seconds!" the woman below shouted.

Eleven to self-destruct. Gloria Tsandi pursed her lips, biting back the years of training and all the promises she'd made to her superiors.

From memory, she navigated the fractured menu options on her broken HUD. Crew authorizations. Xavi Decklan, Navigator. Temporary command. Confirm. Confirm.

"What—" he started.

"No time. Pause the self-destruct," she said, and

hoped he could find it. Only a few seconds left. "Then be ready to get us out of here."

A shape flew past her gaze. Vanessa rocketing up toward the bridge at breakneck speed. As the woman passed Beth she shouted, *"Now!"*

Beth turned the release handle. Gloria could hear the clunk as it slid into position.

Null gravity returned instantly. Gloria counted to three in her mind, her breath held.

Instead of death in a nuclear fireball, she heard the voice of her friend and navigator.

"Buckle up," Xavi said. "We're getting out of here."

Gloria winced as the Scipio tentacle tightened even more. The creature on the hull, trying to hang on. "Beth," she said. "Help."

The engineer had been glued to the airlock window, enthralled with what Gloria could only imagine was a spectacular scene of devastation outside. After a moment the woman turned and flew over to her. She studied the alien limb. "I can't . . . I don't have anything."

"Knife," Gloria managed, pointing vaguely toward where she'd dropped it. She could hardly breathe now. The tentacle wouldn't let her. "Hurry."

There was a brief press of motion to one side as Xavi began to maneuver the ship. It didn't last. Gloria expected a hard acceleration to follow, but nothing else happened. "Xavi?"

"Not yet," he said.

"What are you waiting for?" The words took the last of her breath. Beth reappeared at her side, knife in hand. For a second she studied the silvery tube before her, then gave a small shrug and stabbed hard into the thickest section of it.

Nothing. Beth, face contorted by her own exertions and the spider cracks across Gloria's visor, gave it a twist with all her strength, letting out an almost child-like roar as she heaved on the handle.

There was a whoosh as the tentacle released and slid away, back through its hole.

Gloria Tsandi heaved in a breath. Her stomach tee-tered on the edge of revolt, but that was the least of her concerns just now. Near tears from the brush with suf-focation, she hauled herself over to the airlock window and peered out.

The cable conduit snaked around, now free but still connected at the far end to the Builder ship, groping out toward the *Wildflower* like a ghostly hand. Shreds of white fabric were all that remained of the tube itself, looking like the corroded ribs of some savaged fish, torn up by circling sharks.

Beyond, against the black of space, she saw a cloud of Scipio scouts bearing down on them. Even as she watched they began to flare, bright with nuclear thrust, as they slowed themselves in the instant before reach-ing their prey. Most were bound for the ravaged, desic-cated Builder ship. But plenty were angling for the *Wildflower,* too. She wondered how many more were coming in at angles she could not see. They'd arrived in force now, and would not be denied.

Gloria suddenly realized with cold horror that the *Wildflower* wasn't moving. She'd given Xavi a command, then seen Vanessa fly the length of the ship toward the bridge.

"Xavi! What's wrong?"

A tiny lateral thrust kicked in. Then another. Corrective movements.

"What are you doing, Xavi? Get us away from here!"

"Not sure," he said. "Vanessa said—"

"You're the one in command. *Go!*"

Her navigator must have had his finger on the button. As soon as she said it she was flung bodily into the bulkhead, then across to the other side, as thrusters killed the errant rotation and turned the *Wildflower* to face away from the Builder vessel.

Through some miracle of subconscious thought, Gloria found herself secured to one wall, hands and feet shoved through the ubiquitous stabilizing rungs that studded the interior surfaces of the ship. A split second later, she felt herself become heavy. Very heavy. All she could do was lie against the wall, now the floor, and groan as Xavi piled on the g forces. Gloria warred for consciousness, knowing this would last perhaps hours until they ran out of fuel, but then, abruptly, the acceleration stopped. "What's wrong?" she asked. "Why did you stop?"

"Uh," Xavi replied. "Vanessa's orders."

"What orders? What the hell does she know?"

"She . . . she said she's following the glowing path."

"The *what*?"

"Here we go, boss. Get ready."

Glowing path?

Something happened. Something big. The whole ship screeched and rattled, and Gloria felt as if an elephant had sat on her.

Someone screamed. Maybe it was her.

Then, blackness.

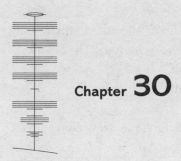

Chapter **30**

The *Chameleon*
6.AUG.3911 (Earth Actual)

SILENCE CONSUMED HIM. The insanity of battle fell away as Skyler Luiken entered a room he'd never seen before.

The secret heart of the ship.

Or perhaps it was more apt to consider it the brain.

He glanced around, taking it in. There were no walls, per se, just a cavity where cables and conduits of all sizes converged on a large, bulbous pocket, each terminating in a canopy of circular slabs that danced with flickering laser light of every imaginable color.

From these thousands of disks, softly glowing hair-like wires, fine as silk strands, curved and looped in elegant arcs down to a single, monolithic black tower in the very center of the room.

Eve hovered before this tower. The projected entity, the embodiment of the ship. Its high mind, as she called it. Her face, still somehow reminding him in some way of each member of the crew, held no expression at all.

The room became still, the silence almost oppressive.

"Why did you bring me here?" he asked, still holding the edge of the wall where he'd entered. "The others . . . the fighting, it still goes on."

"Come closer," Eve said.

"Answer first."

"I brought you here to defend me. Now come closer, we have much to discuss."

Skyler considered arguing. He was either here to defend her, or have a chat, not both. Not with everything going on around them. But something about the tone of her voice—the barest hint of conspiracy, of intrigue—made him push off from the wall and glide across to her.

Though he had no way to stop himself, nothing to touch or grab, he stopped all the same, via some invisible shift in the currents of air, perhaps, assuming the room held any. The net effect was he found himself floating before her, unable to move. The thrusters in his suit were suddenly offline.

"Tania's plan failed," Eve said.

He bristled. "Don't pin this on her, dammit. The plan was fine, and we all agreed to it, you included. Everything was fine until that ship from Earth found us. Who could have predicted that? That they'd beat us here?"

"My wording choice was poor. I simply meant the plan has failed. A new plan was needed."

"Was?" he asked. "Already got one, then?"

"We initiated it a few seconds after you woke me."

He made a show of looking around. "Doesn't seem to

be working so well. The ship is a mess. We're scattered. I don't even know what the hell kind of shape my crew is in because you've isolated our communications."

"Everyone is alive and exactly where they need to be, except the one called Jared Larsen."

Skyler narrowed his eyes. "About that. What the hell were he and Alex even doing here? Alive? You kept them hidden from us."

"I find it interesting that you never even inquired as to the state of those on the losing side of your battle in the key room."

"You said the dead were jettisoned."

"They were. Those I was unable to revive."

"Seriously, Eve? We're going to get into semantics on this? You kept them alive, you hid them from us. Why? Who else is among them? If Grillo is here—"

The hologram shook her head. "We have insufficient time for this. Please know that I only kept Alex and Jared. I needed them in order to protect you and the others."

"Not good enough—"

Eve blinked, and Skyler's words died on his still moving lips. He could hear himself only as one could hear a distant conversation, several rooms away.

"Please," she said, "listen."

Skyler swallowed his sudden anger. There was real urgency in her voice, of that he had no doubt.

Only, Eve said nothing. She just stared at him.

"I'm listening," he said, though he could still not hear himself clearly. Some kind of noise cancellation built into his helmet negated the sound.

She seemed frozen in place. The tiny, almost imperceptible movements that made her seem so human had vanished.

A sudden force pushed Skyler forward, toward her. Some invisible wind or gas. He drifted, unable to stop himself. And he flinched when his face neared Eve's. He passed right through, of course, and could have sworn he heard her whisper something to him in a language he did not know.

Behind her was the tower, only it had opened at its base. Inside was some kind of reddish-orange chamber, and it did not look welcoming. Skyler went to throw his arms wide, to stop himself at the precipice, but the suit would not allow it. His limbs were frozen, the black armor utterly rigid. He slid through the door and then his body rotated 180 degrees. Eve hadn't moved. She still stood, staring at the empty space where he'd been. Then, her form flickered and dimmed before vanishing altogether.

The door irised closed.

She's dead, he thought, a chill coursing through his body. The Scipios must have found a way to power her off. They were trapping him in here. This tower was his prison cell.

Skyler's limbs moved without his consent, forcing him into a seated position as he reached the back wall of the tiny chamber. The red-orange material around him began to puff up, inflating like quickfoam. The material pressed in all around him, forcing his body to hold its position, not that he could have moved the armor if he'd wanted to. His view became nothing but red as the material formed around his visor. He was blind and could not move.

"Eve!" he shouted. At least his voice worked again.

His vision blacked out. Or, rather, the visor, for he could still see the faint blur of the bridge of his nose.

A new view appeared. The room he'd been in. Eve, frozen in place like a mannequin, the glowing fibrous filaments of the room still undulating in brightness and color. He realized he was seeing a remote view from outside the tower. He found if he turned his head his view changed, not unlike a sensory chamber.

"Eve," he tried, to no avail.

The glowing fibers began to brighten. Power, he imagined, surging into them. A system overload, or something like it. The whole room seemed to vibrate with the influx of energy. Blinding, pulsating light filled every corner. And Eve, at the center of it all, shone in pure yellow-white glare.

There was a flash. Something purple, pearlescent. He'd seen that color before. But in a heartbeat it was gone, and then everything around him exploded. He heard it, saw it, but felt nothing at all.

The brilliance around him shattered and shot outward in a million chunks of pure energy and heat, Skyler one of them. He was not at the center of this grand display, but a part of the ejected debris. He hurtled into space, so fast his body should have been crushed instantly, though he felt nothing whatsoever. He only saw.

Along the perimeter of the expanding debris cloud came dozens, then hundreds of smaller explosions.

Scores of Scipio scouts, all closing in for the kill, utterly consumed in fire. The shock wave tore through their numbers, vaporizing everything in its path. In an instant the feeding frenzy died in a terrible, all-consuming hell.

My crew! Oh God, my crew! Where—

Farther out Skyler saw anomalies in the chaos. Huge chunks of the *Chameleon,* embroiled in flame, spreading out in a cone somehow aimed in-system. And among that fractured debris, something else. Pearlescent purple globes, flying outward with the rain of fire. And farther still, as if riding the leading edge of the titanic blast, Gloria Tsandi's ship, tumbling out of control.

One by one the purple spheres flickered, then vanished. Left behind were . . . shapes, racing away from the center of the explosion at phenomenal speed. Dark missiles, hidden among the rest of the wreckage. The ubiquitous matte-gray surfaces the Builders used. Pods, like his? Aura towers, like they'd delivered to Brazil?

"Each of those is like yours," Eve said, startling him. Her voice sounded as if inside his own skull, flawless and crystal clear.

Skyler could still not move his helmet, but he could look around a bit. Not that it mattered. His entire body was still encased in the red-orange cushioning, which was probably what had somehow absorbed the forces being unleashed around him at the moment of the blast.

"What happ—" he started to ask her, but Eve spoke over him. A prerecorded message.

"Tania," she said, and a faint square appeared, overlaid around one of the dark shapes. Each name she said produced another marker. "Prumble, Sam and Vaughn, Tim."

What of Vanessa? he thought, with dread.

"Vanessa is aboard the ship from Earth," Eve said, either anticipating his thought or somehow reacting to it. "I did what I could for them. They may not survive this, however. They are not protected as you are."

He wanted to reach out toward the ship. To fly there and help. Skyler wanted to grab all of them and pull them back. But he could not. He was trapped in here.

"I carefully positioned each of you," Eve went on. "My destruction was inevitable, therefore I harnessed it, turned it into a last chance for the mission."

"Fuck the mission," Skyler growled.

"Each of you was expelled along a precise vector, your pods hidden among my debris. With luck each of you will end up more or less where you need to be to accomplish your part of the greater effort. You will be alone, Skyler. You must remain focused and find your task. Only one of you will be able to communicate with everyone else, and they will have to decide what to share and when. A necessary precaution."

Neil knew. Tania's words, so long ago. Neil Platz had gained some insider knowledge of the Builders' plan, well before the Darwin Elevator arrived at Earth, and told no one. Instead, he used that information to maneuver into position to benefit most from the arrival of the Elevator and subsequent plague.

With this came an unsettling thought, and once considered he knew he would never shake it: Had Eve, indeed the Builders, known this moment would come all along? How much of this calamity had already been foreseen and planned for?

The recording went on, undeterred. "You are fighting for more now than just my Creators. You are fighting for Earth. The arrival of Gloria's ship means the Scipios are now aware of you and know humanity possesses the second piece of the puzzle that is universal dominance. The Scipios have immortality already. Now they know that instantaneous travel between stars is within their grasp. With both they will be unstoppable."

With each passing second Eve's rain of debris spread farther out, and Skyler drifted farther away from his companions, all streaking like comets toward some unseen goal. Carthage, that's what Gloria said humanity had named the world the Builders came from.

All except Gloria, in her wreck of a ship. Which veered away and became too small to see even with the marker his visor provided.

His heart skipped a beat when he realized Gloria's ship would collide with one of the moons of Carthage. Skyler stared at the moon as it receded into the distance, memorizing where they would crash, so he could go back for them. Even if just to bury Vanessa. He owed her that much, and more. He'd even bury Alex Warthen.

Alex. Hell. Skyler did not know what to think about him and his presence here. Twice he'd been an adversary, choosing to follow orders first from Blackfield and then the madman Grillo. Yet he'd paid the price for that, in death, literally at the hands of Prumble. Only, Eve had somehow healed him. Who knew what she'd put him through in the time since. Eve called it experimentation; Alex had called it torture. Skyler could hardly fault him for being more than a little pissed off when he'd escaped during the silent run. If they survived their encounter with that moon, he only hoped Vanessa could talk him into being an ally. If anyone could, surely it was she.

His view turned as the tower he flew inside slowly rotated around.

Ahead loomed the captive world of Carthage. A bluegreen marble, so like Earth, yet almost completely obscured by a network of satellites and space stations. Dozens of massive orbitals ringed the equator, connected to the ground by space elevators that glowed like gigantic searchlights. The space stations formed an artificial ring at the halfway point of the elevator cords, where gravity would be nullified. Moreover, they were linked via some kind of visible energy grid, meshed with thousands of other, smaller installations all around the planet. The net effect was a sort of elongated sphere, the structure of which was primarily beams of energy.

Massive spacecraft—cargo ships, he presumed—were moored at facilities along the main equatorial ring, out at the counterweighted ends of the space elevators where centrifugal force would give the sensation of gravity pointing away from the planet below. Behemoths carrying, according to Tania, the captive bodies of the dual-brained Creators, ready to serve as intermediaries for a mind-transfer process the Scipios held a monopoly on.

As Skyler's tower raced in toward one of these outer

shipyards, he came to another realization. There were hardly any small ships here, in close to the world. Eve must have realized this flaw in the Scipios' defenses. They'd put everything out at the perimeter of the solar system, ready to blockade any incursions. But Eve's explosion, her sacrifice, had not only annihilated every scout in the area, but propelled Skyler and the others at a speed the Scipios could not match. A head start, though just how long it would last he had no idea. Surely the Swarm ships would have sent signals, unless they were unable to differentiate the towers from all the other ejecta.

He zoomed closer to Carthage. As the world began to fill his view of space, the first chunks of Eve's exploded hull began to slam into the world and the space stations above it. Some exploded while still well outside the area, shot down by weapons too distant for his eyes to perceive. Tiny bursts of fire and shrapnel began to flicker all across his view like fireworks. Eve had hidden them among this, and it was working. Skyler looked around for the others, but saw none of their markers now. No Tania, no Sam. Nobody. "Shit. No, *no*! Eve, where—"

"There is one last thing," Eve said over him, a terrible reminder that this was a recorded speech. She could not hear him, could not know the dread that gripped him now that the others had vanished from his display. Skyler swallowed. He forced the last bit of trust he could find for this alien intelligence. They must still be out there. They had to be. Eve's voice went on. Calm, oblivious. "I know you disapprove of what I did with the others. Alex and Jared. But I did learn something that may be important. A difference between immune and nonimmune."

Could he have stopped her voice there, he would have. He didn't want to know. Didn't want to be the one with secret knowledge.

"In one of the experiments, I gave their brains the exact same stimulus, and yet their minds produced different hallucinations. The immune saw a beach, the other a mountain ridge. I do not know why, but this may be useful to you."

He barely heard her. In the chaotic rain of Eve's debris, he spotted something familiar. A tower-shaped object like this, not tumbling like the rest. One of his friends. They had made it through, after all!

Fear crushed his mind as he understood the object's impending doom. A Scipio station, right in its path. He watched in horror, utterly helpless. The station was angular, like a hundred metal boxes welded haphazardly together, and studded with towers and antennae. Lights glowed in thousands of windows of uniform size. He wondered how many Scipios were looking out those windows now, at the projectile bearing down on their habitat. Were they aware of it? How visible was he on their version of radar? Then, only seconds before impact, a purplish sphere blipped into existence around that tower. As Skyler watched, the newly enclosed object collided with the Scipio station, sending brilliant light and a shower of debris out into space.

And then it was all behind him. He'd passed right through that upper layer of Scipio tech. The hue across his visor changed; his tower was now similarly encased. Everything outside appeared to slow down. Skyler could only watch as his own tower approached the target Eve had guided him to. Part of him had to admire the AI's precision in all this. Their paths during the battle had taken each of them to a specific point within her hull so that her final explosion would propel them to a pinpoint location millions of kilometers away.

He watched, utterly transfixed, as he approached the atmosphere. Thick milky clouds rushed toward him and then enveloped his entire view. Seconds later his vessel punched out the other side, but to his dismay no surface was visible below. The air was a choking haze of particulate, limiting his view to a scant tens of meters.

"Good luck, Skyler Luiken," Eve said.

Something pushed through the haze. A massive solid obelisk, dark and inscrutable.

Impact.

Fire and light, all around.

A deep shuddering vibration reached his cocooned form. He heard the rattle and clang of countless impacts. He glanced up and saw explosions ripping through the object above. A building, perhaps Scipio. Walls, doors, windows, and probably living creatures, all being vaporized as his shielded tower burrowed deep into the installation. Fireballs rocked the spaces he passed through, digging a gigantic silo out of the structure's levels.

His progress slowed, then stopped. He came to rest in a charred cavity. Severed pipes around him dripping unknown fluids. Exposed wiring that fountained sparks, which fell and bounced off the tower.

His artificial exterior view winked off, leaving him staring at the red foam again.

The cushioning receded, deflating. Skyler wiggled and moved, pushing it away, suddenly feeling trapped by it. He got an arm free, then the other. Finally, one leg managed to squeeze out, and then he fell. The tower, resting on its side in the pit it had dug, had opened, allowing him to exit.

Skyler landed in several centimeters of oily water. He hoped it was water. He stood and took in the space around him, the enormity of the place and his utter solitude threatening to overwhelm him.

He felt utterly alone. A saboteur delivered behind enemy lines. An agent sent into a prison camp so as to sow its destruction from within.

"I'm a virus," he whispered. An infection.

And if there was one thing the Scipios knew well, it was how to deal with such things.

Acknowledgments

First and foremost I must thank my agent, Sara Megibow, and my editor, Michael Braff (plus everyone else at Del Rey who helps bring my books to life). I'm endlessly grateful for all the hard work that goes into a project like this.

Thanks be to the authors I'm so proud to call mentors, friends, and contemporaries: Chuck Wendig, Delilah Dawson, Peter Clines, K. C. Alexander, Kevin Hearne, Ramez Naam, Django Wexler, Kat Richardson, Scott Sigler, Robin Hobb, Shawn Speakman, Wes Chu, Sam Sykes, M. D. Waters, Alexandra Oliva, and on and on . . . If not for this wonderful community I don't know how I'd get by. You wonderful weirdos are amazing.

My extreme gratitude to Felicia Day, whose support, generosity, and encouragement have kept me motivated while writing these books. You'll get your sequel one of these days!

Thanks to my wife, Nancy, for her constant support. Love you, sugar!

And, last but not least, thank you for reading. In the end that's all that matters.

—*Jason M. Hough*
Seattle, 2017

Read on for a sneak peek at

ESCAPE VELOCITY

the thrilling follow-up to
Jason M. Hough's *Injection Burn*.
Coming very soon from Del Rey Books.

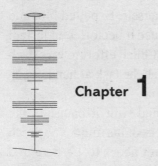

Chapter 1

HE LAY AT the bottom of a deep hole, in a puddle of filthy water that sizzled as bits of molten metal dripped down from the destruction above.

Skyler Luiken remained motionless for a time, just staring up at the column his arrival had carved. He remembered nothing of the actual crash. Couldn't even remember when exactly he'd lost consciousness, or why. Medically induced, probably. Another gift from Eve. Her last? He called out for her. "Eve?"

No response came. But then she'd said he'd be on his own, didn't she?

He took a long, shuddering breath and allowed all the sources of his frayed nerves to worm through his mind. He was a thousand light-years from Earth. Alone. His friends were scattered across the gigantic, planet-spanning apparatus of the Scipios, their exact locations and conditions unknown. All of them had been thrown toward the massive collection of alien space stations in the final explosion of Eve, their host. Eve, the only ally they had, the only one who knew what the hell was really going on here. Now gone. *Holy fuck, she's really gone.* The AI had sacrificed herself. Expelled him and the others on precisely calculated trajectories an instant before her destruction in a last-ditch effort to give each of them a chance to accomplish the task at hand.

He found little comfort in that.

Skyler let his breath out, and with it banished the enormity of his task to the edges of his mind. Too much to grapple with, and he wasn't about to lie here and wallow in overwhelmed shock. He'd deal with his immediate predicament now, and damn the rest of it. He had to survive, take stock, find safety. Find his friends.

"Hello?" he called. "Can anyone read me?"

A terrible silence stretched. He fiddled with the comm menu rendered on the inside of his visor. All channels were already on, but it showed no links to anyone else. He bumped the system to maximum broadcast strength.

"This is Skyler. I'm . . . I've no idea where I am. I'm alive. Obviously. I can't hear any of you, but if you can read me . . ."

What? What to tell them?

"Just stay put," he settled on, no better option coming to mind. "I'll report my location once I know where the hell I am, and wait for you all to join me. Keep trying to communicate. We might just be out of range."

Now what? he wondered.

The answer seemed obvious. He had to scavenge.

Now that, *that,* Skyler could wrap his mind around. He glanced around the pool of fluid and debris in the basin of the pit his arrival had created. The pod had burrowed through some kind of multilevel structure. A space station, no doubt. How deep had he gone? Skyler glanced up. The air above, thick with steam and smoke and a fine particulate like snow or ash, obscured the entry wound, but he figured the hole must have been patched by some automated process or else all that crap in the air would have been sucked out into space. Still, what he could see was at least a hundred meters of the shredded remains of a multilevel structure, as if his little craft had dug its way down through a twenty-story building. There were floors every five meters or so, each sprouting mangled pipes and conduits of unknown purpose, though given that most either leaked fluid or rained sparks, it didn't take much imagination to guess. The cavities in between these, though, were truly unknown. In truth it didn't look much different from a cross section of any Earth-based structure.

He shifted his focus to the remains of his escape pod. It lay around him like a cracked egg, with bits of the foamy orange cushion that had surrounded him during the brief flight now melting away into the soup of knee-deep viscous fluids rapidly filling the space around him. He jumped off his toes, just enough to test the gravity without rocketing himself up into the haze above, and judged it to be about three-quarters of Earth normal. What had Eve said about the gravity on Carthage? Pretty damn close to that, if his memory served. So he must be at a pretty low altitude.

As the last of the cushioning melted away, Skyler saw some gray containers floating amid the wreckage. He picked one up and examined it, puzzled at first. It was

Builder gear, definitely, but its purpose eluded him. He was about to toss it aside when he realized his suit was telling him the answer. In the bottom corner of his field of view, a display on his visor indicated that this was repair paste for his armored suit. He grinned despite himself and picked another. Ammunition, in the form of six pellets that could be inserted into the right or left shoulder of his suit, powering the beam weapons embedded just above his wrists. Skyler's grin widened. Eve may have sacrificed herself, abandoning him and the others to take on an entire sieged planet by themselves, but at least she'd not left them completely naked and defenseless.

Another case held "nutrients." He almost gagged. This would be the rather nasty food Eve had manufactured for them and never quite gotten around to improving. Skyler decided not to look a gift horse in the mouth, as his stomach growled its desire to be filled with the gritty, overly sweet fare. Last, a self-replenishing container for water, filled by pulling moisture out of the very air around him. This he attached immediately to the receptacle on his lower back and then willed the suit to extend the small tube toward his mouth. He heard the thin whir as the little straw extended, and he drank greedily, ignoring the slightly metallic taste. It was cool and wet and somehow grounded him, putting an almost whiskeylike glow of confidence in his gut. He repeated the process with the food, choking a few gulps down.

Skyler tried the comm again. "Anyone out there? This is Skyler. I'm alive, but I've no idea where the hell I am or what to do. Reply if you can hear me."

No response came. The suit's status indicators still showed no connection to anyone else, nor any Builder equivalent of a network at all. He ground his teeth at that, but decided not to spend any more time worrying about it for now. Maybe it was broken, or maybe the others were simply out of range. He left the comm switched on, and set a recurring timer to remind him every ten minutes to try it again.

Finally, he checked himself for injuries. Bruised and battered, but otherwise he felt good. His suit still had integrity, too.

Fed and hydrated, Skyler turned his focus toward his overall goal.

The enormity of which still boggled his mind, but considered in the simplest terms—that he was here to free the world of Carthage from the Scipios—he figured his first task should be to gather intelligence. How did the Scipios hold this world? What were their society and security structure like? Was his crew truly alone here, or could he perhaps rouse some kind of rebellion from within the metaphorical prison walls? The mental image of a worldwide prison riot was almost enough to make him laugh.

A burst of fire erupted into the cavity just a few meters above him, then quickly receded into a small gas-fueled flame like a welder's torch left on. The sound of it somehow woke Skyler's sense of hearing, and he began to listen as much as see. The dripping water, the slosh of his legs in the now-thigh-deep pool, and something else, too. A new sound, rhythmic, that stuttered even as it rose and fell through sweeps of extreme pitch changes. The noise came from all around him. Instinctively, Skyler sloshed over to one side of the pit, pressing himself against a wall made of charred debris, as the volume grew.

Multicolored light tore through the mists above. Beams of violet and yellow. Skyler knew next to nothing about life beyond Earth, but every fiber of his being came to the simple conclusion instantly: security response. He was an intruder here, an *infection,* and the cavalry had arrived to deal with him.

He raised his weaponized arm and waited, forcing even breaths through his clenched teeth. The one thing he could not afford was a shoot-out. Whatever the population of Scipios here was, it was bound to be far higher than he had ammunition for. No, a subtler approach was the only real option if he were to have any hope of reaching the surface, much less accomplishing what he'd come here to do.

The flashing lights above were joined by others, and then a shadow appeared in the rising steam. The curling white murk spread and swirled around the edges of a teardrop-shaped object maybe two meters tall, with four metallic and heavily segmented tentacles moving in a carefully controlled dance as it lowered itself deeper into the pit.

The sight of it barely registered, for it was what Skyler saw beyond this alien that almost overwhelmed his mind. A brief glimpse through the thick haze, but that was enough.

A night sky, half obscured by clouds.

He didn't need to get to the surface. He was already there. The realization left him reeling as his assumptions shattered like glass.

Skyler did his best to keep still, tucked in shadow under a curled bit of torn fibrous metal his arrival had peeled from the floor just above. The creature above him bore an obvious resemblance to the Scipio Swarm that had destroyed the *Chameleon,* though it had fewer tentacles and a more streamlined body of much thinner profile. Made for atmospheric use, perhaps, its existence closer to a support apparatus, rather than the swarmers who lived out their lives in that lonely vigil at the edges of this solar system. Those had been dirty things, rugged and scarred. This was sleek in comparison, with a gleaming white skin or hull that looked almost like porcelain on its top half, covering the lower black and gray areas like a tortoise shell.

With a slight bob the Scipio came to a stop. Its four limbs stretched straight outward to where they grasped whatever support they could find with four-fingered mechanical hands. Much more elegant than the spike-tipped monstrosities their space-faring brethren favored, perhaps because to impale every surface they traversed here would be to damage their own home.

For a time it simply hung there, suspended, crying its odd lilting alarm. Skyler remained motionless, too, ready to unleash hell if noticed, happy to remain hidden if possible.

Another shadow appeared as a second Scipio lowered itself into the deep pit. It came to rest a few meters above the first. This one was slightly larger, and had markings along its side, like a bar code made of skewed and curved lines. Abruptly the shrill alarm stopped as the pair of robotic machines or vehicles—Skyler couldn't be quite sure which—settled into position. He stared at those lines, the markings on the side of the recent arrival. They seemed to shimmer, then warp under his gaze. A trick of the light, perhaps, or just his rattled senses, but before he could puzzle it out the situation changed.

A section of the larger one's belly suddenly extended downward, revealing an array of tubes and connective gear. A turret, his brain warned, and he shifted his aim toward it. Before he could shoot, though, the swivel-mounted cannon revealed its purpose. It swung with precision to one side and burped out a white cloud of foam. The material slapped wetly against one of the small fires licking out from a severed pipe on the wall of destruction. The blaze vanished under the thick goop, smothered instantly. Another quick swivel, another blast from the fire extinguisher. Skyler watched, mildly fascinated, as the machine or vehicle systematically doused each open flame. *An alien firefighter,* he thought. When those closest to Skyler, at the basin of his crash-pit, were out, the thing began to climb smoothly back up toward the top. Every meter or so its cannon would cough out more white mucus. Another flame would vanish.

He shifted focus back to the first Scipio to have arrived, the smaller one. It hadn't moved since its big brother had shown up, and as of yet had not revealed its purpose here.

Skyler cursed himself. With everything else going on he hadn't bothered to check his air levels, and if the air here was breathable. He scanned the information splayed across the corners of his visor, the system tracking his eye movements and thought patterns as a means of navigating the interface. He fumbled his way through the menus until he found what he needed: atmospheric analysis. A quick review told him the only thing he really needed to know: breathable to a human. There were indicators for the various gases present and in what quantity, but that meant little to him. Oxygen was the only one listed in orange, the rest green. Nothing red, so he'd count his blessings and worry about the side effects later.

Besides, the suit acted like a giant gill, from what Eve had said. It could pull the ingredients he would need. Already it had replenished his supply to nearly full—enough to last him twenty hours or so, assuming he left the atmosphere and it couldn't pull in anything more. Still, it gave him some small reassurance to know that even in the event his suit tore, he could still breathe. The air, at least, wouldn't be trying to kill him. Probably.

A brilliant light bored into his eyes, forcing his attention back to the visitors. Skyler raised one arm to shield against the sudden flare before his visor recognized the problem and tinted itself to compensate.

The Scipio, the one that had remained near him, had extended a belly pod of its own. Unlike its larger companion, this one screamed "sensor array." Flickering lasers that swept across the ruined crash site in all directions, along with pulsing spotlights that shifted from one area to another. Several converged on him due to the movement of his arm.

"Shit," he said, and fired without really thinking about it. His beam cannon annihilated the small vehicle in a shower of sparks and shrapnel, as if it had no armor at all. Definitely not built like the Swarm that had attacked the *Chameleon,* then.

For a moment Skyler just stood there, surprised at how easily the enemy had been destroyed, and shocked at how quickly he'd fired on it. Some part of him had assessed, in that instant, that his presence had been noticed. And more important, decided that the little Scipio vehicle was likely transmitting everything its flickering scanners saw in real-time back to some control room. He processed this himself only now, but his suit had reacted to the conclusion and his reflexive decision to fire well before he'd even consciously understood the choice himself. *That,* Skyler Luiken thought, *is going to be a problem.* The last thing he needed was this exotic alien armor going all trigger-happy in a moment where his battle-sense needed to be carefully damp-ened by more strategic needs.

A problem to resolve later when he had a moment to breathe. Right now, he had to get the hell out of here, before this place absolutely crawled with more of these emergency responders or, worse, the Scipio equivalent of a police force.

Back up the way he'd come? Skyler considered that.

The air above had closed back in, unnervingly opaque after ten meters, utterly choked now by the smoky out-pouring of the fire suppression efforts and the explosion he'd just caused.

No, he thought. *Not up.* As much as he wanted to be outside, to survey his surroundings, he could too easily imagine a whole horde of Scipios up there. This hole he'd made was, at the very least, probably seen as some kind of freak natural disaster. A meteor strike or whatever. They'd be all over it, swarming in to plug the hole and repair the damage.

Sideways, then. Flee the scene, get his bearings, find the others if he could.

Skyler pushed off from the wall and climbed up to the first open cavity above him. The ragged pit his arrival had dug looked like a fist that had punched down through a skyscraper, revealing the interior structure—a very Earth-like stack of floors. Their contents were hidden in darkness, unknowable, but that didn't matter. It was a way to go, nothing more. So he jumped and flung himself into the first cavity, aware of several shadows descending into the pit from above and wanting nothing to do with them. Let the Scipios puzzle out the cause of the calamity if they didn't already know.

With any luck, he'd get a few precious minutes' head start before they realized they had a rat on the loose.